COUNTERCLOCKWISE

A NOVEL BY DAVID H. FALLOURE

COUNTERCLOCKWISE

David H. Falloure

Counterclockwise, a novel.

davidhfalloureauthor.com

Designed by
Michael Ratcliff
ratcliffcreative.com

Library of Congress Control Number: 2020918950

ISBN 9780578775562

First Edition: October 2020

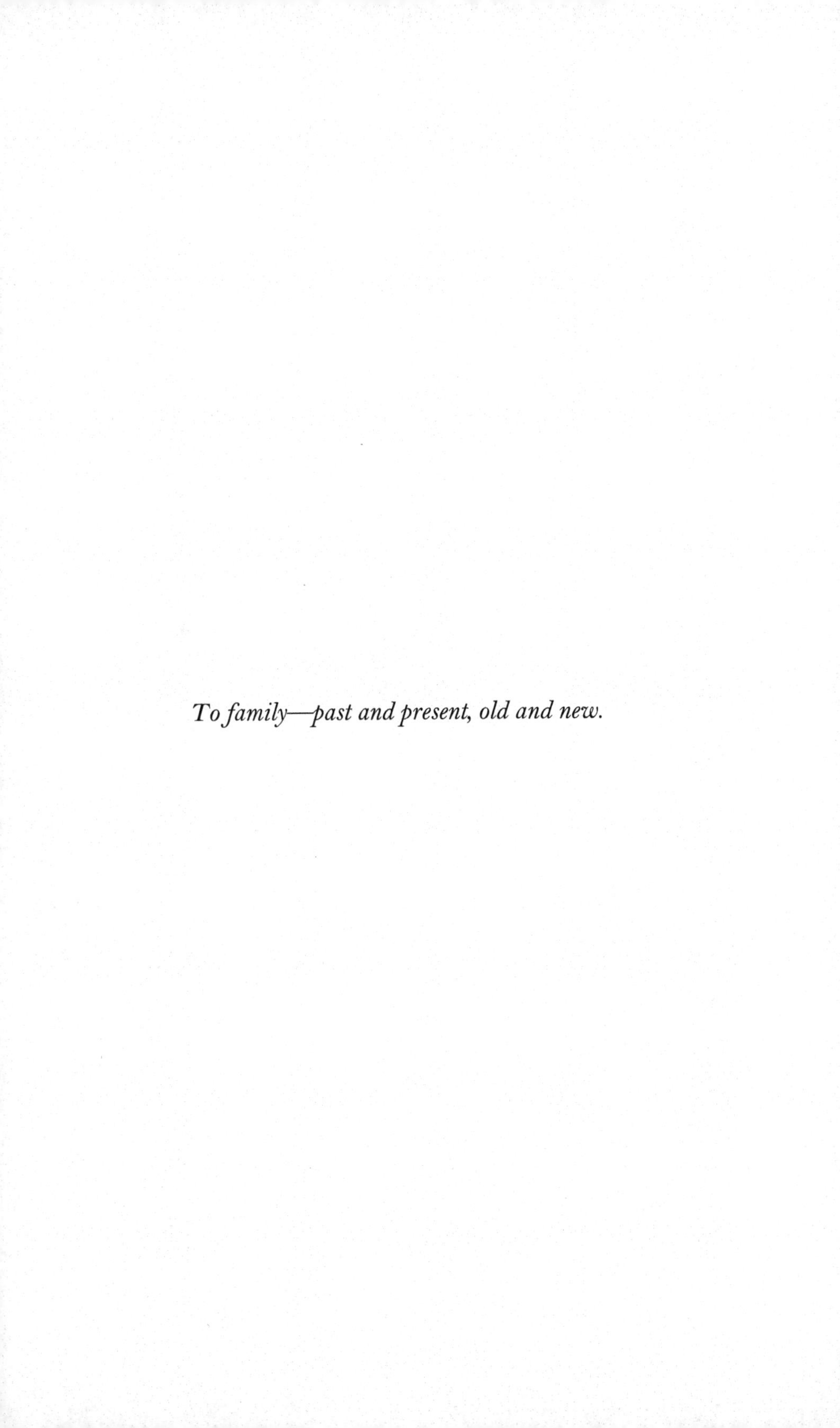

To family—past and present, old and new.

Acknowledgments

Books involve more than just the author, and I don't mean those with any financial interest in the work. There's an army of people who review, critique, discuss, and contribute. So I want to thank some of them, starting with Utpal Mehta. He and I took early steps together on writing our novels, including a weekend jaunt to an agents' convention in Austin, Texas, and I appreciate his discussions with me on my story and style. Steve Erickson is another. His character mapping, supplemental research, and sharp-scalpel editing really firmed up the manuscript. I also have to thank fellow author Russell Little, a great source of publishing process guidance and encouragement. And he introduced me to his publicist, and now mine, Sandy Lawrence. A shout out has to go to Kal Frenzel—both colleague and friend. Among his edits were aggravating comments to flesh narrative into dialogue. He was often right. And there is the Ratcliff family. Madison delivered an honest review of the manuscript and very insightful comments. Michael, your cover nails the feel of Counterclockwise and gives my digital channels a distinctive look. I also can't thank you enough for what you did with the galleys. Your patience is so appreciated.

This book started with family and it ends there. So I have to thank my mom, dad, grandparents, and aunts and uncles for their telling stories of growing up and living life. I listened—probably more than they wanted me to. Then there's my wife's family. She's Italian and comes with a lot of kin, whom I thank for sharing their histories. I listened—probably more than they wanted me to. Thank you to my three sons who read their dad's manuscript and, after recovering from the shock of their father writing certain scenes, gave their honest opinions, advice, and insights. I listened—even when they thought I wouldn't. Finally, to my wife, Ann Marie, who tolerated much while I sculpted this story, and still encouraged me when I was ready to hit delete on the whole thing. I listened—and it meant everything to me.

Counterclockwise: *a direction opposite to that in which the hands of a clock rotate as viewed from in front*

Table of Contents

PROLOGUE

Wednesday, 29 July 1942

Spearhead

Thirty meters below the surface, the sharp bow of U-166 pierced the warm, muddy waters off the Texas coastline. Inside the gray steel bulkheads, Otto Schneider sat on a small desk chair in the captain's cabin—a tight, cramped quarter hardly bigger than a closet with only a draw curtain and a few paces separating it from the control room. U-boat commander Hans-Günther Kuhlmann spread out a chart over the gray wool blanket covering his tiny bunk.

"We are nearing the coordinates," Kuhlmann said quietly, using his finger to pinpoint the submarine at ten kilometers south of Galveston Island. "It will get quite shallow."

The Nazi Schutzstaffell—or SS—officer nodded in response and whispered instructions. "Come to periscope depth and wait, First Lieutenant Kuhlmann."

Kuhlmann said nothing, although Schneider easily read the impatience on the young U-boat commander's expression—his thick black eyebrows low on his forehead. While Kuhlmann commanded the U-166, Schneider was not only in command of the mission, but also carried the much higher rank of sturmbannfürer. After the last sinking of a fishing vessel off Cuba, Schneider ordered Kuhlmann to cease any more attacks on surface vessels as they ventured further into the Gulf of Mexico. Kuhlmann's distaste for the situation was obvious, along with his frustration with having to refrain from hunting American ships.

"The transfer will take little time," Schneider said as he wound his wristwatch. "Soon, you will be able to resume your duty."

"I wasn't aware that I had abandoned it."

"Come now," Schneider began. "We are both military men and trained to loathe spies who slink about, spreading terror from the shadows." The chair squeaked as he leaned back, pulling a small metal case from the right inside pocket of his black tunic. "Of course, there are those who would say a submariner is no better than a spy—lurking in dark waters to sneak up on their victims."

Kuhlmann snorted. "This U-boat's only advantage is its ability for surprise—our presence is revealed the moment we launch an attack." He paused and leaned slightly forward before continuing. "After which we become the hunted. And the resulting battle is, after all, a test between men of honor and duty."

"Your pride is admirable—and appropriately Aryan. But do I see disapproval in your eyes?"

Kuhlmann said nothing.

"Nevermind, it does not matter," Schneider said as he slipped a cigarette from its case and replaced it in his pocket without offering one to his host.

"What I don't understand is how an officer of the SS finds himself on a mission of intrigue," Kuhlmann said as he raised a foot to the edge of his bunk, resting an arm on his knee.

Schneider sat a little straighter, almost at attention, and said, "It is enough for you to know that I have been selected for a specific task—and personally by Himmler himself."

"I meant no offense, only that I thought such things were left to civilian specialists within the Abwehr."

"Rare to be sure, but necessary as the Abwehr has its challenges." From his other pocket, Schneider retrieved a lighter. He traced his thumb over the engraved double lightning bolt insignia. "Guaranteeing loyalty from certain operatives in America has become difficult. Eight of our men were recently captured in New York because one turned on his men."

"No doubt the traitor spent too long in the United States, contaminated by mongrels and vermin," Kuhlmann suggested.

Schneider grunted as he lit his cigarette, the smoke providing momentary relief from the persistent stench of men and petrol.

Kuhlmann looked at the chart beside him and continued, "Operation Drumbeat is all but a complete success, just as Admiral Dönitz planned. Under his leadership, the Kriegsmarine has nearly contained the American merchant fleet, and our U-boats practically sink their ships as they leave port."

"You're asking if my mission is necessary?"

"Yes."

"Interrupting American shipping is like wounding a great beast—but even a wounded animal can still bite or even rage," Schneider said, exhaling smoke. "It must be felled by a swift pierce to the heart—and the heart of America's military is fuel."

Their discussion halted when a seaman knocked on the bulkhead wall on which the captain's bunk was bolted. Mannshaften Herbert Fischer was hardly more than a boy and his voice squeaked as he announced that they reached the designated coordinates. Both men glanced at their watches. Kuhlmann rolled up the chart and hopped off his bunk. Schneider ordered the seaman to retrieve his duffel bag and take it to the forward hatch.

Kuhlmann and Schneider moved into the control room with only a few quick paces. Ignoring the questioning faces of his crew, Kuhlmann gave orders for all engines to stop and to raise the periscope. He also restrained any show of pride in the efficiency of his men during this mystery voyage.

Rumors and speculation about their mission had been inevitable. One weekly shower and a single shared "head," in which fifty-two men urinated or defecated, made for a tightly-knit crew—one prone to gossip. So while Kuhlmann never heard the quiet mutter among his crewmen, the taste of their anxiety was in the recirculated air. Nevertheless, the men of U-166 remained dedicated to their duty.

Within minutes, Kuhlmann squinted into the eyepieces of the periscope. Galveston Island's not-so-distant city lights reflected on the water. He panned five degrees right and spotted a silhouette. He turned a knob, moving a magnifying lens over his eyepiece—it appeared to be a fishing trawler. Kuhlmann noted the time at 00:10 hours and waited.

Three minutes later, a signal came by a light flashing in dots and dashes. Kuhlmann lowered the scope as he barked orders. The normal lights dowsed and the red lamps came on—U-166 was rigged for red. Kuhlmann moved toward the ladder leading up to the bridge atop the conning tower. Leutnant Oppel was already on the top rung with his hand on the hatch handle.

Kuhlmann instructed his dive officer to surface.

The crew maintained silence, as ordered. A circular hand motion from the dive officer told Kuhlmann the conning tower had cleared the surface. He patted young Oppel's leg and the junior officer turned the wheel, releasing the watertight seal. Kuhlmann kept his face down and his shoulders hunched up. Oppel pushed open the hatch, and seawater washed over them, splashing onto the deck plates below.

The two men rushed up through the portal and onto the bridge. Kuhlmann grimaced from the musty stench of the Gulf. These were sour waters compared to home—as sour as his guilt for leaving Gertrude on the day of their second wedding anniversary. He also missed the crisp air of the North Atlantic. The surface was always a break from the stink, heat, and closeness below deck. But off the coast of Texas, the summer air was sticky and oppressive—even in the middle of the night.

"Vessel approaching, Kapitan; bearing zero-nine-five at three hundred meters and closing," whispered Oppel, standing on the starboard lookout's riser-step.

Kuhlmann scanned the horizon off the starboard beam. He focused his field glasses on the approaching trawler and the white dots continuing to flicker from its wheelhouse.

A seaman climbed up onto the conning tower and took position on one of the 20-mm guns mounted at the Wintergarten rail on the platform behind the conning tower, aiming toward the oncoming vessel.

The U-boat commander knelt close to the open hatch and softly called for his signalman, who stood at the base of the ladder.

The signalman emerged, carrying an electric lamp with a louvered lens cover. He set it into a mounting pedestal normally used for targeting binoculars, turned the lamp to face the trawler, and flipped a lever to open and close the louvers that formed the series of dots and dashes. The luminous exchange lasted only a minute.

The submarine's forward hatch opened, and two sailors appeared on the foredeck to take their positions on the deck-mounted gun. Schneider also came up, his blonde hair shimmering even in the dark. Two other crewmen followed the sturmbannfürer, fumbling with a bundle. A sudden pop and hiss broke the quiet as a black rubber raft inflated. Then the crewmen slid the raft into the water.

Kuhlmann batted his attention between the raft and the trawler. The vessel was close—only a few dozen meters away. The low growl of its engines stopped and the trawler drifted. Now the submarine commander could make out details. The shrimp trawler was once green on white, but sun and saltwater had long faded the paint, showing exposed gray wood in some places. Her nets hung empty from the otter boards, which were drawn almost straight up and secured to the mast.

Sturmbannfürer Schneider stepped clumsily into the raft; Kuhlmann turned up one corner of his mouth. Two crewmen rowed the inflatable toward the trawler as someone lowered a rope ladder over the side. On reaching the fishing boat, Schneider climbed up onto the deck. A tall man in a suit walked back from the trawler's pulpit to greet the Sturmbannfürer amidships. Each man raised his right arm into the air. Kuhlmann couldn't hear them say "Sieg Heil!" But he knew they said it just as he knew he would have heard the sound of their heels clicking together.

The tall man and Schneider disappeared into the wheelhouse.

The fishing boat's engines gurgled to life and left behind a small cloud of dark smoke as it moved off from U-166. It faded into a silhouette on the water while the raft and two crewmen were recovered. On the surface, this close to the enemy coast, taking the time to properly stow the rubber raft was an unnecessary risk. Kuhlmann needed to dive. He ordered a crewman to deflate the raft with a knife and leave it to sink. In the meantime, all hands secured the deck and went below. The topside decks of U-166 were deserted except for Kuhlmann and his lookout.

Kuhlmann gave a last look at the trawler disappearing in the distance while his lookout checked the surrounding ocean. They cleared the bridge and went below, where Kuhlmann ordered U-166 to come about 180 degrees and submerge.

The course he plotted was for the Mississippi Delta. That was where, two days before, he had noted a good deal of unescorted shipping. Finally, it was time for U-166 and her commander to resume the hunt.

Kuhlmann retired to his cabin and lowered the desk panel over the sink. He pulled his log from a slot in the wall and opened it to his last entry for review. Scratching the scraggly growth under his chin, he made a new entry:

29 Juli 1942

Ordered all-stop at position 029° north by 094° west. Confirmed location and made prearranged contact with local vessel. Surfaced for transfer of SS Sturmbannfürer Schneider as ordered. Transfer completed at 00:43 hours and observed vessel on course for home port. Ordered U-166 to come about and make for 28.5° north by 89° west, a position of noted enemy traffic.

Leaving the logbook open, Kuhlmann stretched out on his bunk and propped his head on his arm. He shut his eyes to visualize a freighter as he mentally rehearsed torpedo-firing procedures—peering through the periscope to get target coordinates while men loaded the forward torpedo tubes. An officer would confirm coordinates fed into the torpedo guidance system. Kuhlmann would give a command to fire the first tube, then the second. He smiled while imagining the sound of two hits against the hull of his prey. Suddenly, he imagined the shatter of depth charges.

Book of Exodus

The trawler chugged into a canal with aging fishing boats tied all along the pier, passing a vacant berth. A dark-haired woman in a light-colored waitress uniform stood on the dock, her arms folded and her foot tapping a plank. The trawler continued toward the small turning basin as its skipper leisurely wheeled the boat around. He approached his space again and throttled back to neutral, letting the vessel coast to the dockside. Two of his deckhands leaped onto the dock with the bow and stern lines.

The woman didn't wait for the crewmen to tie off the boat. She hopped onto the deck and rushed into the wheelhouse, greeting the skipper with a slap on the face.

"You two-timing bottom feeder!" she said as she slapped him again. "I have to work with her—even the damn dishwasher is laughing at me!" She was screaming, and the trawler captain couldn't get a word in edgewise.

The tall man, the man who chartered the boat, entered the wheelhouse. Behind him was the officer from the submarine—though he had changed into a suit from his black uniform and was finishing the knot of a civilian tie. The wife paused and turned to look at them, barely assessing them before continuing her strafe of the skipper.

"I told you what would happen the next time you did something like this!"

The trawler captain stood speechless as his wife wagged her finger at him. He was stunned. He didn't care that she knew about the waitress. Her timing was bad, and she might draw unwanted attention. Not to mention she'd seen the passengers. The best thing, he thought, was to get her off the boat.

The tall man put his hand tightly over the wife's mouth. Before she could struggle, a long blade sliced across her throat. The tall man said nothing as he let her slump to the deck plank. He stepped back from the pooling blood and, with nonchalance, wiped a red smear from his shoe on the woman's dress. "Dispose of that—discreetly," he said with no show of emotion on his face and an eerie calm in his voice.

The boat captain didn't speak; he merely nodded as he stared at his wife's corpse.

Schneider was impressed. His young associate dispatched the woman both effectively and without hesitation. It was worthy of the Schutzstaffel. Perhaps he, unlike his peers recently captured in New York, had not been fouled by life in the New World.

The code name for Schneider's tall contact was "Moses." It was selected because Moses Austin initiated the colonization of Texas. Despite the fact that it was a Hebrew name, Schneider thought the Biblical reference was more appropriate. On this and two previous occasions, Moses had successfully led Himmler's chosen from the sea.

Schneider followed Moses out as he stepped over the corpse. He said nothing. His bag was on the deck right outside the wheelhouse. Schneider expected his guide to at least pick it up out of respect for his position and rank. He was disappointed when Moses walked past it down to the deck and leaped onto the dock.

The sturmbannfürer picked up his luggage and followed his guide to a maroon Cord parked nearby. Moses opened the trunk and pointed as he went straight to the driver's side, got in, and started the car.

Bait

The aroma wafted up from his sister's house and snuck through the open window of the cramped garage apartment. The sound of old bedsprings creaked as Jack Warren popped out of bed and slipped on the pants he left hanging over the chair the night before. He grabbed his Zippo lighter and pack of Luckies from the bedside table on the way out.

After tapping one end of a cigarette on his wristwatch, he gripped the flattened end between his lips. With a move that was both smooth and practiced, he flipped open the lighter and thumbed the flint-strike.

Jack hurried down the outside stairs attached to the side of the garage. He hopped from the bottom step onto a pea gravel stepping-stone laying in a stretch of dirt separating the backyard from the carport. Two more steps and he opened the screen door, using his foot to catch it before it slapped the doorframe. On the black and white tile counter next to the percolator were three coffee cups and a sugar bowl. Stirring in just a little sugar, Jack poured his coffee.

"Get outside with that cigarette!" Mary Lou's whispered command startled Jack, and he had to slurp the spillover from his wrist before pushing open the screen door with his backside.

Under the carport was a metal table and chairs that used to be white, but the paint had weathered away to primer and corrosion. Jack eased his slender frame into one of the rickety seats and took a tentative first sip of coffee. The morning was quiet, and there was the smell of fresh-cut grass from the empty lot next door. Back on base, it always smelled musty in the morning, and the mornings were always about hustle. But here it was peaceful and pleasant, until his sister came out.

She was tiny, not much more than about five feet tall. Like his, her hair was dark brown, which was stark against the pink housecoat she wore. Mary Lou had crow's feet beginning around her green eyes. That was the price for smoking and years out in the south Texas sun.

"Morning Lou," Jack said. He never called her Mary Lou.

"So, you haven't told me why you're in town."

"The refineries," Jack said as he tapped his smoke on the rim of the ashtray. "I've been assigned to the Navy liaison for the OPC."

"Run that by me again?"

Jack grinned. "Office of Petroleum Coordinator—OPC for short. It's a small part of the War Department. We make sure the Navy gets the right fuel quality and quantity where needed, so we mostly work with refiners and pipeliners." Jack shifted in his seat. "Sometimes I feel out of my league meeting with petroleum engineers."

"They're just college boys, Jack, no smarter than you," Mary Lou said. "Besides, think about all the summers you worked with Daddy out in the production fields and in refineries instead of going to school—that's more than four years of real experience." Then she changed the subject. "How long are you here for?"

Jack shrugged. "Weeks, months, maybe longer."

"Don't you want to get on a ship?"

"No!" Jack said.

"That's what I don't understand, Jack," she said after sipping her coffee. "I get a call from Mother and Daddy that you ran off and joined the Navy, without saying anything to anybody. You hate the water—you don't even like fishing."

"I enlisted last year because it seemed to me that America would wind up in the war anyway." Jack paused to sip from his coffee. "And I really didn't like the idea of broiling in a tank or freezing in a foxhole."

"Ya know, Jack, a lot of men died—"

"I know, I know." Jack said, cutting her off by raising his hand in objection. "Pearl was bad."

Mary Lou looked at Jack and spread her hands.

"Why the Navy?" he asked.

Mary Lou nodded.

"The Navy offers more choices." *And it keeps me far away from Refugio, Texas.*

"I bet Mother and Daddy are glad you're closer to home."

You devious... Jack had put off calling home and his sister knew it. Even though he was on his own—and that grumbling was about all the "ole bastard" could do to him anymore—it was the last thing Jack wanted to hear.

The sound of tires crunching the dry gravel of the driveway was a welcome interruption to Mary Lou's inquisition. Jack turned to see a naval officer step out of the olive drab Chevy, and he stood to attention. Jack stood about five feet and eight inches. And he was lean at about 125 pounds. He and the officer stood almost eye to eye.

Captain Leo Preskin returned the salute and motioned for Jack to sit. "Morning, Chief."

Jack felt uneasy about being out of uniform. He raked his hair into place with his fingers and made sure his undershirt was tucked into his khaki trousers.

"Relax, Jack, this isn't a surprise inspection. Sit down."

Jack thanked his C.O. and introduced him to his sister. Preskin removed his cap and shook her hand. Mary Lou followed by offering the captain a cup of coffee, which he graciously accepted. Mary Lou went off to the kitchen.

"How was Washington, sir?" Jack asked.

"Busy! As you can imagine," Preskin said as he sat down. "I wanted an informal chat away from the office."

Jack nodded.

"You know there's so much U-boat traffic in the Gulf, it's a wonder they don't torpedo each other."

Jack smiled a half-smile but remained silent.

"Here's the score, Jack—" Before Preskin could go on, the screen door squeaked and Mary Lou returned with the captain's coffee. Jack asked her to give them a few minutes. Mary Lou said she needed to check on Corrine anyway.

"Corrine?" Preskin asked.

"She's my six-week old," Mary Lou said. "So, if you please, keep your voices down."

"Yes, ma'am."

The new mother quickly disappeared into the house.

Preskin took a quick sip of coffee. "I don't need to tell you the Texas coastline is vast, and it is simply too much ground to cover with the Federal Bureau of Investigation, Office of Special Services, and the Coast Guard spread out over three coasts—and then there are the Mexican and Canadian borders."

"I'm not sure I follow, sir."

"Here's the deal, Jack," Preskin said, leaning in. "Washington's concern is that Hitler may try another stunt like the Keystone Commandos."

"The German spies in New York?"

Preskin nodded.

"But they nailed those guys."

Preskin scoffed as he turned his cup in place. And he dropped his voice to a whisper. "Capturing the spies was lucky only because the head of the Nazi team turned on his own men."

Jack was confused about the course of the conversation and didn't hide it.

"You're plugged-in, Jack." Preskin leaned back in his chair. "You know the area, the people, and the industry. You can get the scuttlebutt before something happens..."

"So, you want me to be a spy," Jack said sarcastically.

"No, not really—at least not officially," Preskin said grinning. "Just keep your ears to the ground."

"Where, exactly, do I go with this?" Jack asked as he leaned back in his seat. "I mean, alertness is already the order of the day."

"At the moment—wherever it takes you." Preskin leaned in again. "I'm not alone in this, Jack. A few admirals back east agree with the idea that somebody needs to look into this."

"Sir—"

Preskin raised his hand. "The Houston Ship Channel and refinery row are targets far too good to pass up."

Jack wondered if there was something specific, except that Preskin was saying he and the admirals only shared a gut feeling. "Fine," Jack thought, but stepping on the toes of the OSS or the FBI wasn't a wise thing to do. Besides, Jack wasn't sure how he could make a difference. However, this "unofficial" request came not only from his C.O., but also from further up the ladder. "Permission to speak freely, sir?"

Preskin waved his hand in approval.

"Why special attention here?" Jack asked as he tapped his index finger on the table. "For now, the Northeast may be off the table with the eight German spies in custody, but there's the rest of the Atlantic coast and equally attractive possibilities all along the Gulf—I know I'm not brass, but it sounds like this is more than a gut feeling." Jack looked at his C.O., and remembered to add "sir."

"You ever sniff the wind on a blue-bird day and know the rains are coming?"

Jack nodded. He'd spent plenty of time around farmers back in Refugio. Old Man Gonzalez had taught him to tell the difference between approaching rains and just a humid Gulf breeze. Jack straightened up in his seat because it dawned on him what Preskin was trying to say without saying it—airwaves. Transmission must have intercepted—maybe coded ones, but even coded signals can be triangulated to pinpoint who's talking.

"Something is in the air," Preskin said as he nodded back with a grin.

"I'll do my part, sir."

The captain smiled and checked his watch. He reminded Jack they were due at a refinery meeting that morning. Jack excused himself to get into uniform while Preskin finished his coffee.

He hustled up the stairs and, before he turned through the door, he glanced at the southeastern sky. "Red sky in the morning, sailor take warning," he said to himself.

ONE

Saturday, 17 April 1993

Wake

Gray clouds crept up on the blue skies overhead, pushed by a warm breeze blowing in from the Gulf of Mexico. Richard Warren stared down at the grave marker, rubbing a commemorative coin between his fingers. The coin was his father's, the one all GIs and sailors carried to remember the attack in the months following December 7th. Jack Warren, Sr. had survived that war, as well as the many barrages volleyed by three sons.

At least, Richard thought, his father was finally at peace. His parents now lay beside each other, and he shook his head, thinking about their some forty-odd years together. The ones he saw were tumultuous, and he wondered how two such different people came together.

His dad was a small-town boy. Although he was a bit rough around the edges, his blue eyes and easy country style gave him charm. Richard's mom was the eldest of three daughters of an affluent real estate man. She was diminutive, refined, and quietly elegant. Because she was such a devout Catholic, there was a repeated story that had Jack and Margaret not met, she would have become a nun. As a result, Richard and his brothers often joked that each of them must have been the product of an immaculate conception. Richard laughed aloud at the thought.

"What?"

"How the hell'd they ever have three kids?" Richard asked rhetorically.

"I don't know and I don't want to," said JJ, Richard's oldest brother. "Besides, *you* were adopted!" JJ's real name was Jack Warren, Jr., but his nickname cut down on confusion around the house.

Richard and JJ laughed quietly—though only a lone, elderly woman sat nearby on a bench. However muted, they still drew her look, giving Richard a twinge of guilt. But for a moment, he thought the tiny blue-haired woman seemed familiar. Then again, she looked like any of his parents' friends that he was always running into around town. Still, he couldn't shake the feeling of recognition.

"Come on," JJ said as he nodded to the waiting limousine.

They stepped away when Richard halted and spun on his heel. "Damn," Richard said, looking at the freshly etched headstone. The date read April 15, 1993, and he realized he should have filed his return two days ago. JJ's questioning face prompted Richard. "I'm fine. I forgot to send in my taxes."

"Oops!" JJ said. He pulled two cigarettes from a pack. "You're only a few days late; with so much on your plate, maybe they'll grant you a special dispensation."

"Yeah, right—the IRS is so forgiving."

The two laughed again and smoked their cigarettes as they walked across the manicured cemetery lawn. Both men walked in similar fashion—briskly while pounding their heels into the sod. And they were almost identical in height and build to their father when he was younger. But JJ's hair was auburn and Richard's was lighter.

"Let's go, guys. Everybody's waiting at the house," said Tom, the middle brother, who had been waiting in the limo.

"Pipe down," JJ said. Richard chimed in, too, "Ah, you just want a Scotch!" Tom gnashed his teeth as he nodded. So JJ and Richard snuffed out their cigarettes and climbed into the car.

The ride to their parents' house lasted about twenty minutes. The men reminisced about hours spent with their dad watching old war movies. His favorite was a Clint Eastwood and Richard Burton flick called *Where Eagles Dare.* It was a switchback plot of spies, intrigue, and action. JJ pointed out a particular scene where the Germans came up the stairs and Eastwood stood at the top holding two machine guns.

"Aw yeah," Tom interrupted. "They stop and stare at him, and he coldly says, 'Hello,' and then blows 'em away."

"No, he doesn't say anything; but he does in the armory when he pulls the pistol from the briefcase," Richard said.

"Yeah, those were Dad's favorite parts," JJ said.

"Oh, and the part where Eastwood and Donald Sutherland plan the raid on the bank," Tom said.

"No, dickhead. That's *Kelly's Heroes*," said JJ.

"Hey! Have some respect for the clergy."

"Maybe when you're Pope."

Talk of the movies brought up their father's service during World War II. About all their dad ever said was that he was in the Navy, spending most of the war either in Pearl Harbor or San Diego. He also had a standard concluding statement: "A lot of people did their part to win the war, and mine was only a small portion."

"Didn't he serve on a cruiser?" Tom asked.

JJ said he thought he did but wasn't sure if it was for long.

"Whatever he did it got him to Chief Petty Officer," Richard said, looking out the car window at homes passing by. "Not bad for a guy enlisting right outta high school."

"But you know the war doesn't compare to the strafing he's getting now," said Tom. All three cringed and shivered.

"Oh God! Don't you know she's rippin' him a new one," said JJ.

"Can't you just hear it," Richard said. He mimicked his mother's tone and pitch as he shook his finger. "JACK! I told you that your drinking would do this! How many times did I tell you?" Richard rolled his eyes. "Oh man, he gets that for all eternity."

"Hell might be lookin' pretty good," Tom said.

The brothers laughed and shook their heads, then silence. All three remained quiet until the limousine pulled up to their parents' house. It was a small colonial built in the early sixties, with a red brick facade, white columns, and black shutters on the front windows. A few tall pines shaded the front lawn, littered with half-eaten pinecones dropped by squirrels. A mature oak in the backyard was visible even from the street.

Richard followed his brothers in through the front door where a legion of family and friends met them with hugs, kisses, handshakes, and a rush of condolences. The house was full. Chatter rung from each room and activity buzzed for the first time in years. It made Richard think about how his mother loved cocktail parties and entertaining friends. He glanced down at the guestbook on the small antique buffet in the entry. Every name was familiar. Of course, Kurt Hoffman's signature was prominent—almost John Hancock-like. And it didn't take long to find Kurt. He was in the family room by the fireplace, talking with JJ and his wife, Cynthia. It occurred to Richard that Kurt was their father's oldest surviving friend.

Tom quickly made it to the breakfast room, which was where the bar was set up. He poured a healthy glass of Scotch to bolster the faith that comforted him while mourning. Tom being the priest of the family was a source of pride for Jack and Margaret—especially Margaret. It also made Tom the perfect choice for consoling Aunt Mary Lou.

Richard meandered back through the entry and into the living room. A modest, upright Baldwin piano was against one wall, watched over by a portrait of his maternal grandfather. He was a man of some note in Houston real estate circles, and his mother adored the man.

Without warning, although he knew he should have expected it, Richard was surrounded by his mother's friends. They anguished him with stories about changing his diapers or cutesy things he did as a toddler. *Yeah, I feel better*, he thought. *I'm thirty and single, trapped by old women telling me they'd seen me naked as a baby.*

"Rick," Max Taylor said, appearing in the dining room. "I need to borrow you for a second." He liberated Richard, leading him through the kitchen and out to the driveway. He put an open beer in his best friend's hand and said, "You looked like you needed help."

"You're not kiddin'," Richard said after taking a slug from the bottle.

"Amazing how shared hangovers and psychotic ex-girlfriends make you telepathic," Max said.

Richard grunted his agreement while taking another swig.

"You holding up okay?"

"More or less," Richard said between drinks.

"The last time you looked like this was after junior year spring break in Truth or Consequences, New Mexico."

Richard chuckled.

"What was her name—"

"Don't go there or I'll tell your wife how you really got that scar over your eye."

"Change of subject then—what's left to settle for the estate?"

Richard shrugged, "Not much. House goes on the market the next week, anything not split between the three of us goes to charity."

"You need my delivery van to haul anything?" Max asked.

Before Richard could answer, Kurt Hoffman stepped out from the house onto the driveway. "This a private conference or just BS?"

"Both," replied the young men.

Kurt and Max shook hands while exchanging how-do-you-do's. They were about the same size. Like his dad, most of Richard's friends were tall. An imposing attribute should things get sticky in a bar.

"Max, can you grab me something from the buffet?"

Max took Richard's cue and excused himself.

Invitation

Hoffman spouted the platitudes that he could come up with in a pinch, "Getting back to life is the best medicine—so this'll pass quicker than you think." He knew Richard had heard all the same words of advice or condolences from his family, his friends, and his parents' friends. Still, Hoffman felt obligated to offer some words. And when he came up short, Hoffman was relieved when a low rumble from darkening clouds forced a pause.

Pushing away from the wall he'd been leaning on, Richard glanced up at the sky, briefly at Hoffman, then at the ground. "Hell, I don't know, Kurt." Richard tugged on his beer and swallowed. "I really botched this. Every step I made was wrong."

"There *were no right steps*, Rick. Alcoholism was only a symptom, and there's no template or prescription for handling it."

Richard shook his head. "When Mom died, I promised him I'd be there for him..."

Hoffman thought Rick might lose it, but he held his composure.

"He'd relied on her so much for everything."

Although Hoffman and Jack Sr. were distant over the last decade, Hoffman knew the score. When Jack's business went bust in the seventies, he was in his fifties with outdated skills. He wound up job-hopping while Maggie became the primary breadwinner. As Jack slid into a deep hole, Maggie remained his only lifeline. The bottom fell out when she died.

"Instead of listening to him, I was in his face," Richard said. "I criticized him and forced him into rehab. Twice."

Hoffman thought he should have something consoling to say, but he had none to give. Rather, he became distracted. There was something curious about Richard. Perhaps it was his mannerisms that echoed his old friend.

People do that, Hoffman thought, overlaying characteristics of the dead onto children and siblings in some vain effort to hold on to what's been lost.

A tap from inside the kitchen window jolted Hoffman. Cynthia wanted her brother-in-law's attention.

Richard looked at his watch and back up to Hoffman. "I bet people are starting to leave," Richard said as he stepped toward the back door.

Hoffman grabbed Richard's arm and said, "Whatever you do, don't distill your memories of Jack through his vodka bottle."

Richard nodded without saying anything.

"I'm gonna go on but," Hoffman said, smiling, "come by sometime and we'll talk over a glass of wine."

"About an alcoholic..." Richard said with a wry chuckle.

Hoffman grinned as they shook hands and went their separate ways.

TWO

Reminiscence

Scrapbook

Hoffman stared at the page of blurry old photos, but he didn't see them. Jack's death brought the decades rushing in and Hoffman wandered through them, feeling each one with every breath. They gnawed at his joints and pecked at his muscles.

A flash of lightning broke his trance, and he peered out into the darkness trying to pinpoint the source of the distant thunder. Another flash lit the clouds over the skyline.

"What a stupid idea," he said, looking back down at the scrapbook. "All they do is remind you of just how much time has slipped away." He turned the page.

There was more of the same. Images of people long since passed away and places swept under the rug of an ever-changing metropolis. Each a symbol of sins and transgressions for which he was no longer able to repent—except, perhaps, in the thought that maybe his time had come, too.

A faded print caught Hoffman's eye, and he squinted at it. He moved his feet to the floor and leaned up to place the scrapbook on the ottoman. He studied the group shot of people standing around a table. The grainy image made it hard to focus, so Hoffman pulled the stained photograph from its corner holders glued to the paper. Trying to sharpen his vision, he held it at arm's length, slowly bringing it closer, then far away again, as if he were playing a trombone.

Instead, he resorted to the magnifying glass on the lamp table next to him. He recognized that the shot was taken in his original restaurant, a few miles or so from the penthouse where he now sat. At the center stood Hoffman at a café table with his ex-wife, then fiancée, on his left. Jack was right of center with a blonde woman to his right.

On the far left of the photo were two people less easy to recollect. One was a woman he remembered as having had a nice singing voice. *What was her name?* Hoffman sipped a near-empty glass of Bordeaux to jog his memory. "Reina Corte—that's it!" He repeated her name and smiled.

Hoffman pushed off his chair and started toward the wine credenza as he stared at the photo. A memory of Reina coalesced in his mind. She was a petite Italian girl, and he chuckled when he recalled that she behaved like one. Reina was headstrong and saucy; not at all afraid to let you know just how the cow ate the cabbage. But the guy to her left was barely in the frame. It showed only a partial profile because he was looking at Reina, not the camera.

Resting the photo on the credenza, Hoffman reached over to the open bottle of '61 Lafite and tilted the neck over the center of his glass. He stopped. The ink on the label was faint and the paper curled off the bottle. He snorted at the tattered condition of something he held as a symbol of success. Like the photo, something about it taunted his memory.

Hoffman turned and panned the apartment, surveying it. Squinting at a wall of built-in shelves across the room, he carried the bottle and glass as he walked over to the bank of memorabilia. It was full of pictures, including one of Dorothy that he'd saved from the divorce. He touched it where her face was. Almost all the rest were of people of influence and associates, most of whom were now dead or out of his life, but none who were friends. He laughed when he saw the one of him and Nixon shaking hands.

The only candid shot was a picture of Richard and Jack laughing together. Hoffman couldn't remember when or where it was taken. But it made him smile and wish he'd been in on the fun.

He scanned the room and realized he had built himself a gilded cage. The décor and accessories were lovely but more showroom-like than a lifetime's collection of memories.

Hoffman wandered past the sofa toward the terrace, moving like an old grizzly through his last autumn. He slid open the door to find a cool wind, but not as cold as it was inside. Another chill came as he leaned over the rail, watching light rain fall on trees below. He sipped his wine and savored it—the way it glided along his palate and the finish. Staring at the glass of '61 Lafite, he smiled. Hoffman took a final taste and decided to let the glass drop over the rail as if to lead him.

Almost in time with a bolt of lightning in the distance, he was struck with a flash of insight. Hoffman pushed away from the rail and thought about the vintage of the wine, looking through the window to the credenza where he left the photograph. It didn't matter that he couldn't actually see the worn print. The image of the man was now clear in his mind. And remembering his name shook Hoffman to his core.

The phone rang.

Memorial Drive

Richard found quiet refuge from his hovering sister-in-law as he cruised east in his '88 T-Bird coupe. It was his pride and joy, black and sleek with a long front end and silver grille. He thought it was a bit of a throwback to the original design, and the circular taillights capped off the look. He also thought his Ford emulated the 1938 Phantom Corsair concept car, which also had a smooth, stretched hood and small cockpit-like passenger compartment. The interior felt more like that of a 1938 Auburn Cord 812 convertible—it was tight and efficient.

He drove east on Memorial Drive. The bends and curves through pine and old oak trees relaxed him. He always relied on that. His favorite part ran along Buffalo Bayou toward the skyscrapers. They jutted up from a canopy of trees and the sloping banks of the bayou. But the light rain kept his attention on the road in front of him.

Richard took it easy on the curves of the two-lane blacktop. It was slick, and after rainstorms, he often saw cars in the flanking drainage ditches or wrapped around trees. As much by feel as by sight, Richard could sense the road and where he was. It was a path he had taken every day during high school.

The road straightened out as he passed through Memorial Park. It was once an army camp—Camp Logan—back in 1917. Richard was familiar with its dark history from a high school community project to uncover camp ruins. Black soldiers preparing the camp became embroiled in a night of horrible race rioting, triggered by the belief that police unfairly jailed a fellow soldier. Indeed, two soldiers were unlawfully arrested and beaten by two white officers. Tensions rose until about 150 armed soldiers marched into west Houston, erupting into violence. Seventeen people were dead by the time things calmed down. Casualties included four police officers, nine civilians, and two soldiers.

Camp Logan was further cursed in 1918 by several deaths from the Spanish Flu. Ultimately, it was closed and the land sold to the city for a green belt dedicated to those lost in World War I.

Easing down on the brake as a traffic light turned from yellow to red, Richard turned up the song on the radio, but he didn't really listen. He thought about his dad. Why didn't he ever want to talk about the war? Richard never expected heroic tales, just—something.

He leaned on the armrest and stared ahead. Bayou Bend Towers were a little further down on the right. Richard brushed his mustache with thumb and forefinger as he glanced at the dashboard clock; it read 8:15. The light turned green and he drove to the next intersection where another light guarded the private drive leading to the towers.

A valet greeted Richard as he pulled up under the porte cochère. He got out and entered the vestibule where an intercom was mounted on the wall. Without looking at the index of residents, Richard entered Kurt's number on the keypad. A double beep sounded and he heard an elderly man's voice. "Yes?"

"Hey Kurt."

"Rick—you're downstairs?"

Kurt sounded a little startled to Richard. "Yeah. Did I wake you or is this a bad time?" Maybe he was entertaining. Richard admired the fact that, even at Kurt's age, he never lacked companionship.

"No, no. Come on up."

Richard heard a buzz and click. He pushed open the door and crossed the lobby to the elevator bank. Moments later he exited the car on the top floor and walked to Kurt's door. It opened before he could knock. Kurt shook Richard's hand and pulled him through the entry with a pat on his shoulder.

"Now we can finish our talk." Kurt motioned for Richard to sit on the sofa as he went over to a cabinet above the wine credenza. He pulled out a wineglass. "Join me?" Richard immediately recognized the label and smiled his acceptance.

Richard thought it was sad that Kurt lived in Bayou Bend. He remembered

Kurt and Dorothy's home in River Oaks. It was huge, with one unique feature: a custom wine room. Richard loved spending time there with Kurt, learning about wines and how to maintain them, along with the occasional tasting. "You ever go by the old place?"

"No reason to," Kurt said, shaking his head. "Dorothy and I split the proceeds, and she went on her way. She took a few cases and the rest I scattered around my restaurants. I keep a few cases at the club, too." Kurt brought his young friend a full glass. "You boys spent countless hours with me in that wine room."

"It was interesting, and the pay wasn't bad, either."

"To Maggie's dismay..."

"She let us come back."

Kurt settled into an armchair. He was uneasy so Richard glanced around the room.

"I'm alone." Kurt smiled. "What's on your mind?"

"Nothing, really." Richard set the wine glass on the coffee table and stared at the floor. "I'm not even sure why I came by."

"Come on, son—it's just you and me."

Richard clenched his fist, holding back. The tears came anyway.

Confession

Kurt Hoffman stayed quiet; Richard needed to let the emotions out and they came in short bursts—not sobbing, only tears. And it gave Hoffman an opportunity to reconsider his theory. He brought the glass to his lips and paused. He squinted—trying to overlay the boy's face onto the image of that old photo. *Absurd.* Hoffman took a sip.

"Son of a bitch," Richard started. "I told myself I wasn't gonna do this," he said as he wiped his eyes and cheeks to finally look at Hoffman. "I'm sure you wanted to see this."

"Bullshit, son. I'd be more worried if I hadn't seen it."

"Oh God," Richard sighed as he picked up his wine and leaned back.

"Listen, Rick, I won't tell you it's not gonna hurt. You know better. What you have to remember is that you did everything you could for your dad—trust me, he couldn't have asked you to do more."

"I could have listened to him."

Hoffman bobbed his head before responding. "Okay, maybe you could have. But the kind of things Jack needed to get off his chest should have been said to people like me, not you." Hoffman stood up, put his hands in his pockets, and turned to look out the window. "Your dad simply gave up. And of all the people in his life, you were the one who tried. Where was his sister, hmm?" Hoffman turned back to face Richard as he went on, "And you should also be asking me the same damn question. Your father and I were friends for over fifty years—for that reason, and others, I owed him much, much more."

He walked over and sat on the edge of the coffee table across from Richard. "One thing you learn in business is that some debts are transferable. So now, the only way I can repay your father is to do right by you."

"I think the thing that hurts most is how I knew my dad."

"Explain."

"When you're a kid—your dad is Dad. By the time I was old enough to see the man, see past the father, it was too late. I'd like to have met Jack Warren—find out who he was before kids and before things wore him down and peeled him apart."

Hoffman smiled a warm smile as he stood up to get his wine from the lamp table. "You'd have liked him, I think." Hoffman paused to take a sip. "He was a pretty 'hep cat' for his day."

Richard cut in with a laugh.

"Oh hey, he could be a very charming guy when he wanted to," Hoffman said. He took another sip and went on. "He really was a hell of a people person when he turned it on, and then there were the ladies."

"Stop! Thinking about Dad getting it on is just not right."

"Like you said, there was a man beyond the father."

"Sure, but let's not go there."

Hoffman laughed at that but conceded the point.

"Didn't you know him during the war?" Richard said, leaning on his knees. "I mean, how come he never wanted to talk about it?"

"He did talk about the war."

"Yeah, but never much about what *he* did," Richard said.

Hoffman stared into his glass.

"Come on, Kurt, not you, too."

"Those years were very different for me than they were for Jack," Hoffman said, looking off to one end of the room. "I wasn't in the military, so that wasn't our common ground."

Richard sighed.

"Why is that such a big deal with you?" Hoffman sipped his wine while he waited for Richard's answer.

"I guess maybe because it was the one thing he kept so close to the vest,"

Richard said. He leaned back and put a foot on the edge of the coffee table while holding his glass close to his stomach. "It seems like the older I got the less he tolerated questions about it—I know something was there but…"

"You know," Hoffman began, forcing a smile to be convincing, "what would life be without a little mystery to keep us interested?"

Richard shook his head and rolled his eyes.

Hoffman rubbed his face and grunted. "I don't know if it's this Lafite or the time, but I think I'm running out of steam."

"Yeah, I better get moving or Cynthia'll be on my ass," Richard said as he checked his wristwatch.

"Well, we can't have that," Hoffman said as he pushed himself off the chair. He walked with Richard to the door. "I'm glad you came."

"Me, too, Kurt. It means a lot, thanks."

"Give me a call tomorrow. We'll talk some more."

Richard put his hand out and Hoffman took it, pulling him in for a brief embrace with pats on each other's backs. Hoffman watched his young friend walk down the hall to the elevator bank. When Richard stepped out of sight onto the elevator, Hoffman shut the door. He leaned on the doorknob as he pulled the old photo from his pocket.

Hoffman pushed away from the door and headed for the bedroom. He glanced at the terrace, then down at the picture. Indeed, now there was something to *keep him* interested. At least as long as it wouldn't dredge up the secret he hoped he'd buried this afternoon.

Downtown

Richard turned left onto Bagby Street as he entered downtown. Eight blocks or so north was Franklin Avenue, where he turned right. The central post office was on his left.

He parked the Thunderbird at a pair of drop boxes near the end of the parking lot. The lightning was prolific and the rain drizzled. No one was around except a vagrant leaning against a tree. He wasn't in the mood to be hassled for spare change—not to mention he felt a little dizzy. So rather than slip his return through a slot inside the postal center, he decided on one of the drop boxes in front of him.

Richard grabbed his tax return and opened the door. He walked around the long nose of his Ford to the box marked "Stamped Mail." A gust of wind snatched the envelope from his hand and tossed it between the two iron drop boxes.

"Shit!" he said, reaching down, having to squeeze into the narrow space separating the boxes. The hair on his neck tingled as a sudden flash lit the envelope.

Searing pain was the last thing he remembered.

THREE

The Post Office

Up ahead, strobes flashed from several HPD cruisers, a fire truck, and an EMS van. The post office's main parking lot was taped off, and two policemen directed traffic.

Hoffman looked over his shoulder and wheeled his car into a U-turn, parking along the curb in front of the post office building. He started to get out but remembered to grab his mobile phone from the center console compartment.

"This site's restricted," one of the traffic cops said, blocking Hoffman's path.

"I'm here at the family's request," Hoffman said.

"Move on!" the cop demanded.

Hoffman spotted JJ talking with another officer with a clipboard and pen. So he yelled past the traffic cop to get their attention. JJ said something to his officer who yelled to the traffic cop to let Hoffman pass.

With a brief handshake, Hoffman cut to the chase. "What's the word here, JJ?"

"Hell if I know, Kurt," JJ said, throwing his hands up. "His car's over there next to a couple of blasted-out mailboxes—some sort of explosion, but no sign of Rick."

"Excuse me, gentlemen," said the interviewing officer, still writing notes. "Mister Warren, can you give us anything else on his description?"

JJ shook his head.

"Let me make sure I got this right," the officer said, looking back over the information JJ gave him. "He left around seven-thirty or seven forty-five to come downtown, right?"

JJ nodded.

"Do you know if he came straight here or was planning to make a stop?"

"Uh..." Hoffman interrupted. "He came by my place."

JJ snapped a look at Hoffman.

"And you are?" the officer asked.

"Kurt Hoffman."

"Where do you live?"

"Bayou Bend Towers," Hoffman said handing the officer a business card. "Richard showed up around eight or so."

"How long did he stay?"

Hoffman looked down at his feet. How long did it take for them to finish their glasses of wine? "I guess it was about an hour—maybe a bit more."

"Do you know if he came straight here?"

"I'd bet so," Hoffman said with a half-grin at JJ. "He said he wanted to mail something and get home so his sister-in-law wouldn't be on his case."

A camera flash caught his attention and Hoffman saw a group of men hovering with flashlights around Rick's black T-Bird. One was taking photographs, and others were inspecting it inside and out. Others were looking at the mangled mailboxes.

One of the investigators whistled loudly and waved for the interviewing officer to come over. The officer politely excused himself and walked between Hoffman and JJ. They kept their eyes on him as he went over to the investigator. He was holding what was left of a shoe. The officer flagged both men to come over.

"This belong to your brother?" The officer held up a shoe remnant, blistered with a gnarled shoestring broken into segments. Only melted grommets kept the shoelace pieces in place.

JJ said he thought it was the right size.

Hoffman walked around to the driver's side and an officer told him to stay clear. The officer had sprinkled black dust on the steering wheel and on several parts of the dashboard. Using a brush, he cleared the excess powder, which landed all over the interior and the driver's side door.

The last time Hoffman had seen a car dusted for prints was in '42. The FBI had been all over his coupe like white on rice. A brief image popped into his mind—agents rifled through his apartment, tearing it to pieces.

The bumper hung off the car's deformed front end. The hood and grill were mashed as if a giant ball had pushed in the metal. Whatever disfigured the car also left a massive divot in the ground not two feet away. Hoffman thought that if you made a mold it would be almost a perfect bowl shape.

A woman in a parka marked HFD ARSON used tweezers to pick some sort of charred artifact from the divot—maybe fabric. She bagged it and laid it into a bin with several other marked baggies.

One of the mailboxes was still anchored into distorted concrete. Hoffman leaned over to get a closer look.

"Watch it!" the investigator with the tweezers said. She rolled onto the ball of her feet from her knees before standing up. "Check your wristwatch."

It was stuck at 10:30 and the second hand was twitching one tic back and forth.

"It's heavily magnetized, enough to yank a loose filling," she said.

Hoffman nodded. The mailboxes were deformed like the front end of Rick's car. One was still bolted onto the concrete—but now it was a half-moon and nearly all the paint towards the right side was burned off. The other box was ripped from its anchor bolts and lay on its side. The distortions of the two boxes were mirror opposites.

"What did this?" Hoffman asked.

"That's for the evidence to tell us," she said while marking the baggie in her hand. "But the odd thing is the magnetic signature."

Hoffman felt a hand on his arm and he turned. JJ said that HPD was going to add dogs to the search teams scouring the area. "They don't think he could have wandered too far."

"Especially if he's injured," Hoffman concluded.

JJ said he needed to find a pay phone to call Cynthia. "Here," Hoffman said, pulling his mobile from a coat pocket. JJ extended the antenna and started pressing numbers, fighting off his emotions and trying to gather his cool before talking with Cynthia. Hoffman lightly patted him on the back.

Hoffman's attention turned to a policeman talking with a hobo sitting under one of the crepe myrtle trees in the elevated garden at the post office entry. Hoffman mouthed to JJ that he'd be right back. JJ nodded.

The officer was shaking his head and started walking towards Hoffman.

"He see anything?" Hoffman asked the policeman.

"He's so wasted I'm not sure he can even see," the officer said as he continued past Hoffman.

"Mind if I talk to him?"

The officer shook his head no and said for Hoffman to be his guest.

Hoffman approached the man slowly. He was completely stoned—unable to keep his head up and muttering under his breath. Hoffman stopped about a foot away from the man's outstretched legs.

"Spare some green, man?"

"Depends on what you have to say about the car over there," Hoffman said, wrinkling his nose at the stench of wet cloth, old urine, and feces.

The man squinted at Hoffman. "Too old to be a cop," he said as he lost the strength to keep his chin up.

"Never said I was a cop—I'd just like to know if you saw what happened over there." Hoffman'd bet the man hadn't moved from that spot in hours. His clothes were drenched, but his shoes had no fresh mud on the soles or even a wet leaf stuck on the bottom.

"Nuthin'," the man said. "Here mindin' m' business."

"Mm-hmm." One of Hoffman's knee-joints popped as he slowly squatted down. Everyone in the parking lot was busy—not a single person paid attention to Hoffman and the vagrant. "What'd you see?"

"C'mon—give a vet some help, man, and maybe I can help you."

"Vet, huh," Hoffman said as he assessed the man's age. Though he looked ten years older, Hoffman figured the guy was somewhere in his forties—about right for a Vietnam vet.

"Nam, for sure," he said.

Hoffman checked the lot again. He grabbed the vagrant's throat, digging his thumb and fingers on either side of the esophagus while applying pressure. He pulled and then slammed the bum's head against the tree. The vagrant coughed and choked. He couldn't even lift a hand to resist. "Shall we try again?" Hoffman said, easing off on the pressure.

The vagrant nodded. After catching his breath he said, "Dude pulls up and gets out—he leans between the two mailboxes and BAM, he's gone."

"No, no," Hoffman said as he squeezed a little more. "People don't just vanish into thin air." He shook the man by the throat. "C'mon... what else."

"Lightning!"

"What, he got struck?"

"No, one of the mailboxes." The vagrant coughed between words.

"But not him?" Hoffman asked and the vagrant shook his head. "Then which way did he go?"

"Nowhere, man," he said.

Hoffman popped the vagrant's head against the tree again.

"Ball of light! It tore up the car and everything around it," the vagrant said, wincing. "It was like a flash and the dude was gone—poof!"

Hoffman released the vagrant's throat and stood up, having to push on one knee. The mailboxes were too far away for him to see clearly. The vagrant was hacking, and Hoffman could hear the phlegm working up. He reached into his pocket for his money clip. He started to slide out a twenty but stopped. "Do us both a favor," he said, dropping the whole clip of bills in the bum's lap. "Overdose or leave an air bubble in the syringe."

Standing at the steps leading down to the lot, Hoffman had his hands on his hips and stared at the ground. He thought about the picture, and he began to remember a conversation with Dorothy from long ago. She talked about that night in the club when the photo was taken, and how remarkable it was that...

"Kurt!" JJ shouted, bringing Hoffman's attention back to the present.

"Get a hold of your wife?" Hoffman asked as he and JJ met up behind Rick's car.

"Cynthia's a basket case," JJ said, handing Hoffman his phone. Pointing to a man in street clothes, he said, "One of the detectives wants to talk to us."

The policeman who lifted prints from the car cleaned his hands with what smelled like an alcohol wipe. Hoffman asked if he could use one, and the policeman obliged. He cleaned his hands as he walked with JJ over to the detective.

"Mister Warren," the detective said, offering his hand to JJ. "Joe Finan—I'm the lead on this. At least for now." Finan was tall—almost as tall as Hoffman. He had a pencil-thin mustache, and his dark hair was receding from his forehead. JJ shook his hand and introduced Hoffman.

"Listen," Finan said. His voice was deep with an easy, comforting tone. "I know this is difficult, but you should go home."

JJ looked up at Hoffman.

"Even though our only witness on this is questionable, at best, I think we can surmise what happened."

"And what's that?" Hoffman asked.

"We just had a rough thunderstorm, and strikes do happen," Finan said.

"This seems like an awful lot of hubbub for a lightning strike," Hoffman said.

"It is a federal building." Finan hooked a thumb in his belt and added, "Everybody's still skittish from the car bomb at the World Trade Center."

"You think my brother—"

"No, no. I don't," Finan said. He looked around and rubbed his chin. "This is gonna sound callous but, we haven't found any remains, which means somehow he wandered off."

"And why put a bomb in a dropbox when the main lobby was open," Hoffman said.

Finan nodded back and said, "We've covered the scene and immediate area." He started to look uncomfortable. "And we can't drag the bayou until morning."

"What about the hospitals?" Hoffman asked.

"On a Saturday night, sir, there's probably a hundred John Does at Ben Taub trauma center right now—unless we get lucky and the rain kept the loonies inside." The detective's expression was a doubtful one. "Checking each one is going to take time."

JJ was holding it together but barely. To have something like this on the heels of his father's funeral—Hoffman couldn't imagine how that felt. "I think what he's saying," Hoffman began as he put his hand on JJ's shoulder, "is we need to be patient while they run down all the possibilities."

"The other thing, too," Finan said, pausing to take a deep breath, "is that the Federal Bureau of Investigation will be paying you a visit in the morning."

Hoffman and JJ looked at each other, and back at the detective.

"This is really their jurisdiction," Finan said. "They're gonna run a check on your brother—it's routine."

JJ rolled his eyes in exasperation. "Routine for who?"

Hoffman was wondering the same thing. Personal experience taught him that even routine for the FBI meant you came away feeling like a carcass from a wolf pack. The car would be impounded indefinitely, Richard's apartment searched and photographed along with his parents' house. And finally, every person Richard knew would be interviewed to expose even the most intimate of details. The hunt would only end when the evidence demanded it—in that it *could not* support their suspicions, or in that it proved his innocence from whatever crime they deemed this might be.

Finan nodded toward the street. News vans rolled up to the perimeter. The detective said he instructed the uniform cops to keep reporters at bay so JJ and Hoffman could leave unnoticed.

"C'mon, I'll follow you home," Hoffman said.

"Better yet," Finan added. "Drive him yourself, Mister Hoffman, and I'll have a uniform drop Mister Warren's car by later."

Looking at his keys, JJ said, "I don't want to run all the way out to Briargrove Park—I'd prefer to stay close in case Richard turns up, or you find something."

"I tell you what, we can camp out at the original Grille," Hoffman began, speaking specifically to Finan. "It's only a block and a half up. I can keep coffee hot and cold sodas for your people. If any news develops, we're right there."

Finan reluctantly agreed.

Hoffman nodded and JJ handed his keys to the detective. They slipped away while police occupied the reporters.

Waiting for the light to turn at Louisiana and Franklin, Hoffman and JJ were quiet. Another few blocks up, Hoffman could see a light on in the upper back window of what used to be the Pasta Factory.

"Some things never change," Hoffman said.

"I'm sorry?"

"I used to know the owner of that building and she was just as apt to burn the midnight oil." With a grin, Hoffman turned into the alley that led to the back of his restaurant.

FOUR

Wednesday, 29 July 1942

Duress

"Always check your math." Reina Corte shook her head. The ledger was off by only once cent. She spent hours finding the errors. Her manager had added wrong when he made out the day's deposit slip. It was a penny short. The other was a two-cent overage on a bank draft he wrote to a vendor.

Reina looked back through the column of numbers on the paper tape. Reentering the numbers on the ten-key with the grace of an accomplished pianist, she never took her eyes off the ledger. A crank of the handle to crunch the numbers and the machine confirmed what she already knew.

"Finito!" She straightened up her desk, put the ledgers and account books in the top center drawer, and locked it. One look around the room ensured all was in order. Reina lifted her sweater and purse off the rack, flicked off the lights, and went out the office door.

She stepped cautiously down the stairs. Reina didn't want her high heels to catch in a crack between stair planks. Once at the bottom, she walked to the back of the warehouse.

"No class teachin' t'night, Missus Co'te?"

"Clarence!"

"Sorry… didn't mean to give yus a fright." He leaned on his push broom.

"It's all right," she smiled. "Had too much work tonight."

"It be a fine thing ya be doin'."

"Someone did it for me, once." A clap of thunder rattled the warehouse doors. Reina flinched.

"Sounded right o' top us."

That was so close it made the windows rattle and Reina could almost feel the floors rumble. "Not too late tonight Clarence." She smiled. "You should get home before it gets worse."

"G'night." Clarence went back to sweeping the floor.

Reina walked out into the back alley. Something clattered in the trashcans bunched up across the side alley from her warehouse. *Damn cats.* She walked up the alleyway and turned the corner to the side alley leading out to Franklin Avenue. Reina felt a hand on her neck and her back and head hit the wall hard. The rough brick scraped her skin. She gasped for air as she recognized her attacker. *Maceo!*

Vic Maceo held her by the throat and brandished a blade inches from her face. Reina tried to scream but he tightened his clutch. "Scream and I'll cut your throat," he whispered.

Reina stilled.

"Don Parisi has been more than patient, understanding you needed time. He's left a good offer on the table and sent me to help you make the right decision." Maceo leaned in closer while brushing the blade tip along her cheek. The stench of liquor and a stale cigar added nausea to her fear. "He would very much hate for some bad to come to you… or maybe your little one."

Reina panicked inside. She darted her eyes left and right, looking past Maceo in a vain search for rescuers.

"Of course it would be a terrible thing to ruin such a pretty face." Maceo traced her figure with his eyes and hand. "Ah, but some things are equally persuasive. Yes?" He pushed his huge body against hers with a malicious smile. Reina tried to struggle again but he tightened his grip. She couldn't breathe, nor finish the "no" she tried to yell.

"Shhh. It's so much nicer if you don't fight."

Maceo's grip loosened enough to let her inhale. Reina shut her eyes and went limp as his hand trespassed under her skirt.

The Test

Wading through the high water and muck was laborious. Schneider felt something snag on the ankle of his right hip boot; the cold water seeping in made it heavier. He took a brief rest fifty meters from the barbwire fence line to wait for Corporal Werner Neubauer.

Looking over the flooded acreage behind him, the drizzle made halos around the dots of lights from small farmhouses in the distance. There were eerie howls from dogs hiding in the dark. Schneider half expected to see hordes of frontier savages charge at him flinging arrows and spears.

This was a faraway world from the warmth of a room he kept at the Zur Tenne in Kitzbüehel, Austria. It was his favorite inn and where he could hold Ilse as they lay naked in front of the fireplace. Schneider also missed his beloved Gerta. He smiled, remembering the smells of her baked strudel coming from the kitchen while he and their young son, Friedrich, listened to the evening broadcasts.

Standing in the slime interrupted his thoughts. Being in this place was beneath his position, he thought, but it was a demonstration of his commitment. After all, his superiors had faith in him—faith to carry out what only he could be trusted to accomplish. Doing so would quickly return him to the civilization of the Reich, and he would win glory from perhaps even the Führer himself. He would advance his station and his family's.

Neubauer spoke in German as he caught up to Schneider.

"In English, Werner. Always English," Schneider said as they continued their trek toward the property line. "Now, what is your concern?"

Neubauer nodded and apologized before restating his worry. "We may give away our tactic with this exercise."

"Ritter expressed the same doubt before we left," Schneider said, pulling hard to free his right foot from the muck. "As I told him, it is necessary to determine the level of precision we can rely on to achieve our objectives," Schneider said, huffing and puffing. "Given the considerable distance from here to the pipeline river crossing, and the likely outcome, we will be on our way home before any corollary is drawn."

Neubauer lifted on the top wire and stepped down on the bottom one, opening a man-sized gap in the fence. Schneider bent down and squeezed through, then held the opening for the corporal.

In the waiting car on the other side of the drainage ditch, the driver started the engine. Schneider and Neubauer looked at each other, dreading the ride back to the city. Their escort was almost as insufferable as the sump behind them. He was crass and vulgar as Moses had warned.

The trunk lid was unlatched, and Schneider raised it. Neubauer dropped a near-empty pack into the compartment. An unwelcome conversation began as they unhitched their rubbers.

"Y'all tighten the bolts good on the flange?" the man asked with a condescending tone as he got out of the car.

"Of course," Schneider said, sliding off a bootleg.

"And you locked the shack."

"I left everything as it was, and the padlock is in good order," Schneider said while forcing his foot out of the flooded boot. "Though it would have been easier with a key."

"Well I couldn't get the fuckin' key," he said indignantly. "My nigger's a couple of towns up and callin' him in would raise suspicion, now wouldn't it?"

"Obviously."

"The only good thing about the cotton-picker is that he's a helluva bird-dog on a problem—he will figure out the answer." The man spat a black mass that splatted when it hit the pavement. "And the only damn reason we ain't strung him up," he added, wiping a remnant of wet tobacco from the bottom corner of his lip.

What a filthy man, Schneider thought. Neubauer remained silent, though his expression showed agreement.

At least this part of the job was done, and it was the last they would see of this barbarian. Schneider dropped the boots in the trunk and slung his pack over his shoulder. "Shall we?"

"How 'bout my money," the man said.

"Our agreement was when you get us back to the city," Schneider said.

"Then I guess you better haul your butts in the car."

Schneider stopped at the car door, waiting for the corporal to open it. The only light was dim lamp mounted on the pole next to the pump shack. He turned his head to look south-southeast following an imaginary line along the buried path of the pipeline on its way to the river crossing. Based on the oil viscosity and flow pressure against the weight of the components, he calculated that the charge should be tumbling right under a clump of trees in a nearby pasture.

Of course, that was assuming everything worked as it had on the scale model, which was a closed system under strict controls. Despite how flat this terrain appeared, Schneider's concern centered on possible grade variances downstream when the pipe was first laid. Any rise or dip in the line could affect the speed of the charge moving through it—either slowing or accelerating its pace. Still, a detonation within range of his calculations should produce the desired effect. If so, then he could proceed with confidence.

"Time's a tickin', slick!"

The man's voice was as sharp as the lightning Schneider saw in the southeasterly skies. The major closed his eyes and inhaled his last deep breath of fresh air and held it. His personal discipline would be tested over the next few hours. That alone should earn him the Iron Cross, he thought.

Shock

Bone-splitting pain surged through Richard's marrow and radiated outward to muscles that cramped and knotted, wrapped in the sting of singed hair and scorched skin. The swirl of sensations beat him to consciousness while paralyzing his body, leading to a contorted fetal slump among the other refuse lining the brick wall.

The first muscles he moved were his eyelids. Richard shut them hard to endure the anguish. A loud exhale through gritted teeth announced his effort to move a hand. He plopped it palm down in the puddle he lay in, splashing his face with dank water. Another groan relieved the ache of pushing himself to his knees.

Every joint resisted his attempt at standing. The trashcan he used for support tipped over, and he dropped back to his haunches. *Fuckin-A,* he thought, welcoming support from a nearby brick wall on his back.

Richard took a deep breath and blinked several times to clear his sight. Struggling to focus, he made out little in the darkness. The night air wafted over his skin, relieving the sting and bringing a brief chill. He looked down. Things were all too clear close-up. A few charred remnants of fabric clung to his legs and hips. Heavy-stitched loops that were once seams circled his shoulder, waist, and ankles. He peeled a strip from his thigh, and cinder nubs of hair went with it like a Band-Aid left on too long. The skin was red but not blistered. Not much hair remained on his legs or arms.

More hard blinks and deep inhaling helped clear the disorientation, but not the headache. He squinted at the tall weeds across the alleyway that ran along the bayou. Dim lamps lit a few doors and clusters of crates or cartons. Traffic sounds and street noises made him think he might still be downtown.

The brick wall started to feel uncomfortable to the bare skin of his back. Richard leaned forward and knelt on one knee—the dizziness was fading. He placed a hand against the wall to steady himself as he stood. His ascent was slow, and he was careful to preserve what little strength he could muster. Stretching the leg muscles hurt, but not as much as the cramps. His joints cracked and popped in contempt of his every move.

A yelp caught his attention, and he looked around expecting to find someone mortified by the sight of him. He didn't see anyone.

Muffled sounds and whispers came from around the nearby corner. He moved toward them, staying close to the wall but careful not to bump into anything. Past the edge of the building were silhouettes of two people pressed against an opposite wall. Richard darted back behind the corner—smiling even though it hurt. *Lovers from a nearby nightclub.*

"No, pleas—"

Richard cocked his head. His second look was longer and he squinted. The man held a knife to the woman's throat and pinned her to the wall with his body. *Shit! Shit—shit—shit!* Richard leaned against the wall. He wasn't in much of a condition to play the hero; nor did he have the strength for a fight, especially with a guy that big. A call for help might not be heard or responded to, and if it was—ugh!

At his feet were pieces of a broken crate. Richard picked up a loose section of heavy casing. He took a deep breath and bolted around the corner. His swing landed the two-by-four at the base of the man's neck where it met his shoulders. Richard wasn't sure if the crack he heard was from wood or bone. Either way, the man grunted and collapsed, almost pulling the woman to the ground with him.

Drained from the exertion, Richard dropped the plank and propped himself up with one hand on the building behind him. He stretched out a hand to help the woman. She opened her eyes and screamed, "SANTA CLEOPATRA—NUDA! NUDA!" It wasn't English, but Richard understood. And her fist striking his jaw added sufficient punctuation. *Sleep'll do just fine.*

FIVE

Thursday, 30 July 1942

Game Board

Hoffman checked the street below as he tugged on the curtain panel to let in more light. That was the beauty of living in the apartment over his restaurant; it gave him an unrestricted view for three blocks.

He unrolled a sheet of onionskin, positioning it over the area map of Houston and surrounding towns spread across his desk. Registration marks helped him align the two sheets, and he weighted the curled ends using books on both edges.

Black lines inked on the onionskin indicated buried pipelines. They came from every direction, but most originated either from north and northwest or from the east. Nearly all traversed the large area shaded yellow on the map underneath, which highlighted Houston and its city limits. Grids and right angles denoted the main thoroughfares. The inked lines on the onionskin overlay converged and terminated near a few small clusters of grids surrounded by open expanses—these were smaller communities that ran along a waterway marked "Houston Ship Channel." They were the chemical plant and refinery towns of La Porte, Baytown, Pasadena, and Texas City.

Hoffman looked away from the map toward the bathroom door and turned an ear. The water was still running.

He cut a ten-inch section from a second street map of Houston. The cutaway included the two east quadrants of the city as well as Harris County. Hoffman drew register marks—small, precise crosses in pencil on each corner of the section—adding one along each edge between corners.

Hoffman put a piece of blank onionskin over the small map. It was also trimmed to the same dimensions. He traced over the registration marks on the map section underneath and was ready to begin duplicating the plots. The large map and overlay were too large to use while sneaking around fields near pump stations. These small ones would be manageable.

Specifically, he transferred a line that traversed the ship channel. He was careful to adjust for scale and double-checked its orientations against landmarks. Satisfied with his reproduction, he copied the numbers listed next to black squares along the lines.

All he needed now was the final set of plots. Then he heard a squeak from the bathroom and the water flow stop.

Hoffman slid the smaller map and onionskin into his top right drawer. He collected the two books on the edges of the larger one, letting the onionskin scroll naturally. He shoved that one into the center drawer, closed it, and locked it. Folding the larger area map on his desk was a leisurely matter. He knew the city like the back of his hand, but as an excuse, he could say it never hurt to have a map to survey what was around a prospective piece of property.

The door swung open and Jeanine walked out. She had a towel wrapped around her and used another to dry her long, light brown hair that was black when wet. Hoffman smiled at her. "Feel better?"

She purred a "yes" as she walked around the desk and nestled onto Hoffman's lap. Jeanine laid her arms on his shoulders and leaned in for a kiss. "But I didn't mean to stay this long."

"A young girl like you didn't need to be on the streets so late, anyway," he said, bringing her in for another kiss.

"That's what I love about you, *Mister Hoffman*, such care and concern for my reputation."

"I don't think love is what brings you here," Hoffman said, tugging on the tucked corner holding up her towel. It fell to the floor as he lifted her onto the desk. She locked her ankles behind his hips and laid her head off the edge of the desk. Hoffman kissed her neck. He made it as far as her shoulder when there was a knock at the door.

He tried to ignore it but the knocking continued. "Who is it?" There was no answer, so Hoffman repeated the query. He stood up from the desk and motioned Jeanine into the bathroom. She gathered her towel and scurried away.

None of the employees would come to his door, except for Jeanine, and Dorothy wasn't due in town until tomorrow. Hoffman took a revolver from atop the shelf next to the entry. He opened the door the length of the chain and peeked out.

"Good morning, Mo—"

Hoffman held a finger over his lips and bobbed his head toward the lavatory. He slid the chain from the door and stepped out, shutting the door behind him.

"Good morning, Moses," Schneider said quietly and looking somewhat embarrassed. "My apologies for this interruption."

That was one of the last remaining redeeming values in Nazi Germany, Hoffman thought. Even the abominable Gestapo still respected a person intimately engaged—waiting until the moment concluded before making an arrest.

Schneider's intrusion was irritating, but not as much as his apparent delight in behaving surreptitiously. "Just use my name," Hoffman said, shaking his head. "Is Ritter worse?"

"No, the diarrhea has subsided."

"Then, why are you here?"

"Any word?"

Hoffman shook his head. "But I haven't listened to the radio—though I doubt something like that would pass the censors."

The sturmbannfürer was visibly impatient.

"Go back to your room and stay put," Hoffman said firmly. "I'll pick you up after lunch. By then I should know something." He turned to go inside when Schneider grabbed his arm.

"We have a schedule to keep," Schneider said.

Hoffman fixated on Schneider's hand. "Despite your pretenses, I have no divine insight," he said as he removed Schneider's hand and locking eyes with him. "I'm nearly done with the map transfers and I expect the final components tonight, so you should have everything you need to complete your preparations."

"Except verification of our method."

"Wandering around is an unnecessary risk," Hoffman said. He leaned in a bit. "Sit tight until this afternoon."

"Certainly—Moses," Schneider said with an ugly grin.

Hoffman stepped back inside and locked the door behind him. With an ear to the door, he heard Schneider walk down the stairs that wrapped the back curve over the bayou and around to Franklin Street.

He replaced the pistol on the shelf and looked around the apartment. The bathroom door was open, so he wandered into his bedroom. Jeanine's towel was on the floor by the bed, and she was naked on top of the rumpled sheets—sprawled stomach down and smoking a cigarette.

"You're supposed to sell those to customers, not pilfer them from your employer," he said with a grin.

She exhaled a puff of smoke before she spoke. "How can I make it up to you?"

Hoffman knelt on the bed with one knee and rolled her over. He took the cigarette from her hand and dropped it into a near-empty cocktail glass.

The Wounded

Reina used both hands to lift the large pot off the burner. She tilted the edge of the pot over a white porcelain bowl, pouring a little boiling water at first, increasing the flow until she emptied it. Next to the bowl on the breakfast table laid a tray stacked with clean, white washcloths, another stack of gauze pads, and a small plate with freshly picked prongs of an aloe vera plant. Still wearing oven mitts, Reina lifted the bowl by the rim onto the tray.

She slipped off the mitts to grip a cup of coffee on the table, took a sip, and set the cup back down.

The phone rang, and Reina waited to listen to the ring before lifting the tray. The bell sounded two long and one short. It was Mrs. Provenzano's ring, and right on time.

Reina hoisted the tray and stepped lightly down the hall, careful not to spill the water or clop too loudly on the yellow pine floors. She passed the phone nook and glanced at the phone. How the old busybodies on the party line would love to know about her houseguest.

The bedroom door was ajar, so Reina used her shoulder to push it open as she stepped into the makeshift ward. The room had a soft, honey glow from the morning light filtering through the off-white shades. She set the tray on a side chair next to the bed.

She leaned over a small-scale vanity to partially raise one of the shades. The tie of her satin robe tipped a small china cup from its saucer. It was hand-painted with pink flowers, and the gold handle was only big enough for little hands. Reina picked it up and held the delicate cup close to her chest for a moment. She took a deep breath and let it out when she set the cup gently onto its matching saucer.

Her patient lay still on the bed in the same position Clarence had placed him last night—flat on his back over a layer of gauze and with sheets of gauze between his bare body and a light comforter. He looked dead, but his light snoring was reassuring.

Reina sat on the edge of the bed, gathering the lengths of her robe and locking them between her knees. She leaned over her patient and brushed the burnt ends of hair from his forehead with her fingers. He was young, though older than she—maybe in his late twenties. His forehead and cheek were cool to the touch from the back of her hand. He didn't have a fever. She let her fingers follow the contour of his cheek to his jaw—gliding over the slight bruise where she socked him last night. "Sorry about that."

Her fingertip traced a line over to and around his chin, then up to the corner of his Cupid's-bow mouth, and she wondered why he would hide it with a mustache. Her thumb brushed the singed remnants of that mustache and she whispered, "We'll have to shave that off."

She studied his face. "Who are you, and how did you come to be in that alley?" Reina didn't expect an answer, nor did it matter, she was just thankful he was there. "I hope you broke the bastard's skull."

Reina shook off her wonder and building fury to go on with tending to her patient—first folding the comforter down to his waist. She carefully lifted the corners of gauze sheets clinging to the man's body, using both hands to peel each square from his skin.

The burns were mostly first degree. The redness was fading on those. But a few were second degree, and she needed to keep those clean and dressed with another application of aloe vera. Reina dipped her finger into the bowl of water, which had cooled enough to be very warm but not hot. She soaked a white washcloth in the water, wrung it out, and patted the affected skin. First, she worked across his chest, moving outward toward his shoulders and down his arms. His hands were smooth and soft—his nails were trimmed and clean. She could tell he wasn't a laborer.

Reina thought the severity and pattern of his burns were odd. Scorching was worse around his shoulders, wrists, waist, and along his inner thighs. They corresponded to the remnants of seams she had cut or peeled from his body. It appeared to her as if most of the clothing had burned like a magician's flash paper. She once saw such a performance in New Orleans. The thicker seams and waistband of his pants did the most damage by smoldering against his skin. She couldn't imagine what kind of fire he'd been in or where. No alarms or sirens sounded last night.

She completed the sponge bath to his waist, which she noted was slender, and she used another cloth to pat the skin dry. Reina squeezed gel from the spiny-toothed aloe leaf and dabbed it on the second-degree burns. Afterward, she covered the wounds with fresh gauze. To keep her patient from getting a chill, she replaced the comforter over his chest before continuing.

Reina lifted the blanket off his legs and folded it over at his flat stomach. She took a bath towel and draped it over his feet. Starting with his right leg, she lifted gauze squares from both limbs—leaving one square covering his genitals. Each thigh, shin, and calf had singed stubble—just like his stomach, chest, and arms. Working from his hips to his ankles, with the same caution and care as before, she bathed the skin and dried it before reapplying the gel.

From the foot of the bed, Reina repositioned her patient's legs—moving each out toward the edges of the mattress. She sat close to his hips and lifted the square that covered his privates. She wrung out another washcloth and began patting away the old layer of aloe from his inner thighs. It didn't matter that he was unconscious, or that no one was there to see. Reina was uncomfortable and embarrassed when lifting his testicles to clean them and around them. Nor did it help when his body naturally responded to her touch.

Reina scolded herself for being uneasy. "Good Heavens, Reina—you've been married and had a child. And you used to bathe your little brother," she said, shaking her head.

Her attempt at medical detachment was undermined by his body's full autonomic response. "Basta—enough!" She emphasized her command by raising her hands in laughing exasperation, and laughing at herself for talking to an erection as if it would understand. "Men! Even dead you think with your cazzo."

Actually, the erection made it easier for her to clean him. But holding it in her hand—she felt its warmth and its pulse. Her giddiness shifted into grief and remorse. She longed for the love and comfort of her husband; her guilt surged for betraying his memory because, too, her body reacted to the moment.

She quickly dabbed aloe as needed on the burns and covered the area with gauze, and then she folded the comforter back over the patient's legs. Reina wiped the gel off her fingers with a dry cloth, picked up the tray, and left the room.

She set the tray on the table in the kitchen and leaned on its handles, fighting back tears. The young widow dropped onto a chair and laid her head in her arms folded on the table.

Crumbs

Hearing the squeak of the spring on the kitchen screen door and the soft pop of the frame hitting the doorjamb, Jack grabbed his smokes off the bedside table and headed down to the carport.

Phil sat at the table and chairs with a cup of coffee. "A fresh pot's on the stove."

"Yeah, I smell it—be right with ya, ole man," Jack said, tossing his cigarettes to Phil. Jack quietly opened the screen door and went into the kitchen to pour his coffee. A strong odor of last night's fried batter, mashed potatoes, and gravy lingered in the kitchen.

On the counter next to the stove was a cup towel draped over a platter—Jack peeked under it and smiled. He lifted a piece of leftover chicken fried steak and gripped it between his teeth while he doctored his coffee with sugar. A minute later, he sat with Phil. "You're up early," Jack said.

"Long day ahead," Phil said as he puffed a cigarette. "I'll be runnin' like a chicken with his head cut off." Phil looked over at the screen door, chewing the inside of his bottom lip. He scooted the pack of cigarettes toward his brother-in-law. "She was spittin' nails last night," he said, exhaling a breath of smoke.

"Uh-huh," Jack said, finishing the last bite of his leftover steak. "You called, though."

"First thing you learn as a husband—and again when you're a new father."

They both chuckled and Jack licked his fingers. "I'll apologize when she comes out." Jack pulled a smoke from the pack and lit the end from the tip of Phil's—it took a few puffs before he had a good cherry.

"So what kept you so long?" Phil asked.

"Spent the day along the channel talking to refiners—although most of it we spent at the Sinclair facility," Jack said, taking a puff and exhaling it.

"We just machined a few parts for Sinclair." Phil leaned up and flicked the ash from his smoke. "They had us use scrap from their pipelines in Germany."

Jack leaned back in the rickety metal chair. He rested the hand holding his cigarette on the table. His other arm was on the back of the chair so he could twirl the cowlick on the back of his scalp. Frowning, he said, "How's that?"

"Bob Henderson, the purchasing agent over there."

Jack nodded.

"Henderson told me that when Sinclair pulled out of Europe right before the war broke out, they sold all their interests—except Germany. Hitler didn't allow Sinclair to take any cash out of the country. And because he wouldn't pay Sinclair for the hardware and systems they built, the company dismantled pipelines instead and shipped all the scrap and pieces back to Houston."

"No kidding."

"I shit you not. Some of the scrap even had swastikas stamped on 'em."

"Humph. That what kept you out so late?" Jack snuffed out his smoke and finished his coffee.

"No, no. Just the same ole, same ole, catching up on purchase orders for well-taps—replacements on one or two wellheads." Phil took a sip of cold coffee and made a face. "But, I am getting an order from Mac Leroy over at Continental. Evidently a section of a crude line burst outside o' Sealy." Phil said that Mac Leroy griped about some maintenance foul-up on a pump station. The line would have to stay shut down until the breached section was repaired. "Anyway, we're having lunch so he can hand off the order."

Jack picked up Phil's empty cup and got up. "More?"

"Naw, I need to head to the shop." Phil emptied the ashtray into a flowerpot as he followed Jack inside.

Jack rinsed the cups and set them next to the sink. He reached under the cup towel for another piece of chicken fried steak and rested against the counter, taking a bite of the meat and grunting with pleasure.

"Yeah, she makes it as good as your mother," Phil said as he washed his hands. "But don't eat too much of it—it's gotta last another meal or two." He turned off the faucet and dried his hands with a towel as he disappeared through the dining room toward the bedrooms.

With only a hint of guilt about meat becoming more and more precious to civilians, Jack chewed on more of the leftovers as he listened to the voices of his sister and brother-in-law. No doubt Phil promised he wouldn't be late; no doubt Mary Lou strongly suggested he not be. A moment later, Phil plodded back through the dining room, into the kitchen, and toward the screen door.

"Where y'all eating," Jack asked.

Phil stopped to think a second. "James Coney Island," he said as he half pushed open the screen door. "You want to join us?"

"Yeah. I haven't had a good chili dog for a while."

"It'll be a late one—see ya at one," Phil said through the screen door that he eased closed so the frame wouldn't pop on the doorjamb. Then he walked to his car.

SIX

Gremlins

Ingredients

"How's the sauce, Walt?" Hoffman asked his head chef while dipping his finger into the pan for a taste.

"A bit thin, Mr. Hoffman. It needs to simmer more."

Hoffman agreed and turned to face the prep table. He surveyed a large cookie sheet with round cuts of raw meat wrapped in bacon and skewered with metal pins. Hoffman reached over and grabbed the pepper grinder. He held it over the beef medallions while cranking the handle to snow just the right touch of spice. He turned each one over and ground more pepper over them.

A prep cook came for the tray and looked at Hoffman for instructions.

"Cover these and set them in the cooler 'til 5:30. The mayor's reservation is for six o'clock." Hoffman turned back to his head chef. "Walt, I want them on the grill at a quarter 'til."

"Yes, Mr. Hoffman."

Hoffman started toward his office but stopped and turned. "And how's the fresh shrimp I brought in yesterday? There enough for tonight?"

"Yes, sir," Walt replied.

Hoffman continued back to his office. It was a small room, little bigger than a pantry, and crammed with a small, walnut roll-top desk against one wall. The right wall was shelved—each mantel cluttered with stacks of smocks and aprons, boxes with remnants of broken liquor bottles, cartons of spices, and clumps of odds and ends topped with a Civil Defense helmet. On the opposite wall hung clipboards and dangling notebooks.

He sat on the wooden desk chair and swiveled around to face the desk. He scanned the open ledger in front of him. The chair had castors, but Hoffman only had to stretch his arm to retrieve an order pad hanging from a nail on the wall.

The ledger confirmed an earlier comment from the chef that the kitchen stocks were low on lard, oil, and butter. Hoffman leaned back and slid open the center drawer. He pushed loose papers around and checked under them. At the back of the drawer was a small gum-bound coupon book. He grabbed it, closed the drawer, and flipped through the pages. The few left were none he needed. Hoffman tossed the ration vouchers aside and hung the purchase order pad back on the nail. He'd have to scrounge from the black market.

"Mista H, dere's a man…"

"Outta the way darkie," commanded the man. He barged into the small office nook. When he plopped down in the rickety wooden chair beside the desk, Hoffman half-expected the thing to collapse.

"Thank you, Curtis," Hoffman said with a half-smile. "See if Walt needs you."

"Yessuh." Curtis disappeared into the kitchen.

Hoffman turned to his visitor. The man rubbed the back of his skull and neck while he rotated his head as if to work out some kink. Sweat beaded on his forehead and drenched his collar. Hoffman reached back, took a rag off a shelf, and tossed it to the man. "So tell me about it—what happened, Maceo."

"Some son-of-a-bitch blindsided me last night." Maceo wiped his face and neck with the rag. "I never saw who it was."

"Was it business or pleasure?" Hoffman asked, digging around in a pedestal drawer and finding a bottle of Bayer aspirin. He offered it to Maceo.

"Woulda' been both, except for this," he said, gesturing to his head.

"Since you're here, I need a few things." Hoffman scratched out a list of ingredients needed by the chef.

"Past your quota again, eh?"

"Business is good."

"That should please Don Parisi—which is the reason I'm here."

"Mmm. Tell him his cut of the tables'll be higher this period."

Maceo grinned.

Hoffman handed off the list and looked Maceo straight in the eyes. "No skimming."

"Well, this is an easy list," Maceo said, looking at it. He tucked the list into his coat pocket, then opened the aspirin bottle, poured out two tablets, and swallowed them. "But some supplies you've been needing are more difficult to get than others—and with Parisi in town, you may have to lie low."

"Like hell," Hoffman began. "I pay you very well to overcome any obstacles. In fact, Don Parisi would be interested in just how well." Hoffman pulled a bottle of whiskey from a bottom drawer and poured some into a shot glass. "Besides, I have a pretty good idea you'll come out on top if this thing goes right."

"If—if you're successful," Maceo said before drinking the whiskey.

"That much more incentive to hold up your end," Hoffman said. He leaned out the office door and hollered for Curtis before continuing. "Which reminds me, I need to see Allen."

Maceo nodded.

"Yessuh?" Curtis asked, shyly peeking into the office.

"Bring a cup of coffee, please."

Curtis nodded as he left to get the coffee.

"A good boy ya got there," Maceo said.

"Yes, he is. And if you ever call him darkie again, I'll slit your throat. Capisce?"

"What's your beef?" Maceo seemed puzzled. "You don't like 'em any more than I do, and your boss'd just as soon—"

"What I think about *them* is irrelevant; and my boss will do whatever it is he does when the time comes. Until then, Curtis works for me and he works very hard. That alone has value."

Curtis returned with the coffee and promptly left.

"So, we understand each other?" Hoffman's tone was more of a statement than a question.

"Yeah, we do."

"Fine. Now, you have work to do. I need those *other* items tonight. I expect delivery of the list in your hand tomorrow." Hoffman pretended to read the papers on his desk.

Maceo wore a half-grin. He raised his right hand and whispered, "Sieg

Heil, mein Herr."

"On your way, Maceo," Hoffman said, glancing up but not directly at Maceo as he left through the kitchen and out the back door.

Hoffman continued working for a moment but stopped. He tapped his pencil on the ledger, wondering which of two masters he really served.

The Intersection

Jack waited at the corner for the light to change. The long walk of several blocks from the Office of Petroleum Coordination office took more time than he anticipated. Lunchtime traffic was heavy, and the wait at each crosswalk was long—almost making him late to meet Phil and Mac. And the last block was torturous—the aroma of roasted franks and chili made his stomach grumble and his mouth water.

Predicting the light change, Jack stepped off the curb to cross the street. Tires screeched and brakes squealed. Jack suddenly found himself lying on the ground, face to face with the chrome bumper of a maroon '37 Cord.

Jack propped himself up on his elbow and rubbed his throbbing hip. The driver-side door opened and a tall man leaped from the car and ran to the front. "Good God!" the man said as he leaned down. "Are you all right?"

"Yeah," Jack said with a light grunt. "A little scuffed up, but that's all." Jack used the chrome bumper for support as he stood. The driver helped him.

"I didn't see you 'til the last minute…"

"I didn't see you, either," Jack said, brushing himself off. He realized that the driver was a head taller.

A small crowd quickly gathered—and then broke up even faster when a policeman walked up. He asked what happened.

"I came around the corner just as the light changed and I clipped this gentleman."

"Navy, you injured?" the policeman asked Jack.

"No, no I'm fine," Jack said. "But in all honesty, I started to cross before the light. I can't say I was watching what I was doing."

"You sure you're okay?"

"Yes, officer, I'm fine—bruised pride more than anything."

"I should cite the both of you, but since nobody's hurt I'll let it go." The policeman pointed to the car. "Get this outta the way of traffic."

"Yes, sir," acknowledged the driver.

The policeman went on about his beat.

"Kurt Hoffman," the driver said, extending his hand.

"Jack Warren. Heck of a way to meet." The chief petty officer accepted Hoffman's handshake. "But, if I had to be run down, I'd rather this or a Caddy," he said, looking at the Cord.

"Let me make it up to you, buy you lunch. I have a restaurant not far from here."

"Actually, I'm meeting some guys." Jack pointed to the Coney Island marquis.

"Hang on." Hoffman reached into the open window on the passenger side of his car. From the glove box, he retrieved a brass token and handed it to Jack. "I own the Buffalo River Grille."

"Look, uh… I'm on GI pay," Jack said, feeling his face blush. "The Buffalo River's a bit pricey for me."

"Relax," Hoffman said with a smile. "That token'll tell the maître d' you're my special guest. Anytime you want—dinner and drinks are on me."

"This was just as much my fault as yours…"

"Do it as a favor to me," Hoffman said, leaning down a bit. "It's the least I can do."

Jack hesitated but thanked Hoffman. The two men shook hands and went their separate ways. This time, however, Jack made sure there was no oncoming traffic when he crossed the street.

Scuttlebutt

James Coney Island was a small space inside the Beatty-West Building on Walker and Main Streets. The combined kitchen and eating area was equivalent to an elementary classroom. Jack took a tray from a stack near the entrance and slid it along a metal rail attached to the service counter. Without looking at the chalkboard menu over the grill and griddle—he ordered two Number Ones all the way.

Four servers worked an assembly line and each one wore a white envelope hat and white apron stained with years of chili and fixings. Each person had a task building the meal until at the end of the service line, where a man handed Jack a plate with two hot dogs smothered in Texas brick chili, onions, and mustard. Another server asked Jack what he wanted to drink. He said a Coke and the man handed over a six-ounce bottle from the cooler. A man at the end of the rail popped the top using an opener tied to his apron string as he told Jack his total.

Jack dropped two coins into the man's hand and waited for change.

"Have a good day, sailor," the man said, dropping three pennies into Jack's hand. Jack smiled and nodded.

Phil and Mac were sitting in two of the schoolhouse desks lined against the back wall. They waved Jack over. He grabbed several paper napkins from the stack next to the register and turned toward the back wall. Ten paces later, he found an empty desk in the row in front of his lunch partners. Jack turned it to face them and slid into it.

Mac wiped his hand and reached over to shake Jack's. "How are ya?" Mac asked with a mouth full.

"Good, Mac. It's been a long while."

"Mac was just sayin' that the gove'ment's gonna build a refinery down near Bay City," Phil said, looking at Jack, then to Mac.

Mac took another bite, chewing a little and swallowing. "I told Phil he oughta get a piece of the action before Universal Oil Products gets in there."

"Wouldn't that be an awfully tall order for your machine shop?" Jack asked as he lined up his first hot dog for a bite.

"Well, yeah, an entire refinery is out of my league. I'm more interested in auxiliary system components—the stuff too small for Universal. Even a fraction of the job would give me a helluva boost."

Mac said, "Government contracts usually require some local or regional contribution."

"Unless one of those damn Yankee politicians somehow worked in a wartime suspension," Phil said as Jack and Mac grunted.

Between gulps of Coke and mouthfuls of hot dogs, the three explored Phil's options for bidding on parts of the project. They speculated on locations for its construction, what it might mean to the economy of Bay City—a little town hardly a spit southwest of Houston, and how fast the facility could be brought on-stream.

Jack felt uncomfortable when the conversation delved into finance. His economics class at Refugio High was pretty rudimentary. The discussion between Phil and Mac was college boy stuff, so Jack kept quiet and listened, hoping to learn something. He was relieved when the chat resumed a more familiar course.

". . . and we could spur a line straight south, which'd mean additional revenues for Continental," said Mac.

"Speakin' of lines, Phil tells me y'all had a mishap," Jack said.

"One of the damn pump stations—we lost throughput downstream of the one outside of Sealy last night."

"What happened?" Jack asked.

"Don't know yet." Mac said. "All the rain turned the surrounding field into a lake."

"Any idea when you can get in there?" Phil asked.

"Maybe this afternoon, according to the farmer that owns the land. It'll still be mucky but that's when our man is going out," Mac said.

"In waders, I hope," Phil said.

Mac laughed and nodded.

"Think I could tag along?" Jack asked casually as he looked at the last bite of his hot dog.

"I guess so," Mac said, holding his near-empty Coke bottle. "Why?"

"Never seen one."

"A pump station?" Phil was surprised.

Jack shrugged. "I can sketch a rig in my sleep and I know my way around a cracking tower, but I never worked a carrier line."

"Som'bitch!" laughed Phil.

Mac invited Jack to go back with him to the Continental Pipeline office right after lunch. From there, Jack could phone Captain Preskin to check in.

Each man mopped up the last of the chili on his plate with whatever morsel of bread was left, bused his tray, and left the eatery. Neither Mac nor Phil noticed that Jack had a slight limp.

SEVEN

Rationing

Recovery

With his eyes closed, Richard took a deep breath and let it out. The air was fresh with the musk of wet grass and humidity. He could hear birds and the whispers of sounds from outside—there had to be an open window.

He opened his eyes and his first sight was a black fan hung from an off-white ceiling. Its blades were immobile and cast faint shadows from the mellow light. Richard turned his head to the left and frowned, blinking to focus on a little Victorian vanity below a partially open window. Strewn about its surface were a small tea service, a porcelain doll, and a pair of bronzed booties.

A crucifix hung by a door with a glass knob and old-fashioned keyhole. A Shirley Temple doll sat on a small rocker in the corner on the other side of that door. Between the corner and another door, there was a small bookshelf —*Jack n' Jill*, *Mother Goose*, and the *Children's Bible* were only titles he could make out.

Richard felt sticky. He pushed back the comforter to find himself sheathed in gauze. The confused memory of the post office and the alley poured into his mind. He flung the comforter off his body and quickly sat up. His sore muscles and stiff joints instantly punished such quick movements. *Ah jeezus.* Some pads fell away; he peeled off others that hung from his skin. Richard skimmed gel from his arm and rubbed it between his fingers and smelled it. He recognized it as aloe vera—a plant his parents kept around the house for burns.

Areas of his skin felt tight but didn't sting near as bad as they had the night before. Richard grimaced. He used his tongue to feel between his gums and cheek and rubbed the tender jaw with his hand. "Oh yeah," he said to himself with a quiet snort. "No good deed goes unpunished."

Richard took another deep breath and let it out between tight lips, making his cheeks puff out like a blowfish. He decided he was steady enough to stand. Fortunately, the wood floor wasn't cold. More pieces of gauze sagged, so he shucked those as well—dropping the flimsy pads into a wastebasket.

"Hokay, where are ya, Rick?" He tugged on the scalloped shade of the window over the vanity. That released the lock and it rolled all the way up, revealing bungalow-style homes lining the street. Some had picket fences, while others had open yards.

Between the oak trees and the architecture, Richard narrowed his location down to Montrose or the Heights. But he thought the houses were awfully well-kept for areas so run down. He started to turn away and stopped. Something wasn't quite right. He leaned back onto the vanity while being careful not to disturb anything. There was a classic car, in mint condition, parked in front of one of the houses. Another one, but a different make, sat in the driveway of a house a few doors closer.

A little boy appeared in the yard next door. He was dressed in knee pants held up with suspenders. The boy lay on the grass as he slowly rolled a white toy truck over the damp blades. It was metal and looked like an old delivery truck. Richard could make out a green pickle in some sort of round logo.

"This is punishment for doing mushrooms in college—acid flashbacks," he whispered while rubbing his hands over his eyes. Richard thought about lying down again. Then he caught a waft of spaghetti sauce, triggering gurgling sounds in his stomach.

He didn't need a mirror to know he was a sight. All the gauze made him think of that bad Frankenstein mini-series from the seventies with Michael Sarrazin. Richard didn't see anything to cover himself. A small wardrobe was near the bed, but he guessed that was full of little pink dresses or frilly things. A bath towel dangled from the footboard of the bed. He flinched when he wrapped it around his waist and tucked the ends together, which aggravated his burns. "Shit!"

Richard let the towel drop to the wood floor so he could pull back the gauze. A few blisters dotted his skin. One of the doors opened behind him, and he grabbed the corner of the comforter and pulled it over his midsection.

A petite woman stood in the doorway looking startled. Richard didn't know what to say. She didn't say anything either—at first.

In the split-second silence that seemed more like an eternity, he processed a rush of simultaneous thoughts and the image of the attractive woman in front of him. He waited for her to scream or maybe slug him again. Was this her home? Who was she?

She wore her rich black hair pulled back in a ponytail. And she had a widow's peak—a small "V" of black at the top center of her forehead where it dipped below the hairline. He dared not break eye contact to pan up and down her body, but his peripheral vision gathered a pleasing figure outlined by a blue cotton dress.

Holding his breath only made the pounding of his heart more pronounced. Suddenly, his mind went blank.

"You might show a little courtesy for my neighbors—and for me," she said, breaking the awkward silence.

"Pardon?"

"Children live next door." She said it callously as she marched to the window and lowered the shade.

"Sorry." Richard looked down at the floor in embarrassment.

"Mm. Well, since you're going to live, I'll get you something to wear that won't irritate your skin." She left the room, and Richard stunned. She came back in short order with a terry cloth robe and tossed it onto the bed. "I'll be in the kitchen when you're ready." She left again, closing the door behind her.

Strangers

Walking down the hall toward the kitchen, Reina tried not to think about her patient's blue eyes. And she held her hand over her mouth, trying not to laugh aloud at his dumbfounded expression. *What a ridiculous picture,* she thought. He held the edge of the comforter over himself while anyone outside looking in would have seen his bare bottom. It was hard for her not to laugh.

Reina gathered her composure in the kitchen by focusing on the large pot of capellini on the stove and stirring the sauce that was warming in another on the next burner. She used a potholder to pull a warm plate from the oven before dishing up a pile of pasta that she smothered with sauce and small meatballs.

She turned to lay the plate on the table when he appeared—hesitating at the door, darting his eyes from the range to the icebox, and looking like a little boy about to be punished.

"Here." She coaxed him further by pulling a chair out from the table. "This'll do you some good. Sit."

Richard didn't say anything, nodding his compliance as he sat down.

"Good—*mangi*," she said, sliding the plate in front of him.

"Huh?"

"Eat!"

"Yes, ma'am." He took a bite and grunted his approval, twirling more strands of pasta in his fork for a second bite. The pasta wasn't mushy, and the sauce was rich and zesty. "Now that's Italian!" he said in his best accent.

The woman looked at him as if he were a moron. Maybe now was not the time to be a smart-ass, he thought. He took another bite and browsed the kitchen. Everything was from a vintage photograph in an old *Saturday Evening Post.* The refrigerator was small, and the outside was white porcelain. It had a few nicks and mottling, but otherwise, it was shiny and clean. The top door was large and had a silver upside-down handle like the one his grandmother had. Below was a pullout drawer or drop door. The nameplate read General Electric. Stacked on top of the refrigerator were several nested metal mixing bowls.

The cooking range was pretty new. The porcelain and chrome were factory bright and shiny, and the nameplate on it said "Magic Chef," though Richard had never heard of it.

This woman obviously took pride in the appliance. Even with pots still on the burners, she wiped splatter from the surrounding surfaces. And Richard couldn't help but watch her hips swivel from her vigorous cleaning. Her dress accentuated her tiny figure and her ponytail bounced as she worked. He decided to keep his eyes on his plate. "This is really good—thank you."

"You're welcome," she said. "I'm sorry the meatballs are so small, but with rationing and all—well, you know how it is these days."

Rationing?

She turned and leaned against the front of the range, "So, why don't we start with your name."

Richard froze in mid-chew. The outside light coming into the kitchen dimmed, probably because of a cloud. He thought it added to the Twilight

Zone effect. "Um..."

"You have a name, don't you?" She leaned up and went over to an open shelf over a counter. "I'm Reina Corte," she said, having to push up on her toes like a ballerina to reach for a glass and then held it under the faucet. She placed the drink in front of Richard and took the chair next to him.

"I uh..." He tensed up. "Ri... Richard. My name is Richard."

"You don't sound too sure." She rested her chin on her folded hands as she looked right at him. That and her forthrightness made Richard more nervous.

"Honestly I'm not sure of much right now," he said as he stared down at the pasta he twirled on his fork. "Where am I?"

"My house."

"I kinda figured that," he said, looking at her but not in the eye. "What part of town?"

"Rosedale."

He didn't recognize the name and scowled a bit.

She pinpointed their location as between Waugh Drive and Montrose Boulevard, and three blocks south of West Gray Street. "What's your last name, Richard?"

He wasn't sure if it was a good idea to say, nor did he want to lie to this woman. "My mind feels pretty jumbled at the moment," he said, scowling.

"Well, who are your people? Where do you come from?"

Richard closed his eyes and shook his head. "This is all kind of confusing —hell; I can't even tell you how I got here."

For the first time, his hostess was embarrassed. "Well," she said looking down at a place mat and fiddling with the fringe. "After I..." Reina cleared her throat.

"Belted me." He smirked when he said it.

"Yes. After that I—I realized you were trying to help me. That's when Clarence—he works for me at the factory—he must have heard all the ruckus, or my scream. Anyway, he came out and we got you here, although I have to admit we thought about leaving you in the alley. But then you were in a pretty bad way."

"Not that I don't appreciate it but—why not a hospital?"

"Well, you weren't that close to being dead," Reina said with a scoff. She looked down again. "And, I didn't exactly show my appreciation for what you did." She paused for a second and clamped her lips while taking a deep breath through her nose. "Besides, hospitals are breeding grounds for filth and infection —even the new Jeff Davis on Buffalo Parkway, which is the closest one."

Richard started to take a bite but stopped. He remembered that Buffalo Parkway was renamed Allen Parkway in the 60s and that the "new" Jeff Davis hospital closed down years ago. In fact, the last time he drove by it, the building stood empty and boarded up. He set the fork down, leaned his elbows on the table, and put his head in his hands.

"Look, your burns weren't all that bad," Reina said as she let her arms down to fold them. "Only a little blistering, here and there. But if you'd rather a doctor—"

"No, no." He crossed his arms too and cut her off. "It's ok. I'm just really..." Shaking his head, he said, "Befuddled feels like the right word."

Richard noticed her notice his grin. He proceeded with his part of the interrogation. "I take it you have a daughter," he said, cocking his head toward the bedroom.

"Olivia," Reina said with a hurtful smile. "She's in New Orleans for a while, staying with my brother Johnny and his new wife." A bit of pride crept into her demeanor. "He's building liberty ships."

That was the last dot in the line. The cars, the outfit on the kid next door, the antiquated kitchen—those things, along with her mention of Jeff Davis, rationing, and even the liberty ships meant that he wasn't sitting in the kitchen of a faithfully restored home. With a disbelieving titter and mumble, he said, "Not in Kansas anymore, Toto."

"Excuse me?"

"I only meant that I'm fairly convinced I've stepped into a Rod Serling vignette," Richard said, shaking his head. "And, with my luck, your husband is about to walk through that door and blow my head off with a shotgun."

"I don't understand a thing you just said."

"Me either. I—"

Reina suddenly got up and walked over to the stove. Her back was to Richard but it was obvious he upset her. "I lost Vincent a year ago," she said.

"I'm sorry." On top of everything else, this made him feel like the dirt on someone's shoes—no, worse. Then he winced and straightened up from a sudden sting. "Ugh."

Reina turned and saw his physical discomfort. "Where?"

"A twinge on my back."

"Let me see," she said, easing the lapels of his robe off his shoulders and gently exposing his back.

Richard didn't resist, but he felt like a little kid.

"I'd only had a chance to put a dressing on your back once last night. I was going to have Clarence come by to help me turn you, but since you're up..."

Her hands were soft and her touch was gentle—her fingertips caressing around areas that felt tight. Richard closed his eyes and tried to relax.

"Actually they're doing well," she said. "Most of the blistering on your shoulders is down and scabbing over." She slightly touched a few other spots. "There's a little redness."

He felt her finger glide over a tender spot between his shoulder blades.

"Did you fall against something?" she asked.

Richard turned to look at Reina with a raised eyebrow.

She blushed. "I mean before that."

"I remember using a brick wall to hold myself up."

"Come on, let's get your back cleaned up," she said as she gave him a reassuring pat on an unaffected part of his arm. "You can tell me how you came to be my knight in—well, my knight."

Richard hesitated. He knew that the amnesia ruse wouldn't hold. But more immediately, it occurred to him that while she hadn't redressed his back, she must have redressed his front.

"You're looking at me like I'm holding a syringe," Reina said. She rolled her eyes and took him by the wrist. "Don't be childish—it won't hurt and I don't bite. Come along."

Richard went—half hoping to retain what little dignity he felt he had left, and half-hoping that she would bite.

EIGHT

Wet Feet

Wading In

"Damn boy better get here," Gordon Allen said as he rested his foot on the transmission hump of the floorboard. "Sombitch is prolly lolligagin—sittin' in a field somewhere eatin' watermelon."

"I'm sure he'll make it," Jack said as he opened the car door to let in some fresh air. "Mac says he's pretty reliable." He closed his eyes and breathed in as a little breeze wafted through.

"As reliable as one of them can be, I guess," Allen said. He tapped the steering wheel. "You know how they are."

"He mighta misjudged the time, that's all—we are a little early." Jack didn't consider himself colorblind, but he sure didn't like Allen's attitude. He had met plenty of his kind growing up in Refugio. If they didn't bellyache about Negros they griped about the Mexicans. And if it wasn't the Mexicans it was the white trash from the wrong side of the tracks—where Jack's family had to live after 1929.

Clouds rolling in over the prairie reminded Jack of home, though the countryside at home had a bit of salt grass. The scrub was thicker and different from that in front of him, and there were no pine trees there. It all made him think of a girl back home, and he wondered how she was doing.

The chug and clatter of an out-of-tune engine came within earshot. Jack and Allen turned to see a beat-up '37 GMC T-14 pull up behind them. It coasted off the road while its bald tires sank into the mud up to the white walls. The brakes whined as the driver halted the truck.

Jack's shoe squished into the wet dirt on his first step from the car. "There went that shine."

"Where the hell you been, son?" Allen leaped out of the driver's side as he started in on the man. "We're burnin' daylight, damnit!"

"Sorry, Mista Allen," the Negro said, opening his rickety car door. "You said three o'clock, but I guess m' watch mus be slow—it be readin' just a little afta." He climbed out of the dull, two-toned vehicle. The door creaked and popped when he shut it. He was wearing rubber leggings that hitched to a strap around his waist.

"Try workin' a little harder and maybe you can get one that works," Allen said.

"Yessuh."

Jack carefully stepped to the roadside and made it with minimal mud caked on his shoes. He approached the man keeping his hands in his pockets.

"Willie Johnson, this is Jack Warren of the US Navy."

Jack nodded without pulling his hands from his pockets.

"Willie Johnson, suh, nice ta meetchya," he said as he nodded back. He didn't look Jack in the eye, nor did he offer a hand.

"Now that the how-do-ya-do's are over, let's get crackin'," Allen said. He opened his trunk and pulled out a pair of hip-waders. "Gyoddamnit!" He grabbed one of the rubber boots and bent it at the ankle where it widened a slit in the material. "These'll do ya no good."

"I gots an extra pair, Mista Allen." Willie went to the back of his GMC to retrieve them.

Jack walked toward the back of Willie's truck and glanced into the front passenger-side window. On the seat were books on pipeline engineering, calculus, and one titled *Flow Dynamics of Liquid Petroleum.* Underneath were a Big Chief tablet with scribbling and a sketched out diagram Jack couldn't make out.

"Willie!" Mr. Allen bellowed.

"Yesuh?"

"Ya' got yer keys?"

"Yes, Mister Allen."

"You two go ahead on while I go see the property owner," Allen said as he got back into his car. He leaned out the window, spit a black mass onto the road, and said, "He's grousin' about the terms of the lease and bitchin about the line breach. Gotdamn farmer likely couldn't tell the difference between an explosion and somebody with a shotgun hunting armadillos."

"All right Mista Allen… You needs da Service Log? I keeps a copy in da truck."

"I doubt the damn Polack'd care," Allen said, revving the engine. "I'll be back in a bit." He tore off kicking up gravel and mud.

Jack looked at Willie and shook his head.

"Mista Allen has his own opinions," Willie said as he pulled a mud-caked set of waders from under a tarp. He gave them a shake to flake off some of the hardpack. "Here ya are, suh."

"You don't have to call me sir, Willie," Jack said as he leaned on the back of the truck and kicked off a shoe. He kicked off the other one and slipped into the chest-waders. He grimaced at the odor of mildew from the boot.

"Yessuh, Mister Warren," Willie said with a grin.

That was the second or third noticeable slip in Willie's speech.

Willie reached behind Jack, lifted one of the shoulder straps on the bib, and moved it into Jack's reach.

"Whaddya think, Willie?" Jack asked, hooking the metal loop over the button and adjusting the strap on his shoulder. "Gotta twelve-gauge shotgun back there?"

Willie laughed his answer. "Dove don't be flyin' for 'nother couple hours or so, Mister Warren." He felt his pant pocket and reached in for his keys. He looked at them as he said, "A twelv'd tear up a bird. Twenty'd be better."

Jack nodded his agreement.

Willie closed the cargo doors and retrieved the tablet from his front seat, and the two men walked down one side of the drainage ditch and up the other to the barbwire fence. Choosing precisely the right key on the first try, Willie unlocked the padlock of the rickety wooden gate and pushed it open. Jack thought that a little bit more effort would knock the thing from its hinges. Not that they were actual hinges. Two strands of barbwire held the gate frame on one end-post.

Jack plodded through the muck and ankle-deep water, trying to keep up with his guide. Their steps made kerplunk sounds and left swirls of residue to fill each submerged depression as they made a beeline for a levee about a hundred yards up. The pump-shack sat on a gravel pad another 90 yards at the end of the curved levee. Willie trudged up the low slope and turned to wait for Jack.

"Not too much further, Mista Warren."

"Cut the Uncle Tom bit, Willie—Allen's gone."

Willie stopped and faced Jack. "Suh?"

"First of all, you slipped up once or twice in how you talk," Jack said as he paused at the base of the slope. "Mister and Mista, for example." Starting up the slope, he said the second thing was the books in Willie's truck. "All real college stuff."

"And, third?" Willie asked with a poker face.

"That pad you're holding tells me you know a helluva lot more about this pipeline than Allen. Not to mention you backhandedly challenged that prick about your being late. So lay off the dumb nigger routine."

Willie looked Jack in the eyes. Jack wasn't sure if the man was about to punch him. Maybe the "dumb nigger" comment wasn't a bright idea. Fortunately, the man grinned as he held out a hand. "Yes… Mister Warren."

After a mental sigh of relief, Jack took his hand and Willie helped him up as he said, "And I'd bet my bottom-dollar you go by something else at home."

Willie chuckled, twisting the wedding ring on his left hand. "William," he said with a smile. "She calls me William."

"Then William it is," Jack said.

William tilted his head. "You seem pretty observant for—"

"For what?"

"I was gonna say, 'such a young man.' Mind if I ask your age?"

"Nineteen, last May. You?"

"About to turn thirty-eight. Nineteen and you're already a chief! What'd you do, take out a Jap regiment single-handed or something?"

"Not hardly," Jack began. "Just hard work and good CO's. And there were a lot of slots to fill right before Pearl, and even more afterward." Jack panted a few breaths before continuing. He judged the shack about thirty yards away. "And you? Why not sign up?"

"I did a stint in ROTC at Prairie View A&M, Class of '28—and another few years active army after graduation," William said.

"Huh! Maybe I'll apply there after the war."

Both men burst out laughing at the thought of a white man at an all-Negro college.

William stopped as if something caught his eye—a hole in the ground

15 feet from the shack. Stepping up their pace, they reached the rim of a small crater. William grimaced, and Jack could see the gears turning inside the man's head. "Obviously this doesn't look right," Jack said.

"Nu-uh," William said, staring into the four-foot-wide maw. He turned and went for the pump-shack. William pulled out his keys and held up the keyhole side of the padlock on the door. Jack noted that again, William picked the right key on the first try, but he paused and grunted before opening the door.

"What?"

William held the keyhole side up for the young chief to examine. "See those silver marks on the side edges of the slot?"

Jack nodded.

"You usually angle a key in length-wise, or at least I do."

"Me too, I think," Jack said.

"The scratches should be on the top and bottom, not the sides." Closely examining the lock, William said, "Looks to me like it's been picked."

Jack surveyed the open fields and back toward the road. "Could it've been another workman, or maybe the farmer, with a key and just happens to do it differently?"

"Not likely," William said. He continued as he unlocked the padlock. "First of all, who'd want to plow through all that water? It was higher until today. But if it was another Continental man, I'll know from the service log." He unlatched the door and pulled it open. "But then there's that high water again."

William stood just inside the door looking the room over from side to side. "And the farmer, the owner of this land, has no reason to be in here. Not to mention he has no key."

Jack poked his head in.

"I can't imagine he'd know how to pick a lock, or even want to," William said.

Jack snooped around the pump equipment while William went straight for the service log.

"Uh-huh, that's what I thought. I was the last man here—about a week ago and right before the rains came in."

Jack didn't know much about pipeline pumps, but the gauges told him everything he needed to know. "They all read zero and none of 'em are cracked or blown," he said and turning his attention to the valves. "Looks to me like all these are closed."

"They are," William said, walking nearer to Jack. "That's why I was here.

We took this station offline for maintenance work—the part hasn't come in from the manufacturer yet, and she's been bypassed for days."

"So no foul-up?"

"Not from here," William said. He jerked a look at Jack. "Who said a foul-up?"

"Mac Leroy in purchasing."

"That figures. The part requisition probably hit his desk this morning right after the report came in. He put two and two together and thought he got four."

"All right, so you didn't have a back-pressure problem, or at least not at the pump itself, right?"

"This station has a bypass valve that redirects the flow into a spur line circumventing the pump and back through another valve into the main line."

"Where are these valves?"

"One is a few yards north, the other used to be where that hole is out there."

Jack rolled his eyes and leaned his head toward the door. He walked outside and William followed. The two men looked into the hole.

"I think I see part of the valve," William said, stepping into the small crater. He peered into one end of the mangled 10-inch pipe. "I can't be for sure, but I think it's in the open position, and I think the blast pushed it back some." In a squat position, William looked at the surrounding dirt. "I see a lot of scorching."

"From what? There's no spill, so what burned?"

"There is a residue here and there, but not from oil." William ran his finger along the inside of the exposed pipe. "This pitting isn't right, either."

"Pitting?"

"Something smoldered into the surface of the metal," William said with a grimace. He climbed out of the hole and, for a moment, stood with his hands on his hips. He stopped his survey at the inflow bypass valve and went over to it. Barely moving the valve handle, William studied it closely as he did so. "The reason there's no spill is because this valve's still closed."

Jack could see the handle. "But it's set at open."

"Loose set screw with stripped threads," William said as he turned the handle from open to close and back again. "Tight enough to fake resistance but loose enough to not actuate the valve."

Jack looked at William.

"I noted it in my service log and requisitioned the new ball valve assembly, along with the parts for the pump."

"And no outsider would have checked your log." Jack held up his pack of cigarettes to William with a questioning look.

William nodded. "You can smoke."

Jack lit one up and thought a minute.

"Here we go again." William was looking at the valve stem. He crouched down and touched a flange cover. "Fresh tool marks on these flange bolts."

"What about the residue on the pipe?"

"Not sure what that is."

Jack exhaled a drag of smoke. He panned from the road back over the field. After a final shot of nicotine, he stepped out the half-smoked cigarette in the damp ground. "You gonna be in Houston anytime soon?"

William shrugged, "I wasn't planning on it but I guess I could be. Why?"

"Mister Johnson," Jack said as he turned on one heel. "I need a favor."

Both Ends Against the Middle

Maceo leaned down to kiss the ring on Don Parisi's right hand. He kept quiet and waited for the big boss to speak first.

"It's good to see you, Vic." Parisi patted Maceo's arm, then shook his hand. "How's the family?"

"They're all fine—busy with the Balinese Room and Hollywood Dinner Club."

"It shows, too," Parisi said. He motioned for Maceo to sit in the plush lounge chair. "The Maceo family has done well." Parisi eased down onto a sofa against the wall of the hotel room. "Galveston's always been pretty wide open. But I wasn't convinced of its potential until Sam and Rose came to me."

"Thank you, Don Parisi. And they send their repsects"

A knock at the door made one of Parisi's henchmen stiffen up. He stood just inside the foyer of the lavish suite with one hand inside his coat. Another went over to the door and stood to one side, asking who the visitor was.

"Room service."

The henchman opened the door and carefully watched a waiter as he pushed in a cart. It was covered with a pressed white tablecloth and carried a coffee service of sterling silver. Parisi thanked the server and waved him off. The henchman showed the waiter back to the door, slipped him a tip, and pushed him out into the hall before shutting the door.

The discussion resumed over coffee.

"So, what's her answer?"

Maceo tensed up. He couldn't give the answer he knew Parisi wanted and

Maceo felt the eyes of the henchmen pinned on him. "There is no answer, Don Parisi."

"You went to her, yes?"

Maceo nodded.

"And you pressed our offer again, yes?"

"I went to the Factory last night," Maceo said as he scooted to the edge of his chair and leaned on his knees to explain. "I reminded her about the terms of your very generous offer…" He hesitated, glancing at the henchmen closest to him. "But…"

"What happened, Vic?"

"I can't say, Don Parisi," Maceo said with open hands. "I was trying to convince her how important your offer was." He rubbed the back of his head. "But someone from behind—someone I didn't see—knocked me out cold."

With a side-glance at one of his henchmen, Parisi said, "Vic, you are a credit to your family—and you've served me well when I've called on you." He sipped his coffee and stared into the cup. "But these last few years, you've become more heavy-handed than necessary." Parisi looked up from his cup straight at Maceo.

Maceo said nothing as he averted his eyes.

"True, it is sometimes the only way we achieve our goals. But now, more than ever, we have to watch our methods." Parisi set his cup and saucer on the coffee table. "There's a new opportunity. An opportunity to bring real legitimacy to everything we've built."

Maceo kept silent.

"The Attorney General's office proposes that the Families use our resources to uncover spies like the ones in New York."

"And you believe Biddle?"

"I don't expect public endorsements after the war is over, hell no," Parisi said as he leaned back in his chair. "What Biddle did promise was a good deal less scrutiny, besides, protecting the interests of America coincides with the interests of the Families." Parisi reached for his coffee and sipped it before continuing. "Perhaps, finally, we can be seen not as dirty immigrants, but as countrymen. It also means now is the time for expansion—but in the proper manner."

"Yes, Don Parisi." *Fool. They'll never accept us, or you.*

"And do you know why that brings me to the Lamar Hotel for this visit?"

Maceo shook his head no.

"Eight floors down in suite 8-F, men of influence under the guise of legitimacy conspire amongst themselves about this city's future." Parisi leaned up in his chair and spoke softly. "One of them has consented to discuss interests of mutual benefit."

Maceo was curious about which man of influence Parisi meant. It was an open secret who regularly met in that room. Old man Abercrombie, Judge Elkins, Jesse Jones, Gus Wortham, and the Browns—these men and their fortunes, not the mayor or city council, ran Houston. The only one Maceo could easily rule out was Jones. As Secretary of Commerce, most of his time was spent in Washington DC, especially now with the war. He was already responsible for industry ramping up all along the ship channel and in Galveston Bay.

"Apologies, Don Parisi, I don't see the connection to the Corte woman."

"Nevermind, Vic. For now, you and your cousins worry about the Balinese," Parisi said, leaning back. "Get a table ready for me tomorrow night and…" Parisi grinned. "I would enjoy good company, Vic."

"We would be honored by your visit."

"We'll discuss the Corte woman then."

"Good day, Don Parisi." Maceo stood up and bowed slightly at the waist. "Thank you for your patience and understanding." He turned and nodded to Parisi's henchmen as one opened the door. Maceo walked out to the hall and down to the elevator bank. He pressed the call button and the door slid open. They closed behind Maceo as he rested on the handrail, wiping beads of sweat from his forehead. He was relieved—for now.

The Enemy Within

Hoffman leaned half into the driver's side window and handed a Coke to Schneider, who reached over, took the open bottle with his left hand, and turned off the radio with his right.

"Anything on the news broadcast?" Hoffman asked while opening the car door and climbing in. He also handed his colleague the late edition of the *Houston Chronicle*, keeping the *Houston Post* for himself.

Schneider shook his head no.

"I don't expect anything made the papers, but let's see." Hoffman unfolded his newspaper and began reading.

"How long do you think they can keep this up?" Schneider asked as he unfolded his edition to browse the headlines and notices. "Little more than eight months and there is already bickering among your people—and among the Allies."."

"Keep what up?" Hoffman said, scowling.

"Your American *resolve*," Schneider said with sarcasm.

"Careful, Sturmbannfürer. People here have a way of overcoming their differences under the strangest of circumstances," Hoffman said as he casually turned a page. He pointed up the street. "They're cutting the top spires off of the streetlights, and pulling up old trolley rails downtown—all for scrap metal to build tanks, planes, and ships. I'd say those are fair demonstrations of resolve—which Hirohito has already experienced."

"Let the Americans occupy themselves with the Pacific," Schneider said as he glanced up at Hoffman, and back at the paper. "That simply provides us with the time to complete our fortifications against an American invasion."

"Don't forget the British."

"Das Englisch are of little consequence," the SS officer said with a snort. "Without the Americans, they would fall, and when the time comes they will be forced to sue for peace—on our terms."

"Perhaps," Hoffman said, checking his side-view mirror as well as the rearview one.

"You doubt *German* resolve?"

"Not at all," Hoffman said, not looking at Schneider. "That resolve brought the German people from ruin."

"It was der Führer's brilliant vision!"

"But accomplished with the loyalty and sweat of the people." He folded his paper and plopped it on the dashboard. "How did the Führer put it in *Mein Kampf*? 'The thing that matters here is not the vision of the man of genius who created the great idea, but rather the success with which his apostles achieve in shaping the expression of this idea to bring it home to the minds of the masses.' He seems to agree with my assessment—that without the consent of the people no leader can achieve any vision."

"And your loyalty, Herr Hoffman?" Schneider's query was punctuated with a sneer.

Hoffman scoffed. "Don't confuse pragmatism for disloyalty!" He sipped his soda and continued. "As far as my loyalties are concerned, you sitting in that seat and our conversation exemplify my loyalties." Hoffman held the SS officer's stare to reinforce his stated convictions.

"Given recent actions by some of our colleagues, I am forced to always question people's loyalties—both on behalf of our Führer and for my own sense of self-preservation."

"Now you're being a pragmatist," Hoffman said, grinning.

"Perhaps." Schneider smiled back. "Although I believe your uncle would be proud, what brings you to our cause is still undefined."

"Mm," Hoffman grunted as he turned his attention back to the headlines. "I share the Führer's need for order."

"And a capitalist's loathing of the welfare state."

"When Roosevelt took over from Hoover, we were still in the grip of the aftermath of twenty-nine," Hoffman said, shifting to face his body toward Schneider. "FDR reacted in fear—and as a consequence, his socialist precepts took the country down a path almost impossible to reverse." Hoffman paused a moment to check their surroundings before concluding. "Dipping into the public till only breeds more dependence on government and undermines the nation's work ethic. And that infringes on my uncle's legacy—and my livelihood."

Hoffman looked at his wristwatch. "Something's not right," he said, turning the key, then depressing the starter pedal and clutch. "Allen should have been here by now." The engine turned over, and Hoffman set the Cord in gear. He pulled out and turned east from the Texas Company filling station at Westheimer and Hazard streets.

"Agreed," Schneider began. "Allen may be reprehensible on all other counts, however, he is punctual."

"The question is what's keeping him."

"I find it difficult to believe that we've been uncovered so soon—that he has been apprehended."

"Always assume the other side knows what you're up to," Hoffman said, checking his mirrors repeatedly. "That's how you keep from getting caught."

"Surprisingly wise philosophy," Schneider said. "So, what of your precious democracy?"

Hoffman wrinkled his brow as he answered. "This was never a democracy, Sturmbannfürer," he said, glancing once more in his rearview mirror. "This republic, though constructed for the benefit of the people, certainly functions for the pleasure of the few." He briefly looked at the sturmbannfürer, then back at the road. "All societies do so, but some more repressively than others."

"Such as?" Schneider asked.

Hoffman thought it might be a baited question, so he used the Soviets as a prime example of an oppressive society. "Stalin is nothing more than a criminal and mass murderer. It's unconscionable that Roosevelt officially recognizes the Soviet Union and repugnant that he also lauds Stalin." Hoffman's tone became defiant. "That is what defines my service to the cause—to stop

Stalin and to stop his brand of socialism."

"The enemy of my enemy is my friend?" Schneider said.

Hoffman nodded and said, "Such a thread binds Hitler and Hirohito."

"I'm curious about your capitalist's view of the Nationalist Socialist revolution."

"Any state must ultimately be self-perpetuating," Hoffman said, expressionless as he spoke, aware Schneider knew his uncle had declined any contact from representatives of the Abwehr. And it wasn't until 1940 that Hoffman suddenly accepted his current role. Schneider was probably fishing, unsure if Hoffman genuinely held these beliefs or was trying to shore up trust.

"Even Americans must accept at least some state sovereignty to maintain order, regardless of the country's outward self-delusion to the contrary," Hoffman said. "Fascism, to some degree, binds the fiber of all governments and all governed. After all, the shepherd would be moot if the flock were truly capable of self-governance."

Hoffman pulled onto Franklin Street, then into the alley that led behind his building. He let Schneider out before easing into the tight space under the carport.

"I'll expect to hear from you within the hour," Schneider said, looking at his wristwatch.

Hoffman checked his and nodded as he went inside.

Schneider stopped and turned. He scanned across the bayou to the bridge and the parallel street to see if someone was watching. Though he didn't see anyone, he felt an odd but familiar sensation in the back of his head.

It reminded Schneider of Poland when he found himself separated from his unit. Walking along a road, he'd suddenly stopped midstride with the very same tingle. He'd turned around to see a Polish infantryman standing off in the trees—his rifle ready to fire. Schneider had shouldered his weapon for the march.

They stared at each other for minutes until, for no apparent reason, the infantryman lowered his barrel and turned away. Schneider was perplexed by such an act of compassion in war, one that cost the Polish soldier his life. More importantly to Schneider, he's learned to keep his eyes on the trees.

Countdown

Everyone in the kitchen busily prepared for the dinner rush. Waiters and busboys scurried in and out with flatware and linens for the table settings.

Walt was hardly visible within the clouds of steam and smoke coming up from the pots and sauté pans on the burners.

Hoffman walked out to the main dining room looking for Herman. He surveyed the room and tables on his way toward the front podium. The reservation book was open, and among the many reservations was one for the mayor.

"Mister Hoffman," Herman said from behind.

"Gonna be a busy night, Herman."

"Tomorrow looks even better," Herman said as he turned the page to Friday night.

Hoffman smiled. The end-of-the-month boost from booking the new band meant he'd have his best numbers yet. "We're gonna need everybody in tomorrow."

Herman nodded and said Hoffman had several phone messages on his desk.

"Anything important?" Hoffman asked. Herman was silent until Hoffman offered a relaxed smile.

"Miss Dorothy will be in tomorrow."

"That is important," Hoffman said with a grin. "What else?"

Herman listed other calls from patrons and vendors. "And there was an odd one." He scowled. "A Mister Allen said he'd have to cancel his reservation—"

Hoffman looked up from the reservation book.

"Something about being delayed in Sealy because of a pump station malfunction?" Herman ran his hand over the page as he continued. "But he's not in the book for tonight. I thought maybe you knew what he was talking about."

"The name's familiar," Hoffman said, shaking his head. "He leave a number?

Herman said it was on the pad by the phone in Hoffman's office. Hoffman nodded and told his headwaiter to carry on.

Allen had left a number, so he probably wasn't in custody. However, if there was a problem with a pump station, it meant Schneider and his men had botched the job. Hoffman was actually glad—especially for the people downriver from the bypass. The only drawback was that failure was as much an alert to the authorities as if the pipeline had been successfully blown up. He also knew Schneider's patience was about to get much, much thinner.

NINE

Houseguest

Solace

Reina knelt in the pew closest to the confessionals. While she prayed her Rosary, she rehearsed her confession. She would start in the ritual manner. "Bless me, Father, for I have sinned. It has been five days since my last confession."

The priest on the other side of the screen would tell her to continue, and she would have to admit to having impure thoughts. She imagined the horror on Father Allnoch's face.

Reina opened her eyes and made the sign of the cross as she got up and left the sanctuary, forgetting to genuflect. The courtyard next to the church was her favorite place at the parish. That was where she and Vincent exchanged vows almost seven years ago. There was no church then. St. Anne's was a relatively new parish—about ten years old. The school and rectory were the first buildings. Only recently was church construction finished. Against an outside wall of the church was a statue of the Virgin Mary on a pedestal. Being there calmed Reina—another reason she liked the courtyard.

"Reina!" Father Allnoch called to her as he stepped out of the church and extended his arms.

"Good evening, Father," she said with an apprehensive smile.

He took her hand in both of his. "How's Olivia?" he asked with a gentle smile, which helped set her at ease. "Sister Mary misses her very much."

"She's fine," Reina said, not looking him in the eye. "Johnny helps her write letters to me, and he's let her call a few times even though long-distance is so expensive."

"I know it's difficult having her so far away."

Reina looked down at the gravel path of the courtyard.

"This is an especially trying year for you," Father Allnoch said. He used his finger to raise her chin to look her in the eye. "You've faced so much with dignity and courage."

Reina smiled but said nothing.

Father motioned to a bench on the edge of the path. They sat facing each other. "So, what brings you here today?"

Reina stuttered because she couldn't bring herself to come out and say it. Instead, she talked about Vincent. "I still miss him so very much, Father." She closed her eyes and took a deep breath through her nose. "I still smell his aftershave on my pillow and…" She paused, knowing her face grew flush.

"And what, child?"

"I feel his touch," she said, moving her hands across her belly and holding herself. "Then I open my eyes and I'm alone, and I feel a horrible emptiness."

Father Allnoch began to speak, but Reina interrupted him.

"But what hurts more is that I let myself feel something for—" she stopped short of saying it. She darted her eyes between Father Allnoch and the ground.

The priest was silent for a moment. Leaning in, he whispered, "Has someone new entered the picture?"

Reina clamped her lips, still looking away and trying not to cry.

"Whatever you're feeling, it's a part of going on with your life," he said, squeezing her hand. "You've not only honored his memory, but also your marriage together."

Reina almost smiled, but she couldn't.

"Tell me about him," he said.

Father's reaction to her rundown about the assault in the alley was no surprise. He dutifully scolded her for not reporting it to the police, except she knew he understood that prosecuting an attempted rape charge was far more impossible than a full rape charge. Besides which, Maceo had *connections*—and those connections protected both Maceo and Parisi.

She told Father Allnoch how Richard had intervened. And that led to an explanation of how she cared for his wounds. "He had burns all over his body with charred clothing."

"Was there a fire?"

"I don't think so—I never heard about one, which is so odd."

"What happened next?"

"Clarence helped me get him into the house, and to tend to his wounds, we had to cut and remove the scorched garments."

"I take it his wounds were also in sensitive places?"

Reina nodded.

"Are you feeling uneasy, child?"

"Yes, Father."

"The source of your emotions seems pretty clear," Father Allnoch said. He paused, leaving an uncomfortable silence. Reina expected a novena as penance. Father Allnoch shook his head, laughed, and said, "Leave it to you, Reina…"

"Father?"

"Tell me, when you were a girl, did you often bring home stray animals?"

Reina looked at him and said, "We barely fed ourselves, much less an animal."

"Mm. My point is this," Father Allnoch began. "In addition to all your parish work, you spend a good deal of time teaching English to Italians fresh off the boat—taking it upon yourself to employ them, or to find them work. And if all that isn't enough, you take in this man, caring for his injuries when just as easily a hospital could have done so."

"You know how I feel about them."

"Yes I do," Father Allnoch said as he straightened up. "And you know it wouldn't have made any difference with Vincent."

Reina dismissed that. Vincent's pneumonia was compounded by other infections that came from the hospital itself.

Father Allnoch went on before she could dwell on her anger. "Regardless of his actions last night, you don't know this man." He paused and assumed a stern look. "Now listen to me, you of all people have nothing to be ashamed of. You're a young woman, and circumstances being what they are—your feelings are quite natural."

That shocked Reina. Lust may be natural but the church certainly didn't condone it. Father Allnoch smiled at her expression.

"God understands your pain. And it is your capacity for love, physically and spiritually, that is His gift to you."

Reina blushed.

"You've neither acted on these particular feelings nor have you sought out the situation that stirs them."

Reina briskly shook her head to affirm his observation.

"There is no sin here, and no reason for remorse," he said.

Father Allnoch stood up and held Reina's hand as she rose off the bench. They walked toward the drive in front of the church. "You be careful and mindful of the pitfalls," he said with a raised eyebrow. "Don't put yourself into another situation."

"Thank you, Father." She smiled.

"By the way, is he Catholic?"

"I don't know," Reina answered with a quiet laugh.

"Bring him around to Sunday morning Mass, if he's up to it," Father Allnoch said as he guided Reina off the curb of the drive. "Now go home, Reina."

Reina gave Father Allnoch a suspicious smile and he grinned back at her. She turned to begin the thirty-minute walk home. It was just enough time for her to think over everything he had said. And, as well, time to figure out what to do next.

The Munchies

Richard didn't know whether to laugh or cry at his reflection in the mirror. He tried combing his hair, but the more he raked it, the more it frizzed. So he tossed the comb onto the back of the sink.

Turning his cheek and rubbing the stubble under his chin and down the side of his neck, Richard decided to forgo shaving—it'd be another day or so before his skin wouldn't be sensitive to the scraping of a safety razor. However, the burr of his mustache, looking more like a five-o'clock shadow, would eventually have to go.

Reina had provided him with a small, flat jar when he asked for deodorant. He unscrewed the lid and scooped up some cream on his fingertips. He dabbed a bit under his arm and rubbed it in, repeating the process for the other. It was identical to the deodorant his dad used when Richard was little—before roll-ons and even before the aerosols.

He slipped on the jumpsuit Reina had given him and zipped up the front. Her husband must have been a lot taller and a good thirty or so pounds heavier. The outfit hung on him like a muumuu. He felt ridiculous, but the loose fit didn't irritate his skin.

The phone in the hall rang. The tinny ringer sounded two long and one short, which Richard thought was odd. It rang again, so he went into the hall to the phone nook and picked up the receiver. "Hello? Uh, Corte residence." There was no answer. Richard repeated his greeting. Then someone on the other end responded.

"Hello?"

"Yes, hi. Corte residence," Richard said.

"Corte residence my foot," the voice said. "Who is this?"

"Eleanora?" another voice asked.

"Camila? Yes, this is Ellie—who is that man," Eleanora squawked.

"I thought you knew," Camila said.

"No, I don't. Who is this? Where's Reina?"

"This is Richard Warren," he said, trying to follow who was who, but he was lost. *Shit!* "I'm... well... a friend of Mrs. Corte."

"What kind of friend, and what in tarnation are you doing on my line?" Camila asked.

"I'm sorry; it rang and I answered it."

"Oh for Heaven's sake! Obviously this is a party line," Eleanora said.

"Please, forgive the intrusion, ma'am."

"I should say so."

Richard slowly placed the receiver over the hook, listening to the cackle between what sounded like old ladies. In mere seconds, they speculated on whom he was, why he was in "young Reina's home," where Reina was, and how Father Allnoch should know what she's up to. He softly hung up the receiver. "Bye."

He laughed. The whole thing sounded like a bad routine between Lily Tomlin's operator character and Olive Oil from old Popeye cartoons. Then he cringed at having to tell his hostess about the infraction.

Richard slipped his hands into the pockets of the jumpsuit and looked around. He hadn't had a smoke in forever; and he gritted his teeth as he wandered into the front room of the house. The sofa and chairs had exposed wood frames with detailed carvings in a dark finish. The windows had sheers with colorful drapes pulled back and gathered with ties. Looking out the window was tempting, but he chose not to.

In one corner of the room stood a Victrola console. Richard lifted the lid and found a 78-rpm album on the turntable. He rotated the disk so he could read the label. It was deep blue with white letters—a Glenn Miller record. He would love to hear the sound.

There were various levers and what appeared to be switches that protruded from under the turntable. He wanted to crank the handle on the side of the case, but he decided it'd be best not to fool with the thing. He lowered the lid and went on about his survey.

On the wall of the fireplace, built-in cabinets with glass doors flanked the hearth. There were figurines of little animals, some porcelain dolls, and a few sepia-toned pictures of people in uncomfortable looking clothes—expressionless and stiff.

On the mantle over the fireplace was a picture of a bride and groom. It was black and white but had been hand-painted to add tone and hints of color to the subjects. Reina wore a white dress with a long flowing train. She was smiling up at her groom. Richard guessed the man must have stood every bit of a foot over Reina. It wasn't a posed picture. They were happy and natural as if looking forward to their lives together. He gently set the picture frame back in its place.

The small mantle clock softly chimed, and the face read five o'clock. Richard felt a slight pang in his belly.

He walked through the dining room toward the kitchen. Against the partition wall—separating the dining and living rooms—was a secretary. The pull-down desk was open with a newspaper on it. "Don't. You don't want to know," he said aloud, stepping away. Richard stopped and turned back to pick up the paper.

The *Houston Chronicle* was on the masthead, but what stung him was the dateline: Thursday, July 30, 1942. Two headlines of the day were about a debate over new liquor taxes "to Beat the Axis," and a war update detailing "the Allies on the Road to Rome."

Another announced the expanded list of items under wartime rationing. "Now I really need a cigarette." He laid the paper down and, needing to satisfy his craving, went into the kitchen.

It was immaculate. Standing in the doorway, the Magic Chef Range was on the innermost wall. *Very cool,* Richard thought. He admired the white enamel on the surfaces and sparkling stainless steel trim on the sculpted, freestanding unit. The thing had eight burners, two ovens, and a broiler. One chamber didn't seem to have any burners and was where Reina kept larger pots, small ones nested inside the other.

On the top was a built-in breadbox. Richard lifted the lid and found a loaf of Mrs. Baird's bread. He removed it and set it on the table. He reached back and pulled the handle on the fridge. The food brands weren't any he recognized, but he did spot a jar he thought might be mayonnaise—Miss Chuler's Brand Salad Dressing. He was disappointed that it smelled more like Miracle Whip, which people always confused with real mayo. The consistency and texture were totally different, but it was also fixable.

Richard broke a couple of eggs into a small stainless steel bowl. He spooned some of the whip in with the eggs and used a fork to whisk the concoction. Churning the eggs and dressing, Richard curled his upper lip under and onto his top teeth. He spoke in a deep, monotone voice with deliberate and choppy phrases. "Picture a man—an ordinary man, in an ordinary kitchen, making an ordinary meal. But these are no ordinary ingredients. He's about to dine—in the Twilight Zone." Then he performed the iconic melody mimicking the electric strings.

When the mix was just right, he dipped his finger in the bowl for a taste. "Yyeahhh! Now for the peanut butter."

A freestanding cupboard next to the back door was stocked with canned goods and a few packets of baking ingredients—but no peanut butter. Contemplating where Reina might keep a jar, he snapped his fingers and went back to the refrigerator. Nothing obvious jumped out at him. On the back of the bottom rack were several unmarked tins. The first one was half-full of gelatin that smelled like bacon drippings. Another was full of shortening or lard. The third tin had a twist-off lid with remnants of a peeled label. He opened it. "Paydirt!"

With a knife he scrounged from a drawer, Richard stirred the peanut butter to mix back in oils that had risen to the top. He removed two slices of bread—they were thick and the crust was a rich brown. "Toaster?" A quick look around the kitchen didn't reveal one. But there were two sets of tongs over the range.

The pilot lights on the burners were lit. He turned the knobs to crank up fire for two burners. Richard lightly toasted the slices using the tongs and potholders—careful not to burn the bread or make a mess of Reina's sparkling range.

Richard laid the toast on a cup towel he flattened out on the breakfast table. He spread the peanut butter first in a thick layer on one slice. Next, he gave the homemade mayo a quick whip and globbed it on the other slice—spreading it in a not-so-thick layer.

Richard married the two halves of the sandwich and crunched into the first bite. He froze in mid chomp when Reina stepped through the backdoor.

A mouth full of the PBM on toast garbled his attempt at "hello" without spewing half-chewed chunks.

Crossed Wires

"Didn't your mother teach you never to talk with your mouth full?" Reina closed the door behind her and set her purse on top of the cupboard next to the door. She stopped and sniffed at the aroma of toasted bread. "Did you toast the bread?"

"Yep, over the burners," he said with a cheek full of sandwich. "I couldn't find your toaster."

Rare for a man to know his way around a kitchen. "I left it with Charlie Evans," she said, describing him as the Mister Fixit in the neighborhood.

"Ah."

"What in the world are you eating?" she asked, sitting next to Richard as she peered over the mixing bowl and at the ingredients he had out.

"Peanut butter and mayonnaise," he said, holding the sandwich out for her inspection.

"Mayonnaise." Reina frowned.

"Yeah, you know, mayonnaise? The opposite of mustard—a thick white spread to keep from having a dry sandwich?"

Reina said she'd heard about something like it that was back east. "But I thought it was pretty much the same as whipped salad dressing—which I see you found."

"Nuh-uh," he said, following with an explanation about the differences between the two products. Reina smiled at his passion for the subject. Still, the thought of that concoction and peanut butter looked simply disgusting.

"You wouldn't let your daughter turn her nose up at something before trying it?" he asked.

Reina sneered at him. The smart-aleck was trying to use her motherhood against her. He sliced off an uneaten corner of the sandwich and offered it with a mischievous grin. Reina reluctantly accepted it.

Richard got up, took a glass from the shelf next to the sink, and filled it with water. He set it next to her, sat down, and waited with another smirk.

That damn smirk of his, she thought. She also wondered if he could ever deliver on what the glimmer in his blue eyes promised.

Reina warily tasted the bite, but the flavor was surprisingly good. The toasted bread gave it texture, and the peanut butter made her mouth water a bit while the mayonnaise melted around her tongue. She flinched when

Richard raised his hand toward her face.

"Take it easy," he said as he dabbed a bit of the white spread from the corner of her mouth and wiped it on the cup towel.

Gentle.

"See—it never hurts to try something new," he said.

Reina chased down the bite with a drink of water, leaving a smudge of lipstick on the rim. She turned down his offer of another morsel, not from distaste, but from the fact she wasn't hungry.

Once Richard finished off his last bite, Reina started to clear the table. He refused to let her, clearing the table and gathering up what minor mess he made. Over the sound of running water and the clang of metal utensils being washed, the phone sounded two short rings. Reina got up to answer it.

"Um." Richard paused.

"Yes?"

"Go ahead," he said, nodding to the phone as he turned back to the sink.

She picked up the phone halfway into the third set of rings. "Hello?" On the other end was her best friend. "Hi, Carla."

"You missed our luncheon," Carla Bono said.

"I know, I'm sorry—something came up," Reina said.

Reina looked toward the kitchen and started speaking in Italian. She told Carla about what happened in the alley and about her narrow escape. And she explained that Richard was the reason she missed the Ladies' Guild luncheon.

Carla's reaction to the story was anger toward Maceo and his attack, followed by her whispered shock that Reina brought home a naked man. So Reina brought up her conversation with Father Allnoch. While that put Carla at ease about the whole situation, it raised her curiosity.

"Si, bello piccolo," Reina said with a giggle.

"Who is a little handsome?" asked a different voice on the line. "Is it *that* Richard Warren I spoke with earlier?"

"I'm on the line, Missus Provenzano," Reina said, thinking the busybody was listening in the whole time. She coldly stared toward the kitchen as she realized Mrs. Provenzano had said Richard's last name.

"Reina, I need the line open!"

"I'm sure you do, but I need a few more minutes." Mrs. Provenzano clicked the receiver down. The conversation wound down as Carla reminded Reina of plans they made a few days earlier.

"What about tomorrow night?" Reina asked, and then remembered. "Oh for Pete's sake, I'm supposed to meet you and Frank at the Buffalo River

Grille. Or is it the Rice Empire Room?"

"The Grille," Carla said.

"The Woody Wilson Orchestra's playing, right?"

"No, remember? It's one of the guys who used to play with Woody Wilson who's performing—he started his own band."

"Can I let you and Frank know for sure around the middle of the day tomorrow?

"Of course, Reina. Bye."

Reina hung up the receiver, folded her arms, and leaned against the doorjamb of the kitchen entryway. "You have something you want to tell me?"

"I didn't know you had a party line," Richard said, drying the last utensil. "When it rang I just answered it. Sorry about that."

"Well, I'm sure the news is all over town by now that I brought a strange naked man into my house."

"I take it you share a line with the town gossip," Richard said.

Reina glared.

"Well," Richard began, gnashing his teeth. "Fair warning: she'll probably drop dime on you to somebody named Allnoch."

"Drop dime?"

"Uh, rat you out. Tattle."

Reina silently thanked God she'd already seen Father Allnoch. But she wondered where Richard had learned to speak.

"You know, a private line would solve the problem," he said.

"Mm, an unnecessary expense," Reina said. "Besides, now that you know the ring—"

"I know," Richard said as he raised his hands at the elbow. "I'm sorry if I put you in a bad situation."

"Hmm, well, bad situations seem to be my lot, lately," Reina said. She pushed off the doorjamb and sat down at the table. As she pulled out a chair for Richard, she patted the seat and said, "Speaking of which, let's talk about yours—Mister Warren."

TEN

Evening Shade

Tight Lid

"Aye sir, he'll meet us in the morning. Goodnight," Jack said to his commanding officer. He hung up the receiver and went back into the kitchen.

Mary Lou and Phil were almost finished with dinner. Phil scraped some gravy up against his chicken fried steak while he asked, "Everything A-OK, Jackson?"

"Yeah, just finishing up some business for tomorrow."

"How'd your jaunt go this afternoon?" Phil asked.

"Uh, interesting, but I can't really talk about it." Jack gave Phil the "not now" face as Mary Lou paid more attention to her food.

"Lou, this is even better than last night," Phil said.

"Enjoy it, boys—it'll be the last time we see meat for a while," Mary Lou said.

"At least for us civilians," Phil added, nodding his head at Jack.

Mary Lou smiled before asking Jack what his plans were for Friday night.

"I haven't firmed anything up. I was thinking of heading over to San Antonio to see friends, but I think Captain Preskin'll need me close," Jack said as he gathered some mashed potato and gravy on his fork. "So instead, I might go to the Buffalo Grille over on Franklin."

"With some lonely girl?" Phil fluttered his eyebrows.

"Phillip Reilly!" Mary Lou backhanded her husband's shoulder. Jack and Phil laughed.

Phil gave Mary Lou an apologetic look before continuing. "That place is booked—hard to get into unless you have greenbacks."

"I did meet the fella that owns it."

"That the one that damn near ran ya down?" Phil asked, referring to the incident with Hoffman.

"What's this?" Mary Lou clanked her fork onto the plate and glared at Jack.

"Relax, Lou," Jack said as he glanced up then back down at his plate. "He just clipped me a bit. No harm done."

"Yeah, Jack said it was a Cord." Phil grinned. "The character probably has more money than Carter has little liver pills."

"But what's this have to do with a club?" Mary Lou asked.

"This fella, Hoffman, said he owned the Buffalo River Grille over on Franklin at Milam," Jack said.

"Scuttlebutt is there's gambling and liquor by the glass in a private club underneath," Phil said.

"Underground in this town?" Mary Lou asked with a disbelieving tone. "You poke a stick in the ground too deep and hit water."

"I think it's built on a high bank of the bayou and the bottom level drops below street level down the slope," Jack said.

"Well ain't you the cat's meow," Mary Lou said.

"Guess so," Jack said with a smile.

Mary Lou started in on the dishes until the baby began to cry. Phil and Jack took over "kitchen duty" so she could go back and nurse Corrine. They cleared the table and wiped it down. Jack washed the dishes and scrubbed the pots while Phil dried and put them away.

"What the hell'd you find out there in Sealy?"

"I'm not at liberty to say, Phil."

"C'mon Jack, I overheard you talking to Preskin." Phil had a stern look but his brother-in-law didn't flinch. "What's the score?"

Jack looked at Phil with a raised eyebrow.

"Then who is this guy meeting y'all?"

"He's one of the guys responsible for maintaining that particular part of the pipeline," Jack said as he stopped washing for a minute. "He's only coming down at my request to give us his take on what happened."

"So what happened?"

Jack kept washing. "Don't read too much into it, Phil." He looked over his shoulder and said, "There's no cloak-n-dagger stuff goin' on."

"What's Mac Leroy at Continental got to say about all this?" Phil asked.

"Mac had no take because everybody but a handful at Continental is out of the loop, altogether." Jack stopped washing and turned off the water. He lowered his voice as he spoke. "All I can tell you, which is more than I should, is that it's probably what it looks like—a simple foul-up. But until they're sure, everyone had to be tight-lipped about it."

They could hear the baby cry again, and Jack suggested Phil join Lou and Corrine. "I'll finish up here."

"Sure?"

Jack motioned for Phil to go on. Phil laid the towel on the counter and started to leave the kitchen. Jack kept his attention on the dishes but heard Phil's fading steps on hardwood floors down the hall.

With the last of the flatware dried and set in the drawer with the rest, Jack rinsed and wiped out the sink. He lifted the percolator off the stove and shook it. And with his other hand, he retrieved a cup and emptied coffee from the pot, doctored it with sugar and a drop of cream, grabbed his Luckies off the counter, and went out the door.

Climbing the stairs a step at a time, he shook the pack, forcing the end of a cigarette to pop out. He crimped it between his lips, exchanged the pack for his lighter in his pocket, and lit the smoke.

Inside the small garage apartment, an oscillating fan next to an open window panned left then right—rattling a bit when it paused before panning back. It sucked in outside air and wafted pulses of breeze throughout the room. On the table against the wall, Jack set his cup next to a typewriter. A sheet of thin paper was in the carriage, rolled halfway down the page with the strike-guide positioned in the middle of a sentence.

Jack moved the ashtray on the bedside table next to his cup on the makeshift desk. He sat down, puffed his cigarette, and lifted the drooping top of the page to review the paragraphs he typed earlier.

It was titled **SITE REPORT – PRELIMINARY**. A portion of the last word on the page was covered by the strike-guide, which didn't matter because Jack remembered exactly what he had typed. He leaned back, sipped his coffee and took a drag. A sigh accompanied the exhaled smoke out the side of his mouth away from his work area as he reread the page—never taking his eyes off it while he drank and smoked.

Jack crushed out the nub of his cigarette, squared himself in the chair, and typed without looking at the keys. **PROBABLE CAUSE – SABOTAGE**

Black Magic

Hoffman sat at a small table in the far back corner of the Grille. It was next to the last floor-to-ceiling windowpane overlooking Buffalo Bayou. The tablecloth was white and pressed; it matched his double-breasted dinner jacket. On the table was a small chessboard. Hoffman pondered over the pieces as he poured Louis XIII cognac from its Baccarat crystal decanter into a small aperitif glass. He usually reserved cognac for after dinner, but tonight he was in a good mood and felt like treating himself. Besides, Louis Trey is best earlier rather than later. He let it rest in the glass, admiring the copper color and taking in the gentle fragrance influenced by the ancient casks in which the cognac aged. Hoffman sipped the century-old treasure—relishing refined, nectar-rich opulence, like drinking liquid silk.

Activities in the dining room tore him from his indulgence. The restaurant was split-level; the outer tables were on a floor four steps above the center, where most of the tables were arranged. From his perch, Hoffman squinted first at the mayor's table, quickly assessing drink levels and estimating when to signal for the next course.

Music echoed up from the club below the main dining room, serenading many of Houston's dignitaries scattered about the tables. The muffled notes from trombones, saxophones, and assorted other instruments sounded the melody from *Chattanooga Choo Choo.* It drew Hoffman's attention to the club doorway, guarded by his tux-clad bouncer. Only select clientele were permitted downstairs.

Another check of the mayor's table revealed near-empty wineglasses. Noting the crossed forks and knives on bare plates, Hoffman held three fingers over his left lapel as he stared at the waiter he assigned to exclusively service his Honor. Arlen, the Grilles's headwaiter, normally tended to the mayor. But tonight he was pacing a waiting room outside a maternity ward, so Hoffman had to pay special attention to ensure his patron's preferred rhythm.

The substitute waiter refreshed the wineglasses, then signaled the busboy to remove dishes and the unneeded flatware, making space for the dessert course. Hoffman watched the choreography with particular focus on the mayor's expression. His Honor glanced at Hoffman, nodded, and raised a glass. Hoffman nodded back and drank from his cognac.

The tempo of the music slowed, and a clarinet led the orchestra in a rendition of *That Old Black Magic*. That's when the maître d' delivered an envelope to Hoffman. "A gentleman just left this for you."

"Thanks, Herman."

Herman excused himself and returned to his podium at the front.

Hoffman tore open the flap and read the note. "Delivery." It was signed *VM*. He shoved the note in his inside breast pocket and got up. He greeted a few guests at tables along the way as he crossed the room. Once again, the mayor gestured a toast and Hoffman smiled and nodded.

Entering the kitchen, Hoffman approached a slender young woman in a long gown. "Jeanine, pull a few Havanas for the mayor," he said, passing her.

She smiled and said, "Yes, Mister Hoffman."

He briefly turned to admire Jeanine's carriage as he ducked into his office. Hoffman pulled a lockbox from a desk drawer and unlocked it. He stashed a stack of twenty-dollar bills in his coat pocket, secured the lockbox, and put it back in the desk. He walked back through the kitchen and out the rear door.

Standing next to a row of empty produce crates, Maceo was puffing a cigar at the outer boundary of the light from the door lamp. "Looks busy in there tonight."

"At least you stayed low-key." Hoffman looked around the alley. "Half of city hall is in tonight—including the mayor."

"Rationing's good for business, ain't it."

"Yeah, you've said that before—what do you have?"

"For starters, here's your goods from this morning." Maceo pointed to cartons stacked against the wall.

"But you're not here because of butter."

"I told you, Parisi's in town," Maceo said as he twisted the cigar between his teeth. "He told me about some agreement between Biddle and the Families."

Hoffman waited for more.

"Uncle Sam is recruiting us to guard the home front." Maceo drew in more smoke from his cheap cigar and exhaled. "We're supposed to keep an eye on things the feds can't."

"Your point?" Hoffman waved the dung-like odor from his face.

"This is all I can give you right now." Maceo handed Hoffman a nine by twelve-inch envelope. "Inside are the last of the plots you wanted."

"And the rest?" Hoffman opened the flap and peeked inside to confirm the contents.

"With Parisi down from Dallas for a few days, gotta delay bringing the rest of your supplies.

Hoffman scowled and clamped his jaw.

"Your man should've come more prepared," Maceo said.

"He came very well prepared—based on what you promised you could provide." Hoffman was indignant. He tucked the envelope under his left arm and slipped his right hand into his left inside coat pocket.

"I'll keep my promise, Hoffman." Maceo edged closer. "You'll just have to be patient," he said, blowing a little smoke in Hoffman's face. "Hear me?"

The men were similar in size, though Hoffman estimated Maceo at thirty pounds more.

"Now hear this," Hoffman said as he instantly drew a pistol from his coat pocket and cocked the hammer, pressing the barrel to Maceo's crotch. "You've been paid to hold up your end," he said in a low tone through gritted teeth. Then Hoffman increased the pressure of the barrel. "If you don't, I'll shoot it off—you hear me?"

Maceo nodded while staring down.

"I'm damn sure you'd expect no less from anyone who owed you. Agreed?"

Maceo nodded again.

"As for patience, I'll give you 'til Saturday night." Hoffman eased the hammer down and pushed Maceo back, keeping the pistol trained on his target. "How you deal with Parisi is your problem—send him back to Dallas or off your goddamn pier, I don't care which. But be here Saturday night before closing."

"I'll be here." Maceo backed up another step and kept his hands where Hoffman could see. "But you pull a gun on me again, and you'll pay."

"If I do, I'll drop you there and then." Hoffman cocked the hammer again. "No games. There's other players—don't forget that." He shoved the envelope in his belt, then pulled a stack of bills from a coat pocket and tossed the cash to Maceo.

"What da hell is this?" Maceo fanned through the stack.

"You held up on your part of this bargain." Hoffman pointed to the cartons of butter, lard, and oil. "I'm holding up mine, as agreed. And a bit more because, as you said, you're early."

"I don't figure you, Hoffman."

Hoffman backed toward the door. "Don't try," he said, easing the hammer down and slipping the pistol back in his pocket. He gave a hard look to Maceo. "Before closing on Saturday."

Maceo nodded, turned, and walked away. Hoffman watched him to the end of the alley before going back inside.

Nuances

Schneider leaned his shoulder against a wall on the opposite side of the alley. He stayed far enough back to keep outside of the rim of light coming from the lamp over the backdoor of the restaurant. He stood completely still, listening to Maceo and Hoffman.

Hoffman demonstrated remarkable control and cunning as if he anticipated every move Maceo would make. Too, his honor in apparently making good on a business exchange amidst such clandestine dealings was quite revealing—young Hoffman held his honor at high value. And that was precisely what concerned Schneider.

The two backed away from each other and Maceo disappeared down the alley toward the thoroughfare. Schneider studied Hoffman as the restaurateur eyed his nemesis walking off.

Since Maceo didn't have the remaining components, Schneider saw no point in disclosing his presence. Once the door shut behind Hoffman, Schneider flipped open his lighter and lit a cigarette.

Five times, Hoffman's uncle had vehemently denied the privilege of serving the Reich. Young Hoffman himself resisted until the third or fourth time he was approached by the Abwehr. His arguments were convincing enough, but Schneider knew better than to place blind faith in him. He was, after all, an American—a capitalist who, by his own admission, was more concerned with opposing communist forces than with furthering the cause of the Nationalist Socialist Empire.

Schneider slid a hand in his pocket as he slipped out of the alley, blending in with the crowd of pedestrians. The streets were wide here, and so many of the buildings were new. It all made the walk back to his hotel look further than it was.

He took the stairs to the fifth floor because the elevator at the Sam Houston Hotel was in disrepair. Ritter and Neubauer's room was down on the left. He knocked once, then twice. Ritter opened the door a crack before letting Schneider in. He was still frail.

Neubauer was at the desk, wearing a jeweler's loop as he tinkered with a detonator. "Did you get the explosives?" he asked, barely looking up.

"It seems there is a delay," Schneider said as he walked over to Neubauer.

"Mein Herr, our calculations depend on specific weight versus density and flow," Neubauer said.

"I expect we will have the variables soon enough," Schneider said as he picked up a timer. "And I believe the explosives will be in our hands forty-eight hours from now," he said, fiddling with the set-stem. The entire device was about the size of a large pocket watch. He tripped the mechanism and heard the spring-loaded magnet spin within the minute copper coil, causing a small spark between the dangling leads.

"Doing that might put undue wear on the spring," Neubauer said.

Schneider nodded as he turned to Ritter and asked how he was feeling.

"Ready for duty, Sturmbannfürer." Ritter clicked his heels as he came to attention.

Weak yet spirited and determined, Schneider thought. "I'm sure you are, and even more so once we pass this delay."

From his pocket, Schneider handed Ritter a small piece of paper. Ritter was shocked by the message.

"Transmit that at the designated time," Schneider said, adding, "Use the frequency modulation noted at the bottom."

"I don't believe this is used by the Schutzstaffel, Herr Sturmbannfürer," Ritter said, shaking his head.

"It isn't," Schneider said with a nod for Ritter to resume his work.

He left his colleagues to return to his room. His was one flight down on the corner and next to the stairwell. Schneider liked being close to an exit.

On the bedside table was a small decanter of brandy, from which he poured a glass.

Schneider propped himself up against the headboard and began thinking about Hoffman again. Despite Hoffman's achievements—bringing in Ritter and Neubauer as well as Schneider himself, his ability to procure information and supplies, and, too, his immediate dispatch of the woman on the boat—Schneider sensed something, but it was illusory.

He pulled the detonator from his pocket and rubbed his thumb over the crystal. The intricacies of this business were no less than that of the clockwork in his hand. Everything about Hoffman *should* inspire trust, but some nuances pestered Schneider. And those subtleties prompted additional information from home.

The Abwehr dossier on "Moses" was quite detailed; however, there might be something more under the surface. Hoffman was a first-generation immigrant. Certainly, the Gestapo would have details unknown even to the Abwehr, and perhaps, more telling.

"Time," Schneider said to himself as he sipped his brandy and stared at the detonator. "Time will tell."

ELEVEN

Friday, 31 July 1942

First Light

Richard stood on the back stoop with one hand in the pocket of his jumpsuit and holding a non-filtered cigarette in the other. The air was cool and moist. Soft streaks of morning light pierced through the canopies of the oak, pine, and other trees in the backyards to the east. He could see across three or four lots. Although a chain-link hurricane fence enclosed one property, wood picket fences separated the other yards.

Laundry was hung out to dry in the yard next to Reina's. The house behind had a small vegetable garden near the back of the property, flanked by a small shed. In the driveway sat a black '32 Ford with fat, bald white-wall tires.

A deep drag of the unfiltered smoke burned Richard's throat, and he decided that next time he'd take a smaller puff. He picked a shred of tobacco from the tip of his tongue and flicked it away.

Like all the rest on the block, Reina's house was on a pier-and-beam foundation. The piers, however, were nothing more than stacks of cinder blocks. Richard could hear the sound of soft thumping and the creaking of the wood floors. Reina was up.

Richard stepped down off the concrete steps and sat in one of the white metal garden chairs on either side of a matching table. He could see between two houses and through to the next street over. Now and then, a car went by, and he shook his head because none were newer than a '41 model.

Reina pushed open the screen door with her shoulder, holding two coffee cups. Richard watched her take one step at a time, careful not to trip over her satin robe. Her rich black hair covered her face, falling gently over her shoulders with slight curls resting just above the slope of her bust line.

"Morning." She offered Richard one of the cups. "You're up early."

"I've had enough sleep to last fifty years," he said, taking a cup and smelling the steaming aroma. He tested the temperature with a sip. "Mmm, nectar of the gods." He drank more. "And I was starting to feel a little claustrophobic," he admitted.

Reina smiled, closed her eyes, and tilted back her head. The sun lit her olive skin and her nostrils flared as she breathed in the fresh air.

"It is a nice morning," he said as he mashed his cigarette into the bottom of the ashtray. "More blooms than I'd have expected for this time of year."

"Like a second spring," she said with her eyes still closed. She opened them, slipped her feet out of her slippers, and curled up in the chair with her knees to her chest. "But I'm sure August'll bring back the steamy summer." Reina sipped her coffee.

Richard detected a faint rhythm of clip-clops, reminding him of *Monty Python's Holy Grail*—the scenes where the crusader skips along on foot with his squire trailing him and using two hollow coconut halves to mimic hoof beats. The sound was distant but growing louder. He leaned up in his chair, looking between the houses not quite sure what to expect.

"That'd be the milkman." Reina sipped more coffee.

"Milkman?"

"The milkman." She motioned to the next street over.

Richard turned in time to see a horse-drawn wagon lazily halt. He cocked his head, blinked his eyes once, and stared. A man in a bright white uniform tied off a pair of reins, pressed a foot lever that locked a wagon wheel, and climbed out of the rig. He scurried to the back and removed a small wire rack of four bottles.

Reina waved to him and he gave a short wave back, never stopping as he left the rack at the backdoor of the house behind hers. Richard's mouth hung open as he looked from Reina to the milkman, and again at Reina. He laughed.

She laughed, too. "I know, but maybe it's the one good thing to come out of rationing."

Richard shook his head and reached for his coffee. "Uh-huh."

"It is," she said, tilting her head as her hair fell from her shoulder. "With things so unsure and moving so quickly, maybe something like the wagon slows the pace a bit."

"Just wait a few years. You'll see quick."

"Oh, so I guess you have a crystal ball into the future," Reina said. She sat a little straighter letting one exposed leg hang off the chair. "Wait, don't tell me; you follow those Buck Rogers serials—that stuff is simply nonsense."

"Careful," Richard said with a soft chuckle. "There was a time when Jules Verne's Nautilus was considered nonsense." He took a quick sip of coffee before going on. "Besides, I'm more of a Captain Kirk kind of guy."

"Captain who?"

"Never mind." Richard pulled the pack of cigarettes from a pocket and patted the others, feeling for the matchbox. He found it in the chest pocket and struck a match to light another smoke. "I'm glad you had these things," he said. "I was about to blow a gasket last night." He leaned back and rested the hand holding the cigarette on the table.

"Vincent liked to smoke out here in the morning." She glanced around the yard. "And I have a few friends who like a puff once in a while, so I guess I never broke the habit of picking them up at the market. And—" Reina leaned up and over the table. In the same move, she brushed her hair behind her ear and helped herself to a drag of Richard's cigarette.

Her reach offered Richard a glimpse down her robe. He caught her eyes and knew he was busted, and he blushed. But he also thought he caught a sparkle in her eye. *So, you have a little bit of bad girl in there.* "You smoke?" he asked with both surprise and delight.

"Not really." Reina slowly exhaled the smoke from barely open lips as she looked at Richard. She took a second drag, and gently slid the cigarette back between his fingers. Her hand was warm. She curled back in her chair, picked up her cup with a mischievous grin, and turned her head. "A few puffs now and then," Reina said, her lips caressing the rim of her cup.

Down boy! Richard drew puff but thinking about her lips delicately drawing smoke from the same cigarette fanned the spark. "What's on your agenda for the day?" he asked as he exhaled smoke.

"I need to catch up with work at the business. We're not behind on orders or anything, well, not yet. It's making up for the flour shortages since the government is using so much."

"Can't you go direct to the mills?" Richard asked.

"I already do," Reina said and nodded. "But because my business is relatively small compared to others, I'm at the bottom of the list."

"I get it," Richard said. "You're basically scrounging from too many inconsistent sources."

Reina turned up a corner of her mouth and nodded again.

"What about buying direct from the growers?"

"Yeah—if Texas growers have a second crop or I truck it in from another state," Reina said as she stretched her legs, then brought them back to her chest and tucked her robe between her knees. "But I still have to have it milled."

Richard was stumped and impressed. Reina clearly knew what she was doing. It didn't sound like she kept her business going on the coattails of her husband. She had the angles on what she was doing; and that had to be rare in her day and age.

"What about you?" she asked as she turned to look right at Richard. "Isn't there something you need to do?"

He didn't look up as he puffed his smoke.

"Last night you told me bits and pieces," she said as she sat straight up in her chair and bent a leg under the other one. "I know your name, now, and that you remember graduating from college out of state." She went down the list of items from last night's interrogation.

"I know I was born here but I'm not sure of much else. I'm sorry." Richard hated lying to Reina.

She huffed and opened her hands around her cup. "Richard, you're not in the directory and none of the Warrens in it know who you are."

Her pressing the point made Richard sigh and rub his forehead.

"I'm not saying you're lying to me," she said softly, folding her arms on the table and leaning on them. "And I don't think you'd hurt me."

Richard snapped a look at Reina. Before he could object, she reached over and put her hand on his. "I feel like you're holding something back." Reina held his hand in both of hers. "Yes, I owe you for what you did, but at the very least you owe me the truth."

"You owe me nothing," he said, closing his eyes and shaking his head. "And I've told you everything I'm able to, right now." He turned in his chair and put his other hand over hers. "As soon as I figure all this out, you'll be the first to know. Bear with me."

Reina pulled away and folded her arms, not looking at Richard. She slid her feet into her slippers and marched into the house without a word.

Richard leaned back in the chair and spoke to the star side of the clear sky as if there was a vessel in orbit. He snorted and said, "Now would be a good time, Mister Scott."

Rumors

The bills of lading were in good order, and so were the sales tickets. Having taken a whole day off from the business, Reina expected things to be a disaster when she walked in. There was a bit of cackling between the girls on the production floor, but that was no surprise. News travels fast.

Reina opened the ledger to check her accounts. She stared at the pages but didn't see the entries or columns of numbers. Wednesday night was still vivid in her memory. She could almost smell the cigar and liquor on Maceo's breath. Reina rubbed the front of her neck where he gripped her throat; and she remembered the fear and nausea when his hand touched her down there. The nausea came back.

The entire scene played and replayed in her mind. Then, there *he* was. A strange man out of nowhere who, even stranger, seemed to be from nowhere. "Oh, Reina! What are you doing to yourself?" She tried to focus on the work in front of her, but she couldn't.

"You say something Missus Corte?"

Reina looked up from her desk at Anita. "No, no. Just thinking out loud." Anita Ruggerio's look was the same one on the faces of the girls down on the production floor. By now, every Italian from Houston to Kemah had word of the other night, courtesy of Mrs. Provenzano's eavesdropping.

"Can I bring you something?" Anita asked in a mousy kind of way. "Coffee or a Coke?"

Reina smiled and said she was fine and that it was almost lunchtime anyway. "But ask Clarence to come up when he gets in."

"Yes, ma'am." Anita disappeared into the bullpen.

Reina shut the ledger and began looking over the order tickets. Some would be hard to fill. More and more grain was being appropriated for the GIs, so just the orders in her hand alone would far exceed her commercial rations for flour.

As she told Richard, the Texas wheat harvest already came in around May. But if she was lucky, she might find a few farmers who had managed a second harvest and she could buy direct. The problem with that, however, was that she'd have to have it milled.

An option she hadn't mentioned to Richard was that she could make up some of the difference from the black market, but that came with problems of its own.

One ticket a third of the way into the stack was from the Buffalo River Grille, and it reminded Reina of her plans with Frank and Carla. They were always trying to get her out to meet new people—new men.

She half-smiled and wondered if Richard liked to dance. Did he even know how to dance? Then she immediately scoffed when she thought about this morning in the backyard. Reina no more believed the amnesia nonsense than in the man on the moon. She sensed he was afraid to tell her something, but she couldn't understand what.

Aside from all that, she had to admit it felt good to sit with a man, sit with him—to start the day and chat. It had been so long since she could enjoy being noticed, and Reina liked the way Richard noticed her. She smiled, thinking about his look when she shared his cigarette. She crossed her arms and held herself—half trying not to think about him and half letting his image wander through her mind.

There was a light tap on the door, and Reina opened her eyes as she swiveled her chair around. "Come in."

"You want t' see me Missus Co'te?"

"Morning, Clarence." She grinned at Clarence, and then scowled at her watch. "You're awfully early, today."

"I figgered you be in today," Clarence said as he peered out the doorway and whispered. "You be okay, Missus Co'te?"

"I'm in one piece, Clarence, thank you."

"Dat man, he come up yet?"

"Yes, he's up and around now."

"I know it not my place to be tellin' ya, but you watch yaself with that strange boy."

Clarence had white hair and his hunched-over posture revealed his age and a life of hard labor. Reina wondered how he kept such a gentle demeanor. She pretended to be sheepish when she answered. "Yes, sir."

Clarence smiled back a shy smile. Reina thought she almost caught a blush on his black skin. How many children did he have? Six total—four girls and two boys. She realized Clarence and his wife, Lula Mae, were probably great grandparents by now.

"Did anyone give you a hard time yesterday?"

Clarence looked at Reina.

"None of the hens down there?" Reina asked as she winked.

"Oh no, Missus Co'te," Clarence said with wide eyes—the whites yellowed from decades of tobacco smoke. "They jus' now be cluckin' bout it when I come up."

Reina decided there was no sense in worrying about how it got around. It had, and she accepted that people would say what they would say. She opened a small notepad and jotted down a list. Tearing the sheet from the spiral binding, she handed it to Clarence. "Will you run down to the warehouse to the walk-in crate under the catwalk?" she asked, taking a key from her purse and handing it to him.

"Bring dese up here?"

"Actually, no," she said. She pulled a coupon from her gas-rationing booklet along with two dollars. "Will you take them to my house and see that he gets them?"

"You sure bout dis, Missus Co'te?"

"Like you said, Clarence," she said, grinning. "I have to be careful. I can't have him running around my house the way we found him now can I?"

Clarence laughed. "No ma'am!"

"Besides, with Johnny off in New Orleans, at least someone can get good use of those things."

Clarence nodded and left the office.

Reina picked up the receiver and used the eraser end of her pencil to dial the phone. On the third ring, Carla picked up. Her first words were if Reina had heard the latest.

"No, what?" Reina asked.

"Supposedly, Don Parisi's in town," Carla whispered.

"Is he at the Rice Hotel?"

"I don't know but maybe."

Reina didn't speak as she tapped her pencil on the desk. The Pasta Factory was too small a fish to bring a shark like Parisi down from Dallas. However, Reina thought it might be an opportunity to settle the issue once and for all. The incident with Maceo was the last straw. She was tired of worrying about him and the threats, and the sooner it was over with, the sooner she could send for Olivia.

"Reina, you there?"

"Yes," she said.

"You think it has anything to do with, you know, the thing that happened the other night?"

"Oh, Carla." Reina wanted to change, the subject, in part because she wasn't in a mind to think it through, and also because the wires have ears. So she asked if they were still on for dancing tonight. Carla said yes, sounding a little surprised. She also said that she and Frank would pick up Reina at her house. That was Carla's idea rather than Frank's. And because Carla was "just dying" to meet Richard, Reina had already decided on another surprise for her friend. "Would you and Frank mind if I brought along a guest?"

Stray Cats

Another twist of the screwdriver tightened the hinge enough to level the cabinet door. Richard opened and closed it a few times to be sure it held. "Perfect!" Richard twirled the tool in his hand as a gunfighter would his six-shooter. He looked around for something else to do as he checked off his mental list of chores: the spring on the screen door, the dripping faucet in the bathroom, the cabinet door in the kitchen.

They weren't things Reina had asked him to do; he'd noticed them and wanted at least to earn his keep. It seemed like a good time to take a coffee break, so Richard shook the percolator and upended it over his cup. Then a knock came from the back door. "Can I help you?"

"Yessa," The elderly man said, holding a steamer trunk. "Missus Co'te sent me along wit dis."

Richard opened the screen door and let the man pass. The case didn't look heavy but Richard felt he should relieve the old gent's load. It turned out to be heavier than it looked. "What's she got in here?' Richard asked as he strained to hoist it up and down. "Feels like lead weights."

The old gent explained that the clothes belonged to Reina's brother, Johnny. He and his new bride had left some things with Reina to store while Johnny was off working in a Louisiana shipyard.

Richard was glad; he was getting pretty tired of the jumpsuit and he figured Reina was too. The thing made him feel like a shrinking old man. He opened the trunk to find dress shirts, a suit, a sport coat, slacks, and tie. There were also belts, socks, and a few pairs of shoes—even undergarments. "Everything today's well-dressed man needs, eh?"

"Yessu, I guess so," the old gent said. "Mista Johnny's about yo size. Mebe a bit thinna," he said, looking Richard up and down. "If'n dat possble."

Richard laughed. And realizing he hadn't introduced himself, he held out his hand and said, "Richard Warren."

"Clarence," the old gent said, looking at Richard's hand. Clarence tentatively shook his hand, pulling his away quickly.

Richard waited for a last name. When he didn't get it, he said he was glad to have met the man who helped Reina get him out of the alley. "She's quite a woman, that Reina Corte."

"Yessa, she is."

Richard zeroed in on Clarence's stern tone. He looked him in the eye and said, "And this is where you tell me I'd better behave."

Clarence grunted and chewed on his lip. "Not ma place ta be tellin ya anithin," he said. "But ifin she'uz one ma girls, dat'd be 'bout right."

"And you've known her so long you think of her as a daughter."

"Uh-huh."

Richard smiled and said, "Yes sir!"

"I bes be getting' back, Mista Warren," he said, stepping towards the door.

"Clarence, my name is Richard."

"Uh-huh, I knows."

"You're just not quite sure what to think of me."

Clarence started to reach for the door but stopped. He turned to Richard and explained that Reina was a very hardworking woman. "She and Mista Vincent bought da Pasta Factory and, in six years, make it a nice bidniss. They hire imm'grants and folks in need. And if'n she couldn't hire someone, Missus Co'te find 'em work." Clarence's expression became one of delight as he said, "You know she hold anglish classes for them imm'grants Wednesday nights!" He shook his head. "She musta learnt half dem Italians in town how to talk." Clarence stepped toward Richard. "So it no suprise she took in a stray cat."

"What about Mister Corte," Richard asked. "What was he like?"

"Oh he uz a fine man," Clarence began. He smiled and said, "Mista Vincent was d foreman for old man Ancona, original owner of da Pasta Factory." He explained that's how the two met. Reina came to work for Mister Ancona right out of high school. Vincent Corte ran the production floor and the warehouse. "But I'd say Missus Co'te was'n da one who know da way numbers and thins work."

"Smart lady," Richard said.

"Yessa," Clarence said. "It sad she have a tuff go dis past year."

Richard lifted a shirt from the case then put it back. He fiddled with the collar. "How'd he die, Clarence?"

"Mista Corte gots da newmonya." Clarence didn't remember how he got it, but he kept working, at first. It got bad enough to send him to the hospital.

"He got sicker from 'nuther bug," Clarence said. "He die from it."

Reina had described hospitals as "breeding grounds for infection." *No wonder she brought me home.*

"Ifin dat weren't bad 'nuff, she send missy Olivia away on account her troubles from dat Mista Maceo." Clarence shook his head. "Cain't think o' nuthin more to gives her a heavy heart."

Richard shook his head, feeling guilty about what he himself added to the mix.

"She never complain 'bout it, but all dis war ain't hepin," Clarence said.

"Wouldn't be in her nature."

"No suh!"

That must have been all that was on Clarence's mind. He stopped talking. But it was enough, and Clarence had made his point. Richard felt like he'd just visited with a prospective father-in-law. And it made Richard wonder about Reina's real father. It also made him realize that a few turns of a screwdriver weren't nearly enough thanks for all she'd done for him.

Richard thanked Clarence for bringing the clothes and for telling him more about Reina. He saw the old man out the door.

Even though the cup of coffee he poured was cold, he drank it. With rationing and all, he didn't want to waste it. Unfortunately, it didn't fill the pit in his stomach. There was way too much back-story for all this to be an acid flashback, or for it to be some kind of comatose dream set in an old Grant and Hepburn movie. Still, he couldn't figure out how any of it could be real, believing his current situation was scientifically implausible.

But whatever this situation was, Richard was worried—he might actually have to live it out for the rest of his life. And while Reina presented an alluring companion, would the complications of this given situation, if she were indeed real, be an additional source of pain for her?

Richard laughed. "When did you become a moralist," he said aloud. He closed his eyes for a minute and thought about a lifetime of failures—the most recent being with his father. "Oh, God," he said as he rubbed his face. The family was still in mourning and Richard up and disappears.

Cynthia Marie would be frantic and ready to phone anybody and everybody from the police to the FBI; Richard's brothers would be worried but not ready to panic. This wasn't the first time a Warren boy went missing. Years before Tom had entered the seminary, in the summer after his freshman year at the University of Texas, Tom lost himself in the arms of a girl he met at a bar.

Richard, his brother JJ, and their dad found Tom's beat-up '66 Mustang on a side street near that bar. Both his dad and brother hesitated when it came to opening the trunk. Richard, a 14-year old, popped the lid. He wondered who'd have the honors when they found his car at the post office.

The problem was that Richard wouldn't be turning up two days later with a post-coital grin. He looked at everything around him with a particular focus on the calendar tacked to the wall by the refrigerator. If it was possible that this happened, shouldn't it be possible to reverse it, he thought. But he rolled his eyes because, first, he had no idea how it happened to begin with; and, second, finding the answer probably involved advanced equations—when even simple ones weren't exactly his forte.

Richard was left with one option. "Play it out," he said aloud as he shrugged. "Maybe you'll wake up." He smiled, remembering Reina in the backyard that morning. *Then again, maybe not.*

TWELVE

Name of the Game

Jack had another look at the three-page report he typed single-spaced. He found two typos, so he inked through those, as well as on the carbon copies, and penciled in corrections. But his attention was focused on his conclusions. He tapped the pencil on the desk and chewed his bottom lip.

He let his eyes wander around the office. Standing at a bank of filing cabinets was Preskin's assistant, Ensign Barbara Reese. Her casual lean against an open top drawer accentuated her figure. Jack admired the way her skirt fit and the curve of her legs. One foot was partway out of her shoe and the pose gave her a Rita Hayworth look.

Jack thought he remembered her saying she had graduated from Southern Methodist University in '41, and that she was recruited for a Navy pilot program leading to Women Accepted for Voluntary Emergency Service. He guessed she was around 22 or 23. Since she was older, and an officer, it was risky asking her out. Then again, so were his conclusions about the Continental incident. He took a deep breath and signed off on the document, straightened the pages and closed the file folder. Jack rolled back in his chair and got up.

Ensign Reese pulled a folder from the cabinet drawer and returned to her desk. Jack arrived at the same time and slid his folder in Captain Preskin's in-box marked "HOT." He turned toward the coffee bar and grunted under his breath, holding his left hip.

"Gotta hitch in your get-along, Chief?"

"A minor run-in with a Cord." Jack grinned. "You should see the Cord." He took her smile and concern as an opening. "Join me?" He asked with a nod toward the hotplate.

Reese had a wary expression and paused before getting up. *A girl like that,* Jack thought, *beat the boys away with a stick.* He motioned to the coffee again and she joined him. Reese brushed his hand from the percolator as he reached for it. She filled two cups and handed one to Jack. "So how'd it happen?"

"Not watching where I was going," he said, shrugging and adding that it wasn't serious. He sipped his coffee. "I hear it'll be hoppin at the Buffalo Grille tonight."

"The Grille!" She kept her eyes on Jack's as she sipped. "Pretty high-cotton—*Chief.*"

He flipped the token he took from his pocket and smiled crookedly. "I have connections," he said.

"You know, I have a friend or two at Pearl."

"So do I." Jack winked. "But I'm no wolf."

"Oh, that's not what I hear," she said with an impish grin. She raised an eyebrow and almost kissed the rim of her cup. "Word has it you do bite."

"Only when asked," he said.

Jack leaned in for close-quarter sparring when Captain Preskin burst into the office. The ensign and chief petty officer set their cups down immediately and snapped to attention. Preskin closed the door and walked straight for his office. Barbara and Jack exchanged looks of relief like teenagers caught in the backseat of a father's sedan.

Barbara picked up a file from her box and the file with Jack's report from the HOT box. She took them into Preskin's office and came right back out. Jack doodled on a piece of scrap paper and waited. He mentally reviewed his text, thinking he should have been less definitive.

The captain's muted voice called Jack's name from behind the door. Taking a deep breath, Jack rolled back from his desk, got up, and marched for the door. He rapped on the doorframe.

"Come!"

"You wanted to see me, sir?"

"Close the door and have a look at this," Preskin said, holding an open folder.

Jack took the file and read the top page. The dispatch was a report from Coast Guard escort PC-566.

> **1730 hours; 30 July, 1942–U.S. passenger freighter S.S. Robert E. Lee torpedoed 50 miles south of Mississippi Delta; approximate position 28°37' N 90°45' W; 268 passengers aboard. Turned, dropped 6 depth charges; contact lost; rescue affected; casualties: 15 crew, 10 passengers.**

"Audacious, don't you think," Preskin said. "He slams a fish into a passenger vessel headed for port with a patrol riding shotgun."

"Sneaky is more like it, sir."

Preskin looked at Jack.

"The patrol craft turned after the hit," Jack said, looking at the dispatch. "That puts it, what, a quarter or half a mile ahead? The sub waited to attack from astern of the *Lee*." Jack tapped the papers with the back of his hand. "Then he fired, dived, and ran. Probably a short run. Then, to avoid a pounding from the 566's depth charges, he played possum."

Preskin furrowed his brow at Jack's summary analysis.

"But the real question is—was he inbound or outbound?" Jack closed the file and laid it on the desk. "It's only 300 miles here to there. If he was outbound…"

"He was running silent until the *Lee*." Preskin gave Jack a twisted smile. "Tell me again why you're not on a ship of the line."

Jack lowered his voice even though the door was closed. "I type eighty-five words per minute."

"Mm." Preskin got up and stared out of his window. "Well, I'd say this just upped the ante in your report! It wouldn't be a stretch to think a few friends were dropped off for a road trip to Sealy," Preskin said as he sat back down. "Hopefully Mister Johnson can shed more light on it for us." Preskin checked his watch and added, "We've got about half an hour to cogitate on this thing."

"Sir?"

"Mull it over."

"You want me to leave you to it, sir?"

Preskin shook his head. "I gotta tell ya, Jack, if this turns out to be what you say..." He leaned back in his chair. "You called it right outta the shoot."

Jack hadn't realized the pipelines were so vulnerable. It wasn't until he formed his site report that he understood the potential impact of even one strike. "My first thought was that taking out a line wouldn't amount to much more than an inconvenience."

"Inconvenience, Chief?" Preskin asked with a raised eyebrow and grin. "That's the name of the game—interrupting supplies and diverting men and materiel."

They heard the outer door to the OPC office shut. Captain Preskin motioned for Jack to have a look outside. He opened the door to see a Negro visitor dressed in a two-piece suit and shoes with a high shine. He was carrying a canvas bag.

"May I help you?" Barbara asked without her usual warm tone.

The Negro gentleman introduced himself as William Johnson and told Barbara that Chief Warren requested a meeting there at the OPC office. Preskin checked the time on his desk clock. "Early bird," he said.

"Did a stint in the army," Jack said as he walked out to greet William.

Neither man extended a hand. But each nodded to the other with a casual smile. "That watch seems to work just fine today," Jack said.

William chuckled.

Jack escorted Johnson into the captain's office and made the introductions. Again, no one extended a hand. But Preskin did offer William a seat as he thanked him for coming to town and for being prompt.

Jack didn't sit. He closed Preskin's office door and stood to one side of his C.O.'s desk. He stayed silent while the captain spoke.

"Mister Johnson, Chief Warren's report makes a startling conclusion." Preskin tapped his finger on the closed folder. "A critical portion of it is based on his confidence in your experience."

"That of a Negro maintenance man."

Preskin nodded.

"Extending the basis of your problem is that, despite the validity of his conclusion, he is a very young chief petty officer—and not an expert in this kind of investigation," William said, gesturing to Jack without taking his eyes from Captain Preskin.

"Regardless of all that, the conclusion in itself seems far-fetched," Preskin said.

"Except for the evidence." William reached into his bag and pulled out a small stack of papers. "Those are results of tests performed on a few pieces of metal the chief let me take from the station," William said, placing his documentation on Preskin's desk.

"And?"

"An old classmate from Prairie View A&M now runs the college's chemistry lab. He and I spent the better part of last night testing the residue found on the blasted pipe." William directed Preskin's attention to a formula listed on the top page. "We ran it three times to be sure, and each time we came up with $C_7H_5N_3O_6$."

"I barely remember my periodic table, Mister Johnson," Preskin said.

"Trinitrotoluene, Captain."

"You're sure?"

"Three times, sir," William said, looking to Jack and back to Preskin. "Given that Prairie View is an all-Negro institution, we included affidavits defining our test methods and assuring our confidentiality."

"And you both agree the faulty valve handle kept it from going bad."

"Yes, sir," Jack said, nodding to William. "He noted a stripped set screw in the valve assembly. Fortunately, that kept the bypass flow from being employed."

"A dry pipe, Captain," added William.

Jack spelled it out for Captain Preskin. "A working valve would have sent the charges downstream and, depending on the path of the line, the explosion could have done serious damage. The burn-off would be bad enough, but shrapnel from the rupture would have torn anything or anyone nearby to pieces."

"Not to mention the magnesium," William said.

"Magnesium?" Jack and Preskin asked at the same time. Then Preskin scanned the analysis.

"Precisely what pitted the inside diameter of the pipe," William said as he looked up at Jack who was looking back wide-eyed. "Whoever built this charge was mean."

"Anything and everything around the blast would have burned unquenchably," Preskin said.

"We're lucky this went off underground," William said. "If oil had been in the line or the bypass was on the surface, there'd be a pond where the levee and pump shack are."

"Where's this line run?" Preskin asked.

William pointed to the plot map he included with his documentation. It highlighted a river crossing over the Brazos River between the pump station that blew and the next one downstream.

Jack chimed in by saying that the first thing making this pipeline river crossing so dangerous was a rail bridge that ran a few feet from the pipeline. An explosion could sever that bridge. If it didn't, the magnesium might severely weaken the rails or even the support structure.

The second thing was that the fiery burst would dump gallons of burning petroleum into a flowing river. Running his finger along the blue line denoting the Brazos, Jack pointed out cattle ranches and farms downriver. Further down were industry towns and the coastal town of Freeport. Even if the oil didn't ignite, it would sour the water supply for livestock and irrigation all the way from Sealy to the Gulf.

"Something like this would take unimaginable precision," Preskin said.

"The Germans *have* that reputation—sir," Jack said.

Preskin cocked his head in agreement. "Was there any kind of timer?"

"Nothing apparent yet," William said.

"Since regulations dictate I notify the FBI about this, J. Edgar's men will have to find the timer."

"One other issue concerns us, sir," Jack added, looking over at William and then to Preskin. "The culprit had to have been familiar with the business."

"This type of thing requires a knowledge of oil density and flow rates to calculate the weight of the charge and to derive some sort of time frame for setting a timer," William said.

"Flow rates are fairly easy to figure out," Jack said.

"The last settings are usually logged at each station," William said.

"Or just look at the inflow gauges." Jack shrugged. "Either way, it requires some pretty good math involved."

Jack knew he and William had thrown a lot at Captain Preskin. William followed Jack's lead and kept quiet to let Preskin mull it over as he perused the documentation.

"Is the explosion still being labeled a maintenance foul-up at Continental?" Preskin asked.

"Not sure," William said. "I haven't spoken to anyone about it."

Preskin gathered William's documentation into a stack and placed it in the folder with Jack's report. He leaned forward a bit, resting his arms on the folder. "Please continue to keep this under your hat."

William nodded and said, "Of course, Captain."

"I will also make sure that top men at Continental are aware of just how helpful and insightful their maintenance man has been to the Navy and, in no way, to hold you accountable for this incident."

"Sir, if I may," Jack interrupted.

Preskin nodded.

"Given so few inside the loop, and those being top men only, Mister Johnson's direct supervisor will be his immediate source of difficulties." Jack cleared his throat. "And Mister Allen is a man with very specific opinions, sir."

"He's a bigot, Captain."

"Yes, Mister Johnson, I think Chief Warren made that clear." The captain leaned back in his chair and sighed. "I'll try to preempt any problems when I speak to Continental."

"Thank you, Captain."

"Well gentlemen, I think we've covered it," Preskin said.

"The samples we tested are tagged in this bag," William said, holding up a bag for Preskin to see.

"Leave it with Chief Warren," Preskin said, gesturing toward Jack. "Send in Ensign Reese."

"Aye, sir," Jack said.

William stood up and handed the bag to Jack. The two started for the door.

"Mister Johnson," Preskin said. He stood up and extended a hand.

William shook Preskin's hand and nodded.

Jack escorted William to the outer office. The rest of the staff had arrived and were busy at their desks. Jack told Barbara that Preskin wanted to see her and she went into the private office, shutting the door behind her.

The two men stopped at the door, and Jack opened it as he smiled at William.

"Take care, Chief," William said.

"Call me Jack, William." Jack found himself offering the man a hand.

William looked at Jack's hand then back at Jack's face. He spoke softly with a derisive grin, "Nize ta see ya Mista Jack." He shook Jack's hand.

Jack checked to make sure Preskin's door was shut as he whispered to William. "That son-of-bitch Allen gives you any guff, you let me know."

William smiled as he left the OPC office. Jack watched him stride down the hall for a moment before he closed the door. There were one or two glares, but Jack ignored them. He was more worried about William. No matter what precautions were taken, Allen was likely to treat the man with a heavy hand.

What impressed Jack was that William had gone the extra mile, knowing full well that there would be little, if any, gratitude. He reminded Jack of another Negro he'd met at Pearl. His name was Dorie Miller. Although a cook 3rd class, the man had helped wounded shipmates, including the captain of the *USS West Virginia*, and took up a gun position to defend his ship during the raid on Pearl Harbor. Jack thought he was brave and the most humble person he'd ever met.

Preskin's door opened and Barbara marched out to her desk. She immediately began typing something that Jack guessed was a dispatch to Washington.

The captain stepped into his office doorway and motioned for Jack to come back in. Preskin shut the door and grabbed the now thick folder from his desk. "I've signed off on your preliminary report, and Reese is typing the dispatch." Preskin handed the folder to Jack. "How soon can you have the final ready for me?"

"Before lunch, sir."

"There any way you can stay on this? And I don't mean the report."

Jack wasn't sure how to proceed. "With the FBI notified, sir, their men will be at the site by morning and take charge of the investigation. Ferreting out who's responsible for these sorts of things is their job."

Preskin was disappointed.

"Sir, I have to tell you true on this. We got lucky."

"Remember the old saying, Jack."

Jack nodded. "It's better to be lucky than smart."

"Carry on, Chief."

"Aye, sir." Jack reached for the doorknob but didn't turn it. Based on the suppositions presented just a few minutes ago with William, Jack believed whoever set the charge had to know about the river crossing downstream. That meant the information had come from Continental—someone close enough to the company to know about the crossing. He turned to face his commanding officer and said, "Sir, do you think there's an insider?"

"You're saying the culprit's an employee?"

"Or an employee is in cahoots with 'em," Jack said. Captain Preskin kept quiet, so Jack continued. "A pipeline isn't something visibly traceable and doesn't necessarily run in a straight line. For the most part, they're underground and meander along jagged paths from one ground lease to the next. And it's not unusual for them to have to bend around a refused right-of-way."

"You'd need detailed surveys," Preskin said.

"Exactly," Jack said, nodding. "Some lines out there are over twenty years old. And only the owner would have those plots."

"A minute ago you didn't see a way to press on," Preskin reminded Jack.

Jack didn't have a ready answer. He chewed his lip and looked past Preskin and out the window behind him. "I can try to feel out the guys I know at Continental—"

"Whereas I can with the company brass," Preskin said, finishing Jack's sentence.

"Although the Hoover boys'll lock this down before I get too far."

"Carry on, but—if it turns out that we're treading on FBI ground, then you back off."

"Aye, sir," Jack said, and Captain Preskin dismissed him.

The coffee area was right outside Preskin's office. Jack's cup was still there, and the coffee was warm. Barbara focused on typing a dispatch into the Teletype machine. While Jack enjoyed looking at her for a moment, he was wondering who on the other end would see his report and what they would say.

Things, he thought, were a lot easier when he was just an anonymous petty officer. He had told his brother-in-law there was no cloak-n-dagger stuff going on, but more and more it seemed like there was. And it was this kind of closed-door hubbub that made Jack uncomfortable. He preferred things above table.

Back at his desk, Jack found a small envelope on his chair addressed to *Chief Warren* in elegant handwriting. Inside was a handwritten note on an index card.

See you at eight.

1534 North Boulevard.

B.R.

THIRTEEN

Casablanca

Cocktails at Seven

Richard finished his second try at the double-Windsor knot of his necktie. The tie length fell exactly right—just above his belt buckle. The shirt collar fit perfectly and the sleeves were right, too. But it was a full cut, and the shirttail bunched up in the waist of his pants.

Uncomfortable as it was to the tender spots on his hips, it felt better than chafing from an elastic waistband, which was one reason he decided not to wear the pair of underwear that was in the trunk. The other was that he had no intention of wearing another man's shorts. Besides, he figured no one would notice through the baggy, full cut look of the pants.

He leaned in toward the mirror and looked at his face. Richard hadn't seen the bare skin over his top lip in a dozen years. *What the hell, everybody needs a change.*

He made one final effort to tame his hair. He used as much goop as he thought he could without making it look too greasy. Still, there were a few stubborn locks, so he gave up. He grabbed the tan double-breasted suit coat from the hanger hooked over the doorknob and slipped it on. The pull of the bandages on the skin of his shoulders reminded him to take it slowly.

Richard extended his arms before running his hands down the coat panels as he checked the fit in the mirror. *Not bad, slick.* Before he could try on the hat, a fast-paced instrumental played in the next room.

Olivia's room had two exits—one into the hall and one directly into the living room. He opened the latter. Reina was setting a tray of hors d'oeuvres and glasses on the cocktail table.

"There you are," Reina said, smiling. "They'll be here any time now."

Richard was speechless. Reina was dressed in a black form-fitted skirt with a hem below the knee and matching high-heel shoes. Her top was also black, but it was beaded and had subtly padded shoulders. The neckline wasn't plunging, but it certainly complimented her. Her hair was down and it was parted on her right with the lengths curled under and somehow held behind her shoulders. Her lips were cherry red and very full. He couldn't breathe.

She seemed to light up a bit and she grinned. Her look was almost coy.

"What's the matter," she said, raising an eyebrow and putting one hand on her slender hip. "You've never seen a woman in evening wear before?"

Richard slowly shook his head and smiled. "Not one that ever looked so good," he said. "You're a movie star." He thought she resembled a young Elizabeth Taylor with just a touch of Natalie Wood's sensuality.

"Thank you, Richard!"

"But I'm afraid I feel like a pair of brown shoes in a room full of tuxedos," Richard said.

"You look fine," Reina said as she smiled again and walked over to a console against the wall. Picking up a billfold, she added, "You remind me a little of Humphrey Bogart." Then Reina handed the wallet to Richard. "This belonged to Vincent. I thought for appearance's sake…"

"The man should pay," Richard said, completing her sentence. The initial spell from Reina's appearance subsided and Richard recognized the tune on the Victrola, though he couldn't remember the title. The speaker had a boxy sound, and there were cracks and pops. But the music made him smile. "What's playing?"

"One of Glenn Miller's new recordings." Reina didn't look up as she made sure everything was arranged perfectly on the tray. "American Patrol," she said.

There was a knock at the front door and Carla Bono walked in followed by her husband, Frank. Carla wore an off-white satin outfit. Her brown hair was pulled up in some kind of twirl behind her head. She gave Reina an affectionate hug and the two exchanged giggles and compliments. Reina gave Frank a quick hug and said he looked dashing.

Frank stood a few inches taller than Richard. He had a black patch over his right eye that made him look like a comic book hero. Richard guessed Frank was maybe twenty-seven or twenty-eight. Reina introduced everyone and they all shook hands.

Richard made it a point to give Frank's hand a firm and deliberate grip, just as his father had taught him to do. "Don't try to crush it, but don't hold it like a girl's either," he used to say.

"We've heard a lot about you, Richard," Carla said.

"Really," Richard said, grinning at Reina. "I imagine that was a short story."

Reina gave Richard a wide-eyed look and Carla laughed. Then Reina asked, "Anyone care for a primer before we go?"

"It's only a little after seven," Frank said, looking at his wristwatch. "I think a round's in order."

Reina handed Richard a bottle of champagne to open. Meanwhile, she dropped a pinch of sugar into each of the four chilled champagne glasses and sprinkled an aromatic powder over the cubes. Richard filled the glasses and Reina dropped lemon twists into each.

"Champagne cocktails," Carla boasted. "Aren't we high steppin."

"What's the occasion, Reina?" Frank asked.

"My surrender—I've had enough of Carla's nagging about going out," Reina said with a wink to Carla. Frank shook his head and had a half-grin.

Richard watched and listened as Reina and the Bonos bantered back and forth over cocktails with occasional nibbles on the hors d'oeuvres. He wondered when Reina found time to make them. They were little toasted pieces of bread topped with chopped egg and sprinkled with spices. Did she get the toaster back?

Much of the conversation was foreign to Richard. He had no clue about the people or things they mentioned. Feeling out of the loop, he gulped his champagne cocktail and announced he was stepping out for a smoke. Richard saw Carla shoot Frank a look, and he expected Frank would follow him out. He did.

"The girls want to talk," Frank said.

"I figured as much."

On the front porch, Richard pulled a pack from his pants pocket and offered one to Frank. The two men lit up and Richard asked, "This where you give me a man-to-man talk about Reina?"

"You're old enough to know what's right and what's not," he said, exhaling his smoke. "Besides, Reina's over twenty-one, and I suspect you've learned she's a pretty tough woman."

"That she is," Richard said, rubbing his jaw.

"Yeah, I heard about the right hook," Frank said with a grin.

"Can I ask you a question?"

"How'd I lose the eye?"

Richard nodded.

"It happened some months ago—over China," Frank said, flicking ash over the porch rail onto the shrubs.

"The First American Volunteer Group under Chennault?" *Wow! A real Flying Tiger!* Richard was very familiar with the group known as The Flying Tigers. The squadron emblem became as famous as some of the pilots did—Chennault, himself, as well as Greg "Pappy" Boyington and Tex Hill, although not necessarily everyone in 1942 knew about them. The group was formed when Roosevelt signed a secret executive order authorizing its creation, which is probably why the former Curtiss P-40 pilot looked surprised, too. "So..."

"So, we intercepted a bombing run and their escorts," Frank said, taking a drag and exhaled. "A particular Nate and I exchanged fire."

"A what?" Richard asked.

"A Nate is a very light and maneuverable Japanese plane—the Nakajima Ki-27. They can be a ball-buster in a dogfight. But they're lightly armored, so I managed to get the better of him."

"Then what happened to your eye?"

"Well, like I said, we exchanged fire and a bullet penetrated my canopy and hit one of the instrument gauges. The glass cover shattered, causing a shard to pierce my eye."

"How'd you land?"

"It wasn't textbook," Frank said with a smile.

Frank was grinning, but it was clear he was disappointed to be out of the game so soon after it started. The Flying Tigers weren't flying in China until December of 1941. The first intense engagements came around February and March. That meant Frank was injured during one of his first enemy encounters.

"You're still a fairly young man," Frank said, staring at his cigarette. "What's keeping you out of government issue?"

Richard hadn't seen that one coming. It suddenly occurred to him that he was about the same age as Gregory Boyington—so age wasn't an excuse. Fortunately, Reina opened the door and suggested the group get going to beat the rush of the after-dinner crowd.

The girls grabbed their purses, Reina closed her front door, and they all piled into Frank's '41 Ford coupe. There was no air conditioning, so the windows were rolled partway down—enough to let in a breeze but not so much as to muss the girls' hair.

They drove up Waugh Drive and over Buffalo Bayou to Washington Avenue. The ride was a treat for Richard, and he chuckled. Everything was so different. There were no strip malls, and the bayou was almost untouched. The most striking thing was seeing the tops of distant oil derricks poke up from the trees in the Heights. He had once read that they used to drill there for oil.

Another half mile up and Waugh turned into Heights Boulevard. Richard wished they could keep going so he could see Houston's first master-planned community before the suburban exodus of the fifties. But Frank turned right and headed east on Washington towards downtown. Even then, pockets of dilapidated buildings lined the avenue.

And he had a difficult time suppressing his reactions to the numbers of vintage automobiles on the road. Some were still the spoke-wheeled jalopies from the late twenties and early thirties. Others were the sleek and elegant roadsters and sedans of the mid-to-late thirties. Of course, a few of them were the bulbous hulks that trademarked the forties.

Cruising into the outskirts of downtown, the skyline lacked any of the glass and steel skyscrapers or mega-office complexes of Richard's day. The crystalline landmarks he'd come to know weren't even designed yet. Without Heritage Plaza, the Republic Bank Building, or even the Spindle Top revolving restaurant, the Gulf Oil building was the tallest structure. The only challenge to the Gothic tower came from the elegant dome of the Niels Esperson Building.

"My God!" Richard thought the city popped out of a panoramic scene from a forties movie—except this was in color. Then he realized Frank and the girls were looking at him.

"What?" Reina asked.

Richard looked at Reina, Carla, and Frank. "I cannot get over the Gulf building—it's a big mother."

"That is the tallest building in the South," Frank said.

"I think it's too big, like our city," Carla complained.

As Frank talked about Houston's increasing growth rate since the Crash of '29, Richard wondered if they could ever imagine a sprawling metropolis of four million people.

"Honey, there's Preston," Carla said to Frank.

Frank made a last-minute veer to the right onto Preston Avenue where it forked from Washington. Another five hundred feet up, Frank made another gentle swerve, this time to the left.

Without the I-45/I-10 overpass as a landmark, Richard hadn't quite realized where he was. It was the street sign marked Franklin Street that made his spine tingle. He sat straight up and looked around. Another sign at the approaching intersection was for Bagby Street. Richard locked his eyes onto a rundown hotel next to a boarded-up warehouse across the intersection on the left. He let out a breath and couldn't take his eyes off of them and the precise spot where the downtown post office will be, and the last place he remembered before waking up in the alley.

The feel of his bandages was suddenly noticeable—reminding him of bone-splitting pain and knotted muscles. Richard felt the sweat gathering under the headband of his hat. Nausea churned in his stomach as he remembered a bright flash and, then—this.

He continued his locked view on the buildings until Reina's bewildered expression blocked them and he quickly faced front.

"What did you see?" Reina asked.

"Nothing," Richard said, looking back at Reina but not directly at her. "I thought I remembered that warehouse as something else."

"Here we are," Frank said as he slowed the car where Franklin crossed Milam Street. He pointed to an empty parking spot along Milam. For a guy with one eye, Richard thought Frank parallel parked like a pro. He slipped the coupe into a tight space with one maneuver.

Richard stepped out of the car and looked at some of the surrounding buildings. The Hogg Building was a red brick structure and only about eight stories high. Built by one of Houston's most prominent families in the first half of the 1900s, it featured a lavish, Spanish-style penthouse. It was one of Richard's favorites and he thought the penthouse would make a cool bachelor pad rather than private offices. And at the moment, it was something familiar.

An "ahem" from Carla caught Richard's attention, and he pulled the seat-back forward and helped her out of the car. Frank did the same for Reina on the driver's side.

Crossing the street toward the Buffalo River Grille, the group could see the curved bank of large windows overlooking the bayou. The building was also Spanish-style and had two stories, though it was also capped with a rotunda-like structure on the top.

Richard knew the building well. It was Kurt's original location for the Grille. But any time that Richard spent there was in the basement that Kurt leased out for a dance club. Power Tools was the name and a favorite night-spot from the eighties on into the nineties. While it was a cool place to take a date and be seen, it was also a "meat market." However, the memories Richard had of leaving with someone were only of when he brought them.

Walking with Reina, Richard thought her stride was confident and graceful at the same time. He couldn't help but smile and wink. She moved closer to Richard and slipped her arm around his.

Art of Wine

Whatever Don Parisi wanted, Parisi got. But this was an unsettling change in plan for Maceo, one that caused considerable bickering with his cousins, Sam and Rosario. They had prepared Parisi's favorite meal and set the finest table at the Balinese. And since Parisi's wife couldn't join him this trip, Vic arranged for some very entertaining company.

A rumor that Gus Wortham and the Brown brothers would be dining at the Buffalo River Grille changed Don Parisi's mind. He wanted to be noticed in the same light—seen in the same circles. Maceo had a hunch it was Wortham, himself, or one of the Browns willing to cut some deal. Whatever the reason, Parisi canceled the plans at the Balinese and decided to come to the Grille. The problem was Maceo didn't want Parisi and Hoffman crossing paths for a while. "What's the matter, Vic?" Parisi asked. "You look like you have agita."

"No, Don Parisi," Maceo said with a slight grin. "My stomach's fine."

Parisi leaned closer to Maceo and said, "We'll take the train down to Galveston tomorrow."

"Gentlemen," Hoffman said as he approached the table by the windows overlooking the bayou. "Welcome to the Buffalo River." Maceo batted his eyes between Parisi and Hoffman. Parisi didn't stand, nor did Hoffman offer a hand. He slightly bowed at the waist and nodded.

"Good to see you again," Hoffman said casually to Maceo as he offered a hand.

"Same here," Maceo said as he shook hands.

Hoffman motioned for the headwaiter standing off to the side. "Arlen will give you the off-menu items that feature pastas and, I hope, acceptable sauces.

And while my cellar is light on Italian wines, may I offer a complimentary bottle of 1928 Pauillac?"

Given that Parisi was partial to whiskey, Maceo was surprised when he accepted. While Hoffman ran off to get the wine, the waiter recited the menu and the entrees were selected. Parisi and Maceo would have the veal and a light side serving of al dente pasta and pesto. Parisi's three bodyguards would also have the veal and pasta. Two would be permitted to drink in moderation and the third wouldn't drink at all.

Hoffman returned with a magnum of 1928 Chateau Latour cradled in his arms. Arlen followed right behind rolling a waist-high wooden cart. Hoffman struck a match to light a half-burnt candle.

"What's all this?" asked Don Parisi.

"Normally I'd do this in a dim room," Hoffman said, laying the bottle gently on a towel, keeping it on its side. "But I thought you might enjoy a traditional decanting." He used the tip of the corkscrew to tear the foil around the bottle top, peeling it all away; then, with a handkerchief he wet in a small bowl of water, cleaned the grime from the lip surrounding the cork.

Maceo didn't understand why Hoffman wouldn't just plunge the corkscrew in, turn it, and yank out the cork. Regardless, the whole process pleased Parisi.

Hoffman carefully centered the screw tip and cautiously turned it. He slowly withdrew the cork as he raised the bottleneck to about a twenty-degree angle. When the cork was out, he kept the angle as he raised the bottle over a chemist's funnel inserted into a decanter. Blocking the setting sunlight coming through the window, Arlen handed the candle to Hoffman. He held the flame low on the opposite side of the bottle.

"The purpose of this is what, Mr. Hoffman?" asked Parisi.

"Sediments form as red wines age," Hoffman said as he poured the wine. "The candle allows me to see when those sediments edge close to the bottleneck, which is when I stop pouring."

Hoffman carefully moved the candle towards the neck of the bottle as he poured, looking for the dark spot that was sediment. His eyes darted back and forth between the bottle and funnel to make sure it didn't overflow.

"Decanting is a demonstration of respect for the grower," Hoffman said. "His daily tending of the vines nurtures the finest grapes. It is a nod to the old gent who tediously separates and whips egg whites to fine the wine. Decanting also acknowledges the cask makers who carefully choose and prepare the woods in which the wines ferment. You become part of bringing the wine to its fullest potential."

Maceo thought it was too much sugar for a dime just to drink some hooch. But Hoffman was playing it up for Don Parisi, whose smile made it clear he liked it.

"How'd such a young man get to be so refined?" Parisi asked.

Hoffman grinned and said, "My late paternal uncle raised me. Every few years, he'd take me to Europe to buy wines. One trip was spent solely in the Bordeaux region of France." At that point, Hoffman stopped pouring. He removed the funnel and served a small portion in a glass. Holding the glass up to the light, Hoffman moved it in a circular motion, swirling the wine around the inner surface. Then he handed the glass to Parisi.

Maceo's first impulse was to roll his eyes, but Parisi was enjoying the attention. He also approved of the wine and motioned to serve his associates. The headwaiter filled all but one man's glass.

"Gentlemen," Hoffman began, "I must play both sommelier and host. If you'll excuse me, I should see to things in the kitchen and tend to a few other guests." He again bowed slightly at the waist and smiled. "Enjoy."

Don Parisi thanked him for the demonstration and invited him to join them after the main course. Hoffman said he would be back shortly and walked away as Arlen returned with a tray of stuffed artichoke hearts.

Maceo raised his glass and toasted the godfather. Parisi stopped the glass at his lips, looking past Maceo. The godfather's henchmen snapped a look in the same direction. When Maceo turned fully around to face the entrance, he lost what little appetite he had.

Wingman

When the Bonos, Reina, and Richard entered through the double wood doors, Richard thought he walked right into a scene out of Casablanca. Tobacco smoke overcast the large split-level dining room. There were tables clustered in the center sunken area and, the better tables, which were fewer, lined the windows. The setting sunlight highlighted the grain on the paneled walls and support columns. Waiters wove through the packed tables with their signature white cloths draped over their left arms. Busboys dressed in white button-down coats cleared dishes and reset place settings. There was even a shapely woman with a tray of cigarette packs and cigars making her way from table to table.

Everyone was appropriately dressed for dinner. At the better tables, most men were in tuxes or dinner jackets. The women were all dressed to the nines. The span of attire was a little more mixed in the center section where the table arrangements were tighter. Some people were in after-six garb, but others were in nothing less than coats and ties and cocktail dresses.

Richard half-expected Sidney Greenstreet, Claude Rains, and Peter Lorre to make an appearance. All that was missing was Sam on the piano.

Frank removed his hat and Richard followed suit as they approached the podium a little further in. The tux-clad maître d' greeted them with a Cajun accent. "Good evening, ladies and gentlemen, welcome to the Buffalo River Grille."

"Hello, Herman," Reina said, smiling.

"Missus Corte!" Herman's face lit up with sudden recognition and took Reina's hand in his. "It has been too long."

Reina smiled and turned as she introduced him to the Bonos and Richard.

"The Grille is happy to have you with us," Herman said. "Will you be dining?"

Reina leaned in and quietly said they were there to hear the new band. She opened her pocketbook and searched for something. "I forgot my brass nickel," she said to Carla.

"No need for you, Missus Corte." Herman waved for them to follow him.

Richard and Frank walked behind the girls, who walked behind Herman. They stepped down in the center area and crossed halfway to the back when Reina tensed up and stopped. She was looking toward the windows. Richard couldn't see what—or who—she was looking at.

She marched toward the raised area with tables at the windows.

Richard looked at Frank.

"Parisi and Maceo," Frank said as he cocked his head in Reina's direction.

Richard started to follow Reina but Frank grabbed his arm.

"I don't think that's a good idea," Frank said.

"Would you leave your wingman?" Richard pulled away and caught up to Reina at the steps up from the center section. Within three paces of Parisi's table, the two men at the next table started to get up as they reached into their coats. Parisi never took his eyes off of Reina, but he held out his hand, and the men seemed to stand down. Parisi stood up and addressed Reina formally, almost with respect.

Reina bowed her head ever so slightly—enough for Parisi and Richard to see, though not so much to be obvious to other patrons. She spoke quietly. "Good evening, Don Parisi."

"And who do we have here, young Reina?" Parisi asked, looking at Richard.

Richard left unsaid a tempting *Bond, James Bond,* as he realized Reina hadn't realized he was behind her.

"This is Mister Warren," she said. "Richard Warren, this is Don Parisi."

By instinct, Richard held out his hand—an error in protocol based on Parisi's indignant look. Richard simply nodded and withdrew his hand. He noticed the other man seated at Parisi's table. So, that was Maceo. He was glaring, and he was a lot bigger than Richard remembered. He turned to face Maceo head-on and held his stare, and he was careful not to make any sudden moves. Richard's heart was pounding. His eyes were on his opponent, but Richard tuned his ears on Reina's voice.

"Don Parisi," she started, "We have business between us that needs settling."

"Join me in a glass of wine?"

"No, thank you, Don Parisi."

"Refusing this offer, too?"

"I don't mean to be rude," Reina said, her voice trembling a bit. "But I think this is something better discussed in private."

Ballsy! Richard stayed locked in a staredown with Maceo. He didn't want to look like a deer in the headlights, so he was conscious of keeping his eyes relaxed. Parisi's voice made for an easy distraction. He didn't sound like the Marlon Brando character Richard expected. This Don spoke more like a Texas good ole boy. That is, until he spoke in Italian.

Reina replied in Italian. She didn't sound like an American girl speaking Italian; her accent and speed made her sound like an Italian speaking Italian. Her gesturing, accentuated what she was saying—though Richard was lost to the conversation.

He refocused on Maceo, who held his stare. The son of a bitch looked like a shark ready to attack.

"Everything all right here, gentlemen?"

The voice was unmistakable—though it didn't have the tired edge of an old man. Richard turned and saw Kurt Hoffman—dark-haired, tight-skinned, and trim. He was in his heyday. Richard let himself smile, and he wanted to say, *Kurt, it's me, Rick!*

Questions flooded Richard's mind. Did he have a wine cellar? How was it stocked? What was it like running a business during these years? Then he wondered if Kurt knew his dad at this point. He felt a pang in his belly because he hadn't thought much about his father for the last few days.

"Reina and I are old friends," Parisi was saying.

Kurt's face lit up and gave her a warm hello.

"Good evening, Mister Hoffman," she said with a reluctant smile.

You have got to be kidding! And if it weren't enough that Reina and Kurt knew each other, Kurt was acting friendly with a character like Parisi. Richard's mother never cared for Kurt because he cheated on Aunt Dorothy, and she said he had some seedy affiliations. She never got specific, and he never understood what she meant—until now.

Kurt kept smiling and said that the Pasta Factory and the Grille were old friends. Okay, Richard thought. It made sense since Reina made pasta and Kurt owned a restaurant. Over his shoulder, he saw Maceo still glaring.

"It's been too long since you and your voice have graced our stage," Kurt said.

Richard broke away from the stare-down a second time.

"You're very gracious, Mister Hoffman," she said.

Richard looked at Reina, then at Kurt, and back at Reina.

"Don Parisi, I don't want to disturb you any further," Reina said.

"Until tomorrow afternoon, then," Parisi said.

Richard scowled, wondering how he missed the part of the conversation where they decided on tomorrow afternoon. It must have been when Reina and Parisi had spoken in Italian.

Reina thanked Don Parisi and nodded to him. She smiled courteously at Kurt as she put her hand on Richard's shoulder.

"I'll see you downstairs a little later, Reina," Kurt said.

Richard followed her for a few steps but turned to face Maceo again. He was still staring, and Richard couldn't resist. He slowly raised his hand and, about where he remembered clobbering Maceo, patted the back of his own neck. At the same time, he winked with a smug grin.

Maceo started to stand, but Parisi put his hand on the thug's arm. "Careful, young man," Parisi said to Richard. "My affection for young Reina doesn't in any way translate to you." Parisi held a stern look at Richard while he sipped wine.

A chill shot up Richard's spine. And Kurt's raised brow didn't make Richard feel any safer.

Reina tugged Richard's hand and he followed her back to where Frank and Carla were waiting with Herman. She motioned to the maître d' to continue. When they reached the door, Herman gave the tux-clad bouncer a nod. He opened the door and big band music filled the stairwell.

On the landing halfway down where the stairs turned, Reina stopped, spun around, and faced Richard. "What did you think you were doing?"

"Covering your ass," Richard said, looking her square in the eye.

"Whoa," Frank intervened.

"It's okay, Frank." Reina lowered her eyes. "It was still foolish."

"Pot calling the kettle black?" Richard asked with a judgmental expression.

Reina cut a look over her shoulder at Richard as she marched down the steps. It was nearly as chilling as Parisi's.

The stairs emptied through a door into a low-ceiling basement, which was as elegant in décor as the dining room. At the opposite end was a slightly recessed stage where the band played *Sentimental Journey.* The music was clear but not loud. People were talking almost at a normal volume. In front of the stage was a fair size dance area with couples moving in a counterclockwise flow.

Flanking the long room were two bars with café tables peppered in between. The walls were covered in wainscoting and plaster—the columns too. Soft light came from art deco chandeliers and sconces.

For Richard, it was in stark contrast to how it would look in the decades to come. As Power Tools, the walls and columns would be covered in plaster with black-light paint to make it look like a psychedelic lava tube. The music volume—whether it was live or by Memorex—would be skull shattering.

Richard saw Reina giving Carla a look. Then Carla told Frank she and Reina were going to powder their noses and suggested that he and Richard order drinks. The girls disappeared into the crowd toward the powder room while Frank and Richard plowed their way to the bar on the left.

Richard looked over his shoulder as he leaned on the bar. He could count on one hand, with fingers left over, the number of fights he'd ever been in.

"Expecting a gorilla?" Frank asked.

Richard slowly exhaled.

"I'll say this," Frank said, shaking his head. "You have one hell of a knack for rubbing people the wrong way."

Richard grimaced and nodded in agreement with Frank. "That wasn't exactly a bright idea there at the end."

"You wanna change your skivvies while I order drinks?"

Richard laughed and Frank's good eye twinkled.

"A stiff drink will do fine," Richard said, as the bartender came up and took their order. Frank pointed to an open table not too far from the dance floor. The bartender nodded and left to mix the drinks while Frank and Richard went to claim the table.

And Your Enemies Closer

Hoffman wasn't about to pry into Parisi's business with Reina Corte. However, he was interested in Maceo's reaction to the girl's escort, thinking he must have been the one that cold-cocked Maceo. He found quiet humor in that because Maceo was twice the guy's size. It also meant that Hoffman's pasta vendor was the business that Maceo talked about. The pleasure part he mentioned was obvious and, knowing Maceo, Hoffman figured he took it too far.

"So, you do business with the Factory," Parisi said.

"For some three years now," Hoffman said. "She provides the best."

"And she's a pistol," Parisi said as he motioned to an empty chair.

Hoffman agreed and sat down.

As he partially filled a glass with wine and slid it in front of Hoffman, Parisi asked if he had ever met her husband.

Hoffman shook his head. "Reina has always been my contact. The fact that the business continued and held on through the last year confirmed my expectation that she drives the company."

"You admire her," Parisi said.

"I admire anyone who makes a go of it," Hoffman admitted. "Man or woman, it makes no difference. But perhaps because she is a woman, and widow at that, it makes her success more pronounced."

"Would *you* work for a woman?"

"I prefer to work for myself, Don Parisi," Hoffman said, grinning as he raised his glass. "A man's destiny is best forged by his own hand."

Parisi raised his glass as well.

They drank to their toast and the pause allowed Hoffman to check the room. A few center tables were empty as well as two along the windows. A bright white uniform appearing just inside the front doors stopped his visual sweep. When the serviceman removed his cap and tucked it under his arm, Hoffman recognized the young man he nearly ran over.

"What about the fella with her?" Maceo asked.

"What about him?" Hoffman asked, casually turning his attention back to Maceo.

"He seemed to know you."

"How so?" Hoffman asked.

"He looked at you like you were old pals."

Hoffman didn't like Maceo's accusation, especially in front of Parisi. He shook his head and said, "Whoever the man is, I've never seen him. Besides, he doesn't look the sort to run in the same circles."

"And what circle is that for a saloon keeper?" Maceo said.

"Throwing stones all the way from the Balinese Room, are we," Hoffman said with a raised brow and half grin.

A server with a tray of entrees appeared at Parisi's table. Seizing the opportunity, Hoffman said, "If you'll excuse me, gentlemen, your business is your own, and mine is apparently running a saloon." He smiled as he stood up. "I should see to my other guests." He nodded to Parisi, who nodded back.

Hoffman cut a look to Maceo as he moved off toward the front. The quickest route was past tables along the windows. It was roundabout, but the straight line across the center would force Hoffman to weave through the more tightly packed tables.

At the front, Herman was asking if a couple had reservations as Hoffman approached.

"The Navy has landed," Hoffman said to Jack Warren, putting his hand on Herman's shoulder. "They're here as my guests, Herman."

"Hello, Mister Hoffman," Jack said.

"Call me Kurt, Jack," Hoffman said as they shook hands. "Who do we have here?"

Jack introduced Barbara Reese. She was stunning and just the kind of woman Hoffman thought a young sailor would like to impress. "Are you here for dinner or the entertainment?"

"Both," Jack said.

A table at the fore-end of the windows was empty. Hoffman showed them to their seats as Herman brought over menus. "What kind of business brings you up from Galveston?"

"Actually we're assigned to a liaison office here," Jack said.

"Liaison?" he asked—although it was Jack's use of the plural pronoun that intrigued Hoffman as he held a chair out for Miss Reese.

"Navy attachment to the OPC," Miss Reese said, taking her seat.

"Forgive me, but what is the OPC?" Hoffman asked as he opened a menu for the young woman, though he knew the answer.

"Pretty dull stuff," Jack said.

Hoffman understood the evasive answer and the subtle look Jack gave his date. "Loose lips sink ships" was the motto of the day. And on Jack's single rack of decorations across his left chest was a solid maroon rectangle. It was the Good Conduct Medal and the only one Hoffman recognized, telling him this man *mostly* went by the book.

Reese might well be an officer, which would explain her having the option of not wearing a uniform while off-duty. Hoffman thought he recalled that the enlisted were discouraged from dating commissioned officers. *Interesting.*

"Any suggestions on what's good?" Jack asked.

"The seafood," Hoffman said, grinning. "I have Gulf shrimp fresh-in and some trout." Then he looked at Reese and said, "Just the thing if you're planning a visit to the dance floor afterwards."

Reese smiled at Jack.

"Speaking of which," Hoffman began. "Jake's Phillies is making their debut here. But unfortunately, his vocalist has taken ill."

"I saw Phillips with Woody Wilson, once," Reese said. "His solos on the sax are very sultry." She winked at Jack.

"You have plenty of time to enjoy your meal," Hoffman said as he offered a hand to Jack. "I'll be back in a bit to check on you, and I look forward to seeing you downstairs." Hoffman excused himself and made his way toward the kitchen.

Loose Lips

"Exactly how did you meet him?" Barbara asked.

"He's the reason for my limp," Jack said with a smile. "We literally bumped into each other." He told her what happened at the intersection and, in restitution, Hoffman offered a night at the restaurant.

"Talk about luck," Barbara said, leaning forward but keeping her proper posture.

"Tell that to my hip." Jack stole a casual glance at Barbara's bustline as she scanned the room.

"So, what's with all the closed-door hubbub between you and the C.O.?"

"You're his assistant," Jack said, assuming she had to have the inside track. "You've seen the reports and typed the dispatches yourself."

"Oh, there's more to the story than what's on paper," Barbara said, giving Jack a sly, sideways look.

"Not as much as you think, Barbara."

"Come now, Jack!" she whispered, her drawl more pronounced. "A boy strolls into the office this morning, meets with you two and, afterward, you escort him out like a dignitary. You even shook his hand, Jack!"

"Do we really have to talk shop?"

Barbara held her look at Jack.

"Der cudt be spyz everywhere," Jack said, wide-eyed and smiling.

"That's a lousy accent," she said, grinning. "But point taken." After a few seconds, Barbara asked, "Can we talk about Pearl Harbor?"

"You saw the newsreels," he said.

"The captain said you were there."

"Our transport didn't put to port until the day after the raid." He paused and looked down. "I lost count on the number of bodies still floating in the harbor, and the count ashore was worse. Dozens were pulled from the rubble of destroyed buildings. Machinists spent days with welding torches frantically trying to free the few remaining crewmen left trapped in the mangled ship hulls. Honestly, the initial reports listed only a fraction of the actual number of dead."

Jack shifted in his seat, partly from his hip being sore and partly from uncomfortable memories. "Fires burned and smoldered for days, especially on the Arizona—everything was black, including the water." He looked at Barbara for a moment, and then back down at the flatware and said, "I'd been ashore maybe half an hour when a doctor pulled me into a shack to donate blood." He described being laid out on a gurney and watching his own blood fill a soda bottle.

"I think half the people were in shock, and the other half were terrified of another attack," Jack said. Alerts, he said, sounded for days anticipating an invasion force. "One report stated that on the afternoon of the seventh, our own planes from the Enterprise were accidentally shot down." He shook his head. "The poor guys were just coming in to help, thinking the raid was still happening."

He finally looked up at Barbara, who seemed transfixed and serious. Jack swallowed the emotions welling up. "Anyway, they'll be cleaning up for a good year or more." He smiled but knew it looked as hollow as it was.

"I can't imagine seeing one of those Jap planes diving at me," Barbara said. "Can you?"

"Our transport was strafed by three Zeros on the seventh. We later heard that our carriers were the intended targets at Pearl. I guess the planes attacking us were scouting the shipping lanes and found our ship instead. We were only half a day out from Hawaii."

"What happened?"

"Our radioman received the first calls from Pearl, so we were already at General Quarters," Jack said, sighing. He explained that the transport was steaming at flank speed and zigzagging—which he said was barely faster than a canoe for that tub. "The thing was a rust bucket—built in the early twenties and armed with light defenses." Jack took a sip of water. "Anyway, lookouts spotted planes and all hell broke loose. But lucky for us, the forward gunner grew up duck hunting," Jack said, smiling. "It was ideal training for how to lead a flying target. Two Zeros were downed before they could release torpedoes."

"What about the third one?"

Jack's face went somber. "It didn't have a torpedo but it came in close enough to strafe the deck, which killed our aft gunner and wounded a half-dozen other crewmen."

"Didn't anybody get him?"

Jack shook his head. "He made another run and high-tailed out of there."

"See, that's what I don't understand," Barbara said as she straightened up in her chair. "The Japs are the ones that attacked us, not the Germans. They're just like us, and I don't understand why we're not putting everything into the Pacific."

"Barbara, not all the bad guys have slant-eyes and Coke-bottle glasses," Jack said as he leaned closer to Barbara. "Not to mention the English might disagree with you."

"They need to learn to solve their own problems over there."

"I guess it's a good thing the French didn't say that about us a couple a hundred years ago."

A waiter brought a bottle of white wine to the table along with two glasses. He said it was the compliments of Mr. Hoffman.

A beer or bourbon on the rocks was Jack's preference. However, Barbara's expression meant that the wine would go a long way to achieving tonight's objective. *Thank you, Mister Hoffman!*

They gave their order to the waiter, which was according to their host's suggestions. Jack wondered if the chef could make a passable chicken fried steak, or maybe some fried white squash with mustard greens and bacon. Then again, Barbara might the kind of girl that turned her nose up at those things.

Dallas girls were usually pretty tough nuts to crack. But Dallas was two hundred miles away, as were her family and most of her debutante friends. So as the saying goes, which he learned after boot camp in San Diego, *a girl away loves to play.*

Barbara raised her glass and asked what they should drink to.

Jack tapped his glass to hers, winked, and said, "Friendly maneuvers."

FOURTEEN

Whammy

The Powder Room

"I could just wring his neck!" Reina paced with her arms folded as she growled.

"Which one?" Carla asked as she leaned closer to the mirror and touched up her lipstick.

"You know which one," Reina said. She kept pacing, spinning on her heels.

"Reina, honey, he's right." Carla twisted her lipstick back into its cylinder and put her hands on her friend's shoulders. "Stop your flustering a minute and tell me what on God's green acre you were thinking."

Reina's eyes began to tear. It was bad enough she slept alone, but a quiet house made things worse. And though Olivia was safe, it was killing Reina to have her so far away. "She needs her mother; I want it all over with so I can bring her home."

"Remember who you're dealing with," Carla said as she handed Reina a tissue from the counter. "Nobody confronts a man like Parisi—you have no idea what he'll do tomorrow. Olivia could wind up an orphan. Is *that* what you want for her?"

"She practically is one with the way things are," Reina said, rubbing her stomach.

"So what will you say to Parisi?"

"Whatever it takes for him to leave us and the Factory alone."

"I understand how important it is to you," Carla began. "But is the factory *that* important?"

Reina didn't want to give up the Factory—she enjoyed the work, the people, as well as the novelty of being a businesswoman. It also put Reina in a position to do things she might not have otherwise been able to do. "It's not the money, to me or to Parisi," Reina said. "He wants legitimacy—and I've worked hard for it."

"And Vincent, too. Right?"

Reina sighed. "Yes, of course. We worked hard together. It was a balance with Vincent managing the warehouse and keeping the production floor going, and me dealing with both vendors and customers." Reina leaned against the counter and took a deep breath. "We built up that business together, and Parisi doesn't deserve it," Reina said, holding herself as if she had a chill. "And I want to make sure I have something left of Vincent to give Olivia one day."

"What's that supposed to mean, Reina?"

She looked at the floor instead of at Carla. Tears welled up again and kept her from answering.

"What?" Carla put her arm around Reina's shoulder.

"This morning, I woke up for the first time without thinking of Vincent." She hid her face in her hands. "And I couldn't remember his face."

"Because of—"

Reina nodded to stop Carla from saying his name.

"Boy, he has gotten under your skin," Carla said.

Reina turned and used a hand towel to dry her eyes, being careful not to mess up her makeup any more than she had to. "The last thing I need is a little half-pint trying to interfere," she said, sniffing.

"Oh I don't know, Reina," Carla said. "Imagine if he hadn't interfered the other night."

"So you're on his side, now?" Reina asked, rolling her eyes.

Carla rolled her eyes.

"He's just…" Reina held out her arms and let them drop to her sides. "He's put me on the blink."

"Now you're starting to sound like a song," Carla said, smiling.

Reina laughed and nodded.

Carla laughed with her friend and helped her fix her face. She asked Reina the obvious question.

"Oh God, Carla, how can I be?" Reina laughed, "I've only known him two days."

"So?" Carla took Reina's hand and said, "It's not the time as much as what you know."

"Oh, and he's been such a *wealth* of information."

"I've known him a few hours, and I've learned a lot." Carla counted on her fingers as she recited her list, starting with her index finger. "First of all, he seems pretty concerned with keeping you safe. Second, he makes you feel safe, and I can tell you're at ease with him. Remember what you told me about coffee with him this morning? Part of you is finally ready to move on."

"Is there a third?"

"And a fourth." She took Reina's left hand and held it. "Third is the fact that this is the first time I've ever seen you without your wedding band."

Reina pulled her hand away and rubbed her ring finger. "And what's the fourth?" She asked, staring at her hand.

"You tell me," Carla asked, curling up one side of her mouth. "You saw more of him on day one than I had of Frank before my wedding night."

Reina's eyes grew wide. She smiled and shook her head. "You are such a hussy."

"I'm a good wife," Carla said as she winked. "And Frank's a good husband. You should see the books he brought home from China." She fanned herself.

Reina gave Carla a look.

"The real question is how Richard feels."

"This is crazy," Reina said, getting back to touching up her makeup.

"Why?" Carla asked. "What is scaring you so much?"

Reina spun around and slapped her palm on the counter. "Because the things I'm feeling I didn't feel with Vince!"

"That doesn't mean you didn't love Vince," Carla said with a soft smile as she put her hand on Reina's arm. "Richard's a different man, and only natural he'd rewrite what love means—with him."

"Love! A little fast, don't you think?"

"It happens when it happens," Carla replied, shrugging.

Reina half scoffed and half sighed, though Carla was making sense. "So what makes you so smart?" Reina asked, trying to grin.

"I'm a hussy, remember?"

Reina rubbed her ring finger.

Carla raised Reina's face with a finger under her chin. "Reina, what does your heart tell you to do?"

Chitchat

Reina and Carla walked out into the club while the band played an instrumental. Frank and Richard sat at a table not far from one of the bars. On the table were two champagne cocktails. Frank had a Manhattan, and Richard drank a Martini. Carla sat next to Frank and leaned in to kiss him. Reina sat next to Richard and smiled.

"Am I forgiven?" Richard asked, whispering close to her ear.

Reina turned and whispered back. "I shouldn't have snapped."

"Yeah," Richard said. "You should have. I was over the top."

They sipped their drinks and listened to the band. Richard asked their name, and Reina said *The Jake's Phillies Orchestra.* Jake was actually Jacob Phillips, who used to play the sax and trumpet for Woody Wilson's group.

"Jake prefers the smaller rooms," Reina said. "And he hates road trips."

"And he took Reina under his wing in music appreciation at San Jac," Carla said, grinning.

"San Jac?" Richard asked.

"San Jacinto High School," Reina said.

"I pictured you as a Catholic school girl." Richard smiled.

"I started at Incarnate Word, but when Mama died there was no money for tuition."

"What about your father?"

"I never knew him—only that he was a mechanic on an Italian merchant ship. Mama brought me and Johnny to America from Sicily when I was seven. She worked as a seamstress and helped make pasta when Mr. Ancona owned the Pasta Factory. And then she passed."

"Who took care of you?" Richard asked.

"Me!" Reina didn't understand the look on Richard's face. She was 14 and already worked part-time jobs to help her mother with extra money. She had no other family, so she took things into her own hands. "That's what you do," she said with a casual shrug.

"We all rented rooms in the same building on the north side," Carla said. She glanced at Reina, then back at Richard as she spoke. "We watched out for each other. I babysat Johnny while Reina did her assignments or when she helped out at Nathiel's Dry Goods and Meats."

"Remember the bathroom on our floor?" Reina asked, laughing.

Carla laughed, too, wrinkling her nose. "The roaches and the sour smell during the summer."

"At least you had indoor plumbing—all we had was a *bahkousa* full of spiders," Frank said.

"A what?" Richard asked.

"You'd call it an outhouse, but Italians call it the backhouse. Add a thick Italian accent and you have *bahkousa.* To this day I hate spiders," Frank said, laughing.

"What about your people?" Carla asked Richard. "How'd you come up?"

Richard stared at his drink, clearly uncomfortable with the question. Reina cut Carla a quick grin and Carla winked back.

Richard cleared his throat and said his parents were also gone. When he said his father passed not long ago, Reina thought she caught a break in his voice, and he blinked a few times more often.

"Reina says you went to a Jesuit College," Carla said. "Are you Catholic?"

As Richard said yes, Carla tapped Reina on her foot.

Richard was clearly uncomfortable with answering these questions. He changed the subject by asking what song the band had started playing.

"I've got a crush on you," Reina said.

Richard snapped a look back at Reina.

"It's a Gershwin tune!" Reina laughed. *Yes, you're an idiot,* she thought as he winced. "And nice to dance to, though."

Richard led Reina to the dance floor. She looked over her shoulder at her friends still seated at the table. Carla was giving Reina wide eyes and a toothy grin.

"You should know I'm not much of a dancer," Richard said with a whisper.

"So we'll go to the center of the floor," she whispered back. "No one will notice."

Reina's heart jumped when Richard wrapped his arm around her waist. She put her right hand on his left hand and at the same time, she put her other hand on his shoulder. He flinched but said nothing and smiled at her.

"Do the bandages hurt?" she asked.

He shook his head no.

Reina let Richard lead with a simple box step. His hold around her was firm, and his steps became more fluid with the music. "You're doing fine," she said, smiling, and thinking a little practice could smooth out the rough edges.

Richard smiled back with those eyes. *No. No. No!* She thought her chest would burst open. And with each breath, her blouse tightened. The proper thing to do was keep some daylight between them. Instead, she rested her head on his shoulder.

"This looks nice on you," Reina said, feeling the fabric of Richard's jacket.

"Thanks," he said. "But nowhere as good as you do."

"I can't believe you're such a perfect match to Johnny's size," she said. "Everything fits just right."

"Well, not everything," Richard said.

His devilish grin was taunting. Reina stopped dancing to lean away and look at his suit. Her sudden standstill made Richard bump her hip. Reina gasped. Startled and embarrassed, she darted her eyes around the dance floor, hoping nobody else noticed he was unrestrained, and trying not to look herself. She widened the distance between them.

"That's, that's, that's just so—" Reina said without looking him in the eye.

"Naughty?"

"Brazen," she said under her breath. Reina leered in reply to his mischievous smile.

"Listen," he said as his grin turned sheepish. "Wearing another man's suit is one thing, but—"

Reina's giggle cut him off and she had to put her hand over her mouth to contain it. She had to admit she wouldn't want to wear somebody else's underwear either. Still giggling, she leaned on Richard without meaning to, which exacerbated his condition. She pulled away, trying not to guffaw or break out cackling like a hen. "Let's sit the rest of this one out," she said, leading him off the dance floor by the hand.

"Want anything?" Richard asked, stopping near the bar and pointing to it.

"Air," Reina said still chuckling. She slowly stepped away, and they held hands until each was at arm's length.

Reina smiled and shook her head on the way back to the table where Frank and Carla still sat. Frank was finishing his Manhattan. Reina watched Richard walk toward the bar as she sat down. Richard was still looking at her and she pointed to Frank, signaling for another Manhattan. Richard disappeared behind the light crowd gathering between their table and bar.

"Why so flush, honey," Carla said. "Everything okay?"

Reina waved a hand; she couldn't speak or she'd start laughing out loud. She was almost able to say something to Carla when a tap on her shoulder stopped her. The bandleader greeted her and she smiled, stood up, and kissed him on the cheek. "Mister Phillips!"

"I thought it was you." Jake Phillips smiled and asked how she was doing.

Reina said she was fine. She asked if he remembered Carla and Frank.

"I do. Hello," he said as he nodded to the Bonos. "I'm glad I ran into you, Reina, I could use a favor."

Hook, Line, and Sinker

Richard lit a cigarette while he waited for the bartender. A double sounded good, partly because of how good Reina felt in his arms. And it was terminally cute how she got all flustered and giggly at his going *commando*—quite a novelty in 1942.

The other reason for a stronger drink was he knew Carla would resume her not-so-subtle interrogation. Morsels of truth and a few white lies were fine for now, but they wouldn't hold for long. No matter how much he hated pulling the wool over Reina's eyes, and what eyes she had, the truth was even worse. For the first time in his life, he understood what it meant to be between a rock and a hard place.

On top of all that, there was Kurt Hoffman. Richard half hoped to see him, but the reality of it was weird. He also worried about some kind of temporal impact from interacting with him. Suddenly, not all the classic time paradoxes were so hypothetical, assuming, of course, none of this was a hallucination.

An amplified thump on a microphone and feedback noise turned everyone's attention to the stage. It was a welcome distraction for Richard. The lights dimmed a bit, and a soft spotlight was keyed on Kurt. *Always the consummate host.* Richard grinned and leaned an elbow on the bar while he listened.

Playing emcee, Kurt welcomed the crowd to the debut performance of *Jake's Phillies.* The musicians took their places behind Kurt as he regretfully announced poor health prevented their vocalist from appearing. "However," Kurt said, smiling, "Jake has convinced an old friend of his, and this establishment, to lend a hand for a set, or maybe two." Looking stage right, he said, "Please welcome—Reina Corte."

Richard straightened up and whipped around to look over at the table. No one was there. The audience applauded Reina as she walked to center-stage with casual elegance. Her beaded blouse sparkled in the spotlight, and so did her eyes. Richard was mesmerized with delight as she lowered the mic stand. She nodded to the bandleader, and the music started.

Strings and symbols were followed by bass and a harmonica, giving the melody a sad undertone until Reina started singing as the drummer kicked in with the swish of those wire-tipped sticks. She let her hips move ever so slightly with the beat. Her voice was soft and hopeful as her face lit up with the emotions of each verse about finding love in the mist.

The song was *Skylark.* Linda Ronstadt had done a version of it with Nelson Riddle a few years back. To Richard, Reina sounded every bit as good. There were even similar intonations. *She belongs up there.*

Richard saw the Bonos on the dance floor and smiled. Frank's injury had no effect on Carla. They acted as playful in each other's arms as newlyweds did.

The bartender asked for Richard's order and, never taking his eyes off the stage, he requested drinks for himself and Frank.

Reina smiled when she sang the final refrain while looking out over the room. Her voice faded off as she dipped her chin and closed her eyes. The music trailed off and ended.

The dance floor erupted in applause. There was even a wolf whistle or two. Richard couldn't blame anyone for those. Reina glowed. Her smile was a humble one and it made Richard's heart jump. Then, when she looked over at the bandleader again, another melody began.

Flutes led for a few bars followed by strings again. Richard was familiar with this one, too, but he couldn't place it. Even the first few words from Reina didn't jog his memory. They were about two old sayings, one *that love is blind* and the other to *seek and ye shall find.*

Reina's pining tone pulled together the seemingly disjointed lyrics about looking for a man she loves but has never found. She longingly cried the next verse about finding a shepherd for a lost lamb—*her.*

A sultry beat slid in and Reina matched it with subtle sways of her hips. Along with her expression, her tone went from longing to pouting. Richard suddenly remembered the title, *Someone to Watch Over Me.*

Reina's coy eyes found Richard's and she punched him with the first refrain, turning up the pout as if *she* were the *little lamb lost in the wood.*

Richard's heart raced and he was absorbed into her eyes and her expressions. Teasing the mic stand with her fingertips punctuated Reina's croon about *being good to one who'll watch over her.* Without missing a beat, her look became mischievous. She turned her body enough toward Richard to hint something was coming right at him. And when she oozed out the words about the man not *being what some girls think of as handsome,* she winked and grinned.

Her dimples were more pronounced, and Richard loved the way her nose wrinkled when she smiled. He grinned from ear to ear.

Reina switched back to a full-on pout building into a seductive yearning along with the music rising to a crescendo. She cupped the bulbous microphone in her hands and held it close to her glistening wet lips. The room, the crowd, everything faded away but Reina's voice and what he saw in her eyes. Richard stood there and let her filet him as she wailed the closing lyrics.

Won't you tell him please to put onsome speed
Follow my lead
Oh, how I need someone to watch over me

The applause was louder than after the last song. It hardly fazed Richard. Only repeated pats on his arm broke the trance.

"Your drinks, sir."

"What drinks?" Richard asked.

"Vodka Martini and Manhattan," the bartender said. "Gee pal, she put the starch in my shorts, too. But you, she reeled you in but good."

Richard smiled big. He didn't have to say a word; his answer would have been too easy.

FIFTEEN

Double Whammy

Small World

Reina finished her set and left the stage. The applause was hard to resist. It'd been a long time since she last tasted its appeal, and just as long a time since she practiced her breathing. Her lightheadedness was compounded by her giddiness from the second number.

"It's nice to see you with a big smile, honey," Carla said, waiting for Reina inside the wing exit to the dance floor. She hugged her friend.

"Where's Frank and Richard?" Reina fanned herself.

"They're sitting at the table." Carla patted the perspiration from Reina's cheek with a handkerchief. "I think you gave him apoplexy," she said.

"Maybe I overdid it."

"Not if you wanted to grab him by the cagunis," Carla said, whispering in Reina's ear.

"What has gotten into you, Carla?" Reina asked with a grin. "Does everything have to be about that?"

"Frank and I are still making up for lost time, and maybe you should, too."

"I think you're getting me ahead of myself," Reina said, fanning herself with a napkin. "I'm certainly not ready for…"

"Bet he is now." Carla winked.

Hoffman was waiting when Reina and Carla walked out into the club. "Thank you for filling in, Reina. What a spellbound performance you gave—my stage is open to you anytime."

Reina smiled and said, "Thank you, Mister Hoffman, but still no additional discounts on orders."

Hoffman laughed. "Of course not. And cash on the barrel-head, as always."

Herman appeared with a young woman, who kissed Hoffman's cheek. Hoffman introduced her as his fiancée, Dorothy Malone, and she said Reina's performance was wonderful.

Reina smiled and thanked her.

"Excuse me, Mister Hoffman but the cigarette girl needs Cubans for Mr. Wortham." Herman also asked if a photographer could take a few pictures around the club for the band's promotional circular. "I'll get the cigars, Herman, but tell the photographer no pictures of the bar or cocktail glasses."

Herman nodded and left.

"Don't you ever stop working?" Carla asked.

Hoffman shook his head no and smiled.

"Why don't you let us take care of Miss Malone for a few minutes?" Reina suggested.

The couple agreed and Hoffman said he'd only be a few minutes as he scurried off.

Milling through the crowd toward their table, Reina made conversation with her new ward. "Are you from Houston?"

"San Antonio, originally," Dorothy said.

"How are things there? The same as here?"

Dorothy nodded and told Reina her father owned a furniture store. Since most factories had converted to some part of war production, new goods were scarce, if available at all. She normally spent her summer breaks in Houston with her aunt and uncle working in their five and dime. But this year she'd been helping her father shift to recovering and refurbishing to make up the shortfall.

The only problem with renovating furniture, Dorothy added, was that most fabrics and leathers were hard to get—but not as hard as new frames or replacement parts. Labor, she said, was the only thing her father didn't lack. "His repairmen and upholsterers are middle-aged—past military service age."

"I run a business called the Pasta Factory and having to work around commercial rations for raw ingredients is difficult these days. I have the production labor—it's mostly women from the Italian community, but hard-working men are scarce. So finding warehousemen is a whole other matter."

"Is that how you met Kurt?"

Reina nodded. "He's been a customer for somewhere around three years."

Frank and Richard were talking and cutting up at the table. When Richard saw Reina, he hopped up to hold her chair. She liked the way he smiled and the way his eyes looked at her. And he wasn't exactly shy about how he liked seeing her on stage and how much he enjoyed her singing.

"She does have a lovely voice," Dorothy said.

"I'm sorry," Reina said, realizing she'd erred. "This is Dorothy Malone, Mister Hoffman's fiancée." Reina did a double take at Richard's expression—or his lack of one. She could tell he deliberately avoided looking at her. Reina studied his face a moment more before continuing the introductions, first with Frank and then Richard.

"Warren?" Dorothy asked. "I knew a Jack Warren from Refugio."

Timing

"This is too dangerous!"

"Mmm. Scared?" Jeanine asked.

"No, the timing's just not right," Hoffman said. "Scrutiny is not something I need at the moment."

She stopped and pouted at Hoffman.

"Later," he said, helping her up from her knees. "I'll make it up to you."

Jeanine reached down and pulled up the zipper on his trousers, then ran her hand over his inseam. She sighed and kissed him. "But you'll be with *her*, later."

Hoffman put his hands on her lower back and pulled her in tight to reaffirm his affection. "Dorothy always stays with her aunt and uncle, and nice girls like her don't stay out past midnight."

"So what does that make me?" she asked.

Hoffman smiled and winked, saying, "A very *good* girl." He kissed her and then went to the humidor. "Now, Mister Wortham is expecting these." Hoffman handed her two cigars. "You better go on up."

He held her box-tray so she could loop the strap over her neck without mussing her hair. She pouted, and he smiled while shaking his head. Hoffman led her to the wine room door and patted her backside as she walked out. She turned and tried one more pout. He gave her a crooked smile and nod for her to keep going.

He turned and scoffed at the wooden wine cases stacked here, tucked there, even a few shoved into the empty nooks where bottles should be laid on their sides—one atop the other. "Damnit, David, you left me at a bad time," Hoffman said aloud in disgust.

"Who is David?" Schneider stood in the doorway.

"What are you doing down here?"

"Clearly looking for you—who is David?"

"David Andrews *was* my wine steward," Hoffman said, gesturing around the wine room.

"Another brave volunteer?"

Hoffman grunted his reply. He realized the SS officer must have been wandering around. "How'd you get in here?"

Schneider said he posed as Hoffman's cousin and the man at the door gladly directed him to the stairs leading down.

"I don't have a cousin," Hoffman said.

"Of course you do."

Hoffman looked at Schneider as if the man were an oaf. "There were no other siblings besides my father and uncle."

"I'm speaking maternally," Schneider explained.

"I know little about my mother."

"Perhaps I can educate you at a better time," Schneider said.

Always a game of cat and mouse with you. "She's long dead and we have more immediate issues at hand," Hoffman said. "The problem is your timing is premature."

"My men are sitting idle—paralyzed without the remaining figures and components."

"I have the figures," Hoffman said. "But you were supposed to be here later, and I don't have them on my person, for obvious reasons."

"The components?"

"Delayed until tomorrow night."

"Perhaps if you focused more on the tasks at hand rather than the young woman—"

"Perhaps if you and your men had focused more on what you were doing in Sealy, you wouldn't be feeling the squeeze," Hoffman said, cutting off Schneider.

"How were we to know about the valve stem?" the sturmbannfürer asked indignantly. "Allen should have forewarned us."

"Did you at least check the flowmeter?" Schneider's reaction revealed he hadn't. "Don't fret," Hoffman said, reaching for the doorknob. "You wanted to send a message and you have—the Navy and the FBI heard you loud and clear."

"We have to move quickly."

"Too quickly and we risk exposing ourselves before meeting our goal," Hoffman said. He read on Schneider's face that he was losing patience. But Hoffman didn't see any need for it—yet. "Relax, cousin," he said with a wry grin. "Fortune has smiled on us."

"How so?"

"Upstairs is a Navy representative of the OPC," Hoffman said, pointing to the ceiling.

Schneider was expressionless.

"Office of Petroleum Coordination. And if we are lucky—we'll be able to know what they know." Hoffman checked his watch. It was a little after nine o'clock. "Things'll slow down in about two hours," he said. "Meet me at my apartment then."

"In the meantime?"

Hoffman scribbled out a voucher with a pad and pen he carried in his coat pocket. "Enjoy yourself at the tables." He handed Schneider the cashier's voucher and told him how to find the gaming room.

The Nazi went upstairs and Hoffman scanned the wine room one more time. He leaned against the doorjamb and shook his head. It wasn't the disarray that frustrated him. In one evening, he had comped a full meal for Parisi and his bunch, drinks for Reina Corte and her friends, as well as dinner and drinks for Jack Warren. And now Schneider was off gambling with Grille money. This was one hell of an expensive night.

Boom

"Give me a break!" Richard thought. Aunt Dorothy had come out of left field, and he hadn't realized she and Kurt even knew each other during the war. What's more, Reina was quite the center of influence, which reinforced something his father always said. "Houston may be a big city, but it's sure as hell a small town."

Richard ignored the weight of Reina's stare as Aunt Dorothy mention his dad's hometown of Refugio.

"Have you been there?" Aunt Dorothy asked.

"No." Richard lied.

"It's a little spit of a town just north and a little west of Copano Bay, right between Victoria and Corpus," Aunt Dorothy said.

"Near Aransas Pass, right?" Frank asked.

"Yes," Aunt Dorothy said, nodding. "My mother is from Refugio. In fact, I was down there a few weeks ago visiting family friends. Their daughter is starting at the Lake in the fall."

"The Lake?" Frank asked.

"Our Lady of the Lake College in San Antone," Aunt Dorothy said. "I go to school there and wanted to help our friends' daughter prepare."

Richard gulped from his martini. Our Lady of the Lake was where his mother went to college. He couldn't remember the exact time she attended, but the way his luck was running, he expected Aunt Dorothy to start talking about her.

Carla chimed in. "Dorothy's from San Antonio and visiting her aunt and uncle."

Frank half-joked that a schoolgirl was a bit young for a club.

"Well, the owner is my fiancée," Aunt Dorothy said, grinning shyly. "Besides, I'll be twenty-one in a month!"

Richard smiled. Aunt Dorothy and Kurt divorced when Richard was young, and he didn't recall ever seeing her with any kind of spunk. On the contrary, by the time Richard was old enough to *see* what was going on, Aunt Dorothy was drained of emotion. Her mother died around that time, too. Richard never saw her after she moved back to San Antonio to care for her father.

"So who is this Jack Warren, Dorothy?" Carla asked.

Damn it, Carla! Richard looked at his drink and sipped it.

"I met him through the Harris's," Aunt Dorothy said. "Betty Jean Harris is the daughter I spoke about—the one who'll be a freshman at the Lake this year."

Here it comes, Richard thought. Betty Jean was his mother's best friend.

"I guess Jack's daddy didn't come out of the Depression too well," Aunt Dorothy said. She mentioned the Warrens lived in one of the Harris' rent houses. And the Harrises were down to earth. They never discouraged their children from running with people of different means. "I understand he enlisted with the Navy about two years ago, and the last I heard he was in Hawaii," Aunt Dorothy said.

Whew!

"How'd you meet Mister Hoffman?" Reina asked.

"I walked into a five 'n dime and she threw herself at me," Kurt said, walking up to his fiancé.

Aunt Dorothy smiled and gave Kurt a light backhanded smack on the chest. "We met at my uncle's shop, yes, but I certainly did not throw myself at you!"

Richard was glad the subject changed.

Herman emerged from a crowd behind Kurt and tapped him on the shoulder. Kurt had to lean down a little so Herman could whisper something. He looked at Aunt Dorothy, who was looking at him with disappointment.

"It should be in the first double rack of bins on the left as you walk in," Kurt said. "Look on the right side of the rack in one of the upper bins closest to the door. And be careful, a couple of crates are stacked a bit wobbly."

Herman nodded and disappeared.

Kurt shook his head.

Aunt Dorothy put her hand on Kurt's arm and mouthed, "Thank you."

"Lose something?" Frank asked.

"My wine steward, David," Kurt said, frowning. "The man enlisted, along with everybody else, right after December 7th. He was fanatical about keeping the wine room organized. Although he left it in order, shipments I ordered about the time the war broke out finally arrived."

"I bet getting them here took an act of God," Frank said.

"True, but most of my time has been scrambling to fill my chef's needs and hiring replacements—keeping up with the wine room fell off my list of priorities. David is the only one who can arrange things how I like."

"Just stock your center racks with champagnes, Chardonnays, white Bordeaux's, and anything else you move in quantity," Richard said, staring into his drink. He realized everyone was staring at him, particularly Kurt. "Was that out loud?"

Kurt nodded with both eyebrows raised.

Richard was a little embarrassed but within a split second, he considered an interesting idea. He wanted to do something other than convalescing or loitering around Reina's house. While she didn't seem to need the money, paying for his keep was proper. So maybe he could turn this conversation into a job opportunity—even an interview. After all, Richard thought, Kurt's wine room was made to order. A dark room underground offered a boundary to limit his interactions with too many people while he earned a buck. The only glitch concerning Richard was it meant more contact with Kurt and the opportunity for further contamination. But when Kurt asked about what to do with his reds, Richard charged on.

"Run your celebrated vintages first, by label, and oldest to youngest from the top down," Richard said and named a few for effect, including Mouton, Haut-Brion, Lafite, and Latour. Exactly along the lines Kurt had always instructed, Richard dictated how to arrange the wines. He listed the preferred order of Bordeaux districts, such as Saint-Emilion, Pomerol, Graves, and Saint-Estèphe, which would constitute subsequent groupings. "After your ports, you can clump your Burgundies together next to your off-beat varieties."

"How would you deal with ullage?" Kurt asked.

"Make sure they're placed correctly in the racks so the wine makes contact with the cork, keeping it moist—that's the only trick I know. I'd be more concerned with sediments." Richard said, adding, "I'd be sure to tag the new bottles and date those tags so you would know how long they've been settled."

"Can someone tell me what you two are talking about?" Carla asked.

Richard realized that for a few moments, everyone else in the room faded into the background while he and Kurt talked wines and cellars. It was comfortable. But he ceded the floor to Kurt for the answer to Carla's question. Kurt explained how sediment forms as red wine ages, and the term they used referred to allowing those sediments to settle out. "Shipping tends to mix the dregs back into the fluid, which is something you don't want," Kurt said.

"If you don't let it settle out, it makes the texture of the wine gritty and bitter," Richard said.

"Not to mention they churn your stomach," Kurt added. He turned to Richard. "So how do you handle a stubborn cork?"

Richard gnashed his teeth and said, "Like a nervous bride on her wedding night!" As he said it, he saw Reina raise an eyebrow.

Frank laughed and added, "Coax her, eh?"

Carla poked Frank with her elbow.

Aunt Dorothy blushed.

"With patience," Richard said.

Kurt smiled at everyone at the table, then Richard. "I think we have our new sommelier."

"Why don't I put your cave back in order and we see how it goes."

"All right," Kurt said. "How 'bout tomorrow morning?"

Richard looked at Reina.

She nodded and said, "I can drop you on the way to the Factory."

"And pick me up on the way to our appointment tomorrow afternoon," Richard said, trying to be stern.

Reina nodded.

Kurt smiled and put out his hand and the two men shook on it. "Welcome aboard." Kurt grimaced, smiled, and snickered. "I don't think I know your name."

"Richard Warren."

"Warren," Kurt said, grimacing again.

"Reporting for duty, sir!" From behind Kurt, a young man appeared, looking not much older than a teenager, and wearing a bright white Navy uniform.

Same Difference

Reina saw a man in uniform as he approached Mr. Hoffman. The starched whites were hard to miss and she hadn't seen any other servicemen in the club. *Poor Dorothy,* she thought. The girl couldn't enjoy her fiancé for more than a few minutes without interruption.

"Jack, how was your dinner?" Mr. Hoffman asked.

"Fine, just fine," Jack said.

"Hi, Jack," Dorothy said, surprised.

"Long time no see, Dorothy," Jack said.

"You know each other?" Mr. Hoffman asked.

"We have a mutual friend," Dorothy said, adding, "I was talking about her a few minutes ago."

Reina snapped a look at Richard. His face was white and he was clenching his jaw. She half expected the stem of his glass to break from the way he clamped it. Yet his eyes were far more telling. At first, they were wide and glazed as if he'd seen a ghost. Then he blinked repeatedly. Reina compared the features of Richard and the sailor talking to Mr. Hoffman. *Similar?*

"And this is Reina Corte, Jack," Hoffman said.

"How do you do?" Reina politely asked, finding it hard to glance away from Richard.

"And Jack," Hoffman said, motioning to Richard. "This Richard *Warren.*"

He didn't move, and Reina had to touch his arm. "Richard."

Richard took a breath and blinked a few times. "I'm sorry," he said, smiling —an unconvincing one, Reina thought. He stood up and put out his hand, which was trembling. "My mind was still in Kurt's wine room," Richard said, looking at Mister Hoffman.

"I had an uncle named Richard," Jack said.

"Had?" Richard asked.

"Richard Randolph Warren," Jack said. "I never met him but my father said he died back during the Malaria epidemic in 1912."

"I've been close, but I'm not dead, yet," Richard said, smiling at Reina.

Both men were about the same height and build, Reina thought. The difference was in their faces and hair. Jack's hair was dark and his face was fuller, with a square jaw and a more rounded nose. Richard's hair was sandy. His face was thinner and his nose Romanesque. But to Reina, their eyes were nearly identical. *Twinkling mischievous eyes.*

Jack was also quite a bit younger than Richard. However, he already had the beginnings of the same pronounced furrow between his eyebrows as Richard. Their hairlines were dissimilar. While Jack's hair was combed back, Richard's was somewhat over to the side, yet both receded in the same way.

"What's your middle name?" Carla asked.

"I don't have one," Richard said.

Carla scoffed, "A Texas boy with no middle name? Sacrilegious!"

Richard shrugged.

"You go by Richard, Rick, or Dick?" Jack asked with a smirk.

Richard peered sideways at Jack and said, "Richard, if you want to be my friend."

"Fair enough," Jack said. "Oh, and this is Miss Barbara Reese."

Reina thought it was interesting both Jack and Richard were smart alecks.

"Take my chair," Frank said to Miss Reese.

As the group rearranged itself, a flash, pop, and click surprised everyone. "Sorry," the photographer said. "I wanted a candid shot of Uncle Sam's finest enjoying the Phillies."

Mr. Hoffman quietly reminded him to blackout the cocktail glasses. The photographer nodded and said no problem before asking Mr. Hoffman if he wanted a print.

"Yes," Dorothy said.

Mr. Hoffman smiled at Dorothy and nodded.

Richard leaned over to Reina and whispered, "Why blackout the cocktails?"

"Why do you think," she curiously replied, whispering back and looking at him as if he were crazy. "Liquor by the glass is illegal."

Richard got an "oh, yeah" expression. With another unconvincing smile, he said he'd be back in a minute. He turned and walked in the direction of the restrooms. Reina watched him until she lost him in the crowd.

Parsed Words

A waitress motioned to an exit when Richard asked her where he could get some fresh air. It led to a small cement pad outside a pair of doors in the back of the casino. Casino. It shouldn't have been a surprise. Even the burly guy guarding the doors was right out of the genre. And so was the secret knock to reenter—the one everybody knows: "shave and a haircut, two bits."

The fresh air was only a bit humid but cool. Still, Richard found it hard to breathe, as if his heart and stomach were crammed side by side in his throat. And his teeth hurt from clamping his jaw down to hold back tears. He leaned back against the wall and hunched over with his hands on his knees as he took deep breaths.

Holy shit!

The club was claustrophobic, and when his father—or the man who would become his father—appeared, a panicky and trapped feeling overwhelmed him. Knowing he couldn't hug him or say anything meaningful, the next best thing was to run. Sorting out the torrent of emotions or, at least, letting them settle down was a lot easier out from under Reina's scrutiny.

His dad looked exactly like he did in a picture that sat on a shelf in his parents' family room. Richard let out a sigh as he tried to compose himself. Just days ago he'd wished he could know the man before he was a father. "You got your wish didn't you, stupid?"

"What wish?" Reina asked as she closed the door leading out from the casino.

Crap.

"Don't you think it's time you tell me who you are and what this is about?"

Richard grunted and winced as he turned to rest his forehead on the wall. "Not now, Reina."

"Your behavior tonight is really strange," Reina said. "Not that you're particularly normal to begin with."

Richard turned and leaned back against the wall with his hands in his pockets.

"You owe me the truth!" Reina said, stepping next to Richard and putting her hand on his shoulder.

"You couldn't possibly believe me," Richard said.

"Damnation, Richard!"

Oddly, Richard liked the fury building in her eyes. He thought a minute, and it hit him. "You ever read Mark Twain?"

"What!"

"Mark Twain, you ever read him?"

"*Huck Finn* and *Tom Sawyer*, yes!"

"He wrote a story once about a guy who had to butt heads with Merlin," Richard said.

"Merlin! Richard, what in the Sam Hill are you talking about?" Reina folded her arms and glared at Richard. He felt as if she could penetrate his skull and read his mind. "Miss Malone and Jack Warren aren't strangers to you—I can't explain why they don't know you, but you *do* know them. And what was that with Mister Hoffman? It was like you could read his mind or something."

Richard breathed deeply through his nose. "In all honesty," he said, standing straight and facing Reina. "I can tell you that before this date, I have never met any of those people... no more than I knew you before a few days ago."

"Then what is it, Richard?" Reina asked, moving closer to him.

"I'm occasionally claustrophobic—crowds can heighten my apprehension."

"And yet, you're willing to sit in a dark little room for Mister Hoffman."

"Different things kick it into gear," Richard said. "Besides, as long as I keep busy and step out from time to time, I'll be fine."

Richard was honest about the claustrophobia. Crowds sometimes gave him a penned-in sensation, which also made rooms shrink. However, his reaction tonight was the obvious result of his father's arrival. Somehow, Richard thought, he'd have to figure a way to parse enough of the truth to satisfy Reina.

"Claustrophobia is all fine and good, but it doesn't explain how you behaved in there," she said, pointing into the club. "I'd swear you acted like you saw a ghost."

"Jack..." Richard paused, gritting his teeth to keep emotions from welling up again. He made an effort to smile a half smile and said, "He's very much like someone I knew. So maybe I have seen a ghost."

"Your father?"

Richard nodded.

"When did he die?" She put her hand on his cheek.

"A few days before—" Richard waved his hand between Reina and himself.

"Before we met?"

Richard grunted.

"How did it happen?"

"Time and life mostly. As he got worn down he sank into the bottle, but there was something more driving it. Mom somehow kept him in check until she died—afterward he spiraled." Thinking about it made Richard want to throw up. "But of course I could fix it," Richard said, scoffing at his own arrogance. "The reality turned out to be a shining example of blundering stupidity and ineptitude on my part. In effect, I killed him, as surely as if I drove a stake into his chest." He faced away from Reina.

"He was a grown man," she said. "You shouldn't have to pay for his sins."

"Why not? He paid for mine with his life."

Reina moved around to stand in front of Richard. "Why are you responsible?"

"Because he was my responsibility!" Richard composed himself and lowered his voice. "Honor thy father and mother—that's right smack in the middle of the list."

Reina asked Richard how his mother died.

"You want it all, don't you?"

Reina didn't answer.

"Mom died in a state of grace—a massive heart attack while kneeling bedside and saying her prayers one night. She'd always had a weak heart, but it just happened to give out on a night after she argued with Dad. He thought it was his fault, so he never forgave himself."

"Like father, like son," Reina said.

"What?"

"You're punishing yourself for his death as much as he did for hers." Reina took his hand and squeezed it. "You didn't let him down," she said softly.

"So buck up and move on?"

"Live your life," Reina said with a smile. "Walk away with something good and hold onto it." She leaned in and hugged Richard.

Holding Reina was soothing and he liked her in his arms. For a moment, he didn't hate himself so much. Reina made sense, maybe because she understood his feelings. "Reina," he said.

She raised her head off his shoulder and looked up at Richard.

"How are you at taking your own advice?" Richard asked with a raised eyebrow.

Reina had a soft smile and tightened her hold. "What am I gonna do with you?"

Richard grinned. "You want a written list or a demonstration?"

"You are an absolute scoundrel!" Reina said with a chuckle as she shook her head.

"Scoundrel!" Richard said. "I like the sound of that."

Reina's eyes were hypnotic. They gave him a feeling of being in a holographic movie. Like when she sang to him, there was a split-second image of a child with her same eyes and his light hair.

Without hesitation, Reina lifted up on her toes and kissed him. Her lips were soft and wet and interlocked perfectly with his. She opened her mouth and the kiss shifted into a passionate and electric one as her hand found its way to the back of his neck, her thumb lightly rubbing it.

She breathed heavily with a quiet moan, making him want to kiss her deeper. And it made her press into him more. Richard thought the feel of her body against him might stop his heart. It definitely sent a tingle shooting down his spine, spreading to every nerve in his body.

With a wide-eyed expression, Reina put a little space between their bodies and started to pull her lips from his.

Richard gently held her bottom lip between his teeth for a second as he let it slide from the grip of his mouth.

Reina curled her bottom lip under her top one as if to keep tasting the kiss. Richard liked the way her nostrils flared with every deep breath. She glanced down.

"Does the circulation *ever* go to your brain," Reina said, grinning; now looking up at Richard's face but not his eyes.

"Not tonight," Richard said. *And not with the way you look and feel.*

"Come on, Romeo," Reina said, her eyes meeting his. "Let's cool you down." She led him back into the club.

Geronimo!

SIXTEEN

First Contact

New Friends

What Jack wanted to know was how Betty Jean was doing. But he dare not ask. There was no point, and it'd only be a put off to Barbara. "How's everybody down home?"

"Oh, you know," Dorothy said.

"Same ole seven 'n six?"

Dorothy smiled and nodded. "The Harrises are all fine and, you know, Refugio doesn't change much. Except that a lot of you young men are off fighting the war. No help makes it a rough go for farm families," she said.

"It's the same all over," Carla said.

Everybody's attention turned to the young woman, Reina, and her friend, Richard, when they came back to the table. The guy was a little green around the gills when they shook hands, but Jack figured everything must be okay. They were both smiling as he held out her chair.

Jack didn't think much of sharing the same last name. He'd met two fellas named Warren during basic training in San Diego—four in Pearl—and there was almost a whole page of Warrens in the phone directory here in town with whom he had no remote relation.

Besides, his old man's family came to south Texas from Arkansas by way of Dallas after the Civil War. His only paternal uncle, Richard Randolph Warren, died before Jack was born. There was no way he could have a direct relation this far south.

"Everything okay?" Carla asked Reina.

Reina nodded, and Jack saw her wink at her friend.

"So, what in the world brings you to Houston, Jack?" Dorothy asked.

"Jack says he's a gas jockey for the Navy," Hoffman said.

Jack nodded with a grin. "That'd be about right," he said, looking at Barbara. Without going into detail, Jack explained he was on temporary duty with the OPC, and his job was one of logistics. "Pretty dull stuff, not much to tell."

"How long are you here for?" Richard asked.

"As long as the Navy says I'm here." Jack hated answering questions like these. He'd drawn support duties when it came out he could type. The one thing the Navy always needed in spades were typists and yeomen. Part of him was glad, but another part of him felt guilty for not being on a ship of the line. A dozen guys he trained with at basic died in fighting—six at Coral Sea and the others in scattered battles, including one he just heard about on the USS Houston.

"Have you seen any action?" Dorothy asked.

Jack looked at Barbara for a second.

"Oh, let's not make the chief talk shop," Frank said.

Jack smiled. Frank's eye patch and comment, along with a nod, told Jack what he needed to know. He nodded back.

"Dorothy was telling us how she met our host," Frank said.

"Yeah, I thought you'd be back at the Lake," Jack said.

Dorothy told Jack about her aunt and uncle's five 'n dime, apologizing to the others for having to repeat it. Jack wasn't sure who all were friends with whom, but everybody got along pretty well. But he'd guessed Richard must be a newcomer to Dorothy and Kurt.

"By the way, Jack—how do you and Kurt know each other?" Richard asked.

"He tried to run me down the other day," Jack said.

"He what?" Dorothy said.

Hoffman chuckled before he answered. "A minor mishap during lunch traffic."

"Tell that to my hip," Jack said with a grin.

"Heck of an introduction," Richard replied.

The band started playing *Don't Sit under the Apple Tree* and Frank asked Carla to dance.

Reina leaned in close to Richard and said, "This one should be safe enough." She and Richard laughed as they left the table.

"Ready to cut a rug?" Jack asked Barbara. She accepted.

Dorothy and Hoffman stayed at the table. She seemed happy, and Jack was glad. Not everybody back in Refugio was as accepting of Jack running with the Harrises—including Jack's father. After all, Betty Jean's family owned half the county. And what was Jack, but old man Warren's whippin' post? Dorothy, on the other hand, was always very pleasant and unassuming. So, Jack thought this Kurt Hoffman must be a pretty good man. He was certainly a stand-up guy after the other day.

"Penny for your thoughts?" Barbara asked.

"Oh, they're worth a lot more than a penny," Jack said.

"And what makes them so valuable?"

"You," Jack said with a smirk. "You look like a million bucks."

"Well," Barbara began with a crooked smile and bedroom eyes. "With compliments like that, I can do the difficult right now," she squeezed his hand as she continued whispering into his ear. "But the impossible may take a little while." Barbara wet her lips and her blue eyes shimmered. He held her stare and pulled Barbara in closer. Her body was firm, and she was light on her feet. Barbara also followed his lead; he'd give her the slightest pressure from either hand and she turned exactly on cue.

Jack dipped Barbra as the song ended, and she raised her knee tracking up the front of his leg. In San Diego, Jack learned from another dance partner that a raised inside knee during a dip could be a woman's subtle way of doing reconnaissance on a man.

Barbara lightly bit her bottom lip and smiled. "You gonna let a girl go thirsty, sailor?"

"No ma'am!"

She walked ahead to the table and glanced over her shoulder at Jack. He wondered if she was adding something extra to her sashay. Jack watched her as he veered off for the bar. He bumped into Richard.

Chewin' the Fat

The ole fart could really whirl around the dance floor! Richard had never seen his father do much more than a slow box step with his mother. And the little dip at the end of the song was certainly nothing Richard ever imagined his mom doing. His dad's moves were smooth, confident, and he was charming his date.

He had sort of a Bing Crosby-type cool—along with the ears. The dark hair was in stark contrast to Richard's earliest memories of a father with gray hair. Striking.

Kurt had been right; his dad was a people person. He was able to jump right into a group and mix it up without a hitch. And the blonde with him—Barbara, was it? Wow! She would have turned heads in the future, too.

Richard wished he could somehow tell Max about all this, especially about the blonde—Max had a thing for them. But Max would think he'd lost his mind and Richard wasn't entirely certain he'd be wrong. The surrounding scene was just too vivid to be a dream.

"Whup!" Jack said after bumping into Richard. "Sorry, sir."

The word "sir" sounded horrible, although Richard knew he probably seemed like an old man to his dad. He also had to stop and deliberately think before addressing his father. "Distracted there—uh, Chief?" Richard asked, looking toward the table.

Jack grinned. "I hate to see her leave."

"But love to watch her go," Richard said.

Jack nodded and laughed. "She is a dish," he said under his breath.

The bartender interrupted them to take their drink order. Richard offered to buy Jack's round. Jack refused, and the two men held a friendly debate over who should pay for the round. The bartender settled the argument by telling both men their tickets were the compliments of Mr. Hoffman.

"I guess we're both VIPs," Jack said.

"Evidently," Richard said.

"So, what do you do?"

"As of tomorrow, I'll be working for Mr. Hoffman," Richard replied.

"You must be a heck of a waiter to get the red carpet treatment."

Richard laughed. "Every bit of it is for Reina Corte. She and Kurt do business together—and she did him a favor by singing a few songs earlier."

"She any good?"

Richard shook his head as if he were shaking off a spell. "She could draw sailors to their deaths."

The young Jack let out a chuckle—the one Richard remembered as his dad's signature. It was deep and mischievous, along with a wide grin. It was contagious. Richard couldn't help but smile as they stood at the bar and talked.

"How long have you been in the Navy?" Richard asked.

"Almost nineteen months. I did boot camp in San Diego and was transferred to Hawaii in December of last year," Jack said.

"Before or after?"

"I wasn't at Pearl on the seventh."

"I guess you get a lot of that."

"People see the uniform and assume we were all there," Jack said. He stared at his drink a second and chewed his lip. "Maybe, in a way, we were."

Something more was there, Richard thought. He could tell Jack wanted to go on but was embarrassed. "You want to talk about it?"

Jack shifted his weight on another foot as he leaned on an elbow. His grin was forced. "Ah, boring stuff—not exactly *Red Badge of Courage.*"

"Oh, I don't know, try me."

Neither man said anything. Maybe Jack was surprised someone was truly interested in him rather than some yarn about combat. Richard kept his mouth shut and waited.

"We could see Diamond Head on Oahu from the deck of an old transport," Jack started. He took a breath, cocked his head and said, "Suddenly we heard planes overhead—Japanese Zeros. One by one they rolled over to dive into a strafing run."

Richard was mesmerized. His dad never so much as mentioned he saw a Zero, much less got strafed by one. Jack was trying hard to sound casual but it must have been terrifying.

"Our gunners shot down the first two planes," Jack said, staring at his drink as if he could see his memory through the glass. Richard dipped his head trying to catch his eyes to prompt the young sailor. Jack took a breath as his face went blank. "The aft gunner on our transport was hit—blood everywhere. He was screaming. I was right there, so I took over the gun and tried to fire on the Zero."

Tried?" Richard asked.

Jack nodded. "Nothing happened when I pulled the trigger. I guess the mechanism must have been shattered when the Zero's bullets showered the gunner." Jack leaned in and spoke as quietly as he could. "To be honest, I was relieved it jammed. Killing someone—even a Jap—just isn't something I think I can live with." Jack grimaced.

"But?"

"But sometimes I wonder if that doesn't make me yella."

Richard took a deep breath himself. He was disappointed in himself for never thinking more of his dad's service. "You did your duty, Jack," Richard said. "Not wanting to kill doesn't make you a coward. And you did pull the trigger. Just because it didn't fire doesn't diminish your actions." *You're no coward.*

Jack shook his head slightly. "Funny thing is, my adrenaline really got going when I worked on the wounded with the pharmacist mate."

Richard grinned. He remembered going through his dad's war papers, including certificates for pharmacist mate training. He watched Jack light up.

"Something about treating injuries—helping them—was. . . was…"

"Exhilarating?"

"Yes! And ever since, I've been thinking about requesting a transfer to pharmacist mate training."

"And leave all the excitement of the OPC," Richard said, smiling and thinking he was witnessing the seeds of his dad's decision to become a pharmacist's mate.

Jack laughed and nodded. "It does have its moments," Jack said with a raised eyebrow. "The nice thing, though, is I've had the opportunity to stay with my sister and brother-in-law." He said they lived on the outskirts of town, toward West University and Bellaire.

Outskirts! Those places were in midtown for Richard.

In twenty minutes or so, Richard thought he learned more about his father than he had in over thirty years. He was relaxed, personable, and most notably, not bitter. He was charming and had the sense of humor Richard long missed.

Jack took a drink from the classic Manhattan he ordered. It was his first sip, and quite the opposite of what Richard was used to seeing.

"What'll you do for Hoffman?" Jack asked.

"His wine cellar needs some work."

"Never cared for that stuff," Jack said. "Too sweet."

"All depends on the wine," Richard said.

"That your business?"

Richard grunted. The question was bound to come up, which would lead to another inevitable one. "No, but I'm sort of between things at the moment and can use the work."

"What about working for Uncle Sam?"

"Somehow I don't think I'd pass the physical," Richard said.

"You seem fairly young and healthy."

Fairly? Richard did a quick mental review of childhood injuries. He needed an obvious disqualification. "I'm afraid a fall as a kid injured my back," Richard said. "A second injury as a teenager aggravated it."

"You could apply for back-office work," Jack said.

"I hadn't thought about that," Richard said. "I guess we think of the war effort as strictly you guys in uniform."

"There's always more below the surface," Jack said. "Even though we don't see it doesn't mean it's not there—or important."

"Is this any way to treat a girl?" Barbara playfully complained.

Jack straightened up and apologized to her. He handed her the drink she wanted. "We got to chewin' the fat."

"And you forgot about *me*," she said with a wry look.

"Not hardly." Jack grinned and pointed his thumb sideways at Richard. "Just visiting with my uncle, here."

"I'm getting lonely at the table," Barbara said. She kept her eyes on Jack as she raised the glass to her lips. It was a subtle pause, but Richard thought it was a zinger for Jack. She stepped toward the table and Jack gave her a wink.

Richard picked up his glass to follow his dad and Barbara back to the table.

SEVENTEEN

Last Call

Tactical Reconnaissance

The pause from interruptions by Herman and the other staff was long enough for Hoffman to enjoy a conversation with Dorothy. He appreciated her patience but understood that on her first night in town for more than a month, she'd like his undivided attention.

Hoffman had tried to convince her to hold off her trip for a few days. He needed time to finish his dealings with Schneider and Maceo. However, Dorothy was nothing if not persistent—the one thing her father warned Hoffman about when he asked for her hand. Her uncle, too, once made a passing comment on her tenacity. Auburn hair was the only hint to Dorothy's Irish stubbornness otherwise hidden beneath her veneer of practiced demureness, straight posture, and southern grace. Hoffman never minded when she let it out. It was one of the things that attracted him to her, not to mention a number of her classmates and friends from well-to-do families. Such prospective patrons and allies were keys to Hoffman's plans for the Grille's future.

"I have to open up for the kitchen help and the wine room, first," Hoffman said. "I can swing by and pick you up for breakfast after."

"Bring your part of the guest list, too," Dorothy said.

"Why don't you come up and we'll go over it tonight," Hoffman said, fluttering an eyebrow.

Dorothy blushed with a sideways glance to Hoffman. Her answer was never in question, but he pressed the issue a little more anyway. Hoffman moved in closer and whispered into her ear. "It's only a few months away, so what's the point in waiting?"

"You know I want to save that for our wedding night," she said. "And I promise the wait will be worth it." The corners of her mouth curled up and she leaned up to whisper in his ear. "But I won't let you suffer too much."

Frank and Carla came back to the table along with Reina. Miss Reese followed shortly after. Hoffman could see over the heads of most people in the room, and he was able to see Jack and Richard talking at the bar. *Strange coincidence*, Hoffman thought. Still, more unusual was Richard's familiarity with wines—quite rare in Houston. Indeed, it was unusual in most American cities.

Still, Richard Warren appeared at least near thirty. Hoffman figured he'd probably done some traveling. Regardless, Hoffman was glad; he needed someone to organize the wines room, and Hoffman simply didn't have the time.

The women started in on some meaningless chitchat—at least it was to Hoffman. It led to Dorothy probing about how the other ladies met the men in their lives. Hoffman paid scant attention, but enough to hear they were either incredibly romantic or very humorous. Only when Dorothy got around to Reina did Hoffman have real interest in the discussion. Dorothy asked Reina where she found Mr. Warren. Hoffman thought it curious Reina hesitated and gave an uncomfortable glance to her friends.

"We met only a few nights ago," she said.

Just in time to bust Maceo upside the head, Hoffman thought.

"You seem like a natural couple," Dorothy said.

Again, Reina and Carla exchanged looks and smiles. Hoffman hadn't seen Reina smile for some time, though he'd rarely met with her over the past year. Her few visits were purely business. Reina would personally straighten out some delivery foul up or demonstrate some cooking method to help the chefs authenticate dishes.

Hoffman's introduction to Reina Corte was when he first opened the Grille. Once again, she'd filled in for an ailing singer—that time for the Woody Wilson Orchestra. Hoffman had been fortunate to book them for his grand opening.

Her performance had been elegant from set to set. She'd had a talent for holding the audience in the palm of her hand. She had also been deft at holding his advances at bay.

The next day, she'd marched into his kitchen and, before he knew it, walked out with an order in hand. More than her directness, Hoffman admired Reina for never, ever wavering on a commitment.

Frank looked at the time and nudged his wife, which made Hoffman check his wristwatch. Unofficial curfews were coming up at midnight, which were more of an issue for first-generation German and Italian Americans if encountering some policemen or county sheriffs. "I hate to say this, but things are gonna wind down here in a bit," Hoffman said to Dorothy.

She smiled and nodded.

"And I better go find Jack," Barbara said. She headed off to the bar where Hoffman pointed.

After Hoffman said he'd call Dorothy a cab, Carla suggested that Hoffman's fiancée could ride with them.

"My uncle's house is off Hawthorne and Montrose," Dorothy said.

"We go right by there," Frank said.

Dorothy looked at Hoffman and he nodded, saying to Frank, "I'd appreciate it."

Barbara came back with the two Warrens in tow. Hoffman sized up both men, who he thought could prove advantageous. There were striking similarities in their statures and their strides. Hoffman couldn't narrow it down, but there was something else strange about them.

Jack was a bit coarse and he had the distinctive Texas twang. Richard's accent was less pronounced. Yet, their voices had similar inflections and tones. It was obvious they'd never met before unless Jack was an exceptional actor, which Hoffman didn't see as the case. There was, however, Richard's odd behavior. Of course, tomorrow morning would provide an opportunity for further study.

"Don't forget about our agreement, Hoffman said.

"I look forward to it," Richard said.

Hoffman nodded to Richard, leaned down and kissed Dorothy on the forehead, and said, "I'll see you in the morning." He thanked Frank for seeing her home and took leave of the group.

The crowd was thinning and Hoffman easily made his way into the casino, which was through a door opposite the men's room. He checked with each of his three card tables as well as the roulette table and two crap tables. The dice and the wheel were pulling in the most cash. Two councilmen were playing blackjack at Hank's table—the only card dealer Hoffman had that knew how to let certain VIP's win.

Schneider was playing roulette and losing.

The wheel was spinning when Hoffman whispered into his dealer's ear. "Another hour, then close her down." The dealer nodded. Hoffman caught Schneider's eye, so he darted his eyes up, signaling to Schneider to meet upstairs. Schneider replied with a very subtle nod.

Projects

Hoffman traced his finger along one of the black lines on the map until he stopped and tapped on a square indicating a pump station. "You'll want to be careful here—this first one sits on a levy surrounded by a marsh of salt grass and sticker burrs."

"How far off the road?"

Hoffman laughed. "What road? You'll hike a good mile and a half, so bring lots of sulfa powder," Hoffman said with a grin.

Schneider shook his head as if he didn't understand the comment.

"Sulfa powder minimizes bites from chiggers, ticks, and mosquitoes. Dose your clothes and exposed skin with a healthy spread of the powder. I also suggest you carry a walking stick. You'll find rattlesnakes out there."

Hoffman pointed to two places along a highway where he said the military police might set up roadblocks. "Coastal roads are a particular favorite, so be prepared."

"Ritter can let me out here and he can move off."

"To go where? A car cruising back and forth is suspicious. A simpler solution is to deflate your spare tire so Ritter looks like he's changing a flat."

From his top right drawer, Hoffman pulled a plain brown envelope. He pinched the metal clasps, lifted the flap, and handed it to Schneider. "That's a cut-out of this section along with the corresponding tracing."

Schneider pointed to a short column of numbers next to the square marking the pump station.

Hoffman nodded. "Gives you inside diameter, flow, elevation, and pressure —in that order." He directed Schneider's attention to the map on the desk. "It's the final leg upstream from this tank farm. You and Neubauer check the log this time. You'll find it near the bypass in a boxed pedestal."

"Of course, what I don't have is an exact weight of each stick," Schneider said. From his pocket, he pulled a timer. "This has to be set precisely, so we need to know weight within grams."

"It was your idea to bring only timers and enough charges to perform a test."

"For good reason, Herr Hoffman," Schneider said.

"Yes, yes—the intelligence catastrophe in New York. Not only did both your team leaders turn on their own men, their landing site on the beach was discovered along with all their equipment and explosives."

"Correct," Schneider said sharply. "And it was decided in Berlin I would travel with only detonators and a few bricks of explosives." Schneider sounded irritated as he continued. "Indeed, this was based on your guarantees to procure the TNT and magnesium needed to execute the plan fully. Your proven ability to smuggle in agents up and down the coast instilled high confidence in such promises."

"You'll have your explosives, Schneider."

"I still need the weights and they must be precise."

"Work out your weights based on this," Hoffman said as he produced a single stick of explosive. "Two minutes is all it will take to check your gross weight when all the elements are assembled," Hoffman said. "Which I'd think you'd do anyway."

Schneider concurred with a nod and asked, "Is there additional information from Sealy?"

"Nothing further, although I'm certain a new acquaintance may be more revealing. I've met a representative of the OPC—the Office of Petroleum Coordination."

"Do not arouse suspicion."

"I'm part of the Civil Defense force, so a few questions here and there shouldn't seem too out of place," Hoffman said.

"I must admit, Herr Hoffman, your social skills serve the Reich well."

Hoffman grinned. "Social occasions are only warfare concealed—make people feel at ease with good food and wine, and they'll nearly spill their guts." And Hoffman was particularly proud of his wines, which tripped a thought. "Actually, Sturmbannfürer, it's your skills I could use," Hoffman said. "Meet me here first thing in the morning. I have an interesting side project for you."

EIGHTEEN

A Long Day's Night

A Lazy Stroll

The Ford coupe turned down Montrose Boulevard heading south. Frank had the radio on low, and the music was barely audible through the crackling and squealing of the weak signal. The light from the dial and dashboard lights threw a soft glow on Frank's face.

The three girls were squeezed into the back seat and chattering low. Richard wasn't paying much attention—his last martini had left him in somewhat of a fog.

They passed houses lining the two-lane street. The coupe's tires made a crunching sound as is it rolled over the gravel. As nights on the town go, this one was mild in terms of consumption, but not in drama. Richard didn't think he could have scripted a wilder emotional roller coaster. Every twist, turn, dip, and jolt still reverberated.

Richard stared out the window, yet his father was all he saw. He was a pup of a man—no lines, no jowls, nor gray hair. His stride was smooth rather than a strut. It was surprising how his dad's voice was just as he remembered—masculine and southern. Age didn't wear down that part of him.

After his business had gone sour, Jack had taken a sales position here and there. Richard had summer jobs with him while still in high school. The women in the offices had talked about his father's voice. Young or old it never failed, they found it sexy—something that always grossed out Richard at the time. Tonight, seeing him in action, Richard had to admit Kurt was right—Jack was "hep."

"Who's hep?" Reina asked.

Richard didn't realize he'd said it aloud. "Chief Warren—seemed like an interesting guy."

"How long have you known him, Dorothy?" Reina asked.

"Perhaps six years or so, though I can't say I know him well. Our paths just happened to cross whenever I visited the Harris family."

She changed the subject by thanking Carla and Frank for the ride home. Frank said it was on their way, especially since Reina's was a block off Montrose. Hawthorne Street was only a few blocks up on the other side of Elgin.

"Just pull up to the corner," Richard said to Frank. "It's a short block and half for Reina and me, and I need to walk off my last drink."

Frank nodded and eased the car next to the curb.

"Where do you live, Richard?" Dorothy asked curiously.

"With her," Richard said casually, pointing to Reina. Frank bowed his head trying to hide his smile.

Dorothy looked at Reina, trying to stay composed while hiding her Catholic-girl shock. Richard wasn't sure who was more horrified—Dorothy or Reina. Carla was grinning and grimacing at the same time.

Richard thanked Frank for driving and shook his hand. Frank was still trying not to laugh. Everyone said their good-byes and nice-to-meet-yous as Richard got out and helped Reina climb from the backseat. He closed the car door and waved as Frank drove off. Then began a countdown in his head. *Three… two… one …*

"How dare you!" Reina said, backhanding Richard's upper arm. "She'll think we're living in sin!" She defaulted into loud Italian and backhanded him again.

Richard simpered; the more she got angry the more he liked it. He saw a lot of passion building in her eyes, wondering if her fire extended to the other extreme.

Reina backhanded him once more, this time harder and on the chest.

"All right, all right," he said, grabbing her hands and locking them in his. "Don't get your knickers in a knot. Besides, it'll give Carla something to talk about. And you know she'll make sure Dorothy is straightened out, so relax."

The fury in her glare died down, and Richard knew Reina knew he was right. "You're still a horrible, cruel man," she said.

Richard held out an arm and Reina hooked hers around it as they started walking down the block. Their strides were slow and in step with one another. Croaking frogs and chirping crickets were loud in the absence of the big city noises Richard was used to. There were no streetlights, making the lane almost pitch black. Humidity softened the few scattered beads of light from porch lamps down the way. Several houses had small banners with one or more blue stars hanging in their windows, signifying homes of servicemen. One or two had the same banner but with a gold star, indicating those servicemen who died in combat.

"Missus Rainey's house," Reina said, pointing to a house with a blue star banner. "She worries about her son."

"Where is he?"

"Africa, last she heard from him," Reina said.

Richard didn't say anything, but Mrs. Rainey had every reason to worry. Remembering his history, US troops were being sent to Africa in preparation for a long campaign against Axis forces commanded by German Field Marshal Rommel. Casualties were high on both sides.

Faint sounds of a woman's voice came from one of the houses up on the left. It too had a banner. There were no lights on in the house and her voice was getting louder, but not because Richard and Reina were getting closer. Reina whispered, "She's been excited all week because her husband was coming home on leave."

They heard a yelp.

"Very excited," Richard said with a half-grin at Reina, who averted her eyes, embarrassed. "Oh, come on," he said. "Don't tell me you never made a little noise on a sultry summer night or a cool spring morning." Even in the dark, he could tell she was blushing.

Reina tightened her arm around Richard's and rested her other hand on his arm as well. "So why haven't you ever married?"

Another unexpected question Richard thought he should have expected. He didn't have an immediate answer, so he shook his head and shrugged.

"Answer mine and I'll answer yours," Reina said with a coy smile.

"I don't know," Richard began as he looked down the street. "I guess I never met the right girl at the right time." *Until now.*

"Ah, so was there ever a right girl at the wrong time?"

He chuckled. "Maybe once or twice."

"What were they like?"

"Night 'n' day," Richard said. "One a blonde about your height and build, and the other an Irish brunette."

"No redheads in your past?"

"Strangely—no," Richard said.

Reina had a wry smile. "Left a long trail of broken hearts, I bet."

"Not hardly," Richard said.

Instinctively, they turned up the front walk to the porch steps of Reina's house. Between the left corner of the house and the front bedroom window was a trellis tangled with vines, their pink rose-like buds closed up for the night. Hung from the porch ceiling to the right of the front door was a swing. Richard found himself thinking about wasting away a cool evening next to Reina, swaying back and forth. He shook off the imaginary sound of children.

"What are you thinking?" Reina asked softly.

"You did say you'd answer my question about making noise on a sultry evening if I answered yours about marriage." Richard doubted she'd confess anything so personal. Given, however, that they stood at her door at the end of what was, for all intents and purposes, their first date—it seemed like a good tactical maneuver toward a goodnight kiss.

"Yes, I did," Reina said, standing in front of him. Her smile was alarmingly devious. "I just didn't say when."

Richard gave her a mock sneer.

She cooed and rested both her hands on his chest and said, "I enjoyed tonight."

Richard smiled and they locked eyes. There was a moment of silence before Reina spoke softly. "Tomorrow is a long day and I'd better get some sleep." She leaned in and up on her toes to give Richard a quick and innocent kiss. Without hesitation, she walked through the front door and closed it behind her.

The porch light went out and the deadbolt locked. Richard stood there, perplexed. He tapped softly on the door. "Reina?" Another knock. "Hellooo?"

Signs

Reina let him knock a few more times for good measure. She leaned back on the door, quietly laughing with her hand over her mouth. *That'll show him.* When he'd suffered enough, she opened the door to find Richard with his hands in his pockets and his hat pushed back on his head. He had a meek smile and nodded head. Reina kept her hand over her mouth in a half effort to muffle her laughing.

"You got me," he said.

"You deserved it."

"For a minute there I thought I'd have to camp out on the swing."

"I had to teach you a lesson," she said, leading him in through the door.

"You're a vindictive little minx."

"Uh-huh." Reina kept laughing. "Remember that," she said. She caught her breath and wrinkled her nose. "We smell like a couple of ashtrays."

As she had always done with Vincent, Reina peeled off her top and asked Richard to hang it out over the line on the service porch. Without even thinking, she reached back and unhooked her bra as she walked toward her bedroom.

She froze as the straps popped loose. Reina crossed her arms over her chest to hold the cups in place as she turned. Barely stepping within arm's reach of a stunned Richard, she took back her blouse without looking directly at him. Reina turned back around and briskly walked into her room, tossing her top and bra on the cedar chest at the foot of her bed.

She sat at her vanity, looking at a photograph of Vincent. "What should I do?" she asked. Reina stared at the image of his face hoping for some expression, though she didn't expect to see one. Always an even-keeled man—controlled and calm—Vincent was slow to anger and never smiled without reason. His picture captured that.

Unlike most traditional Italian women, she never prayed for signs of divine intervention. Life had taught her to do what she had to do. If it was right, things worked out. But for the first time in her life, she was truly uncertain of herself. For an instant, Richard had totally displaced the man in the picture. Almost without missing a beat, she could have embraced him in a way she hadn't thought possible for a very long time.

"Be careful and mindful of the pitfalls," Father Allnoch had warned. "Don't put yourself into another situation," Reina repeated aloud. She heard the bathroom door close and a squeak followed by the sound of water flowing through the pipes under the house. She wondered if he was taking a cold shower. "It wouldn't hurt you, either," she told herself.

A good night's sleep was the best medicine, she thought. She undressed and slipped into a short, lightweight nightgown. Rather than sneaking from her room to the back porch to air out her clothes, she put her top on a hanger and hooked it on the knob of her armoire, and she spread her skirt over the cedar chest.

Every night for the past year, Reina dabbed a drop of Vincent's aftershave on his pillow and slept with it against her back. She crawled into bed, reached for the small bottle, and twisted off the cap. It was empty. She held it to her nose and found no hint of the scent. She set the bottle back on her night table.

Reina turned off her light and lay on the bed hugging his pillow. She sighed. On the other side of the wall, Richard was in the shower. Like warm water, she let her mind wander over the topography of his body. She could see the shimmer of his wet skin and the gathering droplets fall over his shoulders, down his back, and off the curves below his waist.

She pulled the hem of her gown up around her hips, tucking the pillow between her knees and cuddling it tight. The sound of the running water churned a torrent of images and ideas in her head, as well as the rush of sensations unsatisfied by something so soft as a sealed envelope of goose down feathers.

The pipes fell silent, allowing Reina to hear the beat of her own heart, and Richard's footsteps on the hollow flooring. Every step told her exactly where he was—he roamed throughout the house at a restless pace.

A brief and faint odor of tobacco wafted in through her open bedroom window. She imagined he was out back having a smoke before bed, and grinned thinking he could be naked. Richard is just the kind of man who would do something like that. "No, no, no," she said to herself while trying to stop thinking about him. He was smoking. He's not naked. He's just smoking.

The floorboards creaked outside her door. Reina closed her eyes and held her breath in lingering anticipation. The seconds dragged on like hours until she heard the door to Olivia's room shut. Reina let out her breath, knowing she should have known better. His behavior could certainly be suggestive, even provocative. But it occurred to Reina *she* was the one initiating things. The question in her mind was whether his bark was worse than his bite.

Humid air seeped into the room and added to her perspiration, making her nightgown cling uncomfortably. Reina flung off the gown onto the vanity bench and threw the sheets over the footboard of her bed. She rolled onto her stomach flipping her hair off her neck to help her cool down. A flow of soothing air cooled her exposed body, which helped her relax and doze off.

It wasn't a deep slumber. She drifted in and out of a groggy half-sleep, sometimes stirred by a critter rustling out her window—maybe a coon or opossum. At one point, she opened her eyes when the predawn light peeped into the room, followed by the crow of Mr. Ginn's rooster, but she dozed off again.

Finally, rattling in the kitchen and the strong smell of coffee made Reina's mouth water, and she opened her eyes to the haze of morning sun reflecting off the white walls. After rolling onto her back and rubbing her eyes, she focused on something beside her bed—a folding tray with a cup and saucer, along with a small dish covered with a lid from a saucepan.

She pushed up on her elbows and noticed a small pink bloom on her pillow. Neatly draped over the back of the bench was her nightgown. Reina looked down at herself then at the closed door, grinning. Turnabout was fair play—after all, she'd seen all of Richard in an unconscious state.

Sitting on the edge of the bed, she lifted the lid off the dish. There was a piece of toast with a poached egg nestled in a round cutout at the center. As Reina sipped the piping hot coffee, she glanced from the empty vial on her bedside table to Vincent's picture on the vanity. His expression was almost approving. Reina smiled back at him and said, "How come you never brought me coffee in the morning?"

Answer to an Unanswered Question

His twenty-minute search for a switch to the attic fan was fruitless. His cold shower wasn't particularly effective either. A cool spot on the sheets worked for short catnaps, but a while later it would be hot and sweaty, and Richard would shift to another one. As much as the thick air made sleeping difficult, even full-blown air-conditioning wouldn't have made a difference. Reina was pulsing through his veins, her image there each time he closed his eyes.

As a distraction, he got up and began writing a letter to his brothers. For a brief moment, it worked as he struggled with how to date it. His solution was to double date it—using one atop the other. Nevertheless, Richard's explanation of events, as best as he could describe them, offered no escape. Reina invaded nearly every thought behind almost every word secreted by each stroke of his pen. She was the catalyst for every experience and everyone he had seen—including his father.

He ended his written confession with a borrowed line: "Resistance is futile." Unable to exorcise her from his mind and frustrated with his lack of creative summation, not to mention the fact that delivering it was impossible, he crumpled each page. One by one, he tossed the paper balls into the wastebasket as if he were making free throws.

Going back to bed was pointless, and it was sunrise anyway. Dreading those silly overalls, he quietly dug through Johnny's trunk for something comfortable to wear while he whipped up some breakfast. And while shocking

Reina by cooking naked would be a kick, he figured it would be too much for her to take. So he slipped on the pair of short-legged pajama bottoms he found.

Now familiar with Reina's kitchen, it didn't take Richard long to pull together a few things for breakfast. He worked quietly, like a culinary ninja as he stealthily lifted the skillet from its place and set it on the stove, cracked eggs, and toasted bread with the tongs. As a teenager, Richard developed skills to navigate creaky floorboards. He put those skills to work when he went out to snip a flower, and he repeated it when he carried the breakfast tray to Reina's room. A soft knock got no response. He debated going in and decided to proceed with caution.. It was a surprise when the door didn't squeak. Richard quietly set the folding tray close to her bed, not wanting to wake her, at least until he saw her sleeping.

The sight of Reina lying completely naked made a firm impression. Her hair was fanned out over the pillow, exposing her delicate neck. It was all he could do to resist the temptation to kiss it and to keep going all the way down her smooth and tapered back, over the gentle slope of her hips to her tailbone, along the curves to just above the back of her thigh, and down to the back of her bent knee. He broke a sweat thinking about going back up again and lingering here and there.

A bolster to what little resolve he had was the still resonant memory of their first meeting. Even if she woke to see her effect on him, Richard felt like her reply might have been the same as it had in the alley. Discretion was the better part of valor.

Once back in the kitchen, he tried to hide under a half-apron. Neither the ties pulled extra tight nor his choice to clean the dishes worked. He stopped washing in exasperation. She simply made his blood boil. It was intolerable when she was in the room, and just as bad when she wasn't. "God, I have a crush on you," he said.

"The flower gave you away."

Richard winced as if her voice were a baseball bat hitting his chest. He couldn't face her but sensed she was standing close from the subtle fragrance of the perfume she wore last night. Reina's light touch on his bare skin started with his back, working her way around to his stomach below his naval. She kissed a spot between his shoulder blades and made caressing circles with the tip of her nose.

"Good morning," she said.

Richard still didn't move. He knew she could feel his chest pounding—

and he was flush with embarrassment and newfound modesty.

Reina kissed his shoulder and thanked him for the morning starter.

"Sleep well?" he asked, not looking at her.

She turned him to face her and looked down at his apron. "About as well as you did, I see."

Her hair was down around her shoulders and the ends rested on her breasts. She wore a satin or silk peignoir barely gathered in the front, and it was obvious she wore nothing underneath.

"That looks awfully tight," she said with a grin as she pulled the string, letting the apron drop to the floor. She stopped staring at the flesh pressing through the front of his shorts by glancing into his eyes, then at his shoulders.

A paralyzing pulse of electricity ignited his nerves when she put her fingers on his shoulders. She lightly moved them to the center of his chest and outward again. Flattening her palm over his pounding heart, she looked him in the eye and smiled. Her hand traced the outline of his body down his sides to his hips.

Reina didn't say anything. She didn't have to. The flame in her eyes was identical to what he saw last night on the corner. She pressed against him and he thought her body would tear through her robe as she took a deep breath through her flared nostrils. Her coordinated attack began with surging a kiss and hands sliding under the waistband of his shorts—first just above his tailbone, gliding around to the sides of his hips and pushing the fabric over the obstacle below.

A young serviceman and his wife stepped off their front porch, leading a pet Scottish terrier by a leash. On the way down to the vacant lot at the end of the block, they walked hand in hand toward the widow's house with pink blooms climbing a corner trellis, which was next to the porch with a swing. The couple heard faint sounds of a woman's voice. It was growing louder, but not because they were getting closer. A yelp startled the terrier, and the husband smiled at his wife. Thirty minutes later, on the walk back, they'd have reason to smile again—and giggle.

NINETEEN

Saturday, 1 August 1942

Framing the Puzzle

The elevator doors opened, and Jack hooked left down the narrow hall. He kept pace with the snappy tune he whistled.

"Good morning, Chief," said one of the civilian office staff who opened the door as Jack reached for the knob. She was a girl about his age, and she carried a small shoe box-like parcel filled with envelopes.

"Morning," Jack said with a smile as he stepped aside to let her by.

Barbara wasn't at her desk. She and another female officer were at the coffee counter leaning close to one another and talking low. When they saw Jack, they exchanged sly looks and split up. The other one said "Morning, Jack" with a Cheshire cat grin. Barbara eased down into her desk chair and shrugged with a timid smile.

Everyone snapped to attention when Captain Preskin came in. "Carry on," he said, so the staff went back to their duties. Preskin took the file of morning dispatches from Barbara, as he always did. She leaned over her desk and said something to the captain as she glanced at his office.

Someone greeted Preskin when he opened the door to his private office.

Jack glanced back at Barbara, and back at the now-closed door.

Moments later, a commander walked out of Preskin's office. He carried an attaché cuffed to his wrist. All personnel came to attention as he briskly exited the OPC office.

Jack slowly sat back down as he stared at Preskin's office. Suddenly, the CO burst out into the bullpen carrying a satchel.

"Chief!" Preskin said, walking past Barbara's desk.

"Aye, sir."

Captain Preskin nodded to the door.

Whether or not anyone actually thought it, Jack was beginning to feel like the teacher's pet. Preskin's confidence was appreciated, but Jack didn't want to be labeled as one of those guys who kissed up to the brass.

He followed his CO out the door and down the hall. They stepped into the elevator and it started down. Preskin pulled the brake knob, stopping the car halfway between floors. He folded down a seat elevator attendants once used to run the car. The satchel he handed to Jack had a latch lock, but it was unclasped. "Open it," Preskin said.

The only thing inside was an envelope with a bold red stamp, SECRET — AUTHORIZED EYES ONLY.

Chief petty officers weren't usually on the look-see list for these kinds of things. Jack was surprised the captain prompted him to open it.

"Skip the cover page and have a look at the second sheet."

It was a mimeograph copy of a decoded transmission.

U-166

OBERLEUTNANT HANS-GUNTHER KUHLMANN

PROCEED TO LORIENT - TAKE ON AN OFFICER OF THE SS - THERE ARE TO BE NO QUESTIONS - FURTHER ORDERS DIRECTLY FROM THE SS OFFICER.

The heading was from an obscure department of something called MI-6 and dated from mid-June. Redacted were parts of the heading referring to what Jack thought was a person's name and an odd word—ULTRA.

He looked up at Preskin who told him to keep going.

There were two more sheets with similar parts of the headings blacked out. One was a consolidated report of transmissions, listing only a series of letters and numbers. Handwritten beside each set was a series of characters, containing a letter and numbers. Jack recognized them as position reports with headings and speeds. Longitude and latitude numbers indicated a steady progression south by southwest, whereas the headings indicated a zigzag course. Two prior reports showed straight headings with the last one dated 28, July 1942.

The final sheet had one transmission from Boat 166.

"Pay particular attention to the dates and positions," Preskin said.

The boat had radioed its report on the same day the *Robert E. Lee* was attacked. The coordinates were east of the last position on the previous page, and nearly where the transport was sunk. But the last line of the communication was circled. It stated her "primary orders" were completed.

Preskin held his hand out and Jack returned the papers. "We were right," the captain said. "The last set clearly showed her off Texas waters, and the next day she's east."

"If I remember the charts right, she was within sight of Galveston," Jack said.

Preskin nodded. "Primary orders complete, she radioed." Preskin rubbed his chin.

Jack slid his hands in his pockets and leaned back on the elevator wall. "But why pass up sweet targets like tankers leaving the bay?"

"The thing drove deep into the Gulf without so much as firing on a vessel." He tapped the satchel as he spoke. "Think about it, Jack. Her prior sinking was over 500 miles away—off Cuba. Suddenly, she goes silent for two weeks after sinking three vessels within a week. "

"And, boom, she hits the transport out of the blue," Jack said. "Everybody and their dog knows she's here and all hell breaks loose." Neither man looked at one another, but they were hit with the same thought.

"The SS officer," both men said simultaneously.

"He didn't want anyone to know he was there," Jack said.

"I'd bet my bottom dollar he wasn't with U-166 on the 30th either. I'll have Ensign Reese contact our batteries on the island," Preskin said and pushed the knob to release the elevator brake.

"I'll start checking with the Coast Guard, although I doubt much will come of it. Trawlers come and go at will," Jack said. With all the fishing villages and marinas, Jack worried it was a monumental task finding how the SS officer may have come ashore. "There was almost a full moon, too," Jack said. "I'm no fisherman, but I gotta believe there were a lot of boats out looking for a good haul that night."

"Let's see if one was fishing for something different," Preskin said.

The elevator reached the lobby. Waiting as the doors slid open was the commander with the attaché. Preskin casually handed him the satchel, which Jack suddenly noticed the CO had relatched. They nodded to each other as Preskin pushed the button to return the car to their floor.

"I told you something was in the air. Remember?" Preskin folded his arms and stepped closer to Jack. "The brass in Washington have been paying very close attention to this—and you," Preskin said with a smile.

"Thank you, sir, but those transmissions, how—"

"You've passed muster, Jack, but even I'm not privy to their source." Preskin folded the seat back and continued. "Now, let's refocus. How do you think our kraut got ashore?"

"A rubber raft," Jack said.

"An awful risk, given their last foul-up is still in the news," Preskin began as he folded his arms. "Besides, an SS officer is one of Hitler's elite and I doubt he'd try to paddle to Galveston beach. The riptides close-in might carry him to exactly where he didn't want to be—near a lot of people."

"They'd also probably know about the emplacements," Jack said.

Jack and his CO marched into the OPC. Preskin called Barbara into his office, and Jack went immediately to his desk. From his center pedestal drawer, the young chief pulled a folder marked, DIRECTORY: HOU-GAL. He opened it and followed his index finger down the list to find the numbers he needed.

Barbara scurried from Preskin's office and arrived at her desk in time to greet a fine-suited gentleman walking through the door. "Can I help you, sir?" she asked.

Jack didn't recognize the man, but he recognized the name he gave the ensign. He was the president of Continental Pipeline. Barbara buzzed the captain and she promptly showed him into the private office. A few minutes later, Barbara peeked out and called Jack in to join them.

The gentleman repeated to Jack what he had told Captain Preskin: an internal dig didn't show any missing surveys for the pipeline that suffered the explosion. To be on the safe side, they checked the files on all the lines. He produced two thick expandable files. One was labeled Cloverleaf - b, and the other Wallisville - 8.

"I know fpr a fact these were surveyed last year, but we're missing the latest plats," the gentleman said, setting the files on Preskin's desk. "The county asked Continental for new ones because of building permit requests that had been filed. One was to expand a neighboring residential area bordering the Cloverleaf line. And the other was for the construction of a private storage terminal along the ship channel near where the Wallisville line crossed a bayou feeding into the ship channel." He pulled the two surveys from each file. The dates were from 1932 and 1937. "We're missing the 1941 surveys for both."

"Who usually handles these records?" Preskin asked.

"Landowners have a set included with their copy of the leases. And landmen or engineers might make their own," the gentleman said. He leaned back in the chair and gestured at the files on Preskin's desk. "These particular files are under the control of a four-eyed, crackerjack file clerk here in the Houston office."

"So how does he explain the missing plats?" Jack asked.

"He can't. But I've known him for fifteen years and I'd vouch for him. He's not the kind of man who would risk his livelihood."

"Somebody was willing to risk it," Preskin said.

"The file cabinets are locked up at the end of every day," the gentleman began, "but honestly, it ain't too tough to jimmy one with a pocketknife. I've done it myself on my own desk lock."

"Are there any differences between these older surveys and the new ones?" Preskin asked.

"Not much. There's hardly been any modifications to the lines relevant to the new surveys. Equipment had been replaced on the old Wallisville line in 1932, but the Cloverleaf was laid down in 1935."

"Can we hold on to these surveys for a day or two?" Preskin asked.

"And you might have a look at those cabinet locks," Jack said.

"I'd like the files back no later than Tuesday morning. Even I have to answer to the clerk," he said with a nervous smile. "And he's in a foul mood these days."

Barbara showed the man out of the private office and walked him to the outer office door.

Captain Preskin snorted. "You'd think these guys'd spread the cheer and pick a line from a different pipeliner."

"I guess if you've only got one cow, you milk her for all she's worth," Jack said, shaking his head. "Still, it does seem pretty stupid."

"Which one's our cherry?"

Jack wasn't sure. Either or both was about all he could say. Both lines crossed bayous feeding into the channel, and both emptied into tank farms. And almost any one of the pump stations would offer a secluded enough spot to make trouble.

"Well, yes," Jack paused. "But they're not looking for just any spot." He slid the surveys side by side and pointed to the icons indicating stations upstream of the bayou channel. "Let's say they're trying to do what we thought they were doing in Sealy," Jack said. He tapped his right index finger on the map to the right. "This one is far enough up from the water to give 'em time to set it and get out. This one over here is too close," he said looking to the map on the left.

"Why not set it at the previous station?" Preskin asked.

"Remember, the charge would get hung up in the pump works." Jack tapped his finger over the pump station again. "Well, unless the downstream bypass is opened up. But I'd guess that's too much sugar for a dime. You'd have to be sure the bypass is open, run back up and insert your explosive."

Chewing his lip, Jack studied the map on the left. Then he saw it. "Bingo!" Jack stood up straight smiling at the map a few moments before realizing Captain Preskin was waiting. "Oh. My brother-in-law once talked about filling an order for this particular section of the pipeline. It was refitted with a larger diameter pipe to accommodate a tie-in from another line. The pump station closest to the water was new and the one downstream was taken offline. This station near the water pushes everything straight into the tank farm," Jack grinned. "It'd be a cherry spot to try and hit this tank farm. Add the magnesium and—pow!"

"You think they're after something that big?"

"I guess they could be looking at this from the mosquito's point of view," Jack said. "But wouldn't you want more bang for your buck?"

"Combine magnesium with burning oil and they'd almost see the fires all the way from Berlin."

Preskin wasn't usually so sarcastic, but Jack understood. Everything, whether in the water or not, would burn and burn hot—igniting more fires and setting off secondary explosions. The aftermath could be on the same level as Pearl.

Preskin pointed to nearby roads, indicating where roadblocks should be set up. He waved his hand over the whole map while saying, "Harbor Patrol and Coast Guard should step up patrols to cover the crossings. Whether this stops them or scares them off is one thing," Preskin said.

"But what we really want to do is catch them with their hands in the cookie jar," Jack said, completing his CO's sentiment.

The captain grinned. "It'd still help if you could get on the horn to the

Coast Guard, and I'll follow up with the observers on Galveston. Finding out who we're dealing with is a long shot, but something might turn up to tip the scales our way."

Jack nodded.

"Hope you didn't have plans for the afternoon, Jack."

"Late Mass, sir, but I can go in the morning."

"Mass?"

"The five-thirty service counts for Sunday. That way it leaves all day Sunday open."

Preskin smiled. "Carry on, Chief."

Jack nodded and went back to his desk.

Meeting Merlin

Richard's arms were already tired, which made fighting the manual steering on Reina's car much more difficult. He insisted on dropping her at the Pasta Factory and taking the car to Kurt's. He wanted no chance of her trying to meet Parisi on her own.

The traffic and cars parked along the streets were no different from a regular workday. Richard remembered his dad saying most people used to work at least half a day on Saturdays and that Sundays were the only true days off. So, he felt lucky when he was able to park in the same spot where Frank had the night before. The short walk meant he could get into the cool wine room before breaking into a full-blown sopping sweat. Even the slightest perspiration stung the reopened scrapes on his back, along with a few new ones.

The mild irritation only served to put a smile on his face and a spring in his step as he whistled a rendition of 'Zip-a-Dee-Doo-Dah.' Contrary to his previous assumptions of pre-sixties intimacy as provincial and sedate—if not puritanical—Reina was anything but. In fact, she was aggressive and uninhibited, as well as extremely vocal. She gave a new definition to the word passionate—to the point where his female contemporaries could learn a thing or two. Or three.

The front doors were locked. Richard snapped his fingers and realized the back would be open. People were staring, but he paid them no mind as he did a soft-shoe dance up the walk and around the corner into the alley, having changed to the refrain from "Singing in the Rain." He decided he had a whole new respect for Debbie Reynolds.

Richard grinned at the thought of the studio editing out nonexistent footage of her rocking Gene Kelly's world on the kitchen floor, and again on the table—which reminded him he needed to pick up new hardware to fix the broken table leg.

He turned the corner to the back door where a man in all white dumped a bucket of dirty water into the weeds along the bayou bank. Richard tried to recover his cool. Too late.

"Mus' be quites a gurl," said the man.

Richard was slightly shocked. "How—"

"Womanz only thang I knowd t' makes a man act a fool."

Richard conceded the point with a grin. The man said if Richard was looking for Mr. Hoffman, he was inside. Richard stepped over an empty crate that smelled like spoiled fish. He stopped, turned, asked the man his name.

"Curtis," he said. "Dishwasha and heppin' hand round hya."

"Thanks, Curtis," Richard said as he went inside. He quickly found a stair that curved behind the freezer and down to the cellar. At the bottom of the stairs, he came to a door. It was old and heavy, made of oak with sturdy iron hinges and a black latch and deadbolt. A muffled voice said "yeah" when Richard knocked—though he wasn't sure if it was Kurt. He pushed hard on the thumb latch, and it made a loud metal clank and pop. It took more than a simple tug to force open the door, which creaked and groaned in protest. A wisp of refrigerated air greeted him.

Inside the square, dimly lit room, the walls were lined from floor to ceiling with square cubbies. Some cubes were packed tightly with bottles, lying on their sides, while others were either half or empty altogether. In the center stood two long walnut wood racks of cubbies, which created three aisles within the room. Stacks of cases took nearly every inch of floor space in between. The tops of the racks had shelves on both sides that came to a peak in the middle. A few magnums and imperials were held in place by rails at the bottom.

Kurt appeared from behind one of the racks. "Be sure to close it tight behind you," Kurt said, without looking at Richard.

"Good morning." He pulled the door and it thumped as it closed. "You look lost."

"A bit confused, now and then, but never lost." Kurt smiled and continued brooding over the wines. "I let this go far too long."

Richard drooled over the trove of what would become incredible grand vintages in his day. *Too bad some of these are still too young.*

"Screw it," Kurt said as he stepped over and squeezed between cases on his way to Richard. They shook hands. "I'll be glad when I can get in here without acrobatics."

"Which is why I'm here," Richard said.

Kurt asked what he needed. Richard said all he could use was a pen or pencil, some small tags he could tie on the bottlenecks, and maybe a little muscle to shift the cases around as needed.

"But the first thing I need to do is see what you have and figure out the space," Richard said.

"I'll bring back tags after breakfast with Dorothy," Kurt said.

"Thanks."

"I'll also send someone down in about twenty minutes to help with the cases."

"That should be about right," Richard said.

"See you in a bit," Kurt said.

The sound of the wine room door closing reminded Richard of the scene with Steve McQueen in *The Great Escape* when the guards locked him in solitary confinement. His character, Hilts, got himself sent to the "cooler" by bantering with the prison camp commandant. The cellar, certainly more pleasant than a cell, felt almost as small and dark from the single bulb hanging only from a wire in the ceiling.

To keep claustrophobia at bay, Richard set to work. The place wasn't in as bad a shape as he had anticipated. The five columns of cubbies to the right of the door were partially stocked with celebrated vintages from various regions. Richard was more familiar with the great vintages from 1929 on. Some of these dated back to the late nineteenth century and the turn of the twentieth century. A few cases were complete years that matched some in the columns. Others were mixed. Totaled together, he figured about a half-dozen cases worth had to be mixed into the first section.

As if he were handling nitroglycerin, Richard moved bottles from one cubby to another—always keeping them horizontal. He'd work the new bottles into the cubbies from top to bottom in the order he described to Kurt the night before. Older vintages of a particular label were on the top and descended to younger ones, so he actually had to start each cubby with a row of younger vintages and load each row in reverse order to end with the older bottles on the top rows.

He left empty cubbies between the end of one label collection and the start of another to allow for expansion from new shipments.

The first section spilled over into a column of cubbies on the perpendicular wall. Again, Richard left an empty space. He began organizing the remaining Bordeaux by region and grouped them by label and by vintage year within each group.

The latch popped and the door creaked. *Good*, Richard thought. A cup of coffee would warm him up a little, and extra hands would help move several more cases around.

"You're just in time," Richard said before looking up. When he did, the man wasn't who Richard expected. And the gentleman's expression made it clear he wasn't there for Richard's benefit. "I'm guessing you didn't bring coffee, either."

"I think not," the man said. He was dressed in a nicely tailored suit, crisply pressed. The knot of his tie was a perfect double-Windsor. "I was looking for Mister Hoffman."

"Kurt darted off to breakfast with his bride-to-be. But I know he'll definitely be back," Richard said as he kept moving bottles around. "Can I give him a message or is there something I can help you with?"

"You refer to your employer by his first name," the man asked. He spoke sharply and with arrogance, and his speech lacked a Texas twang.

Richard chuckled. The man didn't. "I'm just helping out a friend," Richard said, barely looking up at the man. "Kurt and I share a common interest in and a love of wines." He stopped working a moment and surveyed the room with his hands on his hips as he spoke. "One thing led to another, and we agreed I could help put things back in order. But think of me as a freelance," Richard said.

"Are wines and spirits your business?"

It wasn't an unexpected question this time, yet the man's tone was disconcerting, almost interrogative. "I'm sorry, what was your name again?"

"Schneider." His expression was deadpan, and he did not offer a hand. He stood rigid and straight as an arrow, as if he were almost ready to salute. "You are?"

"Warren," he said, half-mocking Schneider and half-playing at being Sean Connery. "Richard Warren." Richard stepped over a case toward a center rack and moved more bottles. "How do you know Kurt?"

"We are cousins."

"Hmm." Kurt had never mentioned family of any sort. Not that cousins necessarily resemble one another, but there was nothing Richard could detect as remotely similar to Kurt.

"You didn't answer my initial question," Schneider said.

His tone further annoyed Richard. "Is it required?" He stopped moving bottles to give Schneider scant attention.

"I simply mean it is unusual to see an able-bodied man out of uniform."

"The same could be said of you, or even Kurt." Richard glanced at one of the cubbies, reached into a case, and resumed stocking bottles. "Although I believe Kurt's deferred or possibly exempt because he's a sole proprietor and people do depend on him for a living."

"I serve my country in my own way."

Richard began studying Schneider's reactions. The man's return volley was equally cryptic to his own. "I guess Uncle Sam'll have to win the war without us," Richard said, going back to the bottles. "Not that we're needed anyway."

"You sound as if it is a foregone conclusion."

"It is!" Richard thought the man stood like a piece of petrified wood. His feet were practically bolted to the floor. Only his eyes told Richard he got a rise out of him. "By the way, you're letting all the cool air out. Mind shutting the door?"

Schneider stepped in enough to close the door. "The war is just beginning for America, whereas the German forces are battle-hardened."

"Against whom?" Richard snickered. "Most of Europe bent over!" While Germany secretly built up for the war, most other nations were all but totally disarmed. "Most of the armies Hitler met were very small, or practically nil, and equipped with out-of-date junk from World War I." Richard continued with moving bottles pretending to be dismissive. "Not much of a match if you ask me—a little like calling a buzzard a bird of prey."

Even in the dim light, Richard could see Schneider's jaw muscles clench, though he pretended not to notice and kept on with his work. Richard wondered if Schneider was pro-German.

"I think the survivors of Dunkirk might disagree with you," Schneider said.

"Probably so, but they'll also admit Dunkirk was a result of doing too little too late."

"So, it is your opinion the cavalry will gallop in at the last moment to save the day as in a western film?"

"Something like that," Richard said. He thought Schneider's attitude was almost defeatist, as if he didn't think the U.S. could pull it off. Possibly convinced it was futile to try.

"I am a practical man. And whatever your assessment of German military skills, it has, in fact, conquered the European continent and is making it heavily fortified. Further, the Japanese have forced a split in attention between the Atlantic and the Pacific..."

"Trying to fight a two-front war, much less win one, seems impractical."

"Precisely," Schneider said.

"Then how do you account for Adolf's march into Russia?" Richard asked. "Aside from the fact it was a case of two demented and disease-ridden, goose-stepping bastards stabbing one another in the back."

Schneider held his composure, except for a vein rising on his forehead and jaw-busting pressure on his jowls. At first, Richard considered Schneider as maybe a pacifist or perhaps an isolationist, at worst a German sympathizer, but this was something else entirely. And if he was right, this was a very small room with only one exit—a tactically bad place to be trapped.

"It is defending against the Communist threat that enabled the chancellor to effectively save Germany," Schneider said.

Save Germany. "Huh. I thought the extermination of the Jews is how he'd save Germany," Richard said. "I wonder if Adolf led his father into the gas chamber."

Richard didn't need to see the man's face turning purple—he felt tremors of tension emanating within the room. Practically all Schneider needed to complete his character was to don a black cape and helmet. Richard half-expected to hear heavy, mechanical-breathing sounds.

The total of Richard's German vocabulary was little more than out-of-context words and phrases picked up from watching war movies. However, on a senior trip to Austria, a word he and Max repeatedly saw on the Autobahn had become a favorite expression. Richard segued into it by suggesting the conversation was leading him and Schneider down a road they probably didn't want to go. With a sarcastic grin, he said, "So why don't we take an *ausfahrt* and agree to disagree?"

Schneider raised an eyebrow.

Richard locked eyes with his opponent.

"You speak German?" Schneider asked.

"No," Richard said. "I've always found German to be—an enigma."

That intensified the disturbance in the 'Force.' Schneider slowly raised his hand and reached into his coat.

Richard had been leaning with an arm on the top of one of the racks, which hid the bottom two-thirds of his body. He gripped a bottleneck protruding from a cubby and slowly withdrew the bottle, never taking an eye off Schneider.

Both men jerked their heads toward the door at the sound of the metal latch and groaning hinges. Kurt walked in. "You down here, cousin?" Kurt asked.

Richard and Schneider casually looked back at each other. Schneider pulled a cigarette case from his coat pocket and pushed the release to pop it open. Richard made sure it was a lighter Schneider would retrieve next after replacing the case in his coat. He also released his grip on the bottle and, as secretively as possible, his breath.

"I interrupt something?" asked Kurt.

Richard shook his head and said, "Just a friendly chat."

"Son of a gun! You weren't in here long and look how much you've done."

"Things weren't as bad as they could have been. Fortunately, your sommelier left me a solid foundation to work with." Richard went back to work.

"Still, this is miles above where it was," Kurt said.

Richard stopped a moment and said, "I still need help with some cases and could use that coffee. And don't forget, I bug out about one o'clock or so."

"Bug out?"

"Leave," Richard said.

Kurt nodded and tossed Richard a packet of tags. He left the wine room with Schneider in tow. As the door closed, Schneider glanced at Richard one last time. Richard made the victory sign and winked.

Once the door shut all the way, he leaned with both arms on the rack and let out another deep breath. "One of these days, Rick, your mouth's gonna write a check your body can't cash."

Girl Talk

The office windows were wide open. Reina and Carla sat side by side with their backs to the front of Reina's desk. Their feet were propped up on a short stack of file boxes, on top of which was a black fan borrowed from the top of a filing cabinet. Each had her skirt pulled up over parted knees so the oscillating air blew underneath.

Carla was the first to start cackling, and it was infectious.

"Shush!" Reina tried to quiet herself down as much as she did Carla. With hands over their mouths, Reina and Carla leaned against one another.

Carla finally caught her breath and holding her stomach said, "Right there in the kitchen?"

Reina scolded Carla to keep it down. The transom over her office door was closed, but they still might hear in the outer office. "Now you know—so hush!"

"Well, I knew it was just a matter of time, but wow!" Carla reached back, grabbing the two sweaty six-ounce Coke bottles from the desk and handed one to Reina.

"Just don't say anything to Frank."

"Oh the heck I won't," Carla said. "He's never brought me coffee in bed or left a flower on my pillow—well, without waking me up I mean." Carla winked as she took a sip of her Coke. Nudging Reina with her elbow and a twisted smile, she asked, "So?"

"So, what?"

"Don't play innocent with me," Carla said with a sarcastic look. "You're about as innocent as Dina Montalbano at our high school spring dance."

Reina gasped. "That is not fair to compare me with the kind of girl who'd swim out to meet troop ships." She lowered her voice and said, "Besides, my dear, I know for a fact you did see more of Frank before your wedding night than you admitted!"

Carla grinned and raised her eyebrows. "Hey! It was only after we were engaged," Carla said, blushing. "And it wasn't until we were married he got the whole shebang!"

Reina chuckled before taking a sip of her drink and smiling. "Vince and I slipped a week before our wedding."

Carla screamed and Reina whispered, "Shut up!"

"You never told me—," Carla said.

"Of course not, otherwise I'd have had nothing to hold over your head for the last few years."

Carla smiled and said, "Richard's right—you are a vindictive girl."

Reina smiled back as she took another sip. "Uh-huh." She swallowed quickly and said, "I thank God I didn't get pregnant with Olivia until almost a year later."

After they giggled, Carla said, "So, speaking of Richard…" She nudged Reina again with her elbow and a twisted smile.

"What?"

"Sooo?" Carla asked.

"So what?"

Carla replied expressionlessly.

Reina scoffed and said, "What more do you want me to say—I left him a curled up ball of drained whimpering naked flesh on the kitchen floor?"

"For starters, yeah."

Reina shook her head. Carla had been like this since in high school when they double-dated the Scalise brothers, who had more hands than a clock shop. Reina missed talking with Carla like this. Before they both married, neither had ever gotten much past a little rumble-seat necking. Once Reina married, the conversations went from mostly speculative to educative for Carla. When Carla and Frank tied the knot, they shared considerable detail—though Carla was the one who usually tended to be the more graphic of the two, which Reina thought was cute since her friend was a librarian.

"I think I did hurt him though." Reina got an impish smile, "when the table broke."

Carla was surprised. "Table?"

Reina nodded. "The second time."

Carla didn't scream but gave Reina a wide-eyed open-mouth smile. They shared another suppressed giggle. "It's good to see you being your old self again," Carla said. "I've missed you."

Reina smiled, looking at her Coke bottle and rubbing the condensation with her thumb. "It feels good to feel these things again."

"I bet!"

Reina jokingly scoffed and shook her head before taking the last bite of her egg salad sandwich.

There was a relaxed silence as each finished off her warm Coke. Carla nibbled the last of her sliced carrot as Reina broke a cookie, offering to share half.

Over the split cookie, Carla asked what Reina's plans were for the rest of the weekend. Nothing Reina wanted to see was playing at the theater, although she said she wouldn't mind catching up on the newsreels. "It's more likely tonight will be a quiet night at home. Besides, I have to get up for Mass tomorrow." Reina put her head in her hands and asked, "How am I ever going to face Father Allnoch?"

"Do what Dina used to do, go to a parish where nobody knows you," Carla said.

"He wants to meet Richard," Reina said with a wince.

"Frank and I'll go with y'all," Carla suggested. "Safety in numbers, you know."

Before long, they made plans to spend the day together and have Sunday dinner. Frank and Richard got along quite well. Since both men were handy in the kitchen, it'd be an easy meal to prepare. The scheme included early morning Mass, and instead of lunch afterward, they'd all graze while cooking.

"I think I've saved enough ration coupons for a nice cut of meat from the butcher—if he has much meat," Reina said as she got up and leaned over her desk to reach into her center drawer. She grabbed her ration book and a stack of coupons bundled by a rubber band. "Santa Cleopatra!"

"What?" Carla asked.

"I don't think I have time to go by the butcher shop before seeing Parisi."

"I'll take care of it."

Reina offered the ration book to Carla, but she refused them until Reina insisted. "Besides, you're gonna make your famous cucuzzas and eggplant."

"Only if you're serving sausage bread," Carla said.

Reina nodded and said, "My last loaf."

The fan was placed back on the filing cabinet and the boxes scooted against the wall. Reina rolled her chair back behind the desk while Carla grabbed the pull to reach up and open the transom. Reina flattened and folded the empty brown paper bag for Carla.

"I better head down before I miss the trolley," Carla said, looking at her watch. "We're highlighting American authors, and I have a lot more books to pull."

"Wait." Reina stopped and thought of something Richard had said last night. "He mentioned a story by Mark Twain."

"Really, which one?" Carla said.

"I don't think he said the title, but..." Reina had to think a minute. She had dismissed what he was saying, or trying to say. "How'd he put it?" she asked aloud, snapping her fingers. "Something about a man butting heads with Merlin."

"*The Connecticut Yankee in King Arthur's Court,*" Carla said. "You want the long synopsis or the short summary?"

"Short please."

"Hank Morgan is an engineer from Connecticut—hence the Yankee part. Anyway, he gets knocked out in a fight and wakes up in six-century England during the reign of King Arthur. It takes a while but Hank realizes he is actually in the past, and he tries using his engineering skills to help people but also make them believe he is a powerful magician."

"You mean he time traveled to the past?"

"Yes"

"How does it end?" Reina asked.

"Not well."

The Shadow

Hoffman didn't like what he was hearing. He didn't like it at all. But it wasn't nearly enough to support Schneider's conclusions. "What would you have him say? A presumption of victory is to be expected and nothing less than patriotic."

"Of course, but read your newspapers," Schneider said. "The sting of last December still lingers. Amidst the rage and swell of nationalism, there is doubt and concern. In contrast, he seems to have accepted the outcome as moot."

"So he's arrogant," Hoffman said, leaning back in his desk chair and putting a leg on the window seat. "Not to mention you found him ill-mannered and insulting, which groups him with about fifty percent of the American population."

"Warren is aware of things about the Reich that make it highly unlikely his presence is a casual happenstance."

"Can you be more specific?"

"He made an innuendo about a device—one I cannot discuss," Schneider said.

"And?"

"This was not a haphazard reference. His inflection was specific and meant as an underscore."

"Either the secret about your device has been compromised," Hoffman said, putting his foot back on the floor and turning in his chair to face Schneider, "or he's an officer of the Reich."

Schneider shook his head, "I find that rather unbelievable. Warren admitted he did not actually speak German—evidenced by his pronunciation of a term he used."

"Then what about your secret device—how does he know about it?

"Unknown."

"Nothing adds up," Hoffman said.

"He must be dealt with," Schneider said.

"You mean kill 'im?" Hoffman shook his head. "Not that I have issue with it, but until we understand who we're dealing with, his sudden disappearance could have more grave consequences. What is he, if not Gestapo or SS?"

"Federal agent or military intelligence," Schneider suggested.

"Then why tip his hand?"

Schneider spoke flawless English, but his scowl showed he had difficulty with such a colloquialism. Hoffman clarified his point by saying he didn't think an agent would reveal himself in that way.

"He did say he was a freelance," Schneider said.

Hoffman grinned. "And the best lies are grounded in truth." Hoffman thought a moment and said, "Warren could be a check-valve sent to ensure follow-through by your team."

The sturmbannfürer took offense to the notion of questioning an SS officer's loyalty. "It is precisely *because* of my loyalty that I was selected—my total allegiance to the Führer and the Reich. One of my men is also SS, and the other is a Wehrmacht officer whose devotion is beyond question."

"Which leaves me," Hoffman said.

Schneider nodded.

"Have I given you reason to doubt my commitment, in any way?"

"I question your motives," Schneider said. He reached into his coat pocket and pulled out a cigarette case. He thought a moment as he tapped the butt of a cigarette on the metal cover. "Your actions, however, undeniably serve the Reich."

"If Warren did know what you suspect he does, you and I should be sitting in individual interrogation rooms—assuming this, this 'Shadow' is a counter agent."

Schneider frowned.

Hoffman chuckled. "I guess Reichs-Rundfunk doesn't include nightly radio broadcasts of pulp-magazine characters."

"Nein."

"*The Shadow* is the alter ego of a fictional man by the name of Lamont Cranston. His mystic abilities enable him to see into the hearts of men," Hoffman said, mocking voice inflections performed at the outset of each radio broadcast. "Cranston harnesses his own darkness to battle the evil around him."

He drew a deep breath and let it out. There just wasn't enough information to go on. Rather than turning in circles with speculation, Hoffman settled on a course of action. "The only way to know what he's angling for is to take the bait and run with it."

"And what of the hook?"

"The hard part about stealing bait is knowing when to spit out the hook *before* he sets it."

It was agreed Schneider would keep his distance—particularly for the next few days. Hoffman also suggested that wines were the way to keep Warren close. "As a matter of fact," he said, checking the time, "I should see what magic he's performed on my cellar."

TWENTY

Dance with the Devil

Richard muscled the car into a right turn at the corner of Main and Lamar Streets. There was a two-car length spot right at the side entrance of the Lamar Hotel. He pulled in and killed the engine.

Looking up at the elegant sixteen-story hotel, Richard wondered why developer Gerald Hines ever razed it. There were stories about the building dubbed the "unofficial capital of Texas." As his dad put it, the city's movers and shakers supposedly met there to cuss and discuss the business of running Houston. He also said two of the city's finest theaters were in the building. Dad and his friends were sad when the building came down.

"You don't have to come in," Reina said.

"I'd feel a whole lot better about this if I did."

Reina was expressionless and her voice was curt. "Then keep your mouth shut and let me handle this." She opened the car door and got out.

In a hurry to keep up with her, Richard smashed his hat on the doorframe. He took it off and threw it in the backseat. Reina was already opening the door to the lobby as Richard hustled around the car to catch up. "Wait up."

What they were about to do was dicey. Richard hoped it was why Reina had hardly said a word since he picked her up and why her demeanor was less than warm and fuzzy. Otherwise, she might be feeling guilty in addition to being nervous.

"I want to get this over with," she said, walking briskly across the lobby to the bank of elevators. The empty car was small and musty, and it lurched when Reina pressed the button for the sixteenth floor. She stared straight at the doors.

The elevator car jolted to a stop and the door slid open. Reina walked out first, slowly. Richard followed close behind. As they passed two men halfway down the hall, Richard glanced over his shoulder at them. They turned and kept pace with him and Reina, corralling them toward a third henchman guarding a door. "My Spidy-sense is tingling," Richard said under his breath.

"What?" Reina asked, sounding irritated.

Richard hadn't meant to say it out loud, nor did he have time to answer.

The guard knocked softly and the suite door opened. Reina stepped in and the two men took Richard by the arms, lifting him from his feet and slamming him face-first against the foyer wall. One pushed hard on the side of his head while someone he couldn't see performed an intimate search for weapons.

"He's clean," someone said.

Richard was spun around and again smashed against the wall, his feet dangling six inches from the floor. Maceo stood a foot or so away with a grin Richard found menacing.

"Remember me?" asked Maceo with a sinister tone and showing an unsettling number of teeth.

"Maybe if you turn around."

Maceo clutched Richard's forehead and cracked his head into the wall. *That hurt, again.*

"Please! Don Parisi!" Reina said, looking at the godfather who was standing by a table.

"This is between me and you, Reina," Parisi said, walking toward her. He scowled at Richard. "And I warned you once already, boy."

Maceo put his body into a backhand elbow punch to Richard's stomach. The henchmen held him so tightly he couldn't double over to absorb any of the impact. Richard felt his stomach and intestines collapse. Maceo struck another blow in the same place before Richard could fully catch his breath.

"Richard!" Reina tried to move toward him, but Parisi grabbed her arm.

With what he thought was his last breath, Richard curled up his legs into a ball and flung them into Maceo—one foot collided with his jaw and the other with his chest. It catapulted Maceo against the opposite wall and left him stunned.

The two henchmen threw Richard to the floor. He felt one knee on his back while the other knelt on his head. But Richard could see Maceo. "Raping defenseless women's a helluva lot easier, huh, dickhead?" More weight was put on the knee crushing his skull.

Maceo pulled a knife and started to his feet until Parisi snapped his fingers.

Parisi said nothing while never taking his eyes off Reina.

"Tell him, goddammit," Richard grunted. If he lived through this, Richard fully expected Reina to kill him. But if Parisi really did have any sort of consideration for her, telling him about Maceo might give her an edge.

Parisi said something to Reina in Italian, as was her response. However she explained it, it was enough for Parisi to signal the henchmen to yank Richard to his feet. Struggling against the aches and pains, Richard tried to translate something from the exchange. Reina was rattling on and using her hands to illustrate her account. Parisi clenched his jaw and flared his nostrils looking at Maceo, also on his feet and looking very worried.

This godfather's demeanor was more like John Wayne than Marlin Brando. With a casual wave, the henchmen released Richard.

Parisi muttered something to Maceo. He repeated it more forcefully the second time and Maceo answered with a submissive nod. A headache kept Richard from shuddering when Parisi's brief glare fell on him.

The godfather stepped around Reina and stood in front of Maceo. Reina turned and hardly glanced at Richard. Her lips were pinched shut and Richard could tell she was chewing the inside of her bottom lip.

Parisi spoke to Maceo in English. "We've talked about this one too many times," he said. Maceo tried to say something, but Parisi held up his hand and silenced him. Parisi pointed to a chair, in which Maceo promptly sat. A henchman loomed next to Maceo.

You're dead, Richard thought. He wanted to smile, but because there was a man left standing beside him, a blank expression was best. Besides, Richard thought, the conversation between Parisi and Reina was more interesting than taunting Maceo. She was comparing herself to him.

"All of us—you and me—have clawed and scratched for everything we've built, not just for ourselves but for family, and me for my daughter—and maybe her child." Reina wasn't pleading with Parisi, she was trying to reason with him. "In a way, we're working for the same things."

Reina paused for a moment. "I remember how lonely and scared I was when I first came to America. I was very young and didn't know the language, but it didn't take long to understand Sicilians weren't always welcome." She raised her head and looked straight at Parisi and said, "Dirty immigrant and garlic-eater were the first words I learned."

Richard listened and thought what a phenomenal woman. Rather than be bitter from her struggle, it drove her to help others learn the language and compelled her to find legitimate jobs for them, sometimes at a personal cost. As he wondered whether the American dream was that strong or if it was something more, Reina answered as if on cue.

"Someone showed me what it was to be an American," she began. "A woman by the name of Connelly took me under her wing when Mama and I settled in town. Missus Connelly was the granddaughter of Irish immigrants and used to tell me stories passed down to her." Reina smiled and said, "Helping each other—that is where the dream lives."

Parisi seemed to be affected. It was then Reina slipped back into Italian and spoke more softly. The henchman beside Richard cocked his ear, but he guessed he couldn't hear either.

Snorting and shaking his head, Parisi leaned up and whispered to Reina. It sounded like he said something about good timing, but Richard wasn't sure. Parisi took her hand as he smiled and said, "Very well, Reina, you've convinced me—the Factory, you, and your family are off-limits." There was more whispering between them. Finally, right out of the Brando flick, Reina curtsied and kissed Parisi's ring.

The henchman guarding Richard was waved off. Reina walked toward the door and nodded for Richard to follow. He passed Maceo, stopped, and turned. Parisi, too, was staring at Maceo. In the split second it took Richard to draw a deep breath, he realized Maceo's death would eventually gnaw at Reina. Picking Maceo's brain might also shed light on a few things about Kurt.

The problem, however, was the inherent risk in asking Parisi for an opportunity to grill Maceo. Richard winced, both from the aches he felt and from not just a little fear. He had only seen the movie once, and he hoped to God it was semi-accurate. The only certain protocol was that with this kind of man, being respectful was absolute.

"He's not your concern, son," Parisi said. He broke his stare at Maceo to glare at Richard. "Don't push your luck."

"Richard," Reina said with a cautioning tone.

He glanced over his shoulder, then back to Parisi. "Sir, may I speak with you—man to man?"

Parisi scowled. "What'd I just tell you?"

"What are you doing?" Reina whispered.

Richard held up his hand. "It's not what you think," Richard said to Parisi. "In fact, sir, just the opposite."

Parisi rested an arm on the back of his chair, his expression one of sarcastic curiosity. Or maybe it was sadistic curiosity; Richard wasn't sure which. Parisi grinned and nodded, saying to a guard at the door, "See Missus Corte to her car and stay with her."

Reina was escorted out. When the door closed, it sounded like a giant prison bulkhead slamming shut. Richard felt the stare from every pair of eyes in the room.

"You either have balls the size of melons or you're the dumbest sombitch in the city," Parisi said, making his henchman laugh, though Maceo didn't.

"Honestly, sir," Richard began with a nervous grin. "I'm feeling more the latter." He was holding the tender spot where Maceo hit his stomach.

"You should," Parisi said, no longer smiling. "Which makes me very interested in what's on your mind." Parisi sneered at Maceo.

"Whatever your plans for Maceo are your business—"

"Agreed," Parisi said impatiently, "and twice you have interfered in family business—the penalty for which is usually definitive and swift."

Richard nodded. "I appreciate your patience, sir."

"Whaddya want 'mericani," Parisi demanded.

"Any chain of command requires discipline, but like you, my regard for Reina is high," Richard said. He motioned to Maceo. "His fate shouldn't rest on her shoulders." It was obvious Parisi and Maceo were perplexed.

Parisi cocked his head and stared at Richard. "Are *you* pleading for his life?"

"More for Reina's conscience," Richard said. "While his demise might have immediate satisfaction for her, we both know she would feel guilty about it later."

"She might disagree with you," Parisi said.

"At first."

Parisi was silent for a moment and squinted at Richard. "And it also keeps the Maceo Brothers off her."

Richard shook his head in ignorance. Parisi said they were Maceo's family—cousins. The godfather held his stare at Richard while drumming his fingers on the back of the sofa. A pounding headache and throbbing belly disguised Richard's anxiety.

"It seems you have an advocate, Vic," Parisi said, looking at Maceo with a smile Richard couldn't quite discern. "Consider this your last call, understand?"

"Yes, Don Parisi," Maceo said with complete bewilderment.

"Your final call, Vic," Parisi said with emphasis. "And yours too, Mister Warren," he added with lifeless eyes.

Richard nodded and said, "Yes sir—and thank you."

Parisi stood and left for an adjoining room followed by the other men. Richard turned and headed for the door.

"Why?" Maceo asked.

Richard leaned on the doorknob. "Exactly why I explained," Richard said.

"No," Maceo said, getting up and walking toward Richard. "There's always something more. And—"

"And now you owe me and really hate it."

Maceo nodded.

"Then tell me about Hoffman," Richard said.

Maceo jerked his head looking at the door to the adjoining room—as if he were concerned Parisi might hear. "So you *do* know him," Maceo whispered.

"No more than I know you," Richard said quietly.

Maceo bobbed his head, signaling Richard to open the door. They walked to the elevator bank past Parisi's watchmen. A car arrived and they stepped inside. Maceo didn't speak until the doors slid closed.

"Hoffman isn't what he seems," Maceo said.

Richard chuckled, "I already know that." Richard thought a second. "You're in as much a pinch with Hoffman as you are with Don Parisi."

Maceo remained silent.

"And Parisi has no clue what you're into with Hoffman," Richard said, starting to grin but stopped by his headache.

Maceo drew a deep breath. He was clearly irritated. "All I can tell you is that he dabbles with the import business."

"So he brings wines in from Europe—I know that."

"Sometimes more than just wines," Maceo said.

Richard waited for a more complete answer. "Well?"

"That's all I can say."

"Bullshit."

Maceo said nothing.

"Then tell me something about Schneider."

Maceo shook his head. "I don't know any Schneider."

The elevator abruptly stopped. Before the doors opened, Richard said, "None of this is enough—you still owe me."

"I can't say anything more about Hoffman."

"Then you need to figure out what you can tell me," Richard said as the doors opened. He stepped out, leaving Maceo in the car.

"Who the hell are you, Warren?"

"The guy who just saved your ass," Richard said. He turned and walked across the lobby and out the doors to Lamar Street.

TWENTY-ONE

Paying the Piper

Good Riddance

"What was all that about?" Reina demanded as Richard closed the car door and pressed the starter.

Richard said nothing, turning to look over his shoulder before pulling into the lane.

"Answer me!" Reina looked him in the eye.

"Can we just head back to your house and talk about this there?" He winced and grunted, rubbing his stomach.

Reina didn't answer. She watched storefronts going by and people on the sidewalks.

For the first time in too long, the weight of the whole mess was lifted and Reina could breathe again. The first thing she wanted to do was go home and call Johnny. Reina wanted Olivia back as fast as the train could get her here. Then she saw the Western Union sign on the corner coming up. "Pull up over there," she commanded and Richard complied.

Inside the small telegram office, Reina stood at a counter and composed a cable to her brother in Louisiana. Her first draft was too long. She discarded it. Reina's excitement got the better of her on the second try as well. On the third, she thought she got it about right.

ALL IS WELL AND READY FOR OLIVIA TO COME HOME - STOP - PLEASE SEND ON NEXT AVAILABLE TRAIN - STOP - GIVE HER MY LOVE AND WILL AWAIT YOUR CALL - STOP - NENA

"Nena" was Johnny's nickname for his sister since he was a toddler. It stuck and would reassure Johnny who sent the telegram.

Reina tore the sheet from the pad and handed it to the teller along with some money. She thanked the teller, who smiled and thanked her. Had there not been bars in the teller window, Reina thought she'd probably have hugged her. Olivia was coming home.

Seeing Richard waiting in the car took the bounce from Reina's steps. She stared for a moment until Richard noticed her on the sidewalk, sighing as she got in. He asked if she needed to make any other stops before they went back to the house. Reina simply shook her head no and stared down at her purse. She cringed when Richard reached over to touch her arm.

Reina wanted to say something, but she didn't know where to begin. Richard turned down West Gray, heading toward Montrose. The closer they got to home, the more nausea she felt. "What did you say to Parisi?"

"Not this again."

"What did you say?"

"I asked him to spare Maceo," Richard said.

"You what? Why?"

"To protect you."

"What he did was humiliating and degrading, something I never wanted to let Maceo have the satisfaction of knowing. Had it been something ordered by Parisi, I didn't want him knowing either."

"Exactly the point," Richard said. "He didn't condone it."

"But you didn't know that."

"It still gave you an edge."

"I didn't need it," Reina snapped. "I told you to shut up—but no, you had to practically get yourself killed."

"Come on, what sealed the deal?"

"I doubt you'd understand," she said.

Richard stomped on the brakes, nearly throwing them both through the windshield. "Wait just a goddamn minute," he said. "I've had my skull caved in and my guts knocked out my ass and you have the gall to say I couldn't understand?"

"None of those things would have happened had you butted out."

"These are the guys who've threatened to take your livelihood for who knows how long and threatened to kill you and maybe your daughter!" Richard shifted in his seat to face Reina and said, "And until today you had no clue whether or not Maceo's actions were condoned. Then suddenly, and somewhat anticlimactically, Parisi goes all warm and fuzzy?"

"Sicilians have a very deep sense of community and obligation," Reina said, scowling. "Honor and dedication have meaning for us…" she paused as she looked directly at Richard, "and so does forthright honesty. Something I know a deceptive little man like you couldn't possibly understand."

Richard said nothing, only nodding and settling back in the seat to start the car again.

The sounds of the car seemed louder. The noises as the wheels rolled over every pebble might easily have been mistaken for bones crushing under the car's weight. They turned onto Willard Street and Richard rolled through the stop sign at Van Buren. He made a wide left turn into Reina's driveway. Stopping just in front of the small garage, he killed the engine and handed Reina the keys.

There was dead silence from the car to the house. Once inside, every step echoed in the emptiness. Reina felt a hollow in her stomach as she passed through the kitchen, locking her eyes first on the floor by the sink, then on the breakfast table with a missing leg. She sprung into a gait down the hall, trying not to think about what happened with Richard this morning.

Reina closed her bedroom door and flopped on her bed, angry because her tears should have been from joy instead of guilt and regret. She swore right then she'd never allow such weakness again.

The thing for her to do now was to get everything ready for Olivia. Richard would have a day or two to find a place. Plenty of rooms were available, and if his mouth didn't ruin it, he had a job with Mr. Hoffman. Her responsibility and debt, she reasoned, were paid in full—and then some.

Looking in the mirror was hard, but Reina didn't want him to know she'd been crying. After regaining her composure, she dried her eyes and touched up her makeup as she rehearsed in her mind what she'd say. She took a deep breath, stood up from the vanity, and opened her door.

Reina called for Richard, but there was no answer. He wasn't in the kitchen when she peeked in there, nor was he on the service porch or in the backyard. The dining and living rooms were empty, and he wasn't out front.

There was no answer when Reina knocked on Olivia's door. She knocked again as she opened it. The bed was neatly made and at the foot was Johnny's trunk. Vincent's wallet and a note were on the trunk lid. All the cash from last night was in the billfold along with a few more dollars than she remembered. Then she read the first few sentences of the note.

Dear Reina,

Thank you isn't enough for everything you've done these past few days. And it means more than you can imagine. It's grossly inadequate but the only way I can repay you is to be out of your way when Olivia comes home.

Reina stopped reading and bolted out to the front yard—no sign of him up or down the block. There were neighbors tending to their hedges or lawns. A group of children chased each other around the trunk of an old oak tree a few houses down. She walked out to the middle of the street to see if she could catch him at either corner.

Not only did he have the last word, which irritated her, but he also left practically in the middle of their argument. Why did men do that? Reina wanted to find him and drag him back to the house just so she could have the satisfaction of giving him the boot.

She growled as she walked back into the house and into Olivia's room. It felt empty, just as it did the day she had to send Olivia away. Reina sat on the foot of the bed and read the note again.

Her throat constricted as she reread through the opening lines, her eyes tearing up as she read on.

Firstly, she'll want her room exactly how she remembers it. And, secondly, she'll need all of your attention and free time. She might not understand a stranger in the house. Not yet, anyway.

Everything is in the trunk except for the trousers and shirt I borrowed. I'll return those as soon as I can. Oh, and there are few dollars I hope covers the food I've eaten.

This is melodramatic, I admit. But I think you'd agree this is best for you and Olivia.

There was no complimentary close, only his signature. He used Rick rather than Richard. Angry, sad, or glad—Reina didn't know which to be. She sighed in exasperation as she threw the wadded note, missing the wastebasket. Then she held up her hands like claws and growled again.

His leaving wasn't what annoyed her, it was that he knew she was going to ask him to leave. She pulled her knees up to her chest and locked them in her arms. Maybe it was for the best, after all, she thought. There were just too many unanswered questions. And the whole thing about the Twain story was simply bizarre.

Reina had been perplexed when Carla summarized the book. She couldn't understand what such a flight of fancy had to do with anything Richard would want to say. In fact, it wasn't until after Carla left that Reina started putting the pieces together. At the root of it was his hesitance at telling her more about himself. Then there was the morning he gawked at the milkman and his gypsy-like fortune telling about the speed of things to come. If all the fantastic space and fantasy stuff he mentioned weren't weird enough, the way he acted at the club certainly was.

Richard being some kind of Rumpelstiltskin in reverse was a stupid idea. His believing it made Reina wonder if he'd escaped from an institution. But then there were the other things. If he were a lunatic, how could…

Reina shook off the wonder. He was gone and that was that—and probably it was the best thing. She composed herself, went over to pick up the wadded note, and decided to go ahead and empty the wastebasket. There were a few other crumpled papers in it, so she picked them out. One was balled up with the writing on the outside. It read "Dear JJ and Tom."

Free Will

Richard sat on the end of the third altar-right pew from the front. The wood still had a fresh finish on it—the sheen yet unworn by three generations of butts sitting, sliding, and kneeling during countless Sunday Masses, weddings, baptisms, and funerals. There was none of the graffiti carved into the seats by bored teenagers or indifferent parishioners.

Everything appeared as it did in his parents' wedding album he'd seen an infinite number of times whenever nostalgia struck his mother. He almost saw the ghostly images of a satin-gowned Maggie and a slightly older, but black-clad Jack kneeling at the altar exchanging their vows.

JJ also married there in 1974. Even then, little had changed except for the addition of a life-sized crucifix. But shortly after, Saint Anne's had undergone a major renovation. The pulpit received new supports, steps to the altar replaced the old communion rail, and new stone laid in place of the old cracked marble. And, of course, air conditioning was installed along with updated lighting.

Despite all that, there was never a change in how the place felt. Sitting in its vintage state, Richard enjoyed a rare and familiar comfort.

In the back of his mind, still throbbing from the earlier pressure of a knee, Richard always assumed he'd someday follow in his parents' and brother's footsteps. Certainly, there were women who had stirred his blood. But until the morning he found himself in a strange bed in a little Montrose bungalow, never had he been ready to plunge headlong into a commitment. Something about her made him picture a life not only as a husband, but also as a father—a vision he saw in Reina's eyes. Tempting as it was, and it was so very much, staying with her would cause her pain, whether from the truth or lies to protect her from the truth.

In a silent prayer, he confessed to being scared, and he apologized for being a hypocrite. Too often, he whispered inside, he lacked the humility to be grateful when things were good, whereas he was all too willing to come begging when things turned sour. With no one and nowhere to turn, he closed his eyes and said aloud, "I could really use advice right now."

Richard opened his eyes and was startled by a man in black standing on the other side of the front pew. Richard had thought he was alone, and he hadn't heard any footsteps.

"Most people who sit here alone are looking for guidance," the priest said. He walked up the center aisle and slid into the second pew to sit in front of Richard. He leaned sideways on the seat back and said, "So what brings you to Saint Anne's?"

"A very long story, Father," he said, sitting straighter.

"Confessions aren't for another hour, and evening Mass isn't 'til five forty-five," he said, looking at his wristwatch. "Although I could go ahead and hear your confession if you like."

Richard chuckled and said, "There *really* isn't enough time to hear my confession. You can pretty much assume I'm guilty of one through nine. Besides, I'm not looking for absolution. Guidance might be a start, though."

"Very well." He made himself more comfortable and prompted Richard, "So?"

"I have no idea how to begin," Richard said. "And please, don't say at the beginning."

The priest grinned.

After a moment, Richard said, "I made a wish once. It was sort of for a second chance."

"However, it didn't come in quite the way you had imagined it would," the priest said.

Richard nodded.

"About par when God answers prayers."

"I grew up Catholic," Richard said. "I'm well aware He doesn't always give the answer we want but the answer we need."

"Then if you recognize that, what's the problem?"

"The answer in itself," Richard said, earning a puzzled frown from the priest. "Depending on how I proceed might cost others too high a price."

"Free will is not so free—is it?"

Richard objected. "This situation wasn't placed in front of me to choose whether or not to enter," he said. "I was dropped into it like a rat in a maze!"

The priest scowled. "Oh, I don't think of God being so malicious."

"Perhaps mischievous would be a better word."

"You sound as if you think He's mocking you."

"I really don't mean to," Richard said. He grinned. "I sometimes wonder if He's not a bit of a prankster." A prime example in Richard's mind being women—the look-but-don't-touch Biblical tenet. A truly devious prank, he thought. But he'd never mention it to the priest. He didn't have to. Richard and his brother, Tom, had gone round and round with that discussion too many times.

"You've gone to great lengths to be very ambiguous," the priest noted. "It leaves me with little or nothing substantive on which to base any advice."

"Therein lies the problem, Father," Richard said.

"What's so awful?"

Richard shook his head. "This isn't about awful. See, if I chose self-satisfaction, then I set off a chain of events resulting in less-than-desirable and possibly unforeseen consequences for others."

"A lot of weight for a man to carry on his shoulders."

"Existential punishment," Richard said with an expression mocking himself as he said it.

"So, you believe your very existence might bring pain to someone else?"

"At this moment, in this place—yes," Richard said. To reassure the priest he wasn't contemplating suicide, he added. "My presence rather than existence is a better choice."

"How can you be so sure of that?"

"Because it's already happened."

"Ah." Father nodded his head and said, "Then there is guilt for something you've done."

"A lifetime's worth." Richard again shook his head but sarcastically. "Aren't we Catholics weaned on guilt?"

The priest chuckled.

"But yes, I only added to her pain, and she's had enough for one lifetime."

"I see," Father said. "You made the decision to remove yourself from her life."

Richard nodded.

"Are you sure it's what she wants?"

Richard nodded again, dramatically.

The priest said to set the woman aside for a minute and got back to Richard's core issue. "Does God make mistakes?"

"Barring mosquitoes and other biting insects, I'd have to say no," Richard said.

"Then, how could your presence be a mistake? If He indeed placed you in such a situation, it must be God's will that you serve His purpose."

"What about free will?" Richard said.

"Ah—the real source of your doubt," Father said. "The guidance you seek is right before you. You can embrace it or run from it."

"It makes no sense He'd want me to choose to hurt someone else," Richard said.

"As cautious as you've been with me, I think you can find a way," Father said. He repositioned himself in the pew and spoke as much with his hands as his mouth. "If there's no difference in risk between action and inaction, which is the better tack?"

"You mean do nothing and I'm assured of nothing, but do something and I possibly get something."

The priest nodded.

Richard nodded back. "I see your point."

"Now tell me about this woman you're so concerned about," Father said.

In the vaguest of terms, he described being lucky to meet Reina, but not by name. In not-so-vague terms, he said he quickly came to know how he felt about her: that in every way, drowning in her would be a blessing.

"She must be quite a woman."

"She is," Richard said. "More than you could know—and more than I've ever known."

"Then give her the benefit of the doubt," Father said.

"Oh, I don't think there's much doubt she wanted me to go."

"Did she say as much?"

"Enough for me to know it was coming," Richard said. "Besides, she has a daughter who needs her full attention." Richard noticed something in the Father's reaction.

The priest eyed Richard for a moment and said, "I'm betting you're Richard."

With an uneasy laugh, Richard introduced himself and said, "And you're Father Allnoch."

They shook hands.

"So you're her mystery man, eh." Father Allnoch appeared to study Richard as if to take stock of him. "At least that fills in a few gaps," he said.

Richard rested his elbows on his knees and his face in his hands. He'd just busted Reina to her priest.

"Relax, son," Allnoch said, putting a hand on Richard's shoulder. "Reina's first impressions about things are, more often than not, black and white." He softened his tone. "Give her time."

Richard leaned back and grinned. Time, he thought, was both the problem and now the answer. He wondered what advice Father Allnoch would offer to Reina when he saw her. She never seemed to question anything about life. It was what it was. Richard, on the other hand, questioned everything and especially the validity of his own faith. "Would you still be this nice if I told you half the time I was an agnostic?"

"Some of my best conversations are with doubting Thomases," Allnoch said with a grin. "Preaching to the choir is easy but nowhere near as fun."

Richard smiled, nodded, and got up slowly. He was trying not to grunt from the tight feeling in his stomach. Once in the aisle he faced the tabernacle and was only half-able to genuflect. He glanced at Father Allnoch once more and turned to leave.

"Will I see you tomorrow?"

With a half turn and sliding his hands in his pockets, Richard smiled and said, "We'll see." He walked out of the sanctuary into the foyer and out the center doors.

It was overcast and the humidity hung in the still air. As much as he wanted to, he couldn't walk back to Reina's. He wondered if the couple of bucks he had left were enough for cab fare to the Grille, then to a cheap hotel, and still be able to pay at least a nightly rate on a room.

"One step at a time," he said to himself. He'd walk to the corner and catch a taxi—if they came out this far. A neighborhood was springing up right around the church, but there were an awful lot of open tracts to the south and southwest.

Richard was standing almost as far west in Houston as was possible at the time. St. Anne's parish had spun-off from Holy Rosary in order to serve the cluster of small farms and settlements by Italian Americans. There was maybe a mile or so between the two. Ultimately, St. Anne's church grounds would annually play host to the second-largest Italian festival in the country, with thronging crowds pulsing through the school courtyard from booth to booth for tastes of traditional foods. Of course, residents of the eventual neighborhoods already springing up would come to hate the traffic and mess and loud music from bands.

The festival was always a fun time. Richard smiled, remembering how he and Max had tried to mine a date or two—and failed. He missed his friend. Richard knew a lot of people, but there were few he believed he could genuinely depend on—and no one more than Max. Unfortunately, no one here fit the bill at the moment.

He pulled a cigarette pack from his pocket and dug in the other one for his matchbook. A smoke would make the trek a few blocks east a little less annoying. He tore out the last match and struck it on the strip. A sudden breeze extinguished the flame right as he got it to the tip of his cigarette. "Shit!"

Just then, an olive-drab car pulled into the dirt circle in front of the church.

TWENTY-TWO

Loose Ends

Strands

Jack flagged Barbara when someone answered the other end of the line. So Barbara got up from her desk and tapped on Preskin's door. He came out as Jack identified himself and asked to speak with the artillery officer on duty last Wednesday night at the Army's coastal gun emplacements along the Galveston Seawall.

"How high is that wall, again?" Preskin asked Barbara.

"About fifteen feet," Barbara quietly began. "The whole island was wiped out by a bad hurricane in 1900. Thousands died, but instead of abandoning the island, residents elevated much of it and built the seawall to protect against future storm surges.

"Fifteen feet isn't necessarily a huge height, but I hope it gave our coast watchers along the wall a better angle on the horizon," Jack added. Just then the artillery officer picked up the phone and said hello.

"Sir, my CO spoke with your CO about something you reported the other night, uh, around midnight on 29, July." Jack listened as the junior officer on the other end described what he saw, jotting down every word.

"My observer thought he caught flashes about ten miles out," the young officer said.

"How were conditions?"

"Clear and with practically a full moon," the officer said. "My man was able to make out only one possible silhouette, maybe a fishing boat. But he said the flashes didn't come from the same boat."

"Then from where?" Jack asked.

"It coulda' been another trawler out there and a swell just made a lantern or cabin light appear like a signal lamp."

"But?" Jack asked.

"The flashes stopped pretty quickly," the officer said. "And you know how the moon on the water can play tricks on ya."

"Can you give me the exact position of your bunker and an approximate bearing of the light and trawler, sir?" Jack scribbled down the numbers and Captain Preskin took the paper over to the wall map. "And you think the range was about ten miles?" Jack asked. He gave a thumbs-up to Preskin and nodded to confirm the range.

"Can you tell me what's up, Chief?"

"You'll have to ask your CO, sir," Jack said. The officer said he understood and if he thought of anything else, he'd get on the horn.

Jack hung up and went over to the map where Preskin plotted the approximate coordinates. The gunnery officer's guess put a trawler right on top of the last position report from U-166 before sinking the Lee. "Ten miles offshore is a fair piece, it could have been anything," Jack whispered.

"Awfully coincidental coordinates, wouldn't you say?" Preskin said as he shook his head.

"Which is what bothers me, sir," Jack said. "Just about every bit we've dug up has been pure luck."

"Better to be lucky than smart any day, Jack." Preskin grinned.

"I'm just surprised they even filed the report."

"The battery commander encouraged reporting anything, no matter how trivial or unlikely. Unofficial reports from his counterparts in Louisiana suggest a certain band of coastal fishermen are running fuel and supplies to U-boats." Preskin paused and thought a moment. "How'd he put it? Coons or Raccoons?"

"Coonasses?" Jack smiled and grimaced simultaneously.

"That's it," Preskin said and shaking his head in confusion.

Without getting into detail, Jack explained the term was often used to refer to some Louisiana citizens. "Whether a good thing or bad depends on who you talk to," Jack said, which made Preskin snicker.

"Are the rumors a possibility?" Preskin asked

"I doubt it."

"What about the fishermen down here?"

"Well, sir," Jack started as he let out a deep breath. "You know as well as I do some people think we should just worry about the Japs."

"And leave Europe to solve its own problems."

Jack nodded to his CO. Preskin didn't say anything, but Jack suspected his CO wondered where he stood. "It just seems to me that if we don't stop them over there, we'll wind up just havin' to do it over here." Jack grinned and leaned in toward Preskin. "Personally, I'd rather leave the mess where it belongs—in Europe. And the same goes for the Pacific."

"You and me both," Preskin said. They turned from the wall map and Preskin handed Jack the sheet with notes. "Now all we need is to hear back from the Coast Guard."

Jack shook his head. "With so much unrestricted traffic in and out of fishing ports, I wouldn't count on anything substantial."

"Then start rubbing your rabbit's foot," Preskin said as an office line rang.

"Captain, the base commandant is on the phone," Barbara said.

"I'll take it in my office," Preskin said as he signaled for Barbara and Jack to come along.

Jack paused to let Barbara walk into the office ahead of him. He stepped in and closed the door as Preskin got on the phone. The two ranking officers quickly exchanged their courtesies and got down to business.

Preskin didn't say much at first. Jack watched him listen intently to whatever the commandant was saying. It was probably a rundown of paranoid reports by island residents imagining the Germans invading the beaches, the almost daily sightings of submarine periscopes—usually turning out to be porpoise fins—and, of course, the ever-constant rescue of small pleasure craft.

Preskin nodded once or twice. Then he said, "I'm looking for anything out of the ordinary on the 29th, say an hour or two either side of midnight?" Captain Preskin scowled as he scribbled notes on a pad. "There's no certainty as to what time the vessel was out?" Preskin kept writing.

Preskin's "uh-huhs" and "I sees" didn't offer much to keep Jack's interest. His attention wandered over to Barbara. She glanced at Jack and he took the opportunity for a covert wink. They made sure Preskin didn't notice.

"And what does the sheriff say about this?" Preskin asked the commandant.

Jack scowled.

"Yes," Preskin said. He said it again, and then he said he appreciated the commandant's help before adding one other thing. "Did you see our dispatch about the channel?" Preskin grinned and nodded. "I'd step it up a bit more since we're heading into the dark of the moon." He nodded some more while repeating his thanks and hung up.

Preskin cocked his head for a second then he leaned back in his chair. The squeak and ping of the springs hung in the quiet. The CO sighed.

With a simple "Sir?" Jack asked Preskin what the commandant said.

Preskin sighed and said, "About what we expected—paranoid reports and reckless small craft operators."

"Anything on the 29th?" Jack asked.

"We may have our mystery lights." Preskin leaned up in his chair and began reading aloud from his notes. According to his statement, a trawler captain's wife fell overboard while they were hauling in their nets. Supposedly, the boat was a man short and she was filling in. The captain was naturally in the wheelhouse, so it was the deckhand closest to her that sounded the alarm. He'd turned to do something and when he turned back around, she was gone. They said they spent hours with spotlights trying to find her. "And they just happened to guess their position wasn't far from our phantom sub."

"Why didn't they radio it in?" Barbara asked.

"Conveniently on the fritz," Preskin said.

"You're not buying it, sir," Jack said.

Preskin shook his head. "Neither is the Seabrook sheriff. The commandant didn't have much detail, but he said the sheriff described this trawler captain as being a *tomcat*."

"Ah," Jack said with an animated expression.

"And apparently the wife knew it," Preskin said. "Just about everyone in Seabrook and Kemah had been witness to the couple's explosive conversations about infidelity."

"So y'all think he killed her?" Barbara asked.

"The spouse is always your first suspect," Preskin said to Barbara.

"But," Jack said, knowing there was something more.

"The other two deckhands corroborated the story. Except for a body, the whole thing seems tight. Which is exactly what bothers me."

"You mean the fact that a trawler was coincidentally near a U-boat position is just too much of a stretch," Jack said.

"Yes."

"Spit and baling wire are about the only things holding this together,"

Jack said.

"We need to get down there," Preskin said, looking at Jack.

"Want me down there tonight or first thing in the morning, sir?"

"Actually, I'll go," Preskin said, adding, "This is one of those times when a little show of brass might help."

Jack grinned and said, "Aye, sir."

Preskin handed Barbara his notes and instructed her to type up a preliminary report before she left for the afternoon. He wanted the rest of the weekend to review it and make any additions following his trip to Seabrook. Barbara acknowledged the CO's orders, and he dismissed both her and Jack.

Barbara went straight to her desk as Jack shut the captain's door. The outer office was empty. Barbara immediately set to typing Preskin's report while Jack cleared his desk. He closed file folders and slid two into the top drawer of his desk and placed another in a file cabinet. Out of habit, he scanned the outer office and then headed for the door.

Barbara stared at Preskin's notes as she pounded the keys on the typewriter at a furious rate. She was fast, but Jack was faster. One or two guys at Refugio High used to rib Jack about being able to type so well. Those same guys secretly paid him to type their end-of-semester book reports. His skill often earned extra silver in his pockets. It also helped get him out of a lot of marching drills in boot camp.

Clerical shortages in the Navy before the war were not quite as bad, but almost. When it was discovered a recruit had any skills such as Jack's, they were immediately put to work as yeomen. And since he had no particular interest in serving on a ship of the line, that suited Jack just fine. It was only after December 7th he felt twinges of guilt about his career path. His experiences on the cruiser made him doubt his contributions.

But his commanding officer at Pearl, Commander Miller, assured him otherwise. He repeatedly said whether at sea or on dry land, every job was important to the war effort. He must have believed it because it was due to Miller's influence that Jack received the Navy Good Conduct Medal. The commendation was normally the result of three years of exceptional performance of duty, whereas Jack was awarded the medal in just over a year.

Even so, Jack's self-doubt persisted. At least until three days ago. Captain Preskin's suspicions had borne out. While he had held no delusions of being a hero, Jack felt crucial to their progress. And it made him walk straighter and with more confidence.

"Night, Barbara," Jack said as he pushed on the balustrade.

"You know, Joyce canceled our plans tonight," Barbara said without looking up as she continued typing.

Jack had his hand on the office doorknob but didn't turn it. "Joyce?"

"My roommate," Barbara said, halting her typing. "She's great but always seems to take a better offer—especially on Saturday nights."

"What'd you have in mind?"

"I hear the Natatorium might change hands again, or maybe even close down," Barbara said.

"Never heard of the place."

"It's a swim facility up in the Heights and it's supposed to be nice. Since things are heating up I thought a dip might cool us down," she said with a coy smile as she went back to typing.

Jack nodded with a smile.

"Come by around sevenish for a light supper before we go."

"See you around seven," Jack said with a wink as he opened the door and left.

Slipknot

Maceo hung up the phone and shattered his half-full cocktail glass against the wall shouting, "Mingnotta!"

A man came rushing into the hotel room. Maceo held up his hand. "It's okay Tony."

"You sure, Vic?"

Maceo nodded. "Fix yourself a drink and give me a minute." Maceo plopped down on the sofa and crossed his feet on the coffee table. Everything was unraveling. Up until the last few days, things were as smooth as silk. He thought he had the favor of Don Parisi—the Balinese Room was raking it in, the girls were cleaning up with all the military ranging from Ellington Air Field down to the bases on Galveston, rationing helped the black market boom—even the family's legitimate businesses were doing well.

Hoffman's little scheme was the fly in the ointment. Maceo had specific reasons for choosing the Continental lines, which perfectly met Hoffman's requirements. Maceo had significant interest in a competing operator—one with nearly identical capacity and would step in to fill the gap left by a Continental loss.

The spike in revenues would speed up repaying Don Parisi, enabling the Maceo family to create an independent corridor from La Porte down to Galveston. In gratitude, Vic hoped, Sam and Rose would help him move gradually east to New Orleans for his own territory. He wouldn't have the biggest pond among the families, but he would be the biggest fish in his and no longer subordinate to anyone.

Things were going according to plan until the Corte job went awry. In itself, it should have been nothing more than it was. Maceo was certain she'd never have mentioned his methods. It was that damn pipsqueak. Had it not been for him, it would all be done and to Don Parisi's satisfaction. But in a blink of an eye, and to his bewilderment, Maceo found himself indebted to the very man he currently hated most.

To make matters worse, Hoffman left a mess for Maceo to clean up. "Dumbass kraut," Maceo said to himself. "So arrogant. So superior. I should let them zero right in on you for murdering the waitress." Unfortunately, the sniveling trawler captain would finger Maceo as well as Hoffman. In fact, that was what the fisherman implied just minutes ago as he begged Maceo for help in dealing with the Seabrook sheriff. Ordinarily, the right amount of cash would sweep the whole thing under the rug. However, people were different these days.

"Vic?"

"Parisi has us booked on the last train out," Maceo said to Tony. "As soon as you drop us at the station, I want you to head straight down to Seabrook."

"Whatchya got in mind?"

Maceo got up off the couch and reached for the phone. "Go down and have the car brought around," he said. "We have a few stops to make, and I'll fill you in on the way."

Tony left.

The hotel operator came on the line and Maceo asked to be connected to the Buffalo River Grille. While he listened to the background noise of the hotel switchboard, he thought about Hoffman. The kraut should be grateful that the goods would be delivered ahead of time. As much as Maceo wanted to stick it to Hoffman, Warren was right—he was in a pinch.

After a few clicks, the Grille phone rang. Someone answered and Maceo asked for Hoffman and heard the thump of the receiver being laid down. Maceo leaned against the table as he waited. Maceo went over the events of last night. Neither Warren nor Hoffman claimed to know each other, but Warren acted as if he did. And this afternoon he was asking questions about Hoffman, risking a lot to ask them.

Maceo didn't care about Warren's reasons, but Hoffman would. And it struck Maceo he might get himself out from between the thorns in his side.

There were two possible outcomes, and either one would be just fine with Maceo. All he needed to set things in motion was a little cooperation from Hoffman. Hopefully, that would come in the next few minutes.

Frazzled

Reina paced with her arms folded. A car door shut and she opened the front door as Carla rushed up the front steps. Reina turned and folded her arms again trying to keep herself together.

"What happened?" Carla asked, closing the door behind her.

Reina glanced at Carla and kept pacing and biting her bottom lip. "He just left."

Carla blocked Reina and stopped her by the shoulders, looking her square in the eyes. Then she repeated her question. Slow and restrained, Reina began to cry until she leaned into Carla's arms and let it out. It didn't last long, and she moved with Carla, still holding her, over to the sofa. Reina sat up and brushed the hair sticking to her wet cheeks.

"Tell me what happened," Carla said, wiping tears from under Reina's eyes.

"We bickered," Reina said.

"Nuh-uh, bickering doesn't leave you a wreck."

In a recap of the meeting with Parisi, Reina said things started ugly and went downhill from there. "Against my wishes, he told Parisi what Maceo did last Wednesday. I needed Parisi to respect my efforts and maybe even me, not pity me like a victim."

"And?"

"And when things settled down, we talked and he agreed to leave me and the Factory alone."

"So now Olivia's coming home," Carla said.

Reina smiled and said yes. "I wired Johnny first thing."

"Have you heard back from him?" Carla asked.

"I doubt my cable has had time to get to him. He'll probably call tonight," Reina said.

"So what started this?"

"Richard spoke with Parisi, privately," Reina said.

"What about?" Carla asked, looking shocked.

Reina said it was apparent Maceo wasn't supposed to do what he did. "And I guess that was the last straw or something because I think Parisi was going to—well, take care of Maceo."

Carla nodded and then said, "And?"

"Richard told me he asked Parisi to not—"

"Oh my," Carla said, looking stunned. "Did he say why?"

"No." Reina started fiddling with her fingernails. "I don't think I gave him the chance. It blew up into other things and then we weren't speaking. I don't care what his reasons were, it was a slap in the face."

"Honey, he may have been right—I don't have to tell you how rough the Maceo boys play," Carla said.

Reina nodded. "So?"

"Well, if something happened to one," Carla began. "Who do you think the family would hold responsible—Parisi or you?"

Reina snapped a look at Carla.

"A Maceo is not going to challenge Don Parisi, but he'd still want vengeance. You can bet your bottom dollar on it," Carla said.

"Oh God, Carla!" Reina put her face in her hands.

"Not to mention the fact you've never had a quiet conscience," Carla added, putting her hand on Reina's back. "But I can't believe he would leave without trying to explain or even saying something."

Reina kept her eyes covered with one hand while she pulled a wrinkled note from her pocket. "He left this." She straightened up as she flipped the hair from her face and sniffed. "Why wouldn't he at least try to say something in there?"

"Would it have mattered?" Carla asked as she read.

Reina stood up and folded her arms. "Why are you always taking his side?"

Carla grinned and chuckled. "I'm not," she said. Carla stretched forward and pulled Reina back down to the sofa. "I just know how you get sometimes—you shoot first and ask questions later, as Frank would say."

Reina stood up. Carla grabbed her arm and pulled her down again.

"As much as you try to hide it, you're very passionate about whatever you're feeling at the moment."

"I can't help it!"

"I know—the Sicilian curse," Carla said. "Did you think the argument was over?"

"No!" Reina started to get up again.

Carla pinned her against the backrest of the sofa. She threatened to tie Reina down if she got up again. Carla rarely gave a stern look—she meant what she said this time. "Now, was it over or just that he got the last word in edgewise?" she asked, holding up the note.

Reina started to get up but stopped when Carla straightened up and shot a glare. Reina leaned back. She kept quiet with her arms folded while rocking the leg crossed over her knee.

"You were going to tell him to go," Carla said. "Weren't you?"

Reina didn't say anything. Tears welled up and she pursed her lips to hold them back.

"I don't understand, this morning you two were—"

"Please don't say it," Reina pleaded. She sighed again.

"You can't pretend it didn't happen."

Reina scoffed and stood up. "It's not about what I did," she said, pointing to the kitchen. "It's about the fact that I did it with a man I know nothing about."

"We talked about this," Carla said, reaching for Reina's arm.

Reina turned to face away from Carla. "It isn't enough that Richard is kind and considerate and protective—sometimes too protective, even to the point of being stupid or abrasive." She turned to face Carla again. "I need more."

"What is it you're not telling me?" Carla asked.

Reina gently sat on the coffee table in front of Carla. She couldn't say what she wanted to say.

Carla cupped Reina's hands in hers. "Obviously your feelings for Richard haven't changed. So, something else is brewing with you. Maybe the Maceo thing set off the argument, but what started it?"

Reina didn't look at Carla. She kept her eyes down. The very thought of trying to tell Carla what Richard believed—the words couldn't get past her throat.

"Is he a convict or something?" Carla asked. Then she got a wide-eyed look. "He's a Nazi spy!"

Reina shook her head. "In a way, I wish he were one of those things. Then I'd know exactly what to do," Reina said.

"Wait a minute; does this have anything to do with Mark Twain?"

Reina didn't say anything.

Carla sighed in exasperation.

"I'm sorry, Carla," Reina said. "The one thing I'm sure of is he doesn't want anyone to know."

"Fine, Reina, so what is it you want to do?" Carla asked, throwing up her arms.

Reina stopped pacing and squatted down to sit on the floor in front of the door. She leaned against it and pulled her knees up to her chest locking them in her arms. "I must be as nuts as he is," Reina said.

"That much is certain," Carla said, which made them both giggle. Then Carla asked Reina where she thought Richard might go.

Where *could* he go, Reina wondered. "I bet he's at the Grille," she said.

"He was there this morning," Carla said.

"Mister Hoffman still needs a somm… somm," Reina couldn't exactly remember the word Mr. Hoffman used. "He wanted Richard to handle the wines." Then it dawned on Reina Mr. Hoffman was the key, though she kept it to herself. Richard was extremely curious about Hoffman. Not only were there comments in the letter to his brothers, but he seemed almost able to manipulate their conversation last night, as if Richard knew…

"What?" Carla asked.

Reina shook her head. "It doesn't matter but the Grille is where we'll find Richard."

"What makes you so sure?"

"I just know. If he is curious about something, he won't let go. Richard's a bulldog like that."

"So, I guess we're going to go get him?"

Reina didn't want to leave because Johnny might call. She wanted to hear Olivia's voice, anticipating the sounds of magical excitement that Reina had missed for so long.

Soon, there'd be sounds to break the haunting quiet of the house. Reina would wake up to little feet running down the hall every morning in a last-minute dash for the potty. She would stand quietly outside Olivia's room and listen to giggles and one-sided conversations with dolls over imaginary tea and frittelle. And on nights when the wind rustled the trees and bushes, a frightened little girl would crawl into her mommy's warm bed for protection from monsters.

"I can't wait until she's actually here," Reina said.

"And what are you going to tell her about Richard?" Carla asked.

Reina thought the thing to do was to take it a little at a time. Let them get used to each other. There had been a lot of changes for Olivia over the last year, and she didn't want to add too much more.

"Think he'll make a good daddy?" Carla asked.

"What?" Reina scowled and grinned at the same time.

"Oh, honey, please," Carla said with an incredulous smile. "Don't tell me it hadn't already crossed your mind."

It had crossed Reina's mind, though she wouldn't admit it. Waking up with him next to her in bed, feeling his back pressed to hers in the early haze of a morning—then hearing the thump of little feet coming into the room and Olivia climbing into bed. She pictured him as a good father, and even in his note to her, he was concerned about her daughter.

"We're getting ahead of ourselves," Reina said with a grin.

"Uh-huh. What's your plan?"

"First you can help me change the linens on her bed," Reina said.

"Then?"

Reina pushed up from the floor. "First we wait for Johnny to call. Afterwards, well, it's a bit tricky."

"How to get Richard back without making it look like you're begging," Carla said, extending her arm.

"Not beg, bait," Reina said, winking at Carla as she pulled her up off the sofa.

Carla gave Reina a sideways look and asked what Reina had in mind.

"A repeat performance," Reina said as they went into Olivia's room and stripped the bed.

TWENTY-THREE

Measure of a Man

Father and Son Talk

Richard flipped the lid closed on his father's Zippo and handed it back. "I really appreciate this."

"My pleasure, sir."

"You know the whole 'sir' bit makes me feel about fifty years old," Richard said. It was far too strange to have his father call him sir. "How 'bout you just call me Rick."

"Fair enough," Jack said, smiling.

Richard continued with the small talk to avoid awkward silence, which he hated. "Will you have enough time to get back for Mass?"

"To tell you the truth, I'm not in much of a mood anyway." Jack said it had been a long day, and he had the sneaking suspicion he'd be called in early tomorrow.

"I guess things are crazy these days," Richard said. He could relate.

Jack grunted.

Richard watched his dad crimp an unlit cigarette between his lips. He flipped open the lighter and thumbed the flint. With the flame held to the tip, he puffed the cigarette to life—all in the same manner Richard remembered.

"Most of what I do is fairly ordinary stuff." Jack took a drag and exhaled. "The funny thing is I really couldn't give two shakes for the oil business," he said, taking another drag before continuing. "But I will say parts of this posting are interesting."

"I'm more familiar with pipelines," Richard said.

"That what you used to do?"

"In a way," Richard said, repositioning himself in the passenger seat. The heat and humidity made his shirt stick to the backrest. "I had a client who developed an additive to improve the flow of liquid petroleum products." He knew the additive was being developed as he spoke.

"How's it work?"

"Fluid turbulence develops as liquids are pushed through a pump and down the line. You inject the additive into the line and it reduces the turbulence, which in turn reduces the drag and increases your flowrate."

"Turbulence?"

"Yeah, the fluid closest to the inner surface of the pipe flows at a slower rate than the fluid in the center—friction causes the drag, which gets worse as deposits build up on the inside surface of the pipe."

"Wouldn't a pig clean out the buildup and help flow just as well?"

Richard shook his head. "Even if you have a smooth pipe—a new pipe—you still get the turbulence caused by the flow disparity. This stuff should help equalize the flow."

"So if you equalize the flow—what do you get?"

"If the research pans out, you could increase your throughput for more revenues or shutdown a pump station and save operating costs."

"What about the additive as a contaminant?"

Richard grinned. Working for the OPC, fuel quality would be the one issue his dad was probably most concerned with, particularly aviation fuel, making his question the first logical one. "It's a petroleum derivative, so it essentially degrades down to its constituent elements."

"So it could be used for both crude and product lines," Jack concluded.

Richard nodded.

"Let me ask you another question since you know a lot about this stuff," Jack said as Richard laughed. "What?"

"Most of what I know is mainly from a marketing standpoint," Richard said. "But go ahead."

"How strong is the flow or pressure—I mean, I know they run pigs through lines and plugs between products," Jack said, looking over at Richard, then back at the road. "But how long does it take to get from one pump station to the next?"

Richard shrugged. "I guess it depends on pipe diameter, pump pressure, and viscosity—probably distance between stations, too. But to be honest, I'm weak at math. Even if I had the numbers, I'd probably get a wrong answer." He cocked his head with a grin. "I was an ad man, not an engineer."

Then Jack shook his head, and Richard asked why.

"Huh? Oh, I was just thinking how engineers love to change things. But the guys who do the work—they hate change," Jack said, sounding aggravated. "At least that's the case in refineries and the fields—those guys need things they can rely on to work, not theory. So it may be a hard sell once you get up and running."

Richard would love to have confirmed his father's observations. He and his client had fought many industry battles over the additive. The single most vindicating point was that the product was used in the Trans Alaskan Pipeline, which wouldn't be built for another twenty-five years or so.

"Sounds like you have a lot of hands-on experience. I'd bet it comes in handy for the Navy," Richard said.

"Well, the experience didn't come by choice, believe me," Jack said, shifting in his seat. "My old man thought I should learn a trade. Naturally, he thought it should be his trade." Jack furrowed his brow briefly and said, "He and I have never really seen eye to eye—but at least this is something I can put to good use."

Richard had always known about the summers his dad spent working with Pampaw, although it seemed like the experience wasn't a cherished memory —a suspicion now confirmed.

Now and then, Jack would tell his sons about how rough Pampaw could be—or they'd overhear those stories. The details were a little fuzzy, but one story that stuck in Richard's mind was the cruel method used to teach his dad how to shoot a rifle. If he missed the mark, Pampaw would inflict some physical punishment.

There were other stories too, which made Richard thankful for his dad. He was a stern father, but never abusive. Nor was he the kind of man to lavish affection on his sons. He could be warm, though. Except much of that waned as the bottle drew him in deeper—making him seem more like Pampaw in later years. But what Richard felt separated his father from his grandfather was humor. Pampaw had none.

"Fathers do tend to play a big part in defining who we are as men, don't they," Richard said.

"God, I hope not," Jack said, exhaling smoke.

"Think about it—men ultimately make the choice either to emulate their father or spend a lifetime trying to be unlike him. A son could choose to blame his father for his own weaknesses and failures or seek out common ground and take strength from it."

Jack flicked his cigarette out the window. He repositioned himself in the car seat and cleared his throat.

Richard chuckled.

"What?" Jack asked.

"Bet you didn't expect a sermon, did you?" Richard asked rhetorically.

"You hear confessions too?"

"Only if it's something good!"

"That remains to be seen," Jack said as he winked.

Richard smiled and snorted. "Another hot date with the blonde?"

Jack grinned, keeping his eyes on the road and nodding. "Too bad you have to work on a Saturday night. What was her name? Reina? You two seemed to be getting along."

Richard grunted as he took a final drag from his smoke, then flicking the butt out his window. He exhaled and said, "Afraid I'm in the doghouse. So I thought I'd try to earn a few bucks and stay outta more trouble."

"How'd you meet Kurt Hoffman?" Jack asked.

"Through Reina, who knows him because she does business with the restaurant."

"There's only a couple of years difference between him and me," Jack said as he wheeled the car around a corner. "And look at him—he's already a successful businessman."

It wasn't envy in Jack's voice—Richard took it as self-doubt. "Yeah, don't hold yourself to another man's standard," Richard said, adding, "To be fair, Kurt had a leg up."

"How do you mean?"

"I believe I heard him say he inherited his restaurant, or at least the property," Richard said as conversations with the old Kurt came to mind—mentions of a German delicatessen belonging to Kurt's uncle. "The point is he didn't exactly start from scratch. You, on the other hand, went into the Navy barely a year or so ago and are already a chief petty officer."

"How do you figure all that?"

"Well, you're friends with Miss Malone and she's college age. So you couldn't have been in the Navy all that long. But obviously your CO's are seeing something they like, otherwise, you'd be a seaman shittin' off a fantail somewhere out in the Pacific."

Jack laughed.

"Look at it like a golf game," Richard said.

"Golf?" Jack asked, confused.

"Yeah. The goal is to hole out in as few strokes as possible. But you can't do it playing the other guy's game."

"You lost me," Jack said.

"Let's say one player is strong off the tee while you might stink but have a deadly short game and be dead-eyed on the green," Richard said.

"The other guy gets to the green sooner."

"Yeah—so what? He may not be able to hole out in regulation," Richard said as he shifted again in his seat. "Forget about the other guy because you're really playing against *yourself*—it's about your own strengths," he said.

"Play a lot of golf, do you?" Jack asked with a smile.

"A round or two over the years," Richard said, then adding, "And I have yet to break a hundred." He realized they were rolling up Milam toward Franklin. Richard hardly had paid attention to the route. The only thing missing from the conversation was a couple of beers. Richard could count on one hand the number of father and son talks they'd shared, although it felt more like their roles were reversed with this one. Nevertheless, old Kurt was right. He did like this Jack Warren.

They turned the corner and Jack pulled over across the street from the Grille. "How's this for curb service?" Jack asked.

Richard opened the door but didn't get out right away. "It doesn't get much better," adding, "unless you offer pick up as well."

Jack checked at his watch and said, "Tell you what, if I show up at closing you'll know how things went on my second date."

They laughed.

"For your sake, I hope you slide into home," Richard said as he got out. "But if not, I'll snag a couple of cold ones for us."

Jack gave a thumbs-up and said he'd see Richard on the flip side. Richard closed the car door and waved as Jack drove off. He felt his eyes water a bit. A deep breath helped him compose himself as he crossed Franklin, looking both ways. The olive drab sedan was still in sight. Richard smiled and said, "Have fun, Dad."

Birds of a Feather

The deadbolt popped and Hoffman pushed the door open for Dorothy. She hesitated. "Come on, honey," he prodded. "It's only for a minute—no spies're lurking to report you." She walked in, giving Hoffman a playful leer over her shoulder.

He tossed his keys on the coffee table as he closed the door behind them. Hoffman went over to his desk and shuffled through papers.

"You don't really have a list, do you?" she asked.

"No, I really do," he said, chuckling.

"Kurt Hoffman—if you're telling me a story."

He laughed and kept digging around his desk and in drawers.

"You should have just brought it with you this morning."

"Here it is!" Hoffman held it up in sarcastic triumph. He took a few steps toward Dorothy, holding the look. She held out her hand and he smirked. "It'll cost you," he said.

Dorothy leaned up and gave Kurt a peck on the lips as she snatched the list from his hand. "What am I going to do with you?"

"Now or on our wedding night?" he asked.

"You have a one-track mind," she said with mock disgust, shaking her head.

"Well, at least I always know where I'm going," he said with a wink.

Dorothy read over the list. "This is very short, Kurt."

"With my aunt and uncle gone, I have no family."

"Most of these are business friends and customers. What about your friends from last night?"

"Other than Reina Corte, they're strangers."

"I'm not sure it would be appropriate to invite her," Dorothy said. She flipped the sheet over but it was blank. "And what about Jack?"

"You know him better than I do," Hoffman said. He eased himself down into his desk chair and crossed his leg over the other. "But why would you say that about Reina?"

Dorothy whispered, "She's staying with that man."

Hoffman laughed. "You don't have to whisper—we're quite alone."

Dorothy rolled her eyes and said, "Well, regardless of the circumstances, two unmarried adults should not be living under the same roof. It sets a very poor example for her daughter."

"Didn't you say her daughter was off visiting relatives?" Hoffman asked, shrugging. "And by the way, you were never very clear about what those circumstances were."

"Mr. and Mrs. Bono only said Reina found him injured from some sort of accident," Dorothy said.

"What kind of accident?"

"They never said. Apparently, she has some aversion to hospitals and cared for his wounds herself."

"When was this?" Hoffman asked.

"Wednesday evening, I think they said."

Interesting. As far as Hoffman knew, the only injury was inflicted on Maceo. And last night, Maceo was ready to pounce on Warren. What's more, this Warren didn't mind pouring salt on the whole thing. He was either very sure of himself or very stupid. "I wonder what caused his injuries?" Hoffman asked.

"The Bonos only said she found him in the alley behind her business. They mentioned he had minor burns, but not if he was in a fire or what kind of accident it might have been."

Hoffman only grunted.

"Oh—and that his memory was like Swiss cheese, which I take to mean Richard has some form of amnesia."

Hoffman sat a minute with a furrowed brow. Warren was definitely the guy who cold-cocked Maceo, which was the only thing that seemed to track. Nothing else about him made sense. Hoffman could see Reina Corte taking him in, especially if he defended her. She had a reputation for putting herself out for other people.

"You can always just send her the announcement," Dorothy said.

"Huh?"

"I know you think well of her, but an announcement would be appropriate."

"If her situation makes you uncomfortable, fine." Hoffman stared out the window a minute. Dorothy asked if he was okay, and he smiled. "I just don't want the list to get out of hand," he said, leaning forward. "The smaller the better."

Dorothy folded the list and stuffed it into her purse. She left it on the sofa as she got up, announcing she needed to use the "little girl's room." Hoffman shook his head. Women always had some euphemism rather than say "bathroom."

Still in his chair, Hoffman wheeled around to see out his front window. He stared at the Houston skyline just a block from his restaurant. The view was like a wall rising up around him.

An olive drab sedan with stenciled lettering emerged from between the concrete and brick canyon walls blocking Hoffman's view further down Milam Street. It slowed on its approach to the intersection and turned east to pull over across the street from the Grille. Hoffman recognized the driver in khaki uniform: Jack. He was talking to someone, but Hoffman couldn't see who it was.

Jack nodded, smiled, and checked his watch. The passenger door hung open for a second. Then Hoffman leaned forward and squinted through a slight part in the sheers to get a good look. Richard Warren appeared.

He wondered if this was a sign the authorities were closing in, except the dots simply didn't connect. This Richard character and Jack had the same name—though Hoffman would concede that as a possible coincidence. However, the joust with Schneider cast a shadow on this all being a random encounter. So the first-time introductions last night could have been a ruse. But was it a ruse—was there a kinship?

Dealing with Richard Warren meant Hoffman might have to do the same with Jack Warren. Strangely enough, Jack was a guy Hoffman kind of liked. Nevertheless, and personal feelings aside, Hoffman's gut was telling him to act. Still, he needed something to nail it down.

He heard the commode flush and jerked around to look toward the bathroom. Dorothy would surely take a moment to put herself back together. Hoffman started to scoot his chair back from the window to the desk but peeked out again to see Jack drive off. Richard Warren waved to the car before crossing the street toward the Grille. He looked up at the building. Hoffman knew better, but it seemed as if Richard Warren was looking straight at him.

Alerted by the door latch, Hoffman straightened up in his chair. Dorothy stood in the doorway, holding something between her thumb and index finger.

"What is this?"

Hoffman couldn't tell what it was. He got up and walked toward Dorothy shaking his head.

"What are you doing with a bobby pin by the sink?"

"It's probably Jeanine's," he said, taking the pin from Dorothy and looking at it.

Dorothy's face was hard.

"I sent her up here to clean her dress," Hoffman said. He handed the pin back to Dorothy and looked her in the eye. "She zigged and a waiter zagged, so she wound up with a plate of red sauce on her dress."

"Why here?"

"You know there's no place downstairs." Hoffman was indignant when he spoke. "She couldn't very well peel off her gown in the ladies' room, now could she?"

Dorothy was silent.

"She's probably downstairs by now—go ask her." Hoffman grabbed his keys off the desk and stood by the front door with his hand on the knob. "I shudder to think what you'd concoct if it were Herman or one of the boys I had to send up."

"Oh, Kurt! How disgusting," Dorothy said.

Kurt nodded and said, "Exactly my point."

Dorothy looked away, then back at Hoffman and smiled. "I'm sorry—I shouldn't have assumed the worst."

"Next time," Hoffman began with a smile. "Just ask me before turning in a verdict." She nodded.

"C'mon," he said as he opened the door. "I'll wait with you at the cab stand."

Casual Interrogation

Hoffman walked through the front doors, and Herman showed him the reservations book for the evening. It'd be a busy night. Word had gotten around about Jake's Phillies. Already, the early birds were dining along the windows to catch the sunset over the bayou. A few older regulars were at the tables in the center.

Herman pointed to the gentleman standing off to one side by the hatcheck counter. Hoffman held out his hand. "Back so soon?"

"I have a few cases left to finish up in the wine room and wondered if you might need a sommelier."

That sounded very convenient. It also created a perfect opportunity to keep Warren close and observe him. "I don't suppose you have a tuxedo," Hoffman said.

Richard shrugged.

If a new waiter didn't have a tux, The Grille usually paid for it and docked his pay. To their credit, a few men turned theirs in when they enlisted after December 7th.

"I think there is one about the right size, Mr. Hoffman," Herman said.

Hoffman cocked his head toward the back office and he and Richard started walking. "You did fine work this morning. But why the empty bins left in places, especially among the older vintages?"

"They give you a little expansion room," Richard said as they walked into the kitchen. "Your older vintages will probably rotate out at a slower pace compared with the champagnes, whites, and younger table reds. So if you trip over a good deal, you don't have to shift everything around when the shipment arrives."

That impressed Hoffman. He searched around the small office, and behind a stack of boxes were clothes hangers with light canvass covers protecting the garments. Hoffman pulled them off the nail and handed them to Richard. "See if any of those work."

As Richard slid off the covers and assessed jacket sizes, Hoffman remembered Warren said wines and spirits were his avocation. "So what's your true profession?"

"In another life I was an advertising account executive," Richard said as he tried on a coat. "It can be somewhat of a glorified combination of salesman and errand boy. But to be fair a good one is invaluable."

"Were you a good one?"

Richard grinned. "Up until the point when it became unsatisfying. I was tired of having to serve two masters. I mean, by virtue of a paycheck, I was responsible to my employer. However, there was the inherent obligation to do the best possible job for the client." He paused a moment to straighten the lapels on one coat, "Sometimes you run into conflicts of interest."

"In what way?" Hoffman asked, trying to sound detached.

Richard's answer was blunt. "Corporate annual reports are an exercise in marketing masturbation. Incredible sums are spent for companies to make themselves look good, well, to themselves. The real story is in the 10-k numbers," Richard said. He continued as he tried on tuxedo jackets. "Certainly, there is a need for any company to market itself in a positive light, even to investors and analysts. Nonetheless, far too much pressure is heaped on the annual report project manager and company head for a document instantly outdated once off the printing press."

This didn't sound like a cover story. Hoffman listened to Richard detail how either printing companies or the design firms would bait and switch clients to increase the profits on these jobs.

"One way is to use a less expensive paper than what was specified in the proposal; it would be slipped in without the client's knowledge. Maybe one-tenth of one percent of the population can tell the difference between a premium grade and a number three grade paper stock, or between a heavy text weight and a light cover weight paper. I could go on, but the point is it's one way to put your thumb on the scale."

"I assume the savings aren't passed on the client," Hoffman said. Richard shook his head, and Hoffman asked if the lesser grade papers had negative outcomes for these documents or the client.

"No, but not really the point." Richard saw a loose label from a wine bottle on the desk. He picked it up and said, "It's like serving a decanter of an off-year vintage to a customer when a fine vintage was requested or promised, or even recommending an off-year vintage as if it were a better one—and charging an inflated price. A customer deserves what they actually paid for."

Hoffman admitted Richard's point was well-taken. But he was curious and wanted to take it a step further. "For argument's sake, let's say there's no harm done."

"C'mon, you know better than that," Richard said as he slipped off one of the jackets. "I'm all for profit, but not profit predicated on a lie—that's called swindling."

"So these kinds of things disturbed you enough to quit," Hoffman said.

"Well, I never lost sleep over them, no—although there were a few heated discussions among colleagues and the boss."

"No you quit, or no you were fired?" Hoffman asked.

"Not fired," Richard said, pulling a pair of matching slacks off a hanger and draping it over his front to measure the width and the length. "I'm sort of on personal leave, and I'm taking the opportunity to reconsider my future." He assessed the pants and said they ought to do.

"They're a bit long, don't you think?"

"Nah, I can just cinch up the braces and no one'd notice under the jacket."

Hoffman grinned and said, "The brown shoes might be the only things to give you away."

"Probably only women will notice," Richard said with a chuckle.

Hoffman agreed and then said, "To be honest you won't be all that busy. Most people don't go in for wines. Champagne moves well. But whiskeys are the most popular."

"Then why all the effort to maintain a wine room?"

"Because I like them. And the wine room puts the Grille in a unique light." Hoffman sat up a bit in the chair and gestured toward all the paperwork on his desk. "There are other restaurants and certainly other places with unspoken entertainment."

Richard scowled a moment then asked, "You mean gambling?"

"Yes. Galveston is a hotbed, but The Balinese Room is the crown jewel. And, then there's Black Palm not far from here. The one I have to work hard to beat is Domain Privee on the outskirts of town. Jake Freedman opened it about two years ago and has a very loyal following of Houston moneymakers. But what he doesn't have—"

"Is a sophisticated wine room," Richard said.

"Exactly. Apart from private country clubs and the better hotels, there are fewer than a handful of truly fine dining establishments in the city—of which the Grille is one. And with a little grease in the right places," Hoffman said, rubbing fingers together, "HPD and the Baptists stay off your back."

"You think they'll ever legalize liquor by the drink?"

"I hope to hell they do," Hoffman said, standing up. "Everybody knows about it—hell, the sheriff comes in here to drink and gamble." Then Hoffman dropped to a whisper. "And it's not unusual to see a minister or two either," he said, winking. "Of course they only order clear liquor mixed with water or served over ice."

Richard smiled.

"The world is full of hypocrites," Hoffman added as he walked out of the office. "See Herman when you get changed." He closed the office door behind him.

What exactly Hoffman could derive from the conversation wasn't clear. Richard's knowledge of that field seemed buttoned-up. And he wasn't shy about his ethics. Hoffman also identified with the tug of war between masters.

Still, in Hoffman's mind, Richard Warren was a flip of the coin. He'd have to wait and be patient. Sooner or later, something would tip the scale. And while it was only a featherweight, one thing did wobble the needle: the man's memory seemed just fine.

TWENTY-FOUR

Future Imperfect

Richard adjusted a suspender strap with his thumb. He'd hitched it tight to keep his trousers up, and it aggravated his still tender shoulder.

The bottle he just decanted reminded him of the earlier conversation with Kurt. Richard remembered hearing about the Domain Privee and The Balinese Room from older Kurt when he was helping in his personal wine room then. The Maceo family was huge in the late 40s and 50s until finally busted by Texas Rangers. Richard smiled at the thought of Vic Maceo in handcuffs doing the "perp walk." Jake Freeman, on the other hand, saw the writing on the wall. While his Domain Privee casino did very well, he knew Houston gambling would end. He left for Las Vegas around 1950 and built the Sands Hotel and Casino.

These were Houston's heady gambling days, and now, Richard was in the middle of it all. He directed his attention back to the decanter and put a top in it, laid a napkin over his arm, and picked up his tray. Herman walked in just as Richard made it to the wine room door.

"One of the guests wants a bottle of champagne," Herman said.

"Anything in particular?" Richard asked and Herman shook his head no.

The less expensive labels were in easy reach. Richard grabbed a bottle and said, "I'll take care of it as soon as I finish with this Bordeaux I'm about to serve. Which table?"

"Missus Esperson."

"Widow Esperson?"

Herman nodded.

"Oh goddamn, Herman!" Esperson was a well-known name even in Richard's time. Niels and Millie Esperson were true Houston movers and shakers. He died in 1922, but she continued influencing the city skyline and development. Richard put the bottle back and climbed up for a better one that he handed to Herman.

As they shut the wine room door behind them, Herman offered Richard a folded paper from his pocket and said, "By the way, I got a phone message for you."

"From?"

"Missus Corte," Herman said.

Richard stopped halfway up the stairs to steady his cargo. He wasn't used to carrying service trays, and Reina's name didn't help his balance. Careful to balance the tray with one hand, Richard took the note from Herman and read it.

Kitchen table needs more attention.

Please drop by after closing

—Reina

Richard nearly tumped over the tray.

"Are you alright?" Herman asked.

"Yeah," Richard chortled as he took tentative steps up the stairway. Maybe Father Allnoch was right, he thought. The girl could shift from zero to sixty in an instant. But if she had come around, then Richard's prospects just became much more pleasant, assuming she wasn't baiting him to actually fix the table leg. Richard grinned. Nah, he thought. If Reina wanted the leg fixed, she'd do it herself out of spite.

The dining room was packed, and Richard carefully weaved his way to his patrons. Arriving at the table of the gentleman who ordered the Bordeaux, he immediately poured the wine into the glass of the man's wife. The couple spoke with accents clearly not Texan. Richard guessed they were originally from Michigan. After filling the gentleman's glass, he set the decanter in the center of the table and ran back to get champagne glasses for Mrs. Esperson.

Mellie Esperson was at a table by the windows. Accompanying her were two couples who appeared to be her contemporaries. Richard set a glass in front of each person, except for one woman who said she didn't drink. He pulled the champagne out of the ice bucket, peeled off the foil, and twisted loose the wire securing the cork. Covering the top with a cloth napkin, he slipped his thumb underneath and popped the cork.

"Pardon me, young man," one of the women said with a cold, smug tone.

"Yes ma'am?" Richard politely asked as he served Mrs. Esperson first.

"I hope your knowledge of spirits isn't reflected by your choice in fashion," the woman said as she glanced at Richard's shoes.

Richard served the snobby hag the next glass, and then he grinned. "The wrapping may be brown, ma'am, but the soles are black patent leather."

Mrs. Esperson giggled along with the third woman and the two gentlemen, one of whom subtly raised his glass to Richard. He thanked the gentleman with a quick nod and finished serving the champagne as Mrs. Esperson resumed the group's conversation.

Replacing the bottle in the ice bucket, Richard silently left the table. He caught sight of Kurt at another table up in the back corner. There was a chessboard in front of him. They exchanged nods as Richard stepped down into the center section, making his way toward the door down to the wine room.

Instead of heading back down to the wine room, Richard passed through the door out to the back. He figured he had a few minutes to catch a smoke.

The back of the building curved along the bank of the bayou, growing with tall weeds. The structure made a sharp angle away from the slope, creating a narrow alley. An intersecting alley led in from Franklin and separated Kurt's building from the one next door to the east. There were puddles everywhere, and garbage was stacked along the wall. It was dark, and the scene reminded Richard of the nightmare he had woken up in just a few days ago.

The shell shock had all but faded, and the reality of his predicament set in. However weird it felt, he was in 1942. How it happened defied answer, so he saw no point in trying. And since he wasn't the star of some episodic adventure, there'd be no miracles, no determined sidekick, or any possible reprieve to help him get back to his own time.

With a fifty-year head start, Richard could make a living. If he worked it right, he could do quite well. The trick would be not to overdo it, knowing full well he'd have to exercise restraint. The downside was he'd be a parasite—taking but unable to give back. Richard could never vote or take any action to impact what should unfold.

While living as a vagrant or hermit was the surest way to eliminate any possible effect, Richard decided he shouldn't have to suffer such punishment since he didn't ask for this situation. And given Father Allnoch's advice, Richard assumed he had the equivalent of a special dispensation.

Puffing his cigarette, Richard paced around the alley behind the restaurant. A maroon Cord was parked under a wood porte-cochère. Sweet, Richard thought. His T-Bird reminded him of exactly that car. The long hood, sleek profile, and coupe-like passenger compartment were similar attributes. "Must be Kurt's," he said aloud.

Kurt was a riddle. Richard couldn't figure what he was up to, and Maceo wasn't exactly forthcoming. He'd said there were "offshore interests," which could mean anything, though Schneider was a good hint. But Richard had a very hard time thinking of Kurt as a Nazi sympathizer.

Richard made a face—squinting with one eye and chewing on his lip. Maybe he was reading too much into Schneider. Kurt had walked in before Richard could get a reading on his last verbal ping at the man. Still, Schneider was suspicious in every way—almost a German stereotype of the era.

Smuggling—that was probably it, or at least what Richard preferred to believe. It seemed a more probable explanation, more fitting to Kurt's personality and his association with Parisi. Sure, Richard thought, Kurt was a practiced host used to being "on" twenty-four-seven. But he treated his people well—Richard thought a Nazi sympathizer would be more aloof with subordinates.

Richard closed his eyes and imagined an old man sitting in his penthouse sipping wine. "Wait a damn minute!" he said, opening his eyes and scowling, then barraging himself with questions: Wouldn't Kurt have remembered? Wouldn't Dad? Is half a century so long a time they'd forget names and faces?

He'd already had the answers. From the beginning, he'd been worried about minimizing contact with people he would eventually know. Apparently, he will have been successful. At least he thought it seemed a logical explanation.

The best way to avoid everybody was by moving out of town, but if his future included a life with Reina, Richard doubted her willingness to move. Not to mention what result her moving might have as well.

"Quit projecting, stupid, and take it one day at a time," Richard said to himself as he crushed out his smoke, twisting the butt into the asphalt with his foot.

No matter how slowly he took it or how carefully he lived from here on, he'd feel the biggest impact. Already he missed his brothers. JJ wouldn't be born for another seven years, and Tom another three years after. A very twisted smile grew on Richard's face, and then he snickered. Suddenly opening up was a whole world of possibilities to exact revenge for a lifetime of pranks, practical jokes, and torment.

He let himself run with the idea for a few minutes. Richard could sneak a peek to witness his own birth. Now that had potential. He could eliminate every woulda, coulda, and shoulda throughout his entire life.

Then, as if an angel appeared on the other shoulder whispering into his ear, he imagined some apocalyptic event or horrid turn of fate if he tried to change his own past. "Shit," he sighed.

Richard frowned. Everyone he left in the future must have been going nuts. He could see Cynthia pacing about and spewing "I told you so's." Somebody would be on the phone with the police. Someone else'd be calling the hospitals. JJ would have called Max, so he'd be there. "I wonder if they'll guess I went to see Kurt?" He doubted it. Why would they?

The letter—that was it, he thought. Richard was going back to Reina's. He could rewrite the letter and leave it with a law firm he knew would be around. They could deliver it on April 18th. Then Richard winced. What would he say? Hi guys, I'm in 1942 and peachy! *Yeah right.*

"Deal with the here and now, Richard," he said quietly. His future lay with Reina; he was certain of that much. She was the silver lining. "So, get through tonight and start fresh in the morning," he said, heading for the kitchen door.

It wasn't much of a plan, and he thought it was awfully Scarlett O'Hara. *But frankly,* he thought, *at this point, I don't give a damn.*

TWENTY-FIVE

Conundrum

Blind Man's Bluff

The smell coming from the seafood crates stacked against the wall was rancid, which brought mosquitoes swarming up from the weeds growing on the banks of Buffalo Bayou. Maceo puffed billows of cigar smoke and swatted the air to discourage the whining pests from their attack.

One of the kitchen doors opened, and a waft of air momentarily disbursed the mosquitoes. Hoffman walked out, looking at his watch, and closed the door behind him.

"Surprised I'm on time?" Maceo asked. Hoffman was expressionless, but Maceo thought he could almost detect a grin. Except it would mean Hoffman had a sense of humor.

Both men made sure they were alone in the alley. It was good and dark, and there was no traffic on the bridge on the other side of the bayou. Hoffman nodded. Maceo flagged the waiting car up the narrow alley leading in from Franklin to the back of the building. Backing in slowly, the glow from the sedan's brake lights added to the hue of the raw brick walls.

The driver cut the engine and squeezed out of the car, tossing Maceo the keys. He opened the trunk and asked Hoffman where he wanted the crate.

"The incinerator," Hoffman said.

Maceo's stared at Hoffman. He can't be that stupid, Maceo thought. You just don't store explosives in an incinerator.

"It hasn't been used in years," Hoffman said, walking over and removing a padlock securing the doors to the firebox. The doors made a scraping sound as he pulled them open. Some bricks were missing and the exposed metal lining had rusted holes. "The stack's clogged and a city ordinance now prevents using these."

Maceo grinned as he lifted the crate and walked over to the incinerator. "And the last place anyone would ever think to look for something like this," he said.

"Exactly."

Maceo slid the wooden box into the firebox, forcing out a cloud of ash. He ducked, and then backed away.

Hoffman closed the doors and replaced the padlock. Then he pulled an envelope from his inside coat pocket. As soon as it hit his hand, Maceo opened it and counted the bills.

"You don't trust me all of a sudden?" Hoffman asked.

"About as much as you've ever trusted me," Maceo said, still counting. "Besides, this time you're short."

"Count it again—it's every bit what we agreed on," Hoffman said, scowling.

"I never agreed to clean up your messes."

Hoffman cocked his head and leered at Maceo.

"The county sheriff is leaning hard on one of my shrimpers," Maceo said, keeping his hands where Hoffman could see them. "From what I hear, his wife has gone missing."

"And?"

"Supposedly the Navy wants to talk with him." That was the first time Maceo had ever seen Hoffman startled. He liked it.

"If they talk to him, they'll talk to you," Hoffman said.

"And you."

"But you're willing to take care of it," Hoffman said, looking at Maceo sideways.

"Double this," Maceo said, holding up the cash.

Hoffman pushed away from the wall toward Maceo.

"I don't want to pick a fight with you, Hoffman," Maceo said as he backed away and with his hands level to his chest. "One, I don't have the time," he said. Then he added, "And two, this is your doing—not mine."

Maceo slowly reached into his pants pocket for a lighter. He relit his cigar to give Hoffman a minute to think it through.

"You're in up to your ass too," Hoffman said, settling back against the wall.

"Yeah, but who are they gonna want to hang first?" Maceo asked as he puffed. "Her blood's on your hands—the hands of a Nazi sympathizer."

"You'd still hang."

"Maybe," Maceo said, taking the cigar from his mouth and exhaling. "But how 'bout I sweeten the deal—as a sign of good faith between business associates."

Hoffman actually grinned. It was sarcastic, Maceo knew. Maybe the guy doesn't have a steel rod up his ass, after all.

"Well since the sheriff and the Navy aren't options for your next move, I can't wait to hear it," Hoffman said.

"Don't be so sure," Maceo said.

Hoffman scowled again. Maceo always thought he did a lot of that.

"Anyone new hanging around these days?" Maceo asked.

Hoffman jerked a look toward the back door, and Maceo understood all too well who Hoffman was thinking about. Maceo savored the moment along with his cigar.

"Our mutual friend is curious about you," Maceo said, grinning and locking his cigar between his teeth.

"What do you mean, curious?" Hoffman asked.

"I mean he's asking questions about you—about things you import," Maceo said.

"Wait a minute," Hoffman said, straightening up then leaning by his shoulder against the wall. "He came to you?

Maceo nodded.

"I find that hard to believe."

"Believe it."

Hoffman stood there without a word. He was squinting at Maceo. Then Hoffman got wide-eyed and started laughing.

"What's the joke?"

"You," Hoffman said. "I only caught the tail end of last night, but I can put two and two together, Maceo," Hoffman said, shaking his head. "Your only link to Warren is the Corte woman—and you two aren't exactly on the same side of that thing."

Maceo frowned.

"So, how'd he do it?" Hoffman asked.

Maceo shook his head.

"Oh come on," Hoffman said, sneering. "Let me guess. It turned out Parisi thought you crossed the line—even by his standards," he said. Nodding his head and pointing his finger at Maceo, Hoffman continued. "The little pecker pulled your fat out of the fire, just to piss you off."

"How or why he came to me doesn't matter," Maceo said, trying to regain his edge.

"The hell it doesn't," Hoffman said. "What'd you tell him?"

"What do you think?" Maceo asked. He held Hoffman's stare.

"I think he has your nuts in a vise, and he doesn't strike me as the kind to back off."

"I gave him nothing," Maceo said, keeping his eyes locked on Hoffman's. "But I can tell you, he knows you're hiding something."

"And?"

"He mentioned someone named Schneider," Maceo said. "Listen, I don't care what or who you're pulling out of the Gulf." He flicked his cigar ash. "The point is I've tied up your loose end. And that was never part of our deal."

"Tied? It's already done?"

"Probably, by now," Maceo said, looking at his watch then back up to Hoffman. "I didn't have time to dawdle." Maceo dropped the cigar nub to the ground. "So how about a trade."

Hoffman said nothing.

"Since I took care of things in Kemah."

"I handle Warren in return," Hoffman said.

Maceo winked as he twisted his foot to crush out the nub.

"So your ass is covered with Parisi and mine with the Navy," Hoffman said.

"We're even Steven—both of us covered all the way around."

Hoffman exhaled through his nose. Maceo wondered if it was hesitation, but decided it was out of character for Hoffman. Then, Hoffman asked, "What about the boat crew?"

"The first mate moves up to captain, and he and the other deckhand earn a larger cut." Maceo added with a chuckle, "They'll stay in line."

The driver had been standing by the car and silent. Maceo caught his wave out of the corner of his eye and realized he needed to get to the train station.

"Do we have an agreement?" Maceo asked.

Hoffman nodded once then stopped. "But—"

"But what?"

"Not right away," Hoffman said. "I have to make sure it won't bring down half the FBI—otherwise we've jumped from the frying pan into the fire."

"I wouldn't wait too long, Hoffman," Maceo said, walking toward the car.

"A day. Two at most," Hoffman said.

Maceo grinned as he opened the car door. Then it occurred to him. Hoffman wasn't likely to go for it, but if he did, so much the better. "Keep in mind," Maceo began as he twisted to bend himself into the car. "He's living with Corte." Maceo shut the door and leaned out the open window. "She probably knows everything he knows," Maceo said as he motioned for the driver to start the ignition.

He looked back at Hoffman but said nothing so it would sink in. He held the look as they drove up the alley. As they turned east onto Franklin toward the station, Maceo smiled to himself. For the first time in days, he had the upper hand.

Hole Card

Maceo's car pulled away and Hoffman was leaning on the wall. He had his hands in his pockets and stared at the ground. Schneider and Neubauer remained quiet, watching Hoffman as he pushed off the wall and position himself close to a wood crate. Suddenly, Hoffman drew back his leg and shattered the flimsy container with one kick. He gave it two more stomps—snagging his sock in the process.

"Damnit to hell," Hoffman said, lifting his pant leg.

Schneider motioned for Neubauer to step further into the shadows. He quietly walked into the light toward Hoffman and said, "I have observed your practiced control and self-discipline enviable by men ten years your senior—until now."

"How long have you been here?"

"Sufficient time to witness how you wrested the upper hand from that oaf then relinquished it," Schneider said, enjoying the surprise on Hoffman's face.

"As much as I hate to admit it," Hoffman began as he shook splinters and wood chips from his shoe. "The 'oaf' is probably right."

"Dispatching the woman was the proper action," Schneider said. "The boat pilot was the weak link." He'd thought they should have killed him as well. However, Maceo corrected the error. His concern was more immediate.

"You wanted something more, and now you have it—action is warranted."

"We've been over this already," Hoffman said. He was using his foot to rake the broken pieces of crate into a pile against the wall.

"Hesitating will only compound the problem."

"Not hesitation—caution," Hoffman said.

"Your own philosophy is to assume the other side knows what you are doing. Richard Warren is the link."

"Something's missing—the pieces don't fit right."

"All the more reason to strike now!" Schneider emphasized the point by dropping his fist on his other palm like a hammer. "It might be days before his superiors realize his silence—giving us the advantage."

Hoffman's resolve appeared to be waning. If so, the mission was in danger of a similar fate to the eight men in New York. "Our success now depends on you," Schneider said.

Hoffman pulled a key ring from his pocket and began working a key off. Schneider followed him to the incinerator. He unlocked the padlock, nodded, and then said, "You're right, it has to be tonight." He handed the key to Schneider but didn't let go. "For both of us."

Decisive or rash, Schneider wondered.

"Make sure you're ready to move fast. But first—" Hoffman pointed toward a public phone on the other side of the eastward building. "Call your men and have them look over both targets immediately."

Again, Schneider was surprised.

"Load up with everything—we'll only have one shot at this."

Finally, Schneider thought. He could complete his work and leave this horrid frontier. And he would give the mongrels a sting almost as painful as the Japanese did in Hawaii. "They will think the world is on fire," Schneider said as he slipped the key into a pant pocket.

"No gloating yet, Sturmbannfürer—if your men see any sign of patrols, then everybody hightails it out of town." Hoffman recommended the border with Mexico because of its porosity.

"So you do think this Warren is here to expose us," Schneider said, wondering what changed Hoffman's mind.

"He's a threat, no matter how you slice it, and he could mean the difference between success and the hangman's noose." Hoffman slipped his hands in his pockets then continued. "Even if Warren is nothing more than happenstance, what he might know could bridge the gap between what the Navy thinks it knows and the truth."

"There is one other connection between the fisherman and us," Schneider said.

Hoffman snorted. "Sooner or later, Maceo will seal his own fate." Hoffman started toward the kitchen doors as Schneider headed for the pay phone. "Just tell me what you find out."

Schneider stopped partway up the alley. His spine was tingling—someone was close by. Hoffman's performance was nearly flawless. But his hesitation, then sudden commitment to dispensing with Warren was, at best, miraculous.

"Neubauer," Schneider said with a whisper.

"Sir!" Neubauer said, rising from a squat position against a wall.

"We are accelerating the schedule," Schneider said, turning to look back down the alley. He waved for Neubauer to follow. "Once we retrieve the charges, I want you to first look over the tank farm."

"Sir?"

"Use the number of that pay phone," Schneider said as he pointed over his shoulder. "Patrols or not, I want to immediately know what you have seen."

"Ja, Sturmbannfürer!"

Schneider unlocked the cinder box doors and wrestled out the heavy crate. He briefly looked around before prying off one of the slats. "Give me the belt from your trousers."

Neubauer's look was skeptical.

Schneider said nothing as he held out his hand.

Neubauer slipped off his belt and gave it to his superior officer.

Schneider strapped three sticks together and tucked the end of the belt under one of the loops.

"Sturmbannfürer?"

Schneider grinned at Neubauer as he replaced the slat. "As the Americans would say, Corporal, I'm covering our bet." He motioned for Neubauer to pick up the crate as he shoved the bundle into his own coattail pocket.

Back down the alley, the corporal set the crate into the trunk of a car. Ritter was inside at the wheel. Schneider leaned in the passenger window after Neubauer got in. "The corporal will explain as you go," he said to Ritter. Then he looked at Neubauer. "Quickly."

Neubauer nodded.

Schneider waved them on, and he watched them turn the corner. The street was empty so Schneider slipped back into the shadows of the alley. He checked his watch trying to remember how long Hoffman said it was before closing.

TWENTY-SIX

New Wrinkle

"This was your idea," Jack said with a grin as he supported her back with his hands.

"I know," she said, leaning back a little to wet her hair. Her hands clasped Jack's neck, and she tightened her legs around his hips. "But this isn't exactly what I had in mind."

Jack slowly swirled them in the dark water and her hair fanned out in the soft wake. She arched her back and Jack lowered his head to kiss her on the chest between her breasts. Barbara let out a sultry laugh and pulled herself up. She rested her elbows on his shoulders and leaned her forehead on his. He rubbed the goosebumps as they formed on her upper arms from a light breeze caressing her bare skin.

Barbara moved her hips around as she kissed him—tightening her legs locked behind his waist. She would stop, smile, and giggle, then kiss him again. "You know what I like about you, Chief," she asked, grinning and rubbing her nose lightly on his.

"What's that?"

"How you snap to attention when an officer is present," she said, squeezing her legs.

Jack had a smirk on his face and fluttered his eyebrows while he saluted. He used the same hand to wave off a mosquito from Barbara's shoulder, and cupped water in his palm to pour it over the same spot. With his finger, he traced from the nape of her neck up to just below her ear and followed the same path down and back across her shoulder. Her skin was fair and smooth as he let his hand glide down below the waterline.

The air went still. The only sounds were those of their kisses blended with the lapping of the water on their bodies; their rhythm was joined by a chirping chorus of crickets and droning frogs in the woods behind the Natatorium. He moved his thumb in just the right way to make her coo.

A high-pitched whining in his ear made Jack pull away from a kiss to twitch his head. The whining resumed before he could kiss her again.

Pests started swarming around them, just over the surface of the water near the unsubmerged parts of their skin. The couple swatted mosquitoes from hovering around each other.

Barbara groaned, and said, "Maybe we should pick up round two at my place."

She got no argument from Jack who was ordinarily immune to mosquitoes. However, he was smeared with Barbara's perfume, or what was left of it, which was no doubt an attraction as well.

They swam the length of the pool toward the opposite end, pulling themselves in easy glides. Barbara was ahead of Jack, and she dove under, raising her backside out of the water. When she came up, she floated face up for a moment before rolling back over. They playfully twisted and turned, reminding Jack of dolphins he'd seen play in the bow wave of ships—flipping and diving under.

When they reached the end, Barbara paused with one hand on the edge and pinched the water from her nose with the other. There were no steps or ladder on that side. "I'm afraid there's no ladylike way to do this," she chuckled.

"Lemme give you a hand." Jack reached under the water and gently held the back of her right thigh. On the count of three, she lunged out of the water and pushed up on the brick ledge. At the same time, Jack pushed. The move was in slow motion and Jack enjoyed watching the water wash down her toned back and off her shiny round backside.

Barbara twisted her body to face Jack as her waist rose level with the ledge. She landed not-so-gently on the ground with her knees together and feet still in the water. But she graced Jack with a view of her breasts bouncing from the impact. And he thought she was very ladylike as she lifted her feet out of the water, her knees still together as she stood.

He braced himself on the ledge and took two practice bounces. Right as he began the third, on which he'd push out, Barbara said with a giggle, "Don't catch yourself on that ledge, Jack."

Jack laughed, and he had to drop back into the water, although he heeded her warning when he tried again.

Barbara was trying to dry herself with one hand and swat at the swarm with the other. "This is the only thing I hate about Houston," Barbara said, quickly rubbing her hair with a towel. "They eat you alive."

"I hope you don't hold the same thing against me," Jack said, shaking the folds out of his towel and drying his hair.

She shook her head with a grin. "You're a bad boy." She jerked straight up and slapped her behind where a mosquito stung her. "They're everywhere."

"C'mon." Jack wadded up their clothes under one arm and pulled her with his free hand. Barbara resisted and asked what he was doing. "We're making a break for the car," Jack said, tugging her.

"Like this?"

Jack tugged her hand again and she followed laughing. They scurried along the side of the pool toward the fenced entrance. Jack leaned on the double gate that was chained. As he had earlier, he pushed it open just enough for Barbara and himself to squeeze through.

They made a half-dash and half-slink up the wooded path out to the parking area. Barbara stopped and yanked on Jack's arm before the clearing. She squatted down and pulled him with her. "What?" he asked, and she pointed. There was a convertible parked across the lot. The top was up and the engine wasn't running.

Squinting through the dark, Jack could tell the windows were fogged up. He closed his eyes and cocked an ear toward the car. He could hear groans and grunts from inside.

"I'm pretty sure they're busy, so they won't see us," he whispered to Barbara. She was wide-eyed and breathing deep through flared nostrils. "Trust me." He winked and smiled, adding, "They won't be looking up."

Jack held her hand tightly and made a run for her car, which was about thirty yards away. Barbara kept pace with him as she glanced at the convertible. They rounded the back of the car so Barbara hid low next to the fender. Jack opened the passenger door, threw the bundle of clothes in the back seat, and helped her into the front. He gently shut the door and bumped it with his hip to latch it secure.

Barbara leaned over and opened the driver-side door for Jack. He quietly shut the door and jerked it to secure the latch. After tipping down the sun visor to drop the ignition key, he put it in the ignition and stepped on the starter. Two heads popped up behind the foggy glass of the convertible, so Jack shifted the car into reverse and backed up enough to make a turn. He shifted into first and gunned it. Pebbles and gravel plinked the underside of the fenders as they drove out and up to Ninth Street.

"Jack?"

"Hmm?"

"If we're stopped, how are we going to explain this to Captain Preskin?"

"Let's not get caught," he said.

"Jack," she began as she reached for the bundle of clothes. Barbara repositioned herself in the seat to rest on her left hip. "We're driving in the middle of town on a Saturday night…"

"Nekkid as jaybirds," Jack said, completing her thought. She had a nervous smile, but at least it was a smile, Jack thought. "I'll run over to North Shepherd and cut over to Kirby—all the way down to North Boulevard." He figured the police would be cruising downtown and the industrial district. The far west side was rural and almost always quiet. It would only take an extra few minutes and there would be less traffic to boot.

"It sounds like you've done this before," Barbara said with a sarcastic expression.

"What—skinny-dippin'?" Jack asked, noticing she'd separated out her blouse and was buttoning it. But her bra was on her lap.

"Uh-huh."

"Most of the time it was just the guys down at a swimmin' hole or irrigation tank on a hot summer day." Jack hardly remembered the last time he went skinny-dipping. It was in the summer of 1940, a month or two before he enlisted. "On one hand I could count the number of times I skinny-dipped with a girl and still have three fingers left over. And you?"

Barbara blushed, which Jack thought was ironic considering her current state of undress. However, the answer he got wasn't unexpected. Everybody had a favorite spot—they had to with Texas summers. It didn't matter whether it was a bayou or creek, a pond or lake, or even a beach—most people had a place to gather with friends to escape the heat and steam of July and August.

"We usually kept something on," Barbara said. "Though sometimes we'd undress all the way naked."

"Ever with a boyfriend?" Jack asked, with an impish grin.

Barbara shook her head and Jack responded with a doubting look. He thought she was almost as unabashed as the girls were in a stag film he once saw. But she held her ground and stuck to her story. Then her expression turned coy. "That's not to say I haven't seen one or two naked."

Jack laughed. "You mean you sneaked a peek!"

Barbara winked as she laid her hand high on his bare leg as she leaned toward him, reaching behind the backrest of his seat. She pushed herself up and had her uniform bonnet in her hand, dropping over his half erection.

Jack shook his head saying rather than asking, "And this does what?"

Barbara shrugged.

Jack shook his head again as he checked his side-view mirror and after that his rearview. No other cars were on the road—so far so good. They were close to the ritzy suburb of River Oaks and starting to run into a little traffic. Barbara nervously crouched down in her seat as she tried to work her stockings over wet feet and calves.

Managing to make all the lights just right, Jack wheeled onto North Boulevard. Barbara stopped trying to dress and held her face in her hands. So Jack rolled through a couple of stop signs, checking everywhere for police. He cut his lights as he turned into the driveway at Barbara's house.

Shifting into neutral, he turned off the engine and coasted the car into the open garage. Jack set the brake, turned in his seat, and set Barbara's bonnet on her head. "Back in one piece," he said with a crooked smile.

Barbara rose up in her seat and glanced around. She let out a sigh of relief and smiled as she climbed into the driver seat with Jack, carefully settling on his lap. She wrapped her arms around his neck and nearly swallowed him in a kiss.

A soft yellow light suddenly lit Barbara's face and they both turned to see someone in the kitchen window. Barbara practically jumped into the backseat, grabbing her skirt from the passenger seat. She tossed Jack his pants almost at the same time she slipped on her skirt without zipping it.

Jack was impressed. She dressed with the speed of a naval aviator scrambling in an air raid. "What's with the general quarters?"

"Joyce," Barbara whispered as she found her purse and stuffed her bra, stockings, and garter inside. Jack shoved his boxers into a pocket. She adjusted the mirror to check herself. "My hair's a mess!" She bunched it up under her bonnet and fixed her lipstick. Jack propped himself against his seat backrest to tuck in his shirt.

They climbed out of the car, and Jack noticed how wrinkled and damp their uniforms were. He rolled his eyes and said, "She'll never know."

"For Pete's sake!" Barbara said with exasperation, trying to smooth out the wrinkles in her skirt and blouse. Then she tried to smooth out the ones on Jack's khaki shirt.

The back door opened before they reached it. Joyce stood in the doorway, silhouetted by the kitchen light. She wore a full-length robe, making sure it was closed and the tie firmly knotted. "Who's that with you, Babs?" she asked.

"Chief Warren from the office, Joyce," Barbara said, making a nervous introduction.

Joyce peered over her glasses, inspecting the condition of Barbara's skirt and blouse. She also looked Jack up and down.

"Evening," Jack said, looking Joyce square in the eyes as he followed Barbara into the kitchen.

"Well, Ensign Reese and Chief Warren," she began with a judgemental tone while walking over to a pad nailed next to a wall-mounted phone. "Your Captain Preskin called and is looking for the both of you." She tore off the top sheet and handed it to Barbara. "He said to call immediately and left a number where you could reach him."

Joyce turned into the hall and paused to grin at Jack. "Don't lose your cargo there, sailor," she said, disappearing down the hall.

Realizing his fly was open, Jack tucked himself back in and zipped up. "Sorry."

Barbara scoffed and covered her face with one hand and gave the message to Jack with the other.

Jack lifted the earpiece off the hook and the operator came on the line. He leaned in close to the separate mouthpiece as he dictated the number. A few moments and clicks later, a man answered with, "Sheriff's Office." Jack identified himself to the deputy and asked to speak with Captain Preskin.

There was silence for a few seconds before Preskin came on the line.

"Jack?"

"Yes, sir." He shut his eyes hard so he could focus on Preskin's faint voice on the other end.

"Listen up," the captain said. Jack could tell he was practically yelling into the phone. "You on a party or private line?"

Jack covered the horn with his hand and asked Barbara about her service. She said it was a private line. "Private, sir." There was silence. "Sir?"

"We're at the end of our rope down here," Preskin shouted.

"Say again, sir." Jack had to shout back and covered his other ear with his hand.

The line crackled then cleared up. The captain must have been able to tell because he dropped to a normal volume and repeated his statement.

"I don't understand, sir," Jack said. The only thing he could figure was maybe the boat pilot slipped out of town. "Did you question the shrimper, sir?"

"We found him hanging around, but he won't be too helpful."

Captain Preskin was beating around the bush. It dawned on Jack that regardless of whether or not this was a private line, the captain was cautious. Suddenly he understood his inflections. Their witness was dead. And Jack had to be careful about his next question.

"Still with me, Jack?"

"Aye, sir," he said. Jack cleared his throat. "Can I assume someone *persuaded* him to keep quiet?"

"That's the consensus down here," Preskin said.

Preskin was saying something else, but Jack let his mind wander a minute until a word jolted his attention. "Say again, sir?" Preskin said the trawler pilot didn't commit suicide. So, now the question was who killed him. "Any leads on known associates, sir?" Jack asked.

"As I was saying, Chief Warren…"

Jack winced. He'd interrupted his CO. The captain repeated what he was saying: he ordered Jack to call the entire staff into the office tonight. All records relating to their inquiry were to be duplicated and prepared to hand over to the FBI by first thing in the morning.

"Sir?" Jack shook his head. He wondered when they'd cross paths with the Bureau.

"Our orders come from Stimson, Jack."

Whoa! That meant the Secretary of the Navy and J. Edgar Hoover must have butt heads over this. That alone was enough to make Jack cringe. He didn't know what to say.

"Relax, Chief," Preskin said, adding, "He's only canceling a previous directive."

Relax? Preskin just hit him with a proverbial two-by-four. Being a small fish in a big pond was no longer a comfort he could enjoy. "We'll jump right on it, sir."

"Hold everything until I arrive," Preskin said. "We're finishing up with a few bystanders from the other night."

"Anything we need to add to the report?"

"Nothing of note, yet," Preskin said. Static on the phone line forced a pause before Preskin could go on. "Everyone we interviewed said the docks were deserted on Wednesday night, as usual. The only tidbit was that two people described what they referred to as a *pretty nice car* parked next to the same pier where the shrimp trawler berthed."

Jack chuckled. He wondered if nice meant expensive or that corrosion from the salt air hadn't set in yet, which was normally the case along the Gulf Coast.

"Of course neither man got a plate number nor the color straight," Preskin said. "One said it was black and the other said it was maroon."

"Any idea on the make?"

"Only one was sure about the make," the captain said. "A late-model Cord."

Jack's stomach jumped into his throat. Realizing Barbara was looking at him, he turned to face the wall. "I'm sorry, sir, I didn't catch that."

"A late-model Cord. That mean anything to you, Jack?"

"Nothing other than it is a nice car, sir," Jack said. He rested his forehead on his arm as he leaned it against the wall.

"The Bureau agents will run it down if it turns out to be anything," Preskin said. He reminded Jack that, in the meantime, have everything ready to turn over to them when they showed up.

"Aye, sir."

"If need be, Jack, you can reach me at the Ellington bachelor officers quarters." Preskin hung up and Jack set the earpiece on the hook.

The weight of Barbara's stare hung on Jack.

"What'd he say?" Barbara asked.

Peeking into the hallway to make sure Joyce wasn't in earshot, he quietly said. "Pull all the Sealy files together and make sure we have copies."

"Tonight?"

Jack nodded as he gave her the keys to the car he had from the motor pool. Before she could say anything, he said, "I need your car to check something out for Preskin. The Navy sedan might be conspicuous."

"To whom?" she asked. "Where are you going this time of night?"

"I'll meet you downtown—just bring everybody in," Jack said as he shut the kitchen door behind him. He opened it again and poked his head inside. "But you might want to change your uniform, first." He shut the door again.

TWENTY-SEVEN

Trigger Point

Waiting Game

The sack was full, and the only thing left was the file of plots. Hoffman shoved it in and packed it down with the rest of the crumpled maps, tracings, and schedules. He rolled the waterproof bag closed and tucked it under his arm as he reached up on the top shelf of the étagère by the door, probing around until he bumped metal. Careful to rest his finger on the outside of the trigger guard, he slipped the pistol into his coat pocket.

One more pan of the living area and a check of his mental inventory told him he had everything. Hoffman opened the door.

"Jeanine!"

She stood on the landing with her hands behind her back, swaying back and forth with a pouty grin.

"Not tonight, baby," Hoffman said, turning the lock on the inside knob and shutting the door behind him. "I have to tally the receipts from tonight."

Jeanine slithered close to Hoffman, ran her arms up his chest, and rested them on his shoulders. She lifted onto her toes and kissed his lips. "Can't all that wait 'til tomorrow?"

"You know better than that," he said, removing one of her arms from his shoulder. "Besides, I have an early call tomorrow." She dropped her head and pouted more. With his hand under her chin, Hoffman raised her head and kissed her. "I'll swing by tomorrow evening and pick you up—maybe head down to a casino in Kemah."

Jeanine's eyes lit up and she threw her arms around Hoffman, squeezing him tight.

"But you have to let me get my work done tonight!"

"Okay," she said.

They walked down the steps to the alley behind the Grille. Hoffman asked if she had cab fare, and Jeanine said she'd catch a ride with Herman.

"Do me a favor," Hoffman said as he opened the kitchen doors. "Ask Richard to meet me down in the casino on your way out."

"Who?" Jeanine asked.

"The new guy—the wine steward."

Jeanine nodded.

Hoffman made up an excuse that he forgot something upstairs. He gave Jeanine another peck on the cheek and said he'd see her tomorrow. She went inside and let the door shut behind her.

He listened at the door for a moment to make sure Jeanine wouldn't pop her head back out. Looking around the alley pavement, he found just what he needed. Over by the incinerator were a few loose bricks and mortar. He unrolled the sack and loaded in the loose brick and mortar scraps to add extra weight. The radio parts and chassis would probably have done it, but it never hurt to be sure.

Hoffman rolled it back closed and sealed it. Temporarily hiding the parcel on the dark side of the incinerator, he angled the dial of his watch toward the light over the back door so he could check the time. Schneider ought to have word by now, he thought.

His long stride made short order of the distance down the back alley behind the building next door. Schneider was smoking a cigarette in the shadows—the amber glow from a drag lit his face. Hoffman curled his tongue against his teeth and made a short whistle sound to catch Schneider's attention.

"Anything," Hoffman asked.

Schneider shook his head. "Any time now," he said, holding the cherry of his cigarette over the face of his watch.

"You heave everything from the incinerator into the bayou if your man has bad news," Hoffman said, pointing a thumb over his shoulder.

"The plots for the second target?"

Hoffman reached into his coat and gave them to Schneider. They nodded to one another as Hoffman backed up and turned. Passing the back doors to the kitchen, he picked up the bag next to the incinerator and stopped to look around—no sign of anyone. Hoffman walked past his car to the set of concrete stairs bisecting the retaining bulkhead. They led down to an isolated pad sunken into the bayou bank and right outside a door leading from the casino. Hoffman kept the pad as a spot for gamblers needing fresh air, though during prohibition it was for bootleggers smuggling booze when the casino was a speak-easy. They would bring it up the bayou on rafts in the middle of the night and offload cases of liquor onto the pad.

One more look around ensured the coast was clear. Hoffman squatted down and unraveled a thin rope, tying one end to the parcel. He flung the bundle into the dark water, keeping his grip on one end of the line. The ker-plunk and splash seemed louder than they were, so Hoffman checked his surroundings. Still alone. He noted the stump closest to the drop spot and tied off the rope to it. Again, he scanned the area.

Hoffman unlocked the door that led straight into the gaming area. He went in and walked over by the blackjack table next to the door leading in from the nightclub. Leaning against the wall on the hinge-side of the door, Hoffman drew a deep breath and waited.

The Lure

"Can I give you a lift?" Herman asked as they walked through to the kitchen from the dining room.

"Yeah," Richard said, holding one of the swing doors for Herman. "If it's not out of your way."

"Missus Corte lives off Montrose and...?"

"A couple of blocks south of Gray."

"My wife and me rent an apartment near there—it's no problem at all."

"Do I have time to change into my regular clothes?" Richard asked

Herman nodded and said he'd pull up to the front.

In Kurt's office, next to the kitchen, Richard lay the wine room key on the desk along with the few dollars he had left. As he shut the door, he stared at the money. He was glad he didn't have to cover a cab ride to Reina's but figured he should probably slip Herman a buck.

Richard chuckled. He'd overheard enough in the dining room to realize a dollar was worth about four gallons of black-market gasoline. Legit, it ran

19 cents a gallon.

His street clothes were on a hanger hooked over a nail in the door. He began to change clothes but stopped to let out an animated and protracted yawn. The suspenders still hurt a bit, so it was a relief when he slipped those off. And Richard didn't bother unbuttoning the shirt. He pulled it over his head and tossed it over the chair on top of the bow tie and dinner jacket.

Heel to toe, he kicked off his shoes and slid off his pants. He matched up the leg cuffs and neatly folded the trousers before he draped them over the chair with the other garments.

The door opened as someone knocked. Richard cupped his hands over his privates and froze.

It was the cigarette girl. Richard couldn't remember her name, not that he cared at the moment. She didn't turn away. Nor did she gasp or scream—nothing Richard expected. She stood two paces away with her hand still on the doorknob.

"Do you mind?" Richard blushed.

The woman wasn't embarrassed, but she slowly turned her eyes away as she spoke. "Kur – uh – Mister Hoffman needs your help in the casino," she said, glancing back sideways.

"Thanks," he said. She didn't move. "Thanks!"

She said good night with a coquettish grin and started to close the door.

"Oh, hey," Richard said as he sidestepped behind the backrest of Kurt's desk chair. "Is Herman still out there?"

The cigarette girl shook her head and said he went to get his car. "I'll see him in a minute, though—he's giving me a lift home."

"Can you tell him I'm gonna be delayed so I'll catch a cab?"

She nodded again and closed the door behind her.

Richard rolled his eyes and sighed. He decided that first thing on Monday he'd go to Sears to buy underwear. Quickly he got back into his clothes. He slipped the canvas cover back over the server's outfit and returned them, hanger and all, to the nail on the back of the office door. Halfway out the door, he remembered the wine room key and his cash.

Most of the lights were turned out, but enough were on to see where he was going. Richard pushed through the swinging doors from the kitchen to the dining area. All the tables were neatly and perfectly set. It was strangely quiet, no dishes rattling or mutters from a dining crowd. Richard paused by the windows, struck by the foreboding darkness hanging over the bayou.

It wasn't his restaurant, but he felt the need to make sure everything was in order before heading downstairs.

A single wall sconce lit the stairwell. He went down and shot out into the club. It was a sharp left and past the restrooms to the secret door. That made Richard laugh inside. *A secret door that everybody knows about.*

He grabbed the oversized knob and pushed through. In that instant, nausea compounded the fact that his heart stopped as cold metal pressed against his right temple, and he heard the unmistakable click of a hammer being cocked.

Sucker punch

"Close the door," Hoffman said as he moved in front of Warren, keeping the barrel trained less than an inch from the bridge of the man's nose.

Slowly, Warren backed up to shut the door. As slowly, he raised his hands shoulder-high while keeping a cross-eyed focus on the end of the barrel.

"Does this satisfy your curiosity?"

Warren grimaced, and then his eyes grew wide again as he darted them from the gun to Hoffman's eyes.

Hoffman nodded. "Maceo is a sneaky bastard, isn't he?"

Warren clenched his eyes shut and shook his head.

"Who are you working for?" Hoffman ground the barrel into the skin of Warren's forehead.

"I'm your wine steward."

Hoffman pulled the gun away then snapped his arm back, smacking the revolving chamber against Warren's skull above the right eyebrow. Warren dropped to his knees with a grunt. Hoffman aimed at his head again. "Who?"

Warren was on the floor, leaning against the wall and pressing his palm against the bloody wound. He held out his other hand for Hoffman to stop. It didn't work. Hoffman cocked back his leg and slammed his foot into Warren's ribs as he repeated the question.

"Okay!" Warren strained when he spoke. "Okay."

Hoffman knelt beside Warren and grabbed the hair on the back of his head, shoving the gun back into his face.

"You're right, you're right," Warren said, coughing and trying to catch his breath. "I'm curious—I can't figure out why a guy like you'd be involved with Parisi."

"Not good enough," Hoffman said, yanking Warren to his feet by his hair. He slammed Warren in the gut before grabbing him by the neck and shoving his face down against a gaming table near the exit out to the bayou.

Hunched over the edge of the table, Warren grunted and coughed as he struggled to breathe. He winced and nodded at the same time. Hoffman released his hold. Warren slid down and sat against the front panel of the table. He held himself by the ribs and looked over at the exit.

"You might as well tell me," Hoffman said. *Make it easy on yourself.*

"Would anything I say make the slightest difference—to either of us?" Warren opened his eyes and looked straight at Hoffman. "Just get it over with and pull the fucking trigger."

Hoffman studied Warren's face. The man's expression turned to what Hoffman thought was disdain, as if Warren could see into his soul and revealed disgust.

Hoffman straightened his arm and drew a bead between Warren's eyes. There was fear in them but also a strange acceptance. So be it, Hoffman thought.

Prowling

Jack cut the engine and sighed. He sat up, looking up and down the block. Downtown was deserted. He exhaled a deep breath, trying to settle his racing heart.

He thought he probably should have said something, at least to Barbara, if not Captain Preskin. The odds of the Cord sighted at the pier being Kurt's were, in Jack's mind, pretty high because there weren't many Cord's running around Houston. He stared at the building. Would a successful person risk everything to side with the enemy? Why? Yeah, his name is German, Jack thought, but Hoffman doesn't seem like a bad guy, like a Nazi. He wondered how Dorothy would marry a man like that.

Making that kind of accusation needed weight behind it. Mere suspicion as a spy would buy Kurt a one-way ticket to internment at the Crystal City camp down near the Tex-Mex border. Innocent or not, he'd lose his business, property—everything but some personal effects and what belongings he could carry.

Jack opened the car door and paused before setting foot on the concrete. He leaned back in the car seat and shut the door, asking himself what he thought he was doing. Chewing on his bottom lip, he stared at the restaurant entrance, then up at the windows on the second floor. The drapes were drawn, and the apartment was dark.

He glanced down to the west corner of the building and over to the eastern one. Jack hoped Richard would pop out so he could give him a ride home and get out of there. But it was long enough after closing that he figured Richard found another ride. It didn't matter, that's not why Jack was there. He got out and quietly shut the car door. He crossed Franklin to the front entrance of the Grille. It was locked.

The bayou bank sloped up to the west side of the building, so Jack turned and walked to the other end to peek around the corner. Empty. He checked back over his shoulder and again up the block. Stepping sideways, foot over foot, Jack snuck his way up the alley.

He stopped at the back corner and slid his hands in his pockets as he looked across the bayou, trying to act nonchalant. It was dark, and he couldn't see anything or anyone. The light behind the restaurant was dim but it was obvious no one was around. He checked east up a dark alley behind the building next door. Again, no sign of anyone. After another glance over his shoulder, he was finally sure he was alone.

His hands trembled as he lit a cigarette and drew in a deep puff. It helped calm his nerves. Barely in the glow of the backdoor light was the front-end of a Cord parked under a wood cover. It was maroon, and he particularly recognized the front right fender.

Something crunched under the first step he took toward the car. Jack lifted his foot off the thin piece of wood. There were stacks of crates against the wall and an odor of dead fish. After all, it is a restaurant, he thought, and restaurants do serve fish.

Jack inspected the car as he circled it, occasionally looking up and around. He didn't know what he'd expect to find, even if he had some idea of what to look for. The car was immaculate. He leaned in and peered through the front passenger window. There was no clutter; nothing left on the seats or the floorboards. Not even a piece of crumpled paper on the dashboard. "Orderly son of a gun," Jack said quietly.

The sound of a phone ringing startled him, and Jack flattened himself against the wall. He only heard it once. There was still no sign of anyone. He decided he was hearing things and headed for the back doors.

Jack stopped as he passed an old incinerator. Nearly finished with his smoke, he dropped the butt through a rusted hole in the metal casing and went on.

One door was unlocked so he stepped inside. The kitchen was vacant—nothing on the burners, the tables were wiped down, no food left out. Almost aloud, Jack asked himself what he was doing, again.

To his left on one side of the kitchen was a wood panel door partly open. He stepped to one side to peek through the opening. It was empty, but he took a few steps closer anyway. The door creaked as he pulled on it. Inside was a small office with barely enough room for the roll-top desk. It was full of cluttered shelves and things hung from nails in the wall.

Jack looked over his shoulder back into the main part of the kitchen. It was eerily quiet, unsettling. Each step toward the swinging doors was a soft one. He peered through the porthole glass of one of the doors into the dining room. His heart was beating fast again, and he had a slight urge to urinate.

Feeling exposed and vulnerable, he picked up a rolling pin off the prep table next to the door. He stared at it and put it back. The iron skillet on the wall was good and heavy. He held it in his hand and gave it a half practice swing. *This'll do some damage.* He slumped his shoulders and hung it back. He wanted something more threatening and manlier.

Jack grinned when he slid a meat cleaver from its wooden block. He nodded, thinking cutlery felt better in his hand—and it might be more terrifying; at least he hoped it would, but to whom he asked himself. Jack wasn't sure what he was expecting to happen. With another look into the dining room, he used his hip to ease open the door.

Skullduggery

Schneider crouched down and kept his hand in the pocket with his pistol, observing the man in khaki uniform lurk about the back of the restaurant. It was too far and too dark to determine what branch of the service he was.

The man lingered by Hoffman's car, walking around it and looking in one of the windows. The phone ringing startled Schneider. He lunged up and pulled the receiver from the hook. "One moment," he said quietly with his hand cupping his mouth and the mouthpiece.

The man in uniform had disappeared. Schneider grinned when a wash of light came from the kitchen door opening.

"Go ahead."

"Motorboat patrols are crisscrossing in front of the tank farm at regular intervals," Neubauer said.

"Sentries?" asked Schneider.

"And foot patrols along the bank of the waterway."

Schneider didn't respond. He stared down the alley as he clenched his jaw. He no longer needed to hear from the Gestapo. It was clear that Hoffman must have alerted the Americans.

"Sir?"

"Leave immediately."

"We can pick you up within the hour—"

"Nein," Schneider said, breaking his own rule of English only. "Take one of the coastal routes south to Mexico."

"Herr Sturmbannfürer—"

"Follow my orders, Corporal. We'll meet again when possible." Schneider hung up the receiver and checked over his shoulder. He stayed close to the wall, being cautious not to bump into someone who might be around the corner. He crossed over to the incinerator and opened the doors carefully, trying to minimize the noise they made.

Schneider pulled the bundle from his pocket and set it atop the cinder box next to his pistol. Next was the detonator.

Leap from the Frying Pan

The pain in Richard's chest went from sharp to dull. And his head was still throbbing, though he didn't expect it to last much longer. Three times he had tempted fate. The first time was with Schneider, the second was with Parisi, and now with Kurt. *Third time's a charm.* He repeated it in his mind as he stared down the gun barrel pointed at him.

How weird to be killed by one of the few people he ever really trusted. Although it occurred to Richard that, like his father's past, Kurt's was a mystery. In some ways, he found his dad to be exactly what he expected—almost to the T who Kurt described. But this Kurt Hoffman was a real surprise.

Feeling dizzy, Richard took a deep breath, but stabbing pain returned to his ribs and he held his chest with one arm. He looked down for a second and tried to catch his breath, and he decided there was no point in seeing the barrel flash. But dangling from his pocket was the wine room key. As scared as he was, all he could do was start chuckling. Kurt again demanded an answer. Richard didn't give one. Nothing he said would likely save him. So he decided to lock eyes with his would-be killer. It was a pointless, meaningless gesture of defiance, except it made Richard feel better doing it.

A saying popped into his head: The true test of character is when you're facing death. So Richard spat his contempt at Kurt by demanding he get it over with. As Kurt took close aim, Richard tossed the wine key to underscore his disgust. It landed an inch or two from Kurt's foot.

Kurt had a puzzled scowl, but his hand was steady as a rock.

Richard stared back, wondering why he wasn't dead yet. Kurt eased the hammer down as he dropped his gun hand to his side. *What just happened?*

Kurt shifted his weight mostly on one foot and continued his leer.

Richard didn't know what to say, nor was he sure it'd even be a good idea. He waited for Kurt to break the silence.

"Just what the hell are you?"

"Scared shitless!" is how Richard wanted to answer, but he didn't. He opened his mouth to talk but froze, simply having nothing to say.

"You're the most confounding son of a bitch I've ever come across." Kurt grimaced as he spoke. "You're not one of Hoover's FBI boys." He shook his head saying he didn't think Richard was Treasury or OSS either. "So I have to believe that maybe you're just stupid."

"I've heard that twice today," Richard said, starting to stand. "And right now I'd say that's the consensus in this room."

"Stay put!" Kurt raised the gun up and Richard complied.

Nothing, Richard thought, could be more awkward than this. He'd hoped Kurt would keep talking, talk himself out of shooting. Instead, Richard got a glare and sensed he didn't have a lot of time to waste.

"You know," Richard began as he repositioned himself to take the pressure off his ribs. "Schneider is the one you need to worry about, not me."

"What?" Kurt didn't lower the gun. He did relax his arm, but he kept the pistol pointed at Richard from waist level.

"He's tooling you," Richard said as he rubbed his ribs—the soreness fading to an ache. "You can't be blind to what he represents—he's a Nazi and you know what those people are."

"You're not helping your case," Kurt said.

"It's not my case I'm arguing."

Kurt squinted.

"Why does a man with your ability and who practically has this town on a string—why would you hook up with a bunch that'll toss you aside the minute they're done with you?"

Kurt snorted.

"You have to know that whatever you and Schneider are cooking up won't make a bit of difference, at least nothing significant."

Kurt half-grinned.

Richard was confused. "Look, you're the guy with the gun," he said. "This is the scene where you're supposed to divulge the insidious plot."

"Not in Charlie Chan movies," Kurt said as he leaned his shoulder against a wall. "Besides, you're doing pretty well."

"If I guess right do I get out of here lead-free?"

"Don't count on it," Kurt said.

Richard scoffed and said, "That puts us back to square one, so why bother?"

Kurt straightened up. He cocked the hammer of the gun as he took a step closer to Richard but froze. Kurt leaned on his back foot and glanced down. So did Richard. Under Kurt's foot was the wine room key. The two men stared at each other. Then Kurt said something in German.

Richard frowned, and held out his hands and shrugged.

"You have no idea what this is all about, do you?" Kurt sighed and answered his own question. "Of course you don't. You're just a goddamn smart-ass playing hero for a girl, pushing his luck to the edge." He eased the hammer back down as he shook his head.

Richard used the gaming table to pull himself up. He stood there looking at Kurt not knowing what to do next and waiting for something more.

"Get out," Kurt said, not looking at Richard.

Richard was shocked. All he could think to do was gesture toward the door with questioning eyes.

"Go! Don't wait for an explanation—I doubt it'd make any sense to you." Kurt chuckled and said, "I'm not sure it does to me either."

Richard started to turn but hesitated. "I guess some debts really are transferable."

"What?" Kurt asked, jerking his head up to look at Richard.

He hadn't realized he said it aloud. "Something someone once told me," Richard said.

Kurt's reaction was a curious one. The statement made a visible impact. He grunted, saying his uncle used to say the same thing.

Richard grinned at the irony.

"Last time—Go," Kurt said, adding, "Before I come to my senses."

Richard didn't hesitate this time. But he backed up to the door and turned when he felt the knob. He turned it but didn't pull, stopping with the snap of a mental light switch. It wasn't Schneider who was doing the tooling. Richard spun around to face Kurt. "You with OSS?" Richard asked.

Kurt scowled and pointed the gun at Richard, gesturing toward the door. Richard quickly shot out the door leading to the bayou and closed it. At the bottom of the concrete steps up the retaining wall, he momentarily leaned on his knees, not sure if he needed to throw up or catch his breath.

Never, ever, ask anybody anything again. The cut over his eye was stinging and still bleeding a bit. He wasn't sure what he was going to say to Reina, but he decided it obviously wouldn't be the truth. Besides, he had the sneaking suspicion she'd have different questions.

Richard exhaled a deep breath and went up the steps as he pulled a cigarette from his pack. When he struck a match, it startled someone by the incinerator.

Flash Blind

From the doorway at the base of the stairs down to the nightclub, the entire room was visible. It was empty and dim like the rest of the place—not a sign of anyone. Jack turned to head back upstairs and stopped when something sounded like a door opening and closing. Holding still, he listened for a second. To be safe, he stuck his head back into the club and panned the room—no one there.

Jack looked up at the ceiling as if he had x-ray vision through to the kitchen. He took a deep breath and jogged up the stairs, skipping every other step. Again, he carefully poked his head through the door. Not a soul was in the dining room, so he tightened his grip on the meat cleaver and moved toward the kitchen.

Walking through the swinging doors and seeing no one, Jack let out a breath and lowered the cleaver. He pivoted on one foot as he made a circle, double-checking the dining room and the kitchen. He laughed at himself for letting his imagination get the better of him.

Jack set the knife down and went out the door to the alley and heard a shout. He flinched against the door from two consecutive loud bangs and flashes like camera bulbs. After a few seconds, his eyes adjusted enough to see the back of a tall man in a dark suit holding a gun. And he recognized the man lying half in the weeds of the bayou bank—it was Richard Warren.

The man with the gun spun around, pointing it at Jack. In that instant, there were two more bangs and flashes, making Jack flinch again. When he opened his eyes, the man with the gun was down on the asphalt.

Another man came out from under the carport into the light. Kurt Hoffman kept his pistol trained on the gunman while slowly approaching Richard.

Jack rushed to the man Kurt shot. Something crunched under his foot when he stepped next to the corpse. He lifted his foot to find what appeared to be the crystal for a timer. Jack leaned down and snatched the dead man's Luger, nudging the body to be sure he was dead.

"Jack," Kurt said softly.

He bolted over to Kurt and Richard. Kurt set his American revolver on the ground as he propped up Richard Warren. Jack and Kurt locked eyes for a second—understanding there were going to be a lot of questions. Kurt looked away first, down at Richard. Jack did as well.

Richard had two rounds in the left side of his chest. The only thing Jack could do was to make him comfortable. As Jack positioned his arm under Richard's head, he told Kurt to roll his jacket into a pillow.

"I gotchya Rick," Jack said gently with a soft smile. "Stay with me."

Richard blinked once, slowly as if he were fighting off exhaustion. He looked up into Jack's eyes and slightly turned up one corner of his mouth. Richard exhaled quietly without taking another breath.

TWENTY-EIGHT

Saturday, 17 April 1993

She sat quietly, staring at the headstone. Tree shadows danced over the worn headstone from a light breeze. Only one date was inscribed beneath the name, August 1, 1942. That had been the end, at least for him. But what wrenched her heart more was that the beginning was yet to come.

In her hands were folded, faded sheets of paper. She squeezed them tighter, which added new wrinkles as she watched a young man, with light hair and a mustache, standing over a nearby grave.

Another man, about the same size and stature, came up to him from behind. They spoke but were too far away for her to hear. They stepped away from the fresh grave and lit cigarettes. Their mannerisms and strides were very similar. She smelled the wafts of their tobacco smoke and heard faint laughter. The youngest man, the one with a mustache, jerked his head up and looked at her. It was paralyzing. She wanted so much to say something, but she understood how it would sound, that he'd react in the same way she herself once had.

And, too, telling him would simply be the first domino. There were others equally deserving of explanations, the result of which would only reopen long-since-healed wounds. She would have to wait. Soon, perhaps in an hour or a day, his nightmare would begin. Gentle tears came with her deep breath as the two men climbed into a black limousine.

The car pulled away as a delicate hand touched her shoulder and a sweet little voice whispered, "Nonny?" She put her hand atop her granddaughter's. "Mommy and Aunt Olivia are wondering if you were ready," the little girl said.

"Yes, sweetie, almost," Reina said. She adored the youngest of her six grandchildren—and what a pistol. There was a lot of headstrong tomboy wrapped up in that little package. Reina brushed the brown hair from her face and blue eyes. "You remind me so much of your mother when she was your age."

The little girl wrinkled up her nose and rolled her eyes. That made Reina giggle. "I'll be right there," she said. The little girl got a familiar and impish grin as she turned and ran back to the car and jumped in. Reina turned and stared at the headstone for a moment. She slowly closed her eyes and pictured his mischievous smile, which made her smile.

TWENTY-NINE

Sunday, 18 April 1993

Secrets

The clock on the wall read nine-fifteen. She kept flipping through the magazine she found on the coffee table, but she paid no attention to any of the pages. A silver Mercedes sedan stopped in front of the outer glass doors. A tall man with gray hair climbed out holding a Styrofoam cup. He entered his code and walked into the foyer, heading straight for the elevators but was stopped by the concierge at the front desk.

The years hadn't changed him much, she thought, except for a few pounds and thinning gray hair. She certainly had. Time never seemed a gentle companion for women.

The man turned and stared at her, squinting. She waited.

"Reina?"

"Mister Hoffman."

"Christ Almighty, I never could get you to call me Kurt," he said. He set his coffee on the reception counter and took her hand in both of his, helping her off the soft, plush sofa. "What brings..." He stopped and straightened up. Right then it was obvious he understood why she was there.

He led her into the elevator and pressed the button for the top floor. Hoffman broke the uncomfortable silence when he asked, "How are you?"

"Well."

"You still have that house in Montrose?" he asked.

"Yes," Reina said smiling. "But I rent it out. I live with one of my girls and her family now."

Hoffman nodded.

"They've given me six grandchildren," she said, smiling bigger as she pulled pictures from her purse and handed them to Hoffman. "Four boys and two girls."

"Fine-looking family," Hoffman said, glancing at the photos before returning them.

The bell sounded their arrival on the top floor and the doors slid open. Reina stepped out first, and Hoffman showed her down the hall to his apartment. Reina didn't ask about his family. It was no secret he had none. His exploits were well published in the society pages, especially his divorce from Mrs. Hoffman.

Hoffman carefully bent down to pick up the morning paper at his doorstep, moving like a tired old grizzly bear. He squinted to find the right key to unlock the door.

Reina walked into the large penthouse and complimented her host on such a lovely place, although she thought it cold and hollow like a museum. Most of the photographs were posed and stiff. She recognized many of the celebrities as well as local and national notables. But none were candid moments captured with family or friends, except one. It was of Jack and Richard laughing together, which made her smile.

"How about some coffee?" Hoffman asked.

"I'm fine, thank you."

"I'm afraid I need a jolt," he said as he rounded the pass-through bar into the kitchen. She followed him and set her purse on the countertop. She giggled when he plugged in an old Corning Ware percolator. "What?" Hoffman asked.

"I haven't seen one of those in years," Reina said.

"I don't know," he said as he got a cup from the cupboard. "The flavor from drip coffee makers has a flat taste." Hoffman doctored the cup with a pinch of sugar and a few drops of cream.

"The price of progress."

Hoffman grunted.

Both stared at the percolator, and it gurgled loudly. Each began to say something and stopped. They both smiled and Hoffman motioned for Reina to go ahead.

"I'm sorry about Jack Warren," she said.

Hoffman nodded and he said, "But you're not here because of Jack." He unfolded the newspaper and plopped it on the bar counter.

Below the fold on the front page of the Chronicle was a panoramic photograph of the central post office with the parking lot in the foreground. It showed the emergency vehicles and all the activity around the site. On one side of the panorama was a headline reading, TERRORIST BOMBING RULED OUT; on the other side there was another, TRAGEDY STRIKES TWICE. Off the lower right-hand corner of the image was an inset photo of Richard Warren. Reina touched the photo above his lips—she remembered the stubble remnants of his singed mustache. She thought about the morning that she had tended his wounds, as he lay unconscious.

A bent and faded photograph suddenly dropped onto the newspaper. It took a moment for the memory of that night to form and flood back into her mind. The image only showed a partial profile of a man, but Reina had no doubts it was Richard.

She felt Hoffman's stare.

"Why dance around it?" Hoffman asked, looking her square in the eye. "Obviously you suspect it. Maybe we both even believe it. And we could go round and round in circles wondering how, and if and when any one of us should have ever figured it out."

"I gave up on those questions a long time ago," Reina said, holding the photograph in her hands.

"I didn't know I should have questions until today," Hoffman said with a scowl. "And, frankly, I still can't believe what we're thinking. Nothing in my experience tells me this is possible."

"How can you say that when you have this?" Reina asked, holding the picture.

"A barely discernible picture of a man we hardly knew for a few days fifty years ago."

"Then tell me, where is Jack's son?"

Hoffman shook his head.

"They're going to have a lot of questions, too," Reina said, tapping on the headline referring to the Warren family. "I'm wondering if we shouldn't give them some answers."

"With what?" Hoffman had a wide-eyed expression. "We show them that picture and tell a cockamamie story," he said with a grimace.

"No." From her purse, Reina pulled a letter that she had saved for half a century. "We let him tell it."

Hoffman took it and unfolded the creased pages of faded handwriting. He opened a nearby drawer and found a pair of drugstore readers. Hoffman was visibly shaken as he read.

The words echoed in her memory from a dozen times of reading it and rereading it. She recited them in her mind and mimicked Richard's inflection. Only once did she look up at Hoffman's eyes to see the emotion welling up in them. When he finished, he leaned on the counter, fighting it back, at the same time shaking his head.

Reina wanted to reach out and touch his hand, but she was too tiny and too old to stretch over the bar. She walked around the counter and put her hand on his arm. He pulled away.

"It'd be better if you just burned those pages," Hoffman said as he handed the letter back.

"I don't..."

"No sane person in the world will believe it, Reina," Hoffman said, not looking at her. "Besides, even if they did, how in God's name would you answer all the questions they'd ask—and I'm guessing you might not want to." He shook his head. "I know I don't."

"I never suggested we go public with this," Reina said, plopping her hand down on the counter. "But I can't understand your reaction—if nothing else it might ease their pain."

"Christ, Reina—*he died!*"

"Yes, he did," she said, gritting her teeth. All too clear in her memory was the Sunday morning when Jack Warren appeared at her doorstep with another official. And she remembered collapsing from the news. As hard as it was to lose Vincent, there had been time to prepare. But Richard was a devastating blow.

"The authorities obscured everything about how Richard was killed. It took days to find out even the smallest details during the torrent of interviews by federal agents about who he was, where he came from—questions I could never answer. They wouldn't even let me discuss it with you or Jack," Reina said, folding her arms and stepping off to face away from Hoffman. "I was forced to accept only that he was gunned down by a man whose name I'd never know or why." Reina turned. "But I do know that it mattered because his death prevented Jack's. And I want to believe Richard understood that before he died."

Hoffman remained quiet as he stared at his feet. She moved within half a step of him and got in his face as best she could. "You were there and you saw," she began. "You have to realize what meaning that had." Again, she put her hand gently on his arm. "You owe it to them—and him."

Hoffman scoffed as he pushed away from the counter. "I owed Jack, I owed *him*, I owe them." Hoffman laughed. "And now you as well." He put his hands over his face. "Jesus, my entire life is a debtor's prison."

"This isn't about me," Reina said, looking at Hoffman. "This is abou—"

"You have no idea what this is about, Reina," Hoffman said, rubbing his face, and then looking at her with a smile betrayed only by disgust in his eyes.

Reina stayed silent. She couldn't understand his self-loathing tone. Something was missing.

"The little bastard would appreciate this moment," Hoffman said, leaning against the counter and nodding his head with a painful smile. Reina started to say something, but Hoffman stopped her. The coffee was ready, and he poured it for himself and one for Reina. She declined.

Hoffman took a deep breath as he handed her the cup. "This is gonna take a while."

A Patriot's Game

Hoffman led Reina over to the kitchen table and held out a chair. He watched her set the cup down first, and with both hands on the table, ease down onto the seat.

"You couldn't have known this," Hoffman began as he sat slowly down. "Rick was a war movie buff, and he especially liked spy plots and intrigue." Hoffman took a sip of his coffee. He got a prideful smile on his face. "Even if he'd seen one a hundred times, he was always able to pick out some new detail."

"Kurt," Reina said as she rested her elbows on the table and leaned toward him. "What does this have to do with anything?"

"Full disclosure," Hoffman said, her sudden familiarity not lost on him. "And settlement of a debt long since incurred."

Reina appeared confused.

"From where you sat, I think I can understand why you thought Richard was the reason for the hush." Hoffman shook his head with a half grin. "What you are right about, though, is how much his death mattered," he said, pausing and looking at his cup. "But not just to Jack."

"Then who…"

"Sturmbannfürer Schneider of the SS," Hoffman said, adding, "The name of the man who shot Richard."

Reina got a wide-eyed expression and leaned back.

"I never knew for sure, but I think his full name was Otto Schneider," Hoffman said, looking up from his cup. "He was the last of about a dozen Nazis I smuggled into the country up and down the Gulf." Hoffman chuckled. "I spent days in a small room reaffirming that he was a cousin from out of state." Hoffman stopped a moment and sipped his coffee. "It was an easy-enough cover with my aunt and uncle gone, and for obvious reasons, no way to verify with distant relatives back in Munich."

Reina sat speechless and agape.

"Still confused?" Hoffman asked with a smirk. She nodded as he expected. "The story worked well enough since Schneider couldn't dispute it, not that he would have."

"But, you sh…" Reina stuttered. She was wincing with disgust. "You were a Nazi?" She asked with a whisper even though they were alone. "My God."

"Not exactly and not quite that simple. You see, my uncle was one of the first members of the Nazi party before Hitler went to prison for treason in 1923. But by the time of the party's rebirth and rise to power ten years later, my uncle had had a change of heart."

Reina was still shocked.

"Age and experience tempered his rage of youth," Hoffman said as he smiled. "That and the fact my aunt was a very gentle and tolerant woman. They also saw what Germany was turning into, so when my father died, caring for an orphaned nephew in America became the perfect opportunity to escape what was coming."

Hoffman reminded Reina that her coffee was getting cold. He went on. "Part two begins in 1939 with Whitaker Chambers."

"Who?"

Hoffman raised a brow and smiled at his coffee. "The Paul Revere of our times," he said. After a quick sip of coffee, Hoffman explained. "Chambers was a dedicated communist until 1938. For various reasons he did a turnabout and, when Hitler and Stalin entered into a non-aggression pact, he saw it as a paramount of evil looming against the United States.

"Now, this is on the heels of a good many people appalled by Roosevelt's pandering to Stalin and official recognition of the Soviet Union. FDR wholly dismissed factual indictments about Stalin's flagrant inhumanity," Hoffman said. He added that Roosevelt's additional sin was the horrifying inroads to creating a state-managed economy. "What broke the camel's back," Hoffman said, "was when then-Assistant Secretary of State Adolf Berle brought Chamber's credible allegations that two dozen Soviet spies and agents operated within Roosevelt's administration. At the top of the list was Alger Hiss."

Reina said nothing. So Hoffman leaned in as he spoke. "The elitist bastard literally told Berle to go fuck himself."

Reina grimaced at Hoffman's language, as he expected.

"To spite Berle for his accusations, FDR promoted Alger Hiss and he was made a top aide to Roosevelt—a position that impacted American foreign policy through the Truman administration."

Hoffman leaned back in his chair and folded his arms. This was a lot of background to throw at Reina. It might have been age, Hoffman thought, but more likely, her eyes were glazing over from confusion.

"So you became a Nazi to stop the communist threat?" Reina asked.

"You're half right," Hoffman said, looking sideways and down at the floor. "FDR's refusal even to consider the allegations raised more than a little ire and frustration within the less-transient ranks of the government and military. But it percolated for, what, the next year, year and a half."

Reina rubbed her forehead and then under her eyes.

"I told you this would take a while," Hoffman said with a grin. He went over to the counter and brought over the coffee pot. He warmed up their cups as he spoke.

"Nobody was particularly tickled with Hitler, but most figured he was Europe's problem," Hoffman said as he sat back down. "So when he turned on Stalin and invaded Russia—well, it was only a couple of bullies duking it out.

"For a few in Washington concerned with Soviet aggression, however, it was the icing on the cake. Given Hitler's march across Western Europe, it was assumed the invasion would be a painful setback for Stalinist Russia."

"And then Pearl Harbor," Reina said.

"That blew the lid off," Hoffman said, nodding. He said he remembered hearing something about Hitler being furious with Hirohito because he felt the timing was bad. "Neither here nor there, but we wound up being pulled into war with both feet."

Reina said none of Hoffman's story explained why Richard was killed. She was looking at her cup and had both hands wrapped around it. "And what you tell me next may be the only thing that keeps me from throwing this in your face."

Hoffman wanted to chuckle but didn't. Reina had mellowed. Fifty years ago, he would have expected that cup to already be in his lap.

"Fair enough," Hoffman said, sipping more coffee before continuing. "So let me bring it all together with one of the big news items of 1942. Do you remember hearing about eight Nazis caught on the East Coast?"

Reina nodded.

"Early on, the Nazi spy service tried recruiting German immigrants in the US. My uncle had been contacted as far back as thirty-five or thirty-six," Hoffman said. He stared at his coffee. "He declined, of course, but after he died I was approached."

Reina glared.

"I reported every contact to the FBI."

Reina got wide-eyed and her mouth dropped open. Then she set an elbow on the table and rested her chin and jaw in her palm.

"Still with me?"

"No."

Hoffman let himself chuckle and asked Reina to be patient a little longer. "Remember those less-transient government officials irritated with FDR?"

Reina nodded.

"I won't name names, but you'd recognize one or two. Anyway, they hatched an unofficial scheme of which I was asked to be a part. And one reason they asked was because I reported the recruiters, and another was that I've never hidden my feelings about communists, which aligned with their politics. The goal was twofold. Their first idea was for me to infiltrate and expose the spy network. The other goal was to help stall America's jump into the European Theater."

"Why?"

"Strategy at the time depended on establishing a course of victory in the Pacific. The Coral Sea and Midway meant we were well on our way, but neither amounted to a guarantee. At the same time, Germany was slugging it out with the Soviets deep in Russia, which is what certain interests wanted. Even in '42, it was obvious to some that we'd lock horns with Stalin. And what better way to weaken him than by letting Hitler do it for us.

"Allowing the Nazis a minor covert espionage victory here and there, though nothing too significant, meant we could penetrate their network while providing needed focus in the Pacific, as well as let Hitler and Stalin divide themselves so we could roll in and conquer." Hoffman nearly exhausted all his breath and had to inhale deeply to go on.

"Wait," Reina said with a scowl. "If you were working for the government, then why interrogate you after the shooting? And how does Richard figure into this with that man?"

"My operation was unofficial—remember? It was separate and distinct from anything that could get back to the White House or anyone considered sympathetic." Hoffman shrugged and added, "I had carte blanche—license to do anything and everything necessary to preserve the integrity of the operation and its goals. . ."

"But?"

Hoffman snorted and said, "The price was high. Aside from occasional status reports, no other contact was accepted. I'd receive no support, and if discovered, no acknowledgment or endorsement. As a result, I'd be subject to whatever the consequences were from the actions I took, regardless of circumstance."

Reina started to say something but Hoffman stopped her. "This is where Richard and Jack come in." He could almost hear the "finally" she must have been thinking.

"Rick set the whole thing in motion when he met Schneider in the wine room. When was it?" Hoffman stopped to remember. He snapped his fingers. "It was that morning—Saturday." He shook his head and told Reina about Schneider's account of the conversation. "He must have instantly figured out what Schneider was," he said, adding, "I'm not sure what it was that tipped him off, but I know at one point he said something to purposely let Schneider know—to bait Schneider."

Reina was tearing up. "That sounds exactly like something Richard would do."

Hoffman used his thumbnail to pick away at flecks of glaze on the coffee cup. "He popped in out of nowhere and pried into my affairs," Hoffman said. "I didn't know what or who he was, but he was a threat, or at least I thought he was."

Hoffman kept picking at the cup. "It was my job," he began. But the next sentence caught in his throat. "It was my job to—eliminate that threat." He took a deep breath before looking at Reina. When he did her tearing eyes turned to horror and he had to glance away.

She sniffed and said with an indignant tone, "You've gone this far, so you might as well give me the rest."

His mouth was dry. He sipped his coffee and licked his lips. It didn't help. "As long as I've kept that night buried, I'm surprised I remember so clearly," he said, still not looking at Reina. "And he faced me down rather well considering..." Hoffman decided not to go into too much detail about what happened in the casino.

"Considering what?"

"Considering I held a gun to his forehead," Hoffman admitted as he took a deep breath.

"But you didn't shoot," Reina said.

"Nope," Hoffman shook his head. "I was ready to. I think I even began to squeeze the trigger," he said. Hoffman's face went blank as he picked more glaze off the cup.

"Why—why didn't you pull the trigger?"

"In that moment, he demonstrated—honor," Hoffman said. "It was an incredibly small thing, but its meaning was enormous." He sat silent, again remembering the conversation in his office between him and Richard. "And, earlier, we had talked about ethics, which you would think was irrelevant to the situation."

Hoffman snorted and shook his head. Only then could he look Reina in the eyes. "I realized the end, however just I thought the cause, could not excuse my means," he said. Hoffman pursed his lips and shut his eyes hard before going on. "He walked out thinking I was working with the OSS," he said as he sipped the last of his coffee. "Another few minutes and he'd probably have begun to—"

"Why did Schneider..." Reina choked up for a moment. "Why did he do it?"

"Rick stumbled onto Schneider planting a bomb at the restaurant. My guess is Schneider began to suspect me as well. All I knew was that there were two shots moments after Richard walked out. When I ran out the back and up to the alley, the first thing I saw was Schneider drawing down on Jack—I didn't even see Richard until after I shot."

"You expect me to believe you had a sudden fit of conscience?" Reina asked sarcastically.

"You wanted to know what happened," he said. Hoffman got up and walked over to the counter with the percolator. "I can't be responsible for what you believe."

"You're responsible for the entire thing," Reina said.

Hoffman glanced her way, not looking her in the eye.

"Saving Jack was simply how you saved your own skin. Like *you* said, what better way than to have someone do your dirty work for you," she said. "Having

Jack testify on your behalf did that quite nicely, I imagine."

"It didn't hurt."

"How much of this did Jack know?" Reina asked.

"Nothing more than my story to the FBI. I guess he bought it, but I'll never know," Hoffman said. "We'd only spoken about that night three times over the years." He turned and leaned on the counter. "A few years later he told me about the OPC investigation that led him there that night." Hoffman closed his eyes. "God, what a waste. He was a man with so much potential."

"The wrong man drank himself to death."

"And the truth shall set you free," Hoffman said with a chuckle.

"What do you know about truth?" Reina asked. "I can't believe that you were doing all this just to be a patriot." Reina spoke with her hands as much as she did with her mouth. "You forget I remember those years. A lot of Germans and Italians found themselves at internment camps, too. The truth is that you were no better than Parisi; your only concern was legitimizing yourself—protecting yourself." She looked right at Hoffman, whispering. "And you let Jack go to his grave believing nothing but lies."

"And what truth will you take to your grave, Reina?"

"Go to hell!"

"That's a given," Hoffman said. He piddled with the spoon he used to stir his coffee. "Besides, I'm not looking for absolution."

"And I can't give it."

"Neither can they," Hoffman said as he reached for the newspaper and held up the front page. "None of this will do anything to ease their pain." He plopped the paper down and picked up the spoon again. He threw it in the sink and waited for the clattering to stop. "It'd only make things worse."

"Worse for whom?" Reina asked. "You're still worried about yourself, not Richard, not what this may have done to Jack." She grabbed her purse, peeked inside, then slid to the seat edge. "Did you ever ask yourself if any of this had to do with his drinking? Did you even care?"

"Th—"

Reina held up her hand as she cut off his answer. "I may be a liar as well," she said, getting up and hooking her purse on her arm. "But never to protect myself—and it never betrayed Richard or his legacy." She went over to the door and opened it. She turned to face Hoffman and said, "You can never say that—and you're left with a debt you can never repay Jack or Richard."

"Reina," Hoffman said. He walked to the door and handed her Richard's letter.

She glanced at it, then at Hoffman. "Keep it," she said, looking around the apartment. "It might be the only thing that has any meaning in such a plush cell."

She closed the door, leaving Hoffman staring at the letter in his hand. He turned and looked around the apartment. He felt a chill.

THIRTY

Monday, 19 April 1993

Hoffman poured another glass of wine and walked back to his desk. He picked up the stack of papers and packed them into a document box with the other files and maps. There was also a one-page letter he'd typed. Without bothering to proofread it, he attached the faded and wrinkled note Reina had left him with a paperclip. He slid them into a different envelope.

The phone rang and he answered it. The concierge said a messenger was on the way up. "Thanks, Paul," Hoffman said, and he hung up. He turned and went over to the coffee table and pressed the power button on the remote. The television clicked and came on.

Dave Ward was citing breaking news on the latest about the explosion at the downtown post office. Hoffman leaned down and switched to another channel where Ron Stone was giving his report. Another punch of the button and Steve Smith was doing the same. Hoffman thought all three news anchors were as old as him. He snorted. "If you only knew the rest of the story," he said, mimicking Paul Harvey's signature tagline.

Hoffman ran through the cable channels at Olympic speed. He had clicked three stations beyond something on one that caught his interest, so he clicked back.

Richard Burton was running from a bridge to an old bus while Mary Ure was blasting away at German troops on the opposite side. Clint Eastwood was setting charges under the bridge.

The doorbell rang. Hoffman pressed the mute button and answered the door.

The messenger boy followed Hoffman to his desk. The kid saw what was on the tube. "*Where Eagles Dare*—cool flick," he said.

"Yeah," Hoffman said as he read over the delivery tickets. The addresses were correct and he handed the tickets to the kid. He also made sure the seal on the document box was good and secure.

"Whoa!"

"Problem?" Hoffman asked.

"It'll be cool going to the Federal building," the messenger said, waving one of the tickets. "You want this one done first?"

Hoffman nodded and checked the time on his watch. He asked if the messenger could get it there before three o'clock.

"This close to downtown?" he said rhetorically with grin. "With fifteen minutes to spare."

"The small one goes to a house out in Briargrove Park right after," Hoffman said.

The kid nodded and laid the envelope atop the box. He hoisted it up and used his chin to secure the tickets as he headed for the door. Hoffman reached past the messenger and opened the door.

"Thanks for the business, Mister Hoffman," the messenger said as he walked out.

"No problem," Hoffman said, patting the kid on the back then closing the door.

He went back to the sofa and plopped down. He turned up the sound on the TV. Richard Burton was at the wheel of the bus. It had a snowplow mounted on the front, and Burton was breaking through a fence while Clint Eastwood blasted away at the German army guarding an airfield. Burton sideswiped a line of parked Stuka fighter aircraft that erupted into fireballs.

Hoffman shook his head and leaned up for his wine. Burton and Eastwood covered each other with machine-gun fire to make their way into the escape plane. The end was near.

Hoffman got up and went over to the built-in shelves to look at pictures. The dialog continued between Burton and the actor playing Colonel Turner, the treasonous bad guy waiting in the plane, but Hoffman only half listened.

He was touching Dorothy's picture. Then there was the picture of Richard and Jack together. Staring at Richard's face, he said, "Schneider pulled the trigger, but I sent you right to him."

Hoffman mockingly complimented himself on how adept he was at playing his roles, so much so he still couldn't resolve which Hoffman let Richard walk away. He wanted to believe it was an honest seeping of humanity. Hoffman thought it was his more likely his subconscious wanted Schneider to do his dirty work. Thinking back, Hoffman wasn't sure if he could actually have forgotten, even briefly, that Schneider was lurking in the alley.

He ran out after Richard before the first shot was fired. Even if it was for the right reason, he failed, then used the whole incident to cover his ass.

The dialog from the movie suddenly became more poignant for Hoffman. Burton had exposed Colonel Turner, who was trying to deny it, saying, "*You're finished Colonel.*" Hoffman wandered past the sofa toward the terrace as Turner spoke. "*A public trial would be embarrassing—even painful, not only for myself, but also for British intelligence.*"

The same thought crossed Hoffman's mind. Today's world couldn't understand his motives, his convictions, and most especially, his actions. Everything would be laid bare and anyone left that he associated with would scurry for cover.

As Hoffman slid the glass door open, Burton's character quipped, "*Perhaps. But not as painful as that long drop to the end of the rope.*" Nor as painful as the knee of the FBI on his chest, Hoffman thought.

By the next morning, he will have traded down for a smaller, more Spartan cell. The question was, for how long? Despite the evidence he was turning over to the FBI, he'd still get life. Even a minimum sentence meant he would probably die in prison, disgraced.

"*Do I have an alternative?*" Colonel Turner said on the television. Hoffman stepped out onto the terrace toward the railing. "*If you want it,*" Burton said to Turner. The wind on the penthouse terrace coincided with the sound effects from the movie, and the rushing of the wind signaled Turner having opened the plane's hatch. Hoffman felt another chill as he leaned over to view the trees and landscape 22 floors below. He sipped his wine and savored its flavor, its finish, and its smoothness. Staring at the glass of '61 Lafite, he smiled. Hoffman took a deep breath as he closed his eyes, holding the glass to his chest until he met the ground.

EPILOGUE

Monday, 9 October 1961

"Hey Dottie, this is Jack." He was leaning against the wall by the pay phone in the hospital lobby. "It's another boy," he said with a grin as he pulled his cigarettes from his pocket. "He's fine, but a tiny little thing. He'll be in an incubator for a few weeks, but they said I could hold him today for a few minutes."

Jack gave Dorothy all the details about weight and length and exactly what time he was born. "Oh yeah, she's doing great," he said. "Except, you know, she really wanted a girl." Dorothy made a joke about running out of boys' names and Jack chuckled. "Why do you think Maggie left his name up to me—she's run out of relatives."

Dorothy asked about the other boys and Jack said they were fine. "They're with Maggie's mom and dad," he said puffing his cigarette. He checked the clock on the wall above the reception station where several nuns were mulling about with files. "Yeah, they want to name him Davy Crockett Warren," he told Dorothy. One of the nuns looked up when he said that. Jack shrugged. He put his hand over the mouthpiece and said to the nun, "I know—too much television." The nun grinned and went back to her duties.

Jack checked the time again. "I only have few minutes, Dottie—is Kurt there?" he asked. She said to hang on. He took a drag and flicked ash in the ashtray within reach of the phone. A woman made a few announcements for doctors and wards over the intercom, so Jack strained to hear if Kurt was coming to the phone.

"Hey, Jack!"

"Hey, yeah. Dottie tell you?" Jack asked. He grinned as Kurt poked fun at him for having another boy and when they were going to try again for a girl. "No, no," Jack said. With Maggie's weak heart, the doctors were browbeating him about even having a third. "Even though she's fine, I think this is it," Jack said.

"Only if you stop using the rhythm method for birth control."

Jack laughed. "How do you think I got three kids!" He did a double take and the nuns at the counter were glaring. Jack grimaced and mouthed that he was sorry.

"Listen, Kurt," Jack started as faced away from the nurse's desk. "Maggie is leaving the baby's name up to me and I wanted to run something up the flagpole." Jack paused a minute. He and Kurt hadn't ever discussed the incident much—maybe twice that Jack could remember off the top of his head. And once was under official circumstances. "I'm gonna name him Richard," Jack said.

Kurt was silent on the other end.

Jack took a drag of his cigarette.

"It's your decision, Jack."

"I know but..." Jack thought a minute. There had been a conversation—one that stuck with Jack all the years since. It had helped Jack come to grips with his role in the Navy during the war and accept that his contribution had both meaning and value. And while he still had a tendency to do it, Jack at least resisted gauging himself against the people around him.

"You're not playing against the other guy, you're playing *against* yourself," Richard Warren once said. It was a piece of advice Jack always kept in mind when self-doubt reared its head. It didn't always work, but to Jack, it was more valuable than anything his father ever told him.

What also stayed with Jack was that Richard's very presence—though he was a man Jack hardly knew—equated to self-sacrifice. Richard's shout distracted Schneider, and his death gave time for Kurt, whom Jack also barely knew at the time, to intervene.

"Yeah, I do like the idea, Jack."

That made Jack grin. "Thanks, Kurt," Jack said as he leaned down to push his cigarette butt into the sand of the ashcan. "I'd like to think he'd approve, too." Jack told Kurt he needed to go and each said goodbye. Jack hung up the phone.

Down the hall and to the right were the elevators, but Jack decided to run up the stairwell. It was only three flights and a lot faster. He pushed open the door into the hall and went straight to the nurses' station. "Excuse me, Sister, have they brought the baby to Missus Warren's room?" he asked.

"A minute ago, Mister Warren," the nun said with a smile as she pointed at Maggie's room.

Jack bolted over to the door and knocked as he walked in. "Hey Darlin'," Jack said to Maggie. She was holding the baby in her arms. Jack figured the baby could fit in the palm of his hand without the swaddling blanket.

Jack leaned in and kissed Maggie's forehead. "I'm sorry it's a boy," he said.

"Oh, honey, no—I wouldn't trade our boys for anything," she said.

"Say that again when they're teenagers," Jack said as he winked.

Maggie giggled and smiled down at the baby. She was still a little pale. But the doctors had reassured Jack she'd be fine. He'd hired a nurse to help her once they'd get home with the baby. And the boys would be a big help, too, he thought.

"You ready?" Maggie asked as she lifted the bundled little boy.

Jack smiled and took him in his arms. He was so light—barely over five pounds.

"Just a few more minutes, Mister Warren," the nun said.

Jack nodded but kept his attention on the baby. Being six weeks premature, he would have to spend time in an incubator. That would be tough on Maggie, but at least he was healthy.

With his index finger, Jack pulled back the blanket from the baby's face. It was all red and wrinkly like the others had been. His bottom lip made it seem like he was pouting. Then a tiny little hand appeared. He hadn't quite figured out how to get that thumb into his mouth yet.

Jack softly rubbed the little hand with his finger. At that moment, the baby opened his eyes for the first time. Jack was just a blur to those little blue eyes. The newborn blinked slowly and Jack smiled, thinking birth was an exhausting process. The baby squinched up his face as if he was smiling.

Out of instinct, Jack cuddled the baby closer. He smiled down at the newborn boy and said, "I gotchya Rick—I gotchya." And Richard exhaled a tiny little breath as he drifted off to sleep in his father's arms.

Non-fiction titles also by David Falloure

Sheer Will: The Story of the Port of Houston and the Houston Ship Channel gives you the story behind the story, not just the facts but the flavor, characters, context, and global forces at work that would turn a tangled patch of sleepy bayou into one of the world's most powerful and strategically critical industrial engines. Available on Amazon.

Brands in History is history like you've never read it. Revealed are the fascinating attributes about groups such as the Spartans, the Samurai, the Red Tails, and the Flying Tigers. Attention is also given to the likes of Caesar, Cleopatra, Churchill, Patton, and Joan of Arc, illustrating just how sophisticated some of our ancestors were at branding themselves. Available on Amazon.

About the author

For his day job, David H. Falloure is an award-winning marketing communicator, working for one of the world's foremost energy service companies. His second career is writing about history and Texas. He spent significant time as a columnist and contributor to several Houston area publications. And he penned articles in the Texas State Historical Association Handbook of Houston launched in March 2017, including an entry he co-authored with one of his sons.

Counterclockwise is Falloure's first novel, but his nonfiction work includes *Brands in History*, the hard copy book based on his long-running blog; *Deep Water: The Story of Beaumont and its Port; The Houston Ship Channel: Open to the World;* and *Sheer Will: The Story of the Port of Houston and the Houston Ship Channel.* Those are long titles but they are long stories, and good ones, too. If you're the YouTube type, catch Falloure in the award-winning documentary, the *Houston Ship Channel: Deep Water Centennial.*

Husband and father of three sons, Falloure makes his home in Texas. He is also an admiral in the Texas Navy—yes, there is a Texas Navy. It's an organization dedicated to preserving state heritage and history.

davidhfalloureauthor.com